In Sheep's Clothing

Edward P. Ciesielski, Jr.

ALL THINGS
THAT MATTER
PRESS

This book is dedicated to:

Joseph A. DeCesaris
and the memory of John M. "Chooch" Solari

Along with thanks to the
Baltimore City Police Department

Special recognition goes to the Baltimore City Fire Department,
especially Engine Company 41 and its retired member,
the dearly departed Edward P. Ciesielski, Sr.

Last, but certainly not least, to the finest group of police officers
found anywhere:
The past and present members of the
Prince George's County Maryland Police Department

GATES OF HELL

By midnight, the wind lessened its portentous howl and the sky began to clear, allowing shafts of moonlight to pass through patchy clouds and create a ghostly spotlight effect. When Paul noticed 'Lucy Baby,' painted in white letters below the pilot's window of the C-47 that would carry him and the other equipment-laden, grease-faced soldiers to their destiny, he said with a boyish grin, "Now ain't that some shit—Lucy Baby." It would have been even more ironic for him to know that at the same time in Baltimore, his wife Lucy had gone into labor with their first child.

While waiting at the heavily guarded British airfield, Paul lit a Chesterfield and watched as the other paratroopers inspected one another's equipment. Guys look just like a bunch a damn chimps checking each other for body lice, he thought as he let go a slight chuckle.

As standard operating procedure required the commanding officer to jump first, followed by the platoon leader, Paul, the third in command, assisted the others in, and then got a shove up from Boetler.

Conversations ceased when Lucy taxied on the runway. When she reached cruising level, the paratrooper's enthusiasm waned as a pall enveloped the passenger compartment; the only sound heard above the roar of the engines was the fillip of Zippos opening and closing. Some of the paratroopers prayed quietly, while others nervously fidgeted with their equipment.

Paul remembered how thrilled he became after shaking General Eisenhower's hand, feeling he was in the presence of an immortal such as Hannibal or Alexander the Great. When he looked at Ike's face, however, he saw a look of reverence in his solemn eyes, and realized he was there to say good-bye to all the brave men who were about to die for their country. He lit another cigarette, and his thoughts drifted to home.

Paul never realized the proper spelling of Highlandtown until it was painted on the overpass above Eastern Avenue. "H-i-g-h-l-a-n-d-t-o-w-n. Hell, that spells Highlandtown, not 'Hollandtown,' " he declaimed the first time he saw it.

He learned there were other vernaculars peculiar to Baltimore: 'zinc' was a place where dirty dishes were put; a 'pockeybook' was a woman's purse; 'wooder' was something to drink; 'sparris' meant sparrows; and Baltimore was pronounced, 'Balmur.'

When the distant sound of anti-aircraft fire was heard, the passenger compartment became energized and the image of his wife's cameo skin and bare breasts melted from Paul's mind's eye. Time for daydreaming was over.

After Lucy entered the killing field of black smoke puffs and responded to the sound waves of the shrapnel-filled ack-ack, Kilmun bolstered his troops' waning confidence when he informed them in a calm and reassuring voice to standby. After what seemed like an eternity, the red light came on and Kilmun shouted like an Evangelist Preacher at a Sunday sermon—"Warriors—on your feet—hook 'em up!" CLICK: fifty-one static-line clamps hit the cable simultaneously. After the green light glowed, Kilmun slid open the door and led I Company into hell.

Shortly after his chute mushroomed open, Paul looked back and saw a fiery streak light up the night sky as Lucy and two other C-47s plummeted. As ground drew closer, he saw small flashes that resembled lights flickering on a Christmas tree. He soon realized it was automatic-weapon fire.

Paul felt pain and thought he had been shot when a canteen hit him in the left shoulder.

Rifles, ammo belts, backpacks, bayonets and other equipment continued to land around him after being ripped from paratroopers as a result of the pilots' failure in reducing speed before turning on the jump light. There was nothing he could do for the moment other than cover himself with his chute for protection and wait.

When the first platoon regrouped and Kilmun saw lights to the north instead of the west, he realized they had been dropped miles from their landing area where their mission was to destroy a German artillery battery and control two exits of Utah Beach. Under the cloak of a shelter half and with the aid of his Eveready and field map, he determined the lights were coming from Foucarville, about fifteen miles away, and close to the battery's location. Kilmun figured if they pushed hard, they could fulfill their mission just before the troops were scheduled to arrive at Utah.

Paul had lost his M1-Garrand and he desperately searched and found another weapon, a Thompson submachine gun on a dead paratrooper who had been impaled on one of the scores of long wooden stakes the Germans had planted in anticipation of oncoming airborne troops. Paul looked at the horrific image and blessed himself while reciting the Hail Mary with extreme emphasis on, 'now and at the hour of our death,' as he snatched the trooper's unfired Tommy and ammo belt.

After reaching Saint-Martin and discovering the battery had been rendered useless by Allied bombing, Kilmun decided to head toward Utah Beach. At noon, I Company saw their first action when they encountered a German column near Beuzeville-au-Plain. After taking out a squad, Kilmun, Boetler, Paul and two others found refuge in an artillery-shell hole.

A few seconds later, a German potato masher landed in their midst. In the two seconds before it went off, Paul's thoughts were of his darling Lucy, his unborn child, the Non-Denominational, Seventh-Day, Alcatrazian, Sun-Worshipping Mother Fuckers from Mars, and the look in Eisenhower's eyes.

When he came to his senses, Kilmun checked the survivors for injuries, then went to Paul's smoldering, mutilated corpse, jerked the dog tags from his neck, kept one, and placed the notched end of the other in the gap between his front teeth that Paul's Lucy thought was so cute. As Boetler crouched and retrieved Paul's St. Christopher medal, Kilmun removed a towel from his backpack in order for them to wipe Paul's blood and fleshy scraps from their faces.

* * *

Before he became a victim of friendly fire from General Patton's 3rd Army at Bastogne, Kilmun wrote a recommendation for Corporal Paul Pinski, 5957771, of the 502nd Parachute Infantry Regiment, 101st Airborne Division, Company I, to be posthumously awarded the Medal of Honor for intentionally covering an enemy hand grenade with his body that saved the lives of four members of his company's first platoon.

After Kilmun's death, Boetler received a battlefield commission to the rank of first lieutenant, and later awarded the Purple Heart and Silver Star. Following Paul's sacrifice, Boetler took a new lease on life and became more tolerant of people.

INDUCTION

Through victories in the Pacific and North Africa, the tide of WWII began to turn in favor of the Allies. Two more years of fierce fighting would continue until the Axis was defeated and the carnage stopped.

For Paul Pinski, his wife Lucy and millions of other working Americans, the war had not been a bad thing. In early 1942, Paul and Lucy were hired as riveters at the Glenn L. Martin Aircraft Factory in Middle River, where Paul started at a whopping $1.10/hour and Lucy at $.90, with assurance of unlimited overtime. The PBY-Catalinas and PBM-Marauders Paul and Lucy proudly assembled were Martin gems, and would prove their worthiness throughout the war.

After beginning employment with Martin, the couple began enjoying a lifestyle unknown to most people who had grown up in the thirties. Paul realized the war was not only the source of his new-found success, but with it came the extreme likelihood of him being drafted as he was twenty-three, able bodied, and had no children. Knowing his deferment as a defense worker wouldn't last forever, he had to come up with a plan.

At fifteen, Lucy had an illegitimate son who was living with her foster parents and sister. As he was the meanest little bastard to ever have drawn breath, coupled with him being competition for Lucy's affections, Paul never cared for him, but disregarded his emotions and decided that adoption would be better than conscription.

* * *

Even though Paul's draft status changed to 2A when Victor became Pinski, he wasn't confident it would be enough; he had to expand his family more.

In September of 1943 when Lucy became pregnant, it pleased her and Paul for completely different reasons: Lucy was happily married with this pregnancy, while Paul figured his chances of survival had been considerably enhanced. When an invasion of Europe became imminent, however, Paul received his 'greeting' letter from Uncle Sam, and although he plead to the draft board that Lucy was pregnant, it didn't change his status as the child was unborn. Paul accepted his fate, and decided to volunteer for the US Army Airborne after reading an article in Life Magazine that said paratroopers got extra pay and received the best possible training.

Paul arrived at the 5th Regiment Armory in his brother Henry's 1932 Ford Roadster he referred to as 'Maggie,' short for magnificent. Maggie was anything but magnificent. In fact, she was a 'heap.' In addition to not having a heater or snow tires, she had rotted floorboards and a piece of plywood placed over a broken-out rear window. Nevertheless, it was Henry's first car, of which he was quite proud.

The sergeant processing Paul's paperwork noticed it was his birthday and sarcastically wished him many happy returns as he stamped US Army inductee next to his name and serial number. After lunch, Paul and ninety-nine other recruits were herded onto two buses and transported to Penn Station, destination Camp Jackson, SC. Before boarding, Paul put the St. Christopher medal Henry had given him around his neck and packed away a carton of Chesterfield regulars.

The following morning, the train pulled into the depot where it was met by a member of the training cadre. "Okay, ya buncha scum buckets, make two groups. Whites on the right and nigras on the left," Staff Sergeant Boetler said in greeting. After carefully examining the assemblage, he said, "Y'all are the sorriest lookin' buncha needle-dicked bug fuckers I ever laid eyes on. Sweet Jesus have mercy, we're in deep shit now."

Before marching to the transport buses, Alan Stein, who had been appointed in charge of the others, approached Boetler and reported a racial incident that occurred on the train. "Git your Christ-killin' kike ass back in formation and shut the fuck up," Boetler barked with a hateful look. No mention of the incident was made again.

* * *

Boetler was an Anglo-Saxon Protestant who came from a long line of impoverished cotton farmers from Nixon, SC. He had no tolerance for Yankees, Catholics, Negroes or Jews. At age seventeen, he joined the army where he got his first pair of new shoes, all he could eat, a warm place to sleep, and a feeling of self-worth and absolute power as a training instructor. Short of killing a recruit, he could do anything to them he saw fit. In addition to his love for the army was Jesus, who gave him the strength to fight and endure.

Boetler was proud of his German heritage and could have modeled for Hitler's Aryan youth, standing just over six feet, with hair as gold as morning sun, and piercing azure eyes. Although he had no idea of his lineage, he maintained his ancient relatives were Teutonic Knights and Prussian aristocrats. As a result of his claim of knighthood, he became known to his recruits as, 'Sir Fucking Galahad.'

When the Germans invaded Poland in 1939, Boetler considered joining the *Wermacht*, but decided against it as he was a buck sergeant and a squad leader assigned to the 1st Infantry Division—The 'Big Red 1.'

After Germany and Italy declared war on the United States, he was forced to remove a photograph of Hitler and a Nazi flag from his quarters.

* * *

The Baltimore group was assigned to Company B, 9th Training Regiment, 2nd Division, located at the foot of the infamous two-mile, four-degree, back-breaking incline known as 'Tank Hill,' so named for the water tank at its crest. As a recruit was not allowed to walk anywhere, one was forced to 'hump the hill.'

Paul's worst fear became a reality after he learned Boetler would be his training instructor. Knowing little of him other than his contempt for Jews, Paul displayed his Saint Christopher medal on the outside of his fatigue shirt fearing Boetler might mistake Pinski for a Jewish name.

When he saw the medal, Boetler, a devout Lutheran, called Paul to the front of the platoon and said, "Do ya believe in the Lord Jesus Christ Almighty, boy?"

"Yes, I do, Sergeant," Paul anxiously answered as Boetler handled and examined the medal.

"Where ya from?"

"Balmur."

"What religion are ya?"

Paul pondered for a moment, and then said to himself, Screw this tow-headed prick. It ain't none of his damn business what religion I am. He then looked Boetler directly in the eyes and replied while saluting, "I'm a Non-Denominational, Seventh-Day, Alcatrazian, Sun-Worshippin' Mother Fucker from Mars—SIR."

How could I have been so ignorant to say somethin' that stupid? A non-denominational what the fuck? he said to himself.

Boetler smirked and replied, "Ya got balls, boy. Big ones."

The next day, he named Paul as one of his squad leaders.

* * *

As a result of his exemplary performance in basic training and display of outstanding leadership and organizational skills, Boetler recommended Paul be promoted to the rank of corporal upon graduating. After receiving his promotion, Paul toyed with the idea of making the army a career—but first he had to survive the war.

When he learned Boetler had also volunteered for the airborne, and they would be training together at Camp Benning, Paul was surprised he had found solace. Although he didn't personally care for Boetler and

7

disagreed with his hard-nosed leadership style, he had gained respect for him as he was an effective teacher and with the recruits through every grueling step.

By the time Paul got home from basic training, Lucy was fully adorned in pregnancy and never looked as gorgeous. When they came in contact, both burst into tears and held one another in death grips. Paul and Lucy enjoyed the best week of their lives; his final day of leave would be the last time they would see one another.

THE LEADER

Paul's commanding officer at Camp Benning was Captain Matthew Kilmun, a West Point Graduate from the Class of 1931. Matthew was born to Stanislaw and Kelo Kilmunciewicz in Warsaw, Poland in 1909. When the family arrived at Ellis Island, their surname was Americanized to Kilmun by immigration officials. Matthew was from Poletown: a section of Detroit, Michigan that bordered its enclave city, Hamtramck, and named after the Polish immigrants who originally settled in the area. The residential section would be destroyed in 1981 by the City of Detroit after claiming eminent domain in order to make way for an automobile plant.

Matthew possessed the heart of a Trojan, and modeled himself after his heroes—the grandiloquent General John Pershing, and the unassuming General Casmir Pulaski—fellow cadets at West Point described him as a cross between Wyatt Earp and George Armstrong Custer.

After graduating ninth in his class and setting school records as a running back, Matthew was assigned to the 82nd Infantry as a second lieutenant. He grew bored in his role as a peacetime soldier and lusted for action. Although the Germans were a growing threat in Europe, a war with them did not seem likely as Britain's Neville Chamberlain continued to offer appeasement.

When Matthew and his wife went home for Christmas shortly before his military obligation was fulfilled, his father-in-law, a top executive with General Motors, offered him a job in the design department with Fisher Body. He thanked him, and informed him he would give it consideration.

Matthew accepted the job at $5,000 a year—three times the amount he had been making in the army. He was up for promotion and a ten-percent increase in salary when the United States got involved in WWII. His dream of going to war had become a reality.

On December 15, 1941, Matthew tendered his resignation to GM. Although upset with his decision to leave, upper management accepted it and assured him his job would be waiting for him when the war was over.

* * *

As he was a West Point graduate with prior military service, Matthew was recommissioned as a captain and assigned to an administrative position at Camp Dix, NJ, where he immediately applied for transfer and was reassigned to the 3rd Infantry Division as a company commander.

After seeing action in North Africa, Matthew volunteered for the airborne in early 1944. Following training at Camp Benning, he was held there in order to assume command of the newly formed I Company, 502nd Parachute Infantry Regiment, 101st Airborne Division.

I Company consisted of 204 of America's finest that were ready, eager and itching for a fight. As he led through example rather than fear and intimidation, Matthew quickly fit in and earned his company's respect. He referred to them as *his people*, and never raised his voice unless it was to offer support or inspiration. Most importantly, he never admonished any in public. Instead, he waited for the opportune moment to offer correction.

While most of the company was in their late teens or early twenties, Matthew was the ripe old age of thirty-five. Despite the age difference, none could physically outperform him. When running the 'airborne shuffle' with them, he literally circled the formation while shouting encouragement to increase the step. He appealed to their warrior spirit, and each was willing to follow him into hell, which was soon to come. They loved him even more when they learned he resigned from a high-paying job to fight in the war.

After jump school, Boetler and Paul were assigned to the 101st and became the squad leader and assistant of I Company's first platoon. When Matthew saw Boetler's unit operate like a well-oiled machine, he decided he would jump with them when the time came.

* * *

After completing training at Benning, the 101st was sent to England in preparation for the invasion of Europe. The agony ended for them on June 4, 1944, when word came down they were taking off at midnight. After a loud cheer, they began packing.

When the mission was postponed due to bad weather, all hell broke loose in the ranks. The level of stress was so unbearable they began fighting amongst themselves, and anyone who got in their way was subject to have their ass kicked, including Eisenhower himself.

Ike knew if the invasion wasn't launched within the following twenty-four hours, it would've had to been put off for a month due to tidal conditions. Of more importance, information received from British Intelligence Headquarters at Bletchley Park indicated German troop concentration was heavy in Northern France and light around Normandy. God only knew where they would be when tidal conditions were right again. A month's delay was not acceptable. Ike made the monumental and agonizing decision they would go on June 6—bad weather or not.

PLEASED TO MEET YOU, HOPE YOU GUESS MY NAME

Paul was killed on June 6, 1944 at noon in France; 6 A.M., Baltimore time—the precise moment his son was born. His birth certificate indicated his arrival as: 6-6-6.

* * *

Lucy and Paul decided to name their child Alec, after Paul's best friend if it was a boy. Alec was killed at the age of sixteen when he fell from scaffolding while resurfacing the inside of a smokestack at Bethlehem Steel in Dundalk.

Lucy never met Alec, but felt a kindred spirit toward him as a result of Paul's tales of their antics. His favorite story was about how they would jump on passing gondola train cars and ride them to Goo-Goo Minnie, located on the Patapsco River close to the shipping channel. No one knew how Goo-Goo had gotten its name or what it meant.

For their amusement, sailors from merchant ships would often throw watermelons overboard for the kids to swim to and float back to shore on, where they would feast on the best melons they had ever eaten and talk about how cool they were.

* * *

Lucy continued to work at Martin until May of 1944, when she and Victor moved in with her foster parents. Her unbridled happiness came to an abrupt halt when the Western Union deliveryman asked for her. "Boy, I hate to do this to 'er," he whispered when he saw her coming to the door.

"Mornin', ma'am. You Lucy Pinski?"

"Sure am."

"Telegram here for ya."

"I don't have any change," she said as she fumbled through the pockets of her housecoat.

"That's okay, ma'am," he answered as he darted away avoiding eye contact.

Lucy never got past the first line: It is with deep regret we inform you of the death of Corporal Paul Pinski, 5957771...

Lucy dropped the message and stared blankly into space. When her eyes rolled back and she began to crumble like Lot's wife, her parents led her to the living room. Although they couldn't read English, they knew what the telegram said.

* * *

At first, Lucy was able to cope with Paul's death. Within a short time, however, she was unable to sleep and displayed hyper energy that lead to aggressive behavior and incessant chatter about God, Satan and the flesh of Christ. When she began running naked and screaming at the top of her lungs in front of her house, the police were summoned. God only knew why he was doing this to her — maybe it was his way of having fun.

When Victor saw his mother handcuffed and being led away, he pulled on one of her legs and was dragged along until an officer pushed him back as she entered the cruiser. An hour after being placed in solitary confinement in one of the basement cells in the juvenile and female holding station at Pine Street, better known as 'the pit,' she was transported to Spring Grove State Hospital in Catonsville.

* * *

Victor was highly intelligent and savvy with tremendous artistic and creative talents. Along with being cunning as a fox, he was able to quickly analyze situations and benefit from them. He liked hanging out with the 'big guys' at the candy store on East Avenue where he acted as a 'gopher' for them and was paid in cigarettes. He learned to cuss from the older group, and could match language with any sailor in Fells Point.

Victor loved John Garfield, Edward G. Robinson and James Cagney, and could do a good imitation of them. When one of their movies opened at the Grand or Patterson, he was the first one in the ticket line.

At the age of twelve, Victor was arrested for unauthorized use of a motor vehicle and sentenced to one year in the Maryland Training School for Boys. After serving three months of the sentence, he ran away while on a corn-picking detail.

On the day of his escape, Lucy got a letter from officials saying that as a result of his good behavior, Victor was to be released nine months early. Instead of being released before his time was up, an extra month was tacked onto his sentence.

* * *

Thirteen months after being admitted to Spring Grove, Lucy was released and placed in the care of her foster parents. As young children were not allowed to visit mental patients, she barely remembered Alec, and was looking forward to returning home and becoming reacquainted with her sons.

A few weeks after she was discharged, an army staff car parked in front of her home. Victor saw the car pull up and met Major Killibrew at the door.

Killibrew introduced himself and asked Victor his name. "What's it to ya what my name is?" he replied.

"Is this the Pinski residence?"

"What if it is?"

"Is Mrs. Pinski in, little boy?" Killibrew answered with a raised brow.

"Yeah, she's here. Wait a fuckin' minute while I find her."

Sweet kid, thought Killibrew. They'll probably end up hanging that little bastard someday.

"Hey, Mom, some asshole from the army wants ya," Victor yelled upstairs.

Nine-year-old Victor, now closely eyeing Killebrew, was an authority on WWII, and could identify every insignia in the US Army. When he spotted the grey-and-blue yin-yang on Killebrew's shoulder patch, he said, "Were you at Normandy?"

"Yeah; twenty-ninth division—second ranger battalion."

"Did ya grease any Krauts?"

Much to Killibrew's relief, Lucy came to the door before he could answer. She politely introduced herself and apologized for Victor's rude behavior, at which Killibrew acknowledged, and asked if he could come in.

When they got to the kitchen, Lucy said, "Care for some coffee?"

"I'd love a cup. Okay if I smoke?"

"Go right ahead. My husband smoked and I like the smell."

When Killibrew pulled out a pack of Lucky Strikes, Victor asked for one. Lucy then made him go to his room.

"I have something here for ya, ma'am," Killibrew said as he handed her a legal-sized envelope with a US Government seal. He explained that his visit was on behalf of the President of the United States and the US Congress to invite her to a ceremony at the White House honoring her late husband and six others for the presentation of the Medal of Honor.

Lucy had been hospitalized shortly after Paul was killed and knew nothing of the circumstances surrounding his death. She wasn't sure if she knew what the Medal of Honor was.

"The contents of the envelope will explain everything," Killibrew said when he saw the confused look on her face. Lucy graciously accepted the invitation and was told someone from the White House would be in contact with her.

After Killibrew left, Lucy went on the back porch and opened the letter. It had been an abnormally warm fall, and there were still a few figs on the tree in the backyard. She picked one and began to eat it as she read.

It shattered her when she got to the gruesome details of her husband's death. Anger took over and she hated Paul after she realized he had willfully covered a hand grenade with his body. "How could he have done such a terrible thing to me? It's bad enough he was killed, but to have done it on purpose, is, is…unthinkable. Did he do it because he hated me?" she said with wet eyes and great agony.

Although he was a hero in its finest form, it would take time for Lucy to forgive Paul for being one.

THE VISIT

Two weeks after Killibrew's visit, Lucy received an engraved invitation signed by President Truman. It included correspondence informing her that transportation and overnight accommodations would be arranged for her and a guest at the Willard Hotel in Washington, D.C. upon receipt of her intention to be present at the ceremony honoring her late husband and the others. At first she was excited, but after thinking about it, her enthusiasm transformed to depression and she returned the RSVP with a polite note stating she would be unable to attend.

After the ceremony, a special-delivery package arrived for Lucy containing Paul's Medal of Honor mounted on a plaque and a letter explaining his children had been awarded a paid scholarship at any university in the United States. Lucy felt guilt at her twinge of solace when she thought that perhaps some good had come of Paul's death.

* * *

Life went on for Lucy and she slowly began to recover from the trauma she had suffered. The true test of her recovery came on a warm Sunday afternoon in March of 1946.

While sitting on the front steps, Lucy looked up after wiping spumoni from Alec's face and noticed a man in uniform walking down Bank Street. When he got to Clinton Street, he looked at the sheet of paper he was carrying, then at the street sign, then turned. When he got close enough for them to see him better, Victor pointed out that his uniform was loaded with fruit salad. Lucy had no idea what Victor was talking about and thought the man had dropped food on his shirt. After Victor recognized his mother's confusion at the comment, he explained that the man was a decorated soldier, and the fruit salad was battle ribbons denoting his war service.

When the soldier spotted Lucy, he immediately recognized her from the photo he had been carrying since the afternoon of June 6, 1944. Upon stopping at their location, Victor saw the Screaming Eagle patch on his shoulder and his face in the spit-shined Corcoran boots. The soldier then extended his hand, and in a deep and trembling Southern drawl, introduced himself as Captain Richard Boetler—a friend of her late husband. At that moment the face of a hardened Trojan warrior transformed into one of a timid school boy.

* * *

When Boetler got to Paul's remains, he dropped to his knees and prayed for the Lord Jesus Christ to take him into his heavenly kingdom. He then retrieved all of his personal effects including the Zippo inscribed with the Screaming Eagle and a spare dog tag GIs carried in their right boot in the event their head was blown off. He removed the Saint Christopher medal, and took a photograph tucked under the webbing of his helmet liner of Lucy standing in front of a B-29 flexing her right bicep like 'Rosie the Riveter.' The last thing he secured was a lock of Paul's hair and put it in an almost-empty cigarette pack.

Boetler considered sending Paul's personal effects to Lucy. Instead, he opted to take a chance on survival and deliver them to her personally, along with his veneration for Paul.

* * *

As Boetler stood at Lucy's feet, his mouth was as dry as the cotton he had picked as a youth, and he was more stressed than when he connected his static line over Normandy. Although he rehearsed what he would say a thousand times, he was totally speechless. When their tearing, glowing eyes made contact and Lucy's hand disappeared in his closed grip, the small gathering sounded off like a pack of wounded coyotes.

"Were you there when my father was killed?" Victor asked.

Boetler couldn't answer; when he nodded, they howled louder.

After regaining their composure, they went inside where Lucy's father broke open a bottle of Dago Red. Victor, of course, wanted a drink and one of Boetler's Old Golds, but settled for a Frostie Root Beer and a stick of chocolate licorice.

When Boetler opened the satchel he was carrying and laid out Paul's personal effects, they broke down again. After spotting a bottle of Old Grand Dad on a shelf, Boetler pulled it down and poured himself a long one, after which Lucy's father followed suit. After the alcohol took effect, they began acting in a more subdued manner.

Lucy's father suggested they have his special marinara sauce and spaghetti for supper, but Boetler declined and insisted on taking them to Haussner's Restaurant. He said he heard of it from Paul and other GIs from the Baltimore area, and understood that German food was their specialty. He knew it was close, as he had spotted it on his way to their house.

Boetler was taken by Haussner's the moment he entered. In the lobby were photographs of famous people who had dined there, including President Truman, J. Edgar Hoover, Clark Gable and Myrna Loy. The restaurant had been converted from four storefronts to one large dining area, and displayed one of the largest private art collections in the world. The collection ranged from small paintings to life-sized marble busts of the Caesars. Shelf after shelf of glass-enclosed cases filled with small carvings adorned the room. Upstairs was a huge mural of the Bengal Lancers on horseback staging for a battle.

Boetler counted 104 entrees on the menu that included everything from hasenpfeffer to barbecued pork chops. After ordering sauerbraten, with a side order of schnitzel, Tyrolean dumplings, spaetzels and stewed tomatoes, he buttered a chocolate-chip muffin.

After dinner, Lucy's father suggested they go back to his house for a shot of ouzo, coffee and biscotti. Boetler wasn't sure what anything other than the coffee was, but acknowledged and accepted.

After they finished the liqueur and dessert, Lucy's father told Boetler he would consider it an honor and privilege if he spent the night with them. When he accepted, Victor, who had become enamored with Boetler, let out a loud, "Hell yeah," and asked him for one of his cigarettes. When he refused, Victor grabbed him by the hand and said, "Come with me, I got some shit to show ya."

When they got upstairs, Victor led him to his bedroom where Paul's Medal of Honor had been mounted on the wall. Boetler stood in stone silence as the entire sordid affair replayed in his mind. "That's good, son. Your dad deserved it," he said to Victor.

Before Boetler left, Victor got the Kodak and took several photos of the group; a collection of tormented souls with little in common a day earlier, that had bonded and formed a relationship none would forget.

* * *

Boetler lived the remainder of his years severely guilt ridden over Paul having given his life to save him and the others. In 1977, he was buried with full military honors at the Arlington National Cemetery.

THE CHEF

A void had been filled in Lucy's life by Boetler's visit, especially when she got the lock of hair. In September, she reapplied at Martin but was turned down as the fat government contracts were gone with WW II. As she had little education and no work experience other than operating a rivet gun, her options were quite limited.

After seeing a sign in Haussner's window advertising for waitresses, Lucy went in. A few minutes later, a man in his sixties with a stern look on his face approached her and said, "May I help you?"

"I'm interested in working here as a waitress," Lucy replied in a timid voice.

Otto Haussner was a German-born, naturalized American citizen, who maintained stringent rules in the operation of his business and employees. The 'table servers' had to be experienced, female, present a neat appearance, have straight white teeth, be of a pleasant nature, their hair rolled into a covered bun, wear a matronly white uniform, and above all, be non-Jewish and Caucasian.

While twirling his 'Snidely Whiplash' mustache, Mr. Haussner looked her over closely. "What your name?" he asked.

"Lucy Pinski."

"Are you a Jew?"

"No, I'm Catholic."

Pinski, where do I know that name? he said to himself.

"Where you live?"

"On South Clinton Street."

When he heard the address, he remembered reading in The Baltimore Sun of a soldier from there who had been awarded the Medal of Honor. "Was your husband in der army?" he said with his eyes cut in her direction.

"Yes, he was a paratrooper and killed on D-Day."

When he hugged her, he morphed into Robert Young from *Father Knows Best*. "When can you start?" he asked with a toothy smile.

"Tomorrow."

* * *

On her first day, it was obvious Lucy was totally inexperienced in table service when she dropped a full tray on her customers then ran in the kitchen and began crying.

"Don't make no never mind, honey. Everybody gotta start sometime," the chef, a man who could pass for Aunt Jemima's twin, said to her.

"I guess I'm fired, huh?" she said to Haussner when he came to her side.

"No, sweetheart. I make things good with customers. Come back tomorrow and start over," he said while wiping her wet eyes.

* * *

Haussner's Restaurant opened in 1938 and Sherman had been the head chef since day one. Mr. Haussner was aware his culinary artistry had created great success for the business and treated him like a partner. Along with other administrative responsibilities delegated to him, Sherman was influential as to who stayed employed, and who didn't.

Lucy immediately became endeared to Sherman as he had a son who had been killed in Europe. He thought at the right time, they would discuss their losses.

When she returned to work, Sherman assigned Lucy as assistant to the head waitress who taught her the ins and outs of serving tables. Before long, she was an ace and regulars began asking for her by name. Lucy prospered, felt good about herself and loved the people around her—especially the chef.

LUKE

After being introduced to him by Mr. Haussner, Lucy said, "Retirement party for one of your friends, huh?"

"Yeah," he replied in an east Baltimore accent, "we're plannin' a shindig for one of the old smoke eaters. He's gonna leave us and go to Florida."

"I've never been to Florida. In fact, I've never been out of Baltimore. No, I take that back, I went to Philadelphia once to visit my husband's relatives."

"Your husband?" he asked, not seeing a wedding ring.

"Yes, he had family in Philadelphia and we went there once."

"*Had* family in Philadelphia? Don't they live there anymore?"

"As far as I know they're still there, but I'm not married anymore. My husband was killed in the war."

Despite his Mediterranean appearance, Luke's face would glow when stressed. "I'm sorry, didn't mean to delve," he replied as he nervously coughed and looked away.

"That's okay. I know you meant no harm."

Although embarrassed by his question, Luke was glad to learn Lucy was not married.

* * *

"And do you, Lucca Mayo Bazey, take this woman, Lucia Maria Pinski for your lawfully wedded wife?"

"I do."

"Now kiss the bride."

Despite his insistence on remaining a bachelor, it was love at first site and the two became one on Valentine's Day of 1950.

* * *

Lucy was reluctant to remarry, as she was not over Paul, and the grief, sorrow and heartache, love and circumstances sometimes bring. Also, she had trepidations as to what sort of father Luke would be, as neither of the boys were his, and at times became frustrated with Victor and his 'little-gangster' attitude. She gave in when Luke convinced her he would be good to her sons.

Although the wedding itself was a small informal affair, the reception was fit for royalty. At Mr. Haussner's insistence and expense, he put on his best show; caviar, champagne and Chateaubriand topped the menu. Sherman baked a five-layer cake and placed fresh strawberries on top shaped in a heart with a bride and groom standing in the middle. When he uncovered it, he said teary eyed, "Now ain't dat purty, it be ma bestest work for ma fav-o-rite gal Lucy and her new hubby. Happy wedding, y'all."

As they posed for a photo in front of the cake, Lucy couldn't help but think of how much she loved Sherman; she then thought about when she married Paul.

Their wedding had been a civil ceremony at city hall, where Paul's brother Henry, stood as best man. Afterwards, they walked to East Baltimore Street where they went to Paul's favorite diner—Pollock Johnnie's. Lucy remembered how Paul loved the hot dogs there, and described them as the next best thing to sex.

PJ dogs were a meal within themselves and famous throughout the city as evidenced by the never-ending line of customers waiting to buy one of the gastronomical nightmares. They were fat, juicy and a combination of meat and various spices consisting primarily of garlic and oregano. They sold for fifty cents apiece, and included a side order of fries. When Henry heard Paul compare the hot dogs to sex, he said, "Brother, you must not be doin' it right. Ain't nuthin' better'n sex."

"What would you know about it, ya little snot? You ain't never had sex with anything 'cept Madame Palm and her five fingers."

Henry smiled as they laughed and finished their meal.

* * *

The newly wedded Mr. & Mrs. Bazey honeymooned in Niagara Falls on the Canadian side. As they passed under the falls and kissed passionately, Lucy was sure she had done the right thing.

* * *

At the time, most Baltimore City Firefighters were WWII veterans and had seen action where they were forced to think on their feet or be killed. It fell in place, therefore, that such a person would have the fortitude to run into a burning building while others were rushing to exit. In addition, many learned skills in the military they were able to apply in civilian life.

Although prohibited by BCFD regulations, nearly all of the firefighters maintained employment during off-duty hours. The rule was overlooked, however, as city officials knew the men were working for slave wages and wouldn't zealously press the issue of pay raises as long as they had another source of income. Besides, the officials needed skilled services on occasion and knew where to find it cheap.

After the wedding, Luke, a top-notch auto mechanic, encouraged Lucy to resign from Haussner's and care for the boys. He told her he would take on more part-time work to offset the income loss. Lucy firmly declined as her job had become a major part of her life and molded her identity. After discussing the matter at length, Luke caved in and they agreed to save money for a house.

Luke made good on his promise to Lucy to treat the boys as his own when he made the decision to adopt them after they agreed not to have children; he felt as though they would feel more like a family if they all shared the same surname. When the NFL Colts moved back to Baltimore in 1953 and were joined by the Orioles in 1954, Luke and the boys became regulars at Memorial Stadium when Luke, a big 'Bombers' fan, converted to an 'O's' addict.

THE MULE

The Bazeys purchased a home close to the Patapsco River in the 'Greektown' section of Highlandtown. The names Papadopulios, Tsolakikius and Colevas were found on marquees, along with an occasional O'Reilly or Stawinski.

Many of the corner houses had been converted to a neighborhood bar, small food market or candy store, where fried codfish cakes or 'coddies,' arranged on serving trays covered with cellophane to protect them from the soot-filled air, were sold. The five-cent price included two saltines and a shot of mustard. Empty glass starch bottles with hinged metal handles were converted to beer containers and filled at the bars for twenty-five cents.

Directly across the street was a candy store named Charlie's, or 'Cholly's' in 'Balmur' lingo, where Frostie Root Beer, Royal Crown Cola and Almond Crush, to name just a few, could be found in the ice cooler. Candy delicacies, such as cherry dollars, strawberry twists, chocolate licorice, malt balls, licorice pipes and candy cigarettes topped the list for Alec, while Victor loved the pinball machine that paid off winners in cigarettes. In the summer, Chesapeake Bay blue crabs or 'Jimmies,' were steamed daily and sold for two dollars a dozen, or twenty cents apiece. Even though the neighborhood was in the heart of the city, it was a great place to live and a lot about life could be learned there.

* * *

Alec was a friendly, cute and quite likeable kid, much like Opie Taylor. His intellect was far advanced beyond a normal eight year old in that he was calculating, highly manipulative and knew the value of a buck.

Herman Panzoukous became one of Alec's best buddies in the neighborhood when he gave him a taste of the gravy-covered French Fries he was carrying in a pan. Alec repaid him with one of the spearmint-leaf candies he had in a small paper sack.

The morning after he met Herman, Alec sneaked out of the house wearing his brand-new, brown-leather, wing-tipped, go-to-church Buster Browns. When he saw him walking up the street, he yelled, "Hey, Herm, wait up."

Herman, the neighborhood bookmaker, on his way to deliver the previous day's receipts, always took a different route. For awhile, he carried the booty stuffed under his shirt, but decided it was counterproductive as it was obvious to even a casual observer he was trying to hide something. Although Herman made good money as a bookie, he was aware of the perils connected with the trade and swore to himself he would go straight and get a real job. He never did, as the rewards highly outweighed the risks.

Alec's call startled Herman and he turned quickly. While running to catch up, it occurred to him for Alec to deliver the goods.

"What ya got in the bag, Herm?" Alec asked.

"Do ya know Mr. Joe up at Click's?"

"Sure, I know Mr. Joe. Click's Pool Room, right?"

"Right. Ya wanna make two bucks?"

"Yeah, what do ya want me to do?"

"Take this bag to Mr. Joe and when you get back, I'll give ya the money."

Before Herman could blink, Alec snatched the rubber-band-bound bag and was on his way. By the time he crossed Eastern Avenue, Herman had reached the corner and watched where he could see his partner, Joe Batta, a policeman's brother, standing in front of the pool room. "Thanks, little boy. Good job," Batta said as he patted Alec's head.

Alec darted back across the busy street and was almost hit by a Sun Cab that came to a screeching halt. "Little cock sucker," the cabbie yelled. "Watch where the fuck you're goin'!" Alec ignored the driver and ran to Herman, who handed him two dollars.

"Gee thanks, Herm."

"No problem, little buddy. Tell ya what, meet me here tamarr at the same time and you can make another deuce."

"All right. See ya tamarr, pal."

Alec immediately ran back to the house to brag to Victor of his new found fortune. "Vic, Victor," he shouted at the top of his lungs.

Luke met him instead and said, "What in the hell are ya yellin' about? And what're ya doin' with your new shoes on?"

"Look at this, I just made two bucks," he answered while waving the money.

"And how did ya accomplish that, Mr. Rockefeller?"

"Herman gave it to me for takin' a bag to Mr. Joe up Click's."

Luke immediately knew what happened and grabbed the two dollars and said, "That fat bastard, where is he?"

"Still outside, I think."

"Hey, Herm, hold up 'ere," Luke shouted when he saw him walking up Fleet Street.

Herman turned in response and saw blood in Luke's eye.

"Ya tryin' to get my kid killed or something? He's only eight years old for Christ's sake. Are ya outta your mind, or just too yella to do your own dirty work?"

"Luke, I'm sorry," pleaded Herman. "I thought I was doin' the kid a favor. Let 'em make a few dollars. You and me go way back, Luke, I'm really sorry. I like Alec, too. It was really stupid of me."

"Stay away from my kids, or I'll beat ya to a pulp, ya fat Greek prick," Luke yelled as he stuffed the two dollars in Herman's shirt pocket.

"No problem, buddy," he said as he scurried up the street and hid in his house the rest of the day.

When Luke got back to his house, he read Alec the riot act. Although Alec assured Luke he understood and it would never happen again, in his mind he had done nothing wrong and was upset over losing the two dollars. Rather than learning the virtues of honesty Luke had intended, he became aware of the value of keeping his mouth shut.

TRIP TICKET

The 'Hawks,' six neighborhood kids ranging in age from twelve to fourteen living within a city block of one another, had dubbed the name of their group from a movie serial about a gang of New York youths from Hell's Kitchen.

Despite the group's motley looks and tough talk, their actions were mostly of a prankish nature. Their favorite trick was to defecate in a bag, set it on fire, and place it on someone's front steps, then knock on the door and run. When the resident answered, they would inevitably tread on the bag to put out the fire while Victor and the others laughed outrageously.

It was the leader's responsibility to assign new members a nickname that related to them in some way: Albert 'Nick-Nick' Nicholson, Kenny 'Monk' Klein, Mike 'Fish' Bass, his younger brother 'Egghead' and Michael 'Reds' Varipapa, whose Irish mother had passed on her rust-colored hair to him, were the present members. As Victor was the leader, he chose the name, 'Cagney.'

* * *

Victor became fascinated with Goo-Goo Minnie when he heard Paul speak of it. After learning it was a few miles from his home, he planned to make a trip there with his flock.

In order to obtain financing for 'necessary provisions,' Victor went on a scavenger hunt and collected sixty-three empty soda bottles, cashing them at Cholly's for $1.26. He came up with $7.50 from his Liberty Bell savings bank, and $6.00 from family members. "Fourteen dollars and seventy-six cents. "At ain't enough," he said after taking stock. "Alec's got a stash, I'm sure of It. Ain't never seen 'em buy nothin' but a soda or candy."

After two hours of searching for Alec's cache, he gave up and decided to do the unthinkable and ask to borrow the money from him.

When Victor got money from the others, he told them it was for the Bible Sacred Heart was selling as a fundraiser. As they had seen the beautiful, white-leather-bound book for sale at mass, they agreed it was a worthy venture and were glad to see him take such an interest in religion. They also realized it was totally out of character for him.

When Lucy offered to buy the Bible, Victor refused and said in Eddie Haskell fashion, "Mother, it's time I grew up and started acting like an adult. Buying the Bible myself would make it more valuable to me."

Lucy was shocked at the answer and gave him money. That night, he and the other hooligans terrorized the neighborhood when they went on a 'shit-stompin' rampage.

Victor was vague when he asked Alec for the loan. After he refused, Victor said, "I wanna buy a Bible for Mom and Dad."

Even though he was constantly exposed to foul language, Alec didn't use it. After hearing the 'truth,' he began to guffaw and said out loud, "Bullshit, give me a break."

"It's true. I wanna buy the fuckin' thing for Mom and Dad," Victor answered with a high degree of indignation.

"No way. You're lyin'."

Victor tried again and Alec held fast. "Bullshit," he repeated with more authority. "You're not gonna buy a Bible. Ya probably want it for cigarettes."

Victor fumed, but knew Alec had his number and came clean.

After hearing about Goo-Goo, Alec became enthralled with the thought of floating on a watermelon. "Tell ya what, I'll *give* ya the money if ya take me along."

"No way, you'd just be a big pain in the ass."

"Okay."

As Alec started to leave, Victor said, "I won't have to pay ya back if I take ya?"

"No, we'll be even."

"Deal. Oh, and one more thing, you can't tell anybody about this, especially Mom or Dad."

"No problem."

THE HERON

When Victor left, Alec went to the backyard and removed a buried coffee bag wrapped in waterproof canvas. After brushing away loose dirt, he emptied the bag, counted its contents and put it in his front pocket.

"Got the money?" Victor asked when he returned home.

"Yeah, I got it," Alec answered as he reached in his pocket.

"How much?"

"Six twenty-four," he said as he threw the money laced with a few blades of grass on his bed.

"Ain't enough."

"Take it or leave it."

"Okay, I'll take it and leave you here," Victor said as he scooped the money.

"If I stay, the money stays."

"Fuck you, I got the money now. What ya gonna do?"

"I'll tell Mom and Dad."

"No, ya won't. They'll be more pissed at you than me for not tellin' 'em before."

After Alec kicked Victor in his balls, he doubled over and said, "Ya ruptured me, I'll never be able to have kids."

Alec then kneed him in the face and kicked him in the solar plexus after he went down. "Stop, God dammit, you can go. I'll take what ya gave me. Caught me off guard," he warily said to Alec for whom he had gained new respect.

* * *

The following day, the Hawks and Alec walked to the shopping district on Eastern Avenue to purchase supplies. The best buys were found at Sunny's Surplus, where military items from every country were found at dirt-cheap prices. When they returned home, they hid the chattels under a wheelbarrow in a rusty metal shed behind Nick's house.

The next morning, the group met at Nick's, where after preparing for their journey they participated in a competitive ritual known as a 'circle jerk.' The ground rules prohibited any form of visual stimulation to be present, and their penises to be soft at the outset; the first to ejaculate was deemed the winner.

As usual, Nick merged victoriously, and came close to breaking his twenty-seven- second record. None of the others were aware he held an unfair advantage over them in that he was a homosexual, and fantasized while looking at the other boy's equipment.

* * *

'Wildly bizarre,' best described the appearance of the group after they donned their new gear. Victor had on a pair of brown combat boots, one-and-a-half sizes too big, a pair of paratrooper's duffel pants fastened to his calves by a set of white military leggings, while a small jumper-cable handle secured the four extra inches in the waistband. Above the waist he wore a khaki shirt with black epaulets, and a tanker's helmet with a thick rubber band wrapped around it holding an ace of spades. His ammo belt was filled with: two packs of Lucky Strikes, ten campfire matches, six Milk-Bone dog biscuits, a small pack of Oreo cookies, a blueberry 'Tastykake' pie, chewing gum, hard candy and two packs of lime Kool-Aid. Also attached to the belt was a first-aid kit containing a suppository pack, bandages and dressing for a sucking chest wound, a small tin filled with water-purification tablets and a bottle of mosquito repellent. Ten packs of sugar, a Pro-Kit, salt and pepper shakers, five tea bags, one Hostess Twinkie, two strips of beef jerky, a box of toothpicks, a deck of playing cards, minus the ace of spades, a set of dice, a flashlight and metal canteen filled with cherry Kool-Aid completed the assortment of supplies. To top things off, he had on a pair of wire-rimmed aviator's glasses and was carrying a loaded, pump-action Red Ryder BB rifle. Victor was fully prepared for any situation and truly a spectacle to behold—he was, 'BAD TO THE BONE.'

Alec wore an aviator's cap, his mother's white silk scarf, short pants, and a pair of high-top-'cathead' PF Flyers. As his ammo belt wouldn't fit around his waist, he carried it over his right shoulder and hooked it together overtop the 'S' on his Superman T-shirt.

Monk had on a German helmet, and three Iron Crosses next to an American Good Conduct Medal pinned to his jungle survival shirt. Fish wore a British helmet, a leather map case around his shoulder filled with chocolate-chip cookies, and a Japanese bayonet attached to his belt. Egghead sported a British pith helmet with captain bars painted on the front, an ammo belt, combat boots, jungle shorts and a hand-grenade pouch filled with rocks. Reds and Nick were less adorned, and only wore American helmets, combat boots, ammo belts and blue jeans. All of them carried army backpacks and a mess kit.

After a final check of their equipment, Victor issued the order, "Synchronize your watches, men," as he looked at his Gruen 'Combat Timepiece,' the costliest item at $2.98.

"Mark. Zero eight hundred and fifty-one minutes exactly."

As Alec was the only other one with a watch, he looked down as the side straps of his aviator's cap dangled to his chest area. He then pulled out the stem and turned 'Mickey's' hands to eight fifty-one, then reset it. The group left the shed and double-timed up the alley, resembling a jailbreak from Looney Tunes.

When they got to the tracks, they hid in high weeds until the last stripped down Sherman-M1 tank was unloaded from a flatcar. " 'Bout fuckin' time. Almost ten o'clock," Victor said.

Before the train started to move, they ran to the locomotive and began waving and yelling for the engineer's attention. When he saw them, he said, "What in the hell is zat?"

"Ya goin' to Goo-Goo Minnie?" Victor yelled.

The engineer cupped his ear and replied, "What? I cain't hear ya, I'm steamin' up for a trip to the river."

"Yeah, can we come?"

"Get your stupid Disney-lookin' asses the hell outta here," he answered as he let out a blast of steam causing them to return to the safety of the high weeds.

When the engine got a safe distance away, they emerged and started running alongside until they saw a gondola at which Victor put his left foot on the step-up, got on board and began helping the others.

When Reds tossed Alec up, he lost balance and began rolling toward the opposite edge of the open-sided car. "See, I told ya you'd be a pain in the ass," Victor said when he snatched Alec's collar as he was about to go over.

After they settled in, Nick suggested another circle jerk in celebration. "What are ya, some kinda fuckin' sex maniac? We just did one. Sit da fuck down and shut up," Fish said.

I wonder what they get outta that. Alec, considerably younger than the others said to himself when Fish admonished Nick. They get all red in the face, wild in the eyes, and seem to lose their wits when they're doin' it, then have to clean up that gooey mess from their 'thing' afterward. I'm never gonna do that 'jerk' stuff, it's stupid and disgusting.

The group basked in the summer sun and took in the scenery as they were cooled from the breeze produced by the moving train. When they crossed over wetlands where local wildlife was abundant, a heron appeared. The majestic creature glided perfectly and seldom flapped its wings; in motion, the bird was truly a magnificent sight.

Acting as though it felt obliged to perform for its enthralled audience, the heron tucked its wings while diving and plunged head first into a pond. "Did ya see 'at shit?" Monk said when the bird surfaced with a fish secured in its beak.

"Cool," answered Victor.

35

When it swallowed the fish whole, Alec thought, that fish didn't have any idea its life was about to end and that bird did it with no warning at all. Stealth, another of life's lessons was learned by Alec at that moment.

When they saw gray threads of smoke billowing above the horizon from the Bethlehem Steel Plant, Alec deciphered a sign that read: GO ON MINI SPEED. "Goo-Goo Minnie," he said.

"We made it," they shouted out in unison.

When the train slowed, they jumped off into a sandy area where they saw the river on the opposite side of a marsh. After a grueling trek, they set up camp on a clear, sandy beach at the water's edge.

"Beats shit stompin," Monk said as he tarried in the seventy-five-degree water.

When a ship drew within two-hundred yards, the boys began yelling at the top of their lungs for the sailors to throw watermelons. The crew waved back and then began heaving them over the side.

After returning to the beach with one melon apiece, Victor declared as Paul had, that they, too, were the coolest sons of bitches on the planet as they feasted on their prize.

TROUBLE IN PARADISE

Victor noticed it was three thirty and remembered Paul said the train made its return at four. "We gotta start back, it's gittin' late," he told the others.

"One more swim?" Alec asked.

"No, the train'll be comin' by soon. We gotta go."

It had been twenty years since Paul's last trip, and although the train still made a run *to* the river, it didn't return on the same route. When it hadn't arrived by four thirty, Victor began to worry. "Probably runnin' behind," he said in an attempt to bolster his slipping confidence. An hour later, he began to panic. "Where's 'at damn train?"

"Probably runnin' behind," echoed Alec.

"Shut the fuck up, ya little weasel."

"It'll be here soon."

Alec's assurance calmed Victor and made him realize how 'un-Cagney' he was acting. "Yeah, you're probably right. We'll sit it out," he said calmly.

Another hour came and went. What would James Cagney do in a spot like this? Victor thought. There was only one alternative: they would have to start walking. He figured if they hustled they could make it home before dark.

"All right, men, saddle up," Victor said, mimicking Sergeant Stryker played by John Wayne in *The Sands of Iwo Jima*.

"What?" asked Reds.

"Ya heard me, saddle up. We're gonna start walkin'."

"Walk where?"

"Home, ya moron. Where do ya think?"

"No fuckin' way."

"Then whadda *you* suggest, Einstein?"

"Wait here 'til somebody finds us."

"Here, is the middle of no fuckin' where, dickhead. Ya gotta damn phone in yer pocket? How the fuck would anybody find us? Now pick up yer shit and let's git the hell outta here."

It was twilight and the flock made good time following the tracks. After he smelled the city dump in the thick humid air, Victor knew they were about a mile from their deliverance and said, "Come on, men, we're almost there."

When they got to the area where they had seen the heron, disaster struck after they realized the tracks with cross ties wide enough to fall through were on a trestle fifty feet above a murky swamp. "What the fuck now? I wish I hadda brought the Bible," Victor said as he looked down the steep embankment.

"I wish I was home watchin' Rootie Kazootie," said Alec.

* * *

As Luke shook a colander full of spaghetti, he said, "It's six thirty and supper's almost ready. Don't they know that's what time we're supposed to eat?"

"Yes, they know. Can't imagine what's keeping them," Lucy answered.

"Probably stopped along the way to play pin ball or somethin'. They'll be here soon. I'm sure they're gettin' hungry."

When they weren't home by seven, Luke said, "Where in the hell are they? Supper's gettin' cold—hell with 'em, let's eat."

At eight, Luke's anger changed to worry. "It'll be dark in an hour. Where can they be?"

After checking with the boy's-friend's parents, Luke and Lucy drove through the neighborhood in search. "I don't know what else to do," Luke said.

"Let's call the police," suggested Lucy.

"Good idea."

"City poleece," the call taker said.

"Yeah, this is Firefighter Bazey from Forty-one Engine, wanna report my kids missin'."

"How long 'ey been gone?"

" 'Bout five hours."

"How many?"

"There's my two and at least five of their friends."

"Gimme your name and address and we'll send a radio car right over."

"Ten-four; really 'preciate it."

* * *

Car #561, an all black '51 Ford with gold police badges painted on its front doors, arrived a few minutes later. The vehicle was occupied by Sergeant Dominic Sabitini and Officer Leander Jones who created a 'Mutt and Jeff' appearance. Before getting out, the two accidentally switched hats, giving them an even more comedic look. After trading head wear, they chuckled and proceeded.

'Dom' and Luke were first cousins and had grown up next door to one another on Boston Street. Dom was Luke's best man and loved Lucy and the boys who in turn were crazy about him.

While vacationing at Ocean City, Dom earned the nickname 'Uncle Blowfish,' when he found a dead one on the beach and held it next to his face, crossed his eyes, filled his cheeks with air and stuck out his tongue. They laughed at the bizarre sight and took a photo for proof of his insanity.

When he was a foot patrolman, Dom walked a beat in the area of Forty-one Engine, and would often stop in to visit Luke. "You fuckin' deadbeat cops," Luke would complain as he served him a bowl of his famous 'three-alarm chili.' "Always lookin' for a free meal. Eat that and you'll shit your brains out."

An hour later with his gun belt draped over his shoulder, Dom dashed past Luke on the watch desk. "Chili got ya, huh?" Luke said grinningly as Dom scurried by.

"Damn near shit myself," he said when he got back.

"Yeah, fixed up a *special* batch knowin' you'd be by."

That night, Dom didn't return to patrol and stayed in the firehouse close to the commode.

* * *

"Damn, I'm glad to see you, cuz," Luke said.

"Yeah, I'm not workin' your area tonight, but when I heard your name come out on the call, I volunteered for it. What's happenin', man? The boys are missin'?"

"Yeah, they were due home at six. We're outta our minds. Can ya do anything?"

"Don't worry, we'll find 'em, pal. By the way, this is my new partner, Jones. They made me his trainin' officer."

Luke was glad to see a black person other than the garbage collectors or those on *Amos 'n Andy* in Highlandtown. "Glad to meet ya, Jones. I'm Luke and this is my wife, Lucy."

"Hi, Jones, glad to meet you."

Jones played center field for the Bowie Black Sox in the Negro League until he injured his shoulder, then joined the BCPD. His graduating class was the first where black officers were assigned to districts in white neighborhoods.

"Glad to meet y'all." In an attempt to hide his nervousness, he said, "Guess you're not use to seein' my kind 'round here."

Lucy answered with a defiant tone, "Not so, young man. I work with the best chef in the world at Haussner's and he's a Negro. Sherman's his name."

"Sherman? He ma uncle. Got me a job bussin' tables 'fore I went in da navy."

"I'll be sure and tell him I met you. What's your first name?"

"Jus' tell 'em Lee, he know who ya mean. Now be sho' and do dat, but firrs we gotta fine 'em boys."

"Please find them, Lee. I'm so worried."

"We git 'em, ma'am."

Dom then went to the radio car and put out a description of the missing youths. He notified the teletype section, then called communications and told them to repeat the lookout every hour.

When he returned to the cruiser he heard the dispatcher, "All cars be on the lookout for..." When the radio transmission was complete, Dom broke in and said, "All units be advised, two of the youths are a city firefighter's sons and he's a relative of mine." Baltimore City Police Officers and Firefighters are members of the AFL-CIO and a close-knit group. "That oughta make 'em look a little harder," Dom said.

"Good work. Thanks, man. Love ya," said Luke who felt some relief.

"We'll find 'em, don't worry, we'll find 'em," Dom said confidently.

* * *

At first light, Detective Bloodsworth from the BCPD Southeastern District Investigative Section, and his rookie partner, Dimitri 'Jimmy' Saukas, met with the Bazeys at their home. Bloodsworth was from Denton, a rural town on the Eastern Shore of Maryland, and Jimmy had grown up in Highlandtown.

After introductions, Bloodsworth said, "I understand Sabitini's your cousin."

"Yeah, he is."

"Promise I won't hold that against ya," Bloodsworth said in jest.

" 'Preciate that," Luke said with a slight grin.

"Semper Fi, brother," Bloodsworth said after seeing a framed photo of Luke and several Marines.

"Semper Fi. But I wasn't in the Corps. I joined the navy and got shanghaied into becoming a corpsman and went in on Iwo. Stayed there for twenty days then went back to the signal bridge on the Guam."

"Don't matter none, you were there. So was I, went in on the first wave with the fourth division."

"Went in with the fifth on the fifth."

"The fifth? Did ya ever meet Hayes, Gagnon, Stranck, Franklin, Bradley or Block?"

"No. Was too busy patchin' up you Girenes when they put up the flag."

"And a fine job ya did, sailor."

40

When Bloodsworth noticed a plaque on the wall, he said, "Is that, the *Star?*"

"Yeah, that's it. Didn't do anything a thousand other 'docs' didn't do. Just so happened I did a patch job on a Marine whose brother was a colonel and there at the time. So he wrote it up and they gave it to me."

"They don't give 'em things out for nothin. Ya had to earn it."

"Got lucky, I guess. Wasn't tryin' to be no hero."

Luke got caught up in the moment and said, "Follow me."

"Don't tell me that's yours, too," Bloodsworth said when he saw the Medal of Honor.

"No, it's my youngest son's natural father's."

"Lord Almighty, I never seen one before. Is that one of the boys who's missin'?"

"Yes, sir, it is."

"Daylight's burning. We got work to do."

Luke liked Bloodsworth and had confidence in him. When they got to the kitchen he introduced him and Jimmy to Lucy. "Good morning, gentleman. Coffee anyone?" she asked.

"Don't mind if I do," Bloodsworth answered.

"None for me," Jimmy said.

"Cream or sugar?"

"No, ma'am. No self-respecting Marine would ruin good coffee with cream and sugar. Okay, what're their names?" Bloodsworth said as he pulled out a pen and note pad from his seersucker suit.

"Victor and Alec Bazey. B-a-z-e-y."

"How old?"

"Vic'll be sixteen in February and Alec nine next June. June sixth in fact, he was born on D-Day."

"Ever run away before?"

"No, they've *never* ran away."

"Just had to ask, no offense intended."

"None taken."

Along with being an excellent investigator, Bloodsworth was an outstanding judge of character and keen observer. He noticed Lucy's reaction when Luke mentioned D-Day and could tell it was a sensitive area for her. He knew Luke was the boys' stepfather and was aware a stepparent is often responsible for foul play when kids come up missing. Luke wasn't sending subliminal messages, however, he maintained good eye contact, showed no facial twitching, made no nervous gestures, spoke direct and with confidence, and seemed to be sincerely concerned for the boys' welfare.

"Do ya have a recent photo of 'em?"

"Sure do. Just got 'em back from Read's yesterday."

"Good. Jimmy, call the evidence guy at the station, what's his name?"

"Alberts."

"Yeah, call Alberts and tell 'em to come over right away and make twenty copies of each."

"Right, boss."

"The phone's right over there," Luke said as he pointed.

GOAT MAN

When the horizon around the setting sun began to turn varying degrees of violet and orange, Victor decided they had no choice but to spend the night and wait for the train to come by in the morning. "I don't see no way 'round it," he said as he slipped off his backpack and ammo belt, "we're stuck here 'til mornin'."

"How 'bout if we crawl across?" Egghead asked.

"I thought we called you Egghead 'cause your head's pointy. Now I know it's 'cause yer stupid. What'd happen if a train came by while ya were out there, asshole? Forget about it and start gatherin' wood for a fire," Victor sarcastically answered.

After settling in and starting a campfire, they heard rustling in the bushes. "What's 'at?" Monk said saucer eyed.

Fish placed his forefinger over his lips. "Shhh."

Suddenly, a hulk of a man wearing tattered clothes and smelling like a dead animal appeared from the darkness. In his back pocket was a pint bottle that sloshed as he walked. When he spoke, the distinct odor of whisky could be smelled.

Reds had heard stories of a half-man, half-goat creature that roamed the area they were in. "Goat Man," he said when he saw the ersatz figure, "it's gotta be him."

"What ya boys doin' here?" the subhuman-looking creature with a snarled expression and raspy, daunting voice asked.

Reds was surprised to hear Goat Man talk. When none answered, he raised his voice and repeated the question in an irritated tone.

"We're stuck here, sir," said Nick. "Can ya help us get to the other side of the swamp?"

"I'll help ya all right, ya little fuck," he roared as he balled his huge fist and punched Nick in the nose. The others watched in terror as the man began kicking him in the face, scrotal area and ribs. After rolling him onto his stomach, the man tightened his belt around Nick's neck. "Git dat mother before he kills 'em," Victor yelled.

As Nick's face turned blue, Fish stabbed the man in the back: once, twice, three times, while Victor delivered six blows to the man's head with his Red Ryder. After being stabbed four more times, he sucked in his last breath.

In a timid voice, Alec asked, "Think he's dead?"

"I think he is," answered Victor as he gazed at the bearish figure lying at his feet.

"So do I," said Monk.

"What's gonna happen to us now?" Fish asked as he wiped the bloody bayonet on his trouser leg.

Alec thought about the times he got in trouble by telling what he had done, then about the stealth of the heron. "Nothin'll happen to us if nobody knows," he said.

After a long pause, Victor said, "You're right. We'll bury 'em at sunup and keep our mouths shut when we get home." They took an oath and quoted Tom Sawyer: "Mum's the word," they all chanted while their faces glowed from the fire as they overlooked the body.

* * *

Immediately after being awakened by honking sounds from a flock of Canadian geese, Fish, using the 'murder weapon,' assisted Victor in digging a grave with a pick tip he found on the opposite side of the tracks. "That oughta do it," said Victor after the body was covered.

When they finished the last of the Milk-Bones and Kool-Aid, they sat by the trestle and waited.

* * *

When Jimmy saw the photo of Victor, he said to Bloodsworth, "I know this kid."

"Yeah? From where?"

"I can't remember, but I'm sure I know 'em."

"Think about it, maybe it'll come to ya."

When Jimmy returned from checking for the group in Patterson Park in the area of the Pagoda where kids sometimes camped out, he said to Bloodsworth, "Now I remember. I popped Victor and another kid about three years ago in a stolen car. When I noticed that the driver was barely able to see over the steering wheel, it made me suspicious and I stopped 'em. I locked 'em up and I think they did some time in Maryland Training School. I don't exactly remember what it was, but I don't think his last name was Bazey."

"You're right. It wasn't Bazey three years ago, it was Pinski. This guy Luke Bazey adopted him and the other one not too long ago."

"Yeah, Pinski, that's it. Lived on Clinton, right?"

"I think so."

"All right, now I remember. Got anything goin'?"

"No, nothin' yet."

"Listen, somethin' else struck me."

"Yeah?"

"This Victor kid's a wild sort. A little gangster if I remember right."

"Yeah, that's what Bazey said. Thinks he's James Cagney."

"I was kinda the same way."

Bloodsworth interrupted and said facetiously, "I never would have guessed it, a nice little 'Gleek' boy like you."

Jimmy liking the innuendo, smiled and replied, "We use to jump a train downa street here and ride it to a place called Goo-Goo Minnie where we'd go swimmin'."

"Goo-Goo, what?"

"Goo-Goo Minnie, it's on the river about five miles down the tracks close to the shipping channel. If we got lucky, sailors would throw watermelons over the side, then we'd swim out and bring 'em to shore and eat 'em. It was a real hoot."

"Goofy fuckin' kids," Bloodsworth replied while shaking his head. "That's why I stayed a bachelor. Go on."

"After, we'd catch the train at the same spot where we got off and would ride it back. Made for a great day. Didn't cost nothin' and we'd eat free. Stopped doin' it about eight years ago when the train changed its route and didn't come back anymore. The train would leave from Nybalt at ten, it's nine thirty now. What say we run down and check it out?"

"Can't hurt, got nothin' else to go on."

When they got to Nybalt, Jimmy ran to the locomotive and introduced himself and Bloodsworth to the engineer, Cecil Parrish, from Mount Hope, West Virginia. When he said, "What can I do for ya'll fellers today?" and Jimmy looked at him closely, he was put in mind of Casey Jones.

"Ever seen either of these boys?" Jimmy asked.

"Yeah, I seed 'em. I talked to this'n yesty. He was wiff a bunch a utter young-uns. They was dressed up all weird 'n crazy lookin' in 'em army clothes. Damndest lookin' sight I ever did see. Tried ta bum a rod wiff me to Goo-Goo Minna, jus down a tracks here aways, but I runned 'em oft."

"What the *hell'd* he say?" Bloodsworth asked.

"He said we found 'em, boss."

After Cecil confirmed the train didn't make a return trip, Jimmy asked, "How would they get back without ridin'?"

"They'd have ta walk I guess."

Cecil removed his hat and scratched his nearly-bald, melon-shaped head and said, "Rough groun' twix here 'n there. Trussle down yonder 'bout a mal crosses a swump. Not lockly dey'd be able ta git cross by foot."

"Is there another way they could go?"

"Onliest utter way I kin think of be ta walk 'round. Swump goes 'bout four, five mals in bofe 'rections. Be a hard-assed walk, ah gar-own-tee. My guess they'd wait to the trussle for me to come by. Y'all wanna run down 'n see?" Cecil said as he twirled his handlebar mustache.

"Okay, boss?"

"When do we leave?"

As Cecil released the brake and pushed the huge throttle handle forward, he said, "Ain't supposed to carry no passengers. In this case I'm sure it'll be okay."

* * *

"Wish we had one of those watermelons with us now," Alec said through parched lips as the July sun advanced its intensity.

Victor looked at his Gruen whose crystal had been cracked during the fight and said, "Ten-thirty, train's runnin' late."

"It'll be here soon," Alec said.

At that moment, the headlight on the locomotive came into view. "It's here," shouted Victor, "it's finally fuckin' here!"

When he exited the train and saw their bizarre attire, Bloodsworth thought, the engineer was right, they are weird looking. "Been lookin' for you boys," he said. "Is this all of ya?"

"Yeah, we're all here," replied a pitiful-looking Victor.

"What happened to you?" Bloodsworth asked Nick.

"He fell and hurt himself," Victor answered, avoiding eye contact. "Patched 'em up the best we could."

"Where'd ya fall from?"

When Victor started to answer, Bloodsworth said, "Let him tell me."

"That tree right over there."

Bloodsworth looked at the tree and estimated it wasn't over seven feet tall. Not likely he got injuries that severe falling from that height, he thought. "What were you doing up there?" he asked.

"Lookin' 'round for help."

"Did you find any?"

"Any what?"

"Help."

"No, just an old drunk that passed by."

Why in the fuck did he say anything about the drunk? Victor thought.

"Did ya tell *him* ya needed help?"

"No, he just yelled at us and left."

"Which way did he go?" Jimmy asked.

"Right over there," Nick answered, pointing in the direction where the body was buried.

That stupid ass. Did he forget about the oath, or does he wanna get caught? thought Victor.

In actuality, Nick did want to tell. After he realized they killed the man, he felt guilt when he looked at the body and experienced joy when he saw his abusive father lying there.

"Right over where?" Jimmy asked.

Nick pointed directly at where the body was buried and said, "Right there."

When Jimmy sensed Nick was trying to tell him something, he remembered reading in Caputo's book, *The Art of Interrogation*, that suspects, especially youths that are emotionally disturbed, often respond to human contact. "Ouch," Nick said when Jimmy put his arm around his shoulder, although he liked the touch.

"Kinda sore, huh?"

"Yeah, hurts a little," Nick answered as he rubbed and grimaced in pain.

With a kind and concerned look on his face, Jimmy asked him his name. Bloodsworth knew what Jimmy was up to and watched intently. This kid's got a future as a detective, he thought.

"Albert Nicholson, but everybody calls me Nick-Nick or Nick."

Jimmy moved his hand to Nick's lower back and began to rub. "Show me exactly where the man was," he said.

Nick now belonged to Jimmy; he led him directly to the grave and pointed. "Right there," he said.

"Where?"

"We killed 'em last night and buried 'em there."

"What did you say, son? You killed 'em?" Bloodsworth asked.

"Yeah, he jumped us and started stranglin' me."

Bloodsworth bunched the boys together and told them not to move. "Y'all are under arrest. Keep an eye on 'em. If they try to run, shoot to kill," he said to Jimmy with a wink and smile.

"Sure thing, boss," Jimmy answered with a return wink.

"Don't worry," said Victor. "Ain't none of us goin' nowhere."

Bloodsworth then got a shovel from the train and began digging. After removing two scoops, the image of a man appeared. "Is that him?" Bloodsworth asked Nick.

"Yeah, that's him."

Stupid cock sucker, thought Victor.

He shouldn't have showed him, thought Alec. We're in for it now.

BIG TROUBLE

Upon discovery of the body, Bloodsworth said, "Let 'em be for now, save 'em for homicide."

"Let me call in 'n tell 'em what's a happnin'," Cecil said. A short time later he yelled to Bloodsworth, "Dispatch wants to perlabble wiff ya."

"What?"

"I think the dispatcher wants to talk to ya," Jimmy said.

A small population of West Virginians seeking employment at the industrial complexes had migrated on the east side of Highlandtown in an area that became known as 'Hillbilly Heights.' As Jimmy had regular contact with them, he was familiar with their vernacular.

"Oh," said Bloodsworth as he walked toward the engine. "Keep 'em covered."

"Aye, sir."

"Dispatch sayed I gotta git this 'ere train a movin', 'hind schedule now," Cecil said as he handed the radio transmitter to Bloodsworth.

"This is Detective Bloodsworth from the city police, who's this?"

"Dispatcher Chauncey Alcock," the male dispatcher answered in a prissy voice. "That train has a schedule to keep, Detective. Forty-five minutes late already, sir."

"Little faggot, what's his fuckin' problem?" Bloodsworth said to Jimmy. He then rekeyed and said, "Chauncey, consider this here train commandeered. We're workin' a murder and need help. Now send me the railroad police."

"No railroad police available, they're out at Camden Yards on a wreck."

"Can't ya shake a few of 'em loose? We got a serious situation here — seven suspects under arrest."

"Standby, Detective. I'll talk to my supervisor."

"Call Captain Shultz at southeastern and tell 'em we located the missin' juveniles. Have 'em send the search team and homicide to our location. Got all that?"

"I *said*, standby, sir."

"Unless you wanna take responsibility for one or all of 'em gettin' shot, ya better get your sugar ass in gear."

Bloodsworth then informed Cecil he was under his command. "Yesir, I'm all yorn, cap'n," he said as he rendered a snappy salute.

"You're a good man, Cecil. Now let's go lock those boys up."

As Victor climbed into an empty boxcar, Cecil handed him a gallon bottle full of water and said, "You yunguns' look lock you might be a needin' this, mighty hot back 'ere."

Once inside, the boys removed the metal cups from the base of their canteens and filled them with water. After Victor swilled down the last of his share, he looked contemptuously at Nick and said, "Why da fuck did ya tell 'em?"

"Thought it was the best thing, they'd a found out anyways."

"How the hell would they have found out?"

"Somebody woulda found the body."

"You stupid shit, you're a real asshole," answered Victor while shaking his head and wiping his dripping brow.

The exhausted group then lay down and drifted off to sleep as they contemplated their fates.

Fifteen minutes later, the dispatcher came on the radio. "Headquarters to Detective Bloodsworth, headquarters to Detective Bloodsworth, come in Detective Bloodsworth," he said, sounding more like a female impersonator than a railroad dispatcher.

"Bloodsworth here."

"Help's on the way, Detective. Your team and homicide have been notified and are enroute. Our police have finished up and should be there within an hour. Anything else I can do for you, sir?"

"I think that's it for now. Good job, Chauncey."

"Call if you need anything else."

"Sure will," Bloodsworth said, as he smirked and blew a kiss in the mike.

As they sat under the shade of the willow waiting for the others, Bloodsworth said, "Great work, kid. Ya not only found the boys, but maybe closed a murder, too. Good job, especially for a dumb Gleek."

Jimmy beamed with pride, as he respected Bloodsworth and knew he didn't pass out compliments arbitrarily.

* * *

When he found out he would be breaking Jimmy in, Bloodsworth said to his boss, "I had the last pain-in-the-ass rookie. None of 'em know shit from apple butter; in this case, piss from ouzo."

"You got no choice in the matter, Blood. Order came down from the mayor's office you'd been handpicked for the job; seems like this rookie's father's got some drag in city hall. When he heard you were the best dick in the house, he called the mayor and asked for you to break in his kid. Ya should feel honored, might get a promotion outta the deal."

"Promote this," Bloodsworth replied as he reached down and grabbed his groin area and shook it.

Jimmy's father, a big campaign contributor to the mayor, owned the Garden Bar and Garden Bakery located on opposite corners at the intersection of Ponca Street and Eastern Avenue. "No problem," the mayor told the elder when he made the request for his son to be assigned to Bloodsworth.

"Election year ya know, Jimmy."

"I know, Tommy, I'll take care of ya."

"I know ya will, Jimmy. Talk to ya later."

* * *

"What about the dead guy?" Jimmy asked.

"What about 'em?"

"Ya think Nick was telling the truth when he said he started beatin' on 'em?"

"Hard to say. I can't imagine they would've picked a fight with 'em. Could be though."

When Bloodsworth went to the cabin for a drink, the railroad police called and requested Cecil to pull the train forward in order for them to move their 'buggy' over the trestle.

When they got to the opposite side of the trestle, Detective Sergeant Stan Conroy, the lead investigator from homicide, and his partner Kenny Rogers, were greeted by Bloodsworth and Jimmy.

Conroy was a native Baltimorean and had a break in his police service when he served with the US Army 8th Air Force as a ball-turret gunner on a B-17. He was one of the lucky few who survived twenty-five bombing missions during daylight hours over Germany from 1943-1945.

Rogers was also a native Baltimorean and a seven-year veteran of the BCPD. Conroy became suspicious of him when he said he hadn't served in the military as he was flatfooted and had been turned down by the army. No one got turned town by the *army* during WWII; the army took Audie Murphy after the other services rejected him, he thought.

"Gunner, how the hell are ya, boy?" Bloodsworth said.

"Couldn't be better, Blood."

"Great to see ya, been awhile."

"Yeah, it has. Think the last time was when Kusak routined that stiff on his footie by the underpass, right?"

"Yeah, think so. What a stinker he was. Been dead four, five days in all that heat. Old Jack blew lunch when he saw all 'em maggots workin'."

"Yeah, he did. Big green wooly chunks if I remember right. Just scrounged some wrapped grape leaves from the Eastern House. When the ambo got there they had to give him oxygen." They all guffawed until their eyes watered.

51

"What ever happened to old Jack?" asked Conroy.

"He's a turnkey down central cellblock. Been there about two years. Found 'em a home."

"Good, Jack's a great guy. Have to drop in on 'em one of these days."

"This is my new partner, Jimmy Saukas."

"Glad to meet y'all," Jimmy said as he shook Conroy's hand.

"Kenny Rogers here," Conroy said as Rogers nodded.

"What ya got goin', Blood?" Conroy asked.

"Seems as though some runaways killed this guy and buried him over there. Kids said he attacked 'em and nearly killed one of 'em."

"How many kids?"

"Seven."

"Where are they now?"

"Locked up in a boxcar down near the front of the train."

"How long they been in 'ere?"

" 'Bout an hour. We locked them up right after we found the body."

"Get some of your people to take 'em to southeastern before they die from the heat. Hell, must be a hunnert degrees. After we examine the body and check out the scene, we'll come up and talk to 'em."

"Roger. How many of my guys you think you'll need?"

"Four or five oughta do it. Cut the rest loose."

"Ceec, how 'bout unlockin' the boxcar for the transport team?"

"Tin-four, cap'n," he answered with another salute.

Bloodsworth looked to the team and said, "You're in good hands here with old Cecil. He's a good man and one of West Virginia's finest."

Cecil's face turned as red as his neckerchief and said, "Thankee, cap'n. I always try ta do ma best."

"Homicide helpers again," complained Detective Jordan when Bloodsworth assigned him to assist Conroy. "That's all we ever do—help homicide. How in hell are we supposed to get our own work done?"

Jordan was a Prima Donna whose father served on the Baltimore City Council. He was a University of Maryland graduate who majored in sociology and had gone on the police department because he thought it would sound good on his resume. After a few years of 'real-world' experience, he planned to return to college and attain his PhD and open a practice.

When Bloodsworth heard Jordan make the comment, he got nose to nose with him and said in typical Marine Corps fashion, "Get over there and help Conroy and Rogers before I kick your apple ass. I don't care if your father's the fuckin' governor, go do it, asshole." Jordan didn't reply and followed the order.

After getting out, the boys were handcuffed together and looked like a Georgia chain gang as they marched single file. After entering the buggy, the engineer put it in reverse and began slowly backing up until they reached Foster Avenue where Detective Monahan went to his cruiser and called for the paddy wagon—'Mariah,' as it was better known, looked like a black ice truck and had gold police badges painted on its sides. One was on the back door that split in half when opened; in the back, twelve sets of handcuffs were laced to an iron bar above two steel benches. When Mariah pulled up, Officers Michael Grogan and Richard Kowalski—the 'Mick' and the 'Dick,' exited.

Kowalski had boxed at the Red Shield Boys Club where he competed in the Golden Gloves tournament nine years earlier. He made it to the semi-finals in the welter-weight division but was eliminated from further competition when Tyree 'The Terrible' from Cherry Hill on the west side, plugged in his 'electric fists' and knocked him cold in the first round.

"What ya got there, Monny?" Kowalski asked while looking down at the group squatted on the sidewalk.

"Seven murder suspects. Blood's downna tracks aways with Conroy and Rogers checkin' out the body. Figure they'll be 'ere awhile."

"Rogers, 'at's at weird guy. Usta be a dick at northern, right?"

"What do ya mean weird?"

"I don't know exactly, he just kinda strikes me as an odd duck."

"Don't know, never met him 'til today."

Kowalski wiped the sweat from his brow and said, "Better get these delinquents rollin' 'fore they melt out here."

* * *

When the buggy returned, Bloodsworth said to Cecil, "You're officially relieved from duty, sir."

"Been my pleasure, cap'n. Hopin' ta see y'all boys again sometime."

"Call me if we can ever help *you*," Jimmy said as he handed him a business card.

"Surely will," he said as he tucked the card safely in his shirt pocket.

"See y'all," Cecil shouted over the noise of the engine as he waved good-bye.

As the train pulled away, Bloodsworth said to Jimmy, "That Cecil's a great guy."

"Sure is, and he doesn't sweat much for a fat man."

"You are *truly* an asshole," said Bloodsworth, now grinning and shaking his head.

Bloodsworth and Jimmy then went to the gravesite where the body had been removed from the ground. Conroy counted seven stab wounds to the corpse's back and neck and observed blunt-force trauma on its forehead. "They did a pretty good job on this ol' boy. Looks like they got

53

him from the back."

"How tall ya figure he is, boss?" Jimmy asked Bloodsworth.

"Six two, six three, maybe."

"Yeah, that's what I figure, too. Ya think he was standing when they got 'em?" Jimmy said to Conroy.

"Probably lyin' face down, judging by the location of the stab wounds on his back. Would've been lower if he was standing; probably got him while he was sleepin'."

Jimmy looked closely at the head wounds and thought to himself, if the guy was lying down when he was killed, seems like his head wounds would be in the back instead of the front. "Think they stabbed and beat his head in all at the same time?"

"Probably. Why do you ask?" Conroy replied.

"I know you're the expert, but I disagree. I think he was crouched. Seems like if he was lyin' down, the head wounds would likely be in the back like the stab wounds are."

When Jimmy disagreed, Bloodsworth thought he crossed the line. He said to himself, Who does that fuckin' rookie think he is, Sherlock Holmes or somethin'? Conroy's investigated a hunnert homicides or more. It then occurred to him Jimmy's theory was more logical than Conroy's.

"Ya might be right, kid. They would've had to roll 'em over to beat his head there. Doesn't make sense they'd done that. Good call, Jimmy," Conroy said.

Rogers found a half-full pint bottle of I. W. Harper, a pack of Camels with three cigarettes, a book of matches, two paper clips and twenty-two cents on the corpse. After rubbing it with spit, he was able to make out a photograph and indentifying information from a military I.D. card he found in his watch pocket: Casper Alfred Olszewski; Private—US Army; 5956123; date of birth: 02/10/22; date of issue: 23/12/41.

Rogers saw an opportunity to impress the others with *his* powers of observation as Jimmy had, and said, "Looks like some dumb-ass clerk made a mistake and transposed the month and day of issue when he typed the card. Wonder what the twenty-third month of the year is, Octacember or somethin'?"

The comment irritated Conroy, and he thought, at least that dumb-ass clerk served. "No, dickhead. The military puts the day first, followed by the month, then the year. You'd a known that if your fuckin' feet weren't flat," he said.

Bloodsworth smiled and said to himself, Atta boy, Gunner.

After examining the card, Conroy repeated the name, "Casper Alfred Olszewski. Any of you guys ever heard of 'em?"

"Sounds like one of that Pollock wagon-man Kowalski's relatives. We'll have to ask him when we get back," said Bloodsworth.

"Mind if I see that?" Jimmy said.

"Know the guy? Hell, you've done everything else around here today, might as well identify the body while you're at it," Conroy said as he smiled and handed Jimmy the card.

Conroy's an asshole, Rogers thought. I'll talk to the captain about changing partners when we get back.

Bloodsworth was glad Conroy seemed endeared to Jimmy and hadn't taken offense when he questioned his theory on how the man was killed. He had a feeling of uneasiness around Rogers, however. Something strange about that guy, he said to himself. I'll have to get with Gunner later and see what he has to say.

Jimmy looked at the card closely then placed it next to the dead-man's face. He waited for a roar after opening the eyelids as the large, stunning tiger blues shined lucid and seemed to bring the corpse back to life. "Where do I know this guy from?" Jimmy whispered.

"We almost done, Gunner?" Bloodsworth said when they finished a grid search.

"Yeah, soon as the ambo crew gets here for transport we can go. Damn, it's hot as blazes. Must be a hunnert with ninety-percent humidity," Conroy said as he fanned his face with his clipboard.

"Smitty, call back and tell 'em we're ready."

"Sure thing, Stan."

"Jimmy told me two of the boys are a fireman's sons. Is that so?" Conroy asked Bloodsworth.

"Yeah, seems to be an all right Joe. Was a corpsman on Iwo. Won the Star there. Nice wife, too."

"The Silver Star?"

"Yeah. The youngest one's real father won the 'big one' with the hunnert and first in Normandy."

"The Medal of Honor?"

"Uh-huh, saw it myself in the older-boy's room."

"Damn, family full of heroes. Too bad the kids're in all this trouble."

Just as Bloodsworth was about to ask Conroy about Rogers, Jimmy came running. "I remember, I remember," he said in a dither.

"Calm down, son. Remember what?" asked Conroy.

"The stiff, I use to see him up on Ponca panhadlin'. Use to come in the bar and bakery lookin' for a handout. They said he was some kinda war hero. Got taken prisoner in the Philippines by the Japs. Put him on one of them 'Hell Ships' and kept him in Tokyo 'til the war was over."

Bloodsworth stared in silence and remembered.

* * *

Japanese soldiers during WW II lived under the Samurai Bushido Code—the way of the warrior. The code demanded loyalty, devotion to duty, honor to death, and required its followers to commit suicide rather than surrender or be captured. Accordingly, prisoners of war taken by Japanese forces were held in disdain.

Allied POWs were transported to Tokyo in cargo ships *not* marked as carrying prisoners as was required by the Geneva Convention. Consequently, these 'Hell Ships,' were often attacked by their own forces. Upon arrival at their destination, the prisoners were dispersed throughout Japan in slave-labor camps where they were subjected to torture and death. A few ended up in the infamous *Camp 131* in Manchuria where they were used as human guinea pigs involving diabolical experiments that made those of the notorious Nazi war criminal, Dr. Mengele, look like Mother Teresa.

Casper Alfred Olszewski, a Patterson Senior High School dropout, enlisted in the US Army on December 8, 1941 and was assigned to the 161st Infantry Division in the Philippines. When the Islands fell to the Japanese, Cas and other prisoners were put in the cargo hold of the *Noto Maru*, a Japanese Hell Ship. The hold was filled so far beyond its capacity, prisoners were forced to stand during the entire four-day journey and given no food or water on the way. With no room to fall, they remained standing after death. When a corpse was discovered, it was lifted above head level and transferred hand to hand and stacked in corners with other bodies.

After remaining in a POW camp in Tokyo until the end of the war, Cas was liberated and shipped to Pearl Harbor where he recovered from a host of maladies, then returned home. Heavy drinking made it impossible for him to keep a job or maintain relationships. Eventually he found his way to the area of the railroad trestle and built a lean-to for shelter and found food wherever he could. Ironically, his life ended at the end of a Japanese bayonet in Baltimore.

* * *

Bloodsworth shot the corpse a slow salute and said, "You didn't deserve this, GI. Sorry, brother." He then walked to the buggy and filled a ladle with water from the giant cooler. "Sure as hell glad you remembered to bring this," Bloodsworth said to the engineer.

"Wouldn't be caught without it. A body dries up quick on a day like this. Hell, it's a hunnert and two," the engineer said as he tapped a thermometer.

When he finished the second drink, Bloodsworth handed the ladle to Conroy and said, "Want some, Gunner?"

"Yeah, my whistle *is* kinda dry, thanks. If it's true what Jimmy said, surprised ya don't know the stiff."

"Never had contact with 'em—guess he kept to himself."

"Some shit. Poor bastard went through all that and ends up dyin' out here like a dog."

"Worse'n dog."

"Life's a bitch sometimes, ain't it, Blood?"

"Sure is, Gunner."

When the dispatcher advised the engineer the ambulance crew had arrived on Foster Avenue, he asked Conroy if they were ready to leave.

"Yeah, we're ready, Smitty. Blood, you and Jimmy stay with me and Rogers and we'll go back after they load the body. Okay?"

"Aye, sir."

"Don't gimme any of that 'aye' shit. I wasn't no fuckin' swabby. Sorry, I wasn't a fuckin' seagoin' bellhop."

"No, your Irish ass was out flyin' 'round on one of those luxury-liner seventeens."

The two laughed as Rogers looked on. They're *both* assholes, he thought; a couple a old fuckwads. Jimmy looked on and said to himself,

Those two are really something. Sure hope I grow up to be just like 'em.

As Detective Jordan entered the buggy, he took a parting shot. In his usual arrogant and surly manner, he waved and said, "Anytime I can be of service to homicide, *Please* be sure and call. I'll drop whatever I'm doing and rush right over. Bye now."

"Only thing you'd drop is somebody else's dick from your hand, ya shit for brains," Bloodsworth answered.

"What the fuck is *his* problem?" Conroy said.

"Aw, he's one of those fuckin' intellects, thinks he's better'n us. Graduated from Murlin with some kinda bullshit degree. Thinks he's Sigmund Fuckin' Freud or somethin'. He's gonna catch me wrong one day and I'm gonna fuck him up good."

"Call me when it happens. I wanna be there to see it."

THE TATTOO

When the ambulance crew arrived, Conroy said, "Snake, glad to see ya could make it, buddy. Didn't disturb ya did we?"

"Fuck you, Gunner," he replied with a slight grin below his David Niven mustache.

* * *

Snake had served as a combat medic during WWII with the 29th Division. After his discharge, his medical experience led him to the position of Baltimore City Fire Department Ambulance Attendant where he became acquainted with Conroy through the many 'clients' for whom they had offered their services.

He acquired his serpent nickname for two reasons: first, because it rhymed with his given name, Jake; second, and even more importantly, because of an incident that took place at 'Fred's Beds' Motel in Rosedale. While in a drunken stupor and suffering a flashback of his landing on the Normandy Beachhead, his escort knocked him cold with a lamp when he began choking her. Upon arrival of the Baltimore County Police, Snake was grasping his erect penis and singing the Star Spangled Banner. At 'so gallantly streaming,' he stroked his erection and sang louder.

After discovering he was a firefighter, the officers notified Baltimore City Fire Department officials. "Roberts'd fuck a snake if ya held its head," one commented after he saw the ugly woman. From that day forward he was known as the 'Snake.'

* * *

"Snake, been with any beauty queens lately?" Conroy asked.

"Man, it's too hot out here to fuck around. Where's the stiff?"

"Right over there."

"What the hell happened to him? Looks like somebody used 'em for a pin cushion."

Conroy didn't go into details for fear he would know the boys' father. "Not sure yet, still workin' on it."

After fastening the buttons on a body bag, Snake and his partner grabbed the front handles. Jimmy pulled one of the back handles from Bloodsworth and said, "I'll get that, boss. Gotta take care of you old guys."

Little suck ass, Rogers said to himself.

When they arrived on Foster Avenue and unloaded the body into a new Cadillac ambulance, Conroy said, "What happened to the old Henry J, Snake?"

"Haven't ya heard? Economy's boomin'. Won't give us a fuckin' raise though."

"Glad Cas is finally getting some first-class treatment," Bloodsworth said as the ambulance drove off.

Bloodsworth's thoughts were interrupted when Conroy said to him, "Me and Rogers are gonna go have a little 'chat' with the boys. Meet y'all at the station?"

"Be there shortly. Gotta go by and tell the Bazeys what's goin' on."

"Good idea, forgot about 'em. Take your time, see ya when ya get there."

When Bloodsworth and Jimmy pulled up, Dom met them at the sidewalk. He had worked midnights and planned to join the search team after catching a few hours of sleep. He was rudely awakened by a call from the state's attorney's office and informed his presence was immediately required at the courthouse. After advising the caller he was involved with a family emergency, the clerk said, "If you're not here within an hour, a bench warrant'll be issued for your arrest, family emergency or not."

Dom sat outside the room where the grand jury met until the clerk who threatened him emerged and said he was free to leave. "What the fuck. I thought this was a do or die situation," Dom said.

"Watch your language, Sergeant—you're in a public place in case you've forgotten," the termagant answered in a wry tone. "Would've been do or die for *you* had you not shown up." Dom cussed her in Italian then proceeded to Luke's house.

"Good to see ya on the case, Blood. Find 'em yet?" Dom asked.

"Yeah, they're all safe and secure at the station."

"At the station, why didn't ya bring 'em here?"

"They were involved in a killing. Stabbed a derelict with a Japanese bayonet. Said it was self-defense."

"Where'd this happen?" Luke asked as the veins in his neck appeared.

" 'Bout a mile down the tracks on the other side of a railroad trestle."

Luke was familiar with the area as he had fought a field fire there a year earlier. "What in God's name were they doin' there?" he asked.

"Not sure yet. Homicide's talkin' with 'em now, Detective Conroy. You know 'em, Dom—Gunner."

"Why do they call him Gunner? Does he go around shooting people?" Lucy asked.

"No, ma'am, he's a nice guy. Got two kids of his own. Got the name

60

Gunner in the air corps. Don't worry, he'll treat 'em right," Bloodsworth said with assurance.

"Certainly hope so," said Lucy with some relief.

"We're headed out to meet Conroy now," Bloodsworth said.

"We'll meet ya. Pine Street or southeast?"

"Southeast."

"What in the hell were they doing at the railroad trestle? That's a god forsaken and dangerous place," Luke said after Bloodsworth and Jimmy left.

"Can't imagine," answered Dom.

When Lucy began to cry, Luke said, "It'll be all right, honey. Bloodsworth said it was in self-defense."

"Self-defense. Yeah, he did say that," Dom replied. "Probably attacked 'em or somethin'. It'll be all right, Blood'll take care of 'em," he said in an attempt to reassure the others as well as himself.

"But they killed him," said Lucy. "How will they be able to live with themselves knowing they murdered a man?"

"Didn't say which one did the killin'. Besides, if it *was* self-defense, it's not murder."

"What is it then?" asked Luke.

"Just like killin' Japs on Iwo, Lukey. It's justifiable."

* * *

"Hungry, boss?" Jimmy asked Bloodsworth on the way to the station.

"Yeah, I could eat. Don't think we have time, though. Gotta get to the station and help Conroy and Rogers."

"Pull over here and I'll get some day olds," Jimmy said as they approached the bakery.

"That's right, your old man owns the place, don't he?"

"He owns it, but Fritz and Audrae got a co-op deal goin' with 'em. They're cool, they'll give us some 'nuts."

"See if they got enough for the boys. I'm sure they're hungry, too."

"Ten-four, boss. Be right back."

"I'll go with ya, won't hurt to meet the management."

"Heard ya was always lookin' for a freebie, boss."

After being introduced to Fritz and Audrae Meindorf, Bloodsworth was surprised when Fritz said, "Pleased to meet you, Detective," in unbroken English. By their names, he assumed they were displaced persons who made their way to the United States from Germany after the war. He detected a Midwestern sound from them and thought, Illinois, but not Chicago, too much of a twang.

"Bet y'all are from southern Illinois," Bloodsworth said.

"Not exactly, but close," replied Audrae in surprise. "We're from

Carthage in Hancock County. Ever heard of it?"

"Certainly. That's where the Prophet Joseph Smith, founder of the Latter Day Saints, and his brother Hyrum, were murdered at the jail in 1844. Carthage's not far from Bentley and Basco."

"Right, how in the world did you know that?"

"I have an aunt who lives in Nauvoo. Mother used to write to 'er. Never met 'er myself."

"What's your aunt's name?"

"Shirley Perkins. Sound familiar to ya?"

"Can't say it does. How could you tell where we're from?"

"Just a little hobby of mine. I pick up on people's dialects and can usually tell from where they hail."

"I can see why you're a police detective."

"The best," Jimmy added as Bloodsworth blushed and looked away.

"I bet," said Fritz. "Now what can we do for you gentleman on this fine day?"

"Like some day olds if ya got any to spare. Locked up some kids this mornin', figure they're hungry 'bout now."

"I can handle that. Was just about to put that tray in the day-old rack and reduce its price. Looks like about three dozen. Think that'll do it?"

"Yeah, that's plenty."

Bloodsworth noticed Fritz was wearing three-quarter-length sleeves, and thought, that's odd on a day this hot. When he placed the tray on the countertop, Bloodsworth read, 1077394, tattooed on the inside of his right forearm. When he looked closer, he noticed that there was a horizontal line across the middle of the sevens, as they are written in Europe.

"Anything else I can do for you guys?"

"No, that's plenty," answered Jimmy. "Put 'em on Dad's account."

"He'll love that," said Fritz. "They're on me. Nice meeting you, Detective. Stop in anytime."

"Been a pleasure. Thanks for the hospitality."

"Nice people, huh, boss?" Jimmy said in the car.

"Yeah, sure are. Do ya know if Fritz was ever in the military?"

"Couldn't tell ya," Jimmy said as he chomped down on a jelly filled that oozed its contents from the fill hole. "Want one?"

"Yeah, gimme one of 'em crullers."

"How come ya asked about Fritz havin' been in the military?"

"No reason, just wonderin'. Know anything about 'em?"

"You know as much as me, boss," Jimmy answered as he grabbed a chocolate custard.

* * *

Bloodsworth suspected there was more to Fritz than met the eye—his suspicions were correct. The population of Fritz Aldo Meindorf's hometown was dominated by persons of German extraction, who had immigrated to the United States after WW I. When WW II began, many of them encouraged their American-born male offspring to defend the Fatherland. Fritz was one of them.

As he was fluent in English and German and held a degree in mechanical engineering, Fritz was welcomed by the *Wermacht* with open arms. After his racial purity was verified and he denounced his American citizenship and vowed unconditional loyalty to the Nazi Party, he became a member of the *Schutzaffel* or *SS*. He was marked for life when his *SS* serial number was tattooed to the inside of his right forearm.

Fritz was directly under the command of Heinreich Himmler and assisted in the design of the *Final Solution*. He helped organize the *Waffen-SS*, where he attained the rank of major. The *Waffen-SS* evolved into a second German Army within the *Wermacht* and gained a reputation for barbarity. Its units helped wipe out resistance in the *Warsaw Ghetto Uprising* and the *Warsaw Uprising*.

Fritz fought in the *Battle of the Bulge* and was an active participant in the *Malmedy Massacre* where eighty-four American prisoners were murdered near the Belgian town of Malmedy.

When it became apparent that Germany would be defeated, Fritz clandestinely contacted his parents in the United States and desperately sought their assistance in order to desert the army. His father, a wealthy dairy farmer, then sent a messenger to Bern, Switzerland who opened a bank account in a false name and smuggled in counterfeit identification and a passport for his son. After deserting, Fritz met the messenger and obtained the credentials then posed as an American businessman from Chrysler. After the war, he returned to Carthage.

In 1947, Fritz married his childhood sweetheart, Audrae Zimmer. When an American-German deserter from the Wermacht was arrested by the FBI in nearby Denver, Illinois, they relocated to Baltimore where Fritz had relatives who offered them safe haven.

Fritz obtained employment at Lever Brothers as a production engineer and lived in the Mars Apartment Complex in Dundalk. Audrae found work at the Garden Bakery where Fritz offered her occasional assistance.

At first, Fritz always wore sunglasses and kept his arms covered. When questioned about his attire, he said a rare skin disease and eye malfunction forced him to protect himself from the sun. After four years, he let his guard down and began removing the sunglasses indoors and wearing cut-off shirts on hot days. If asked about having served in the military, he explained he was classified 4F as a result of his maladies.

Fritz's superior Aryan attitude would not allow him to remove the tattoo. He took pride in having been a high-ranking officer in the *SS*—an organization he considered the most elite in all of history. He felt that if Germany had won the war, he would have joined Himmler at the top ranks of the organization. He was right, for little did he know that one of Himmler's last acts was to promote him to the rank of general. The promotion was rescinded when Fritz's German wife reported his desertion.

* * *

When Bloodsworth drove into the parking lot of the station, he saw the BCPD's Commissioner's unmistakable cruiser pulling into the reserved section. The vehicle was an impeccably clean, '52 black Buick Roadmaster with four vent holes on the upper back of the front fenders and an air siren mounted on the right side.

"Uh-oh, looks like the brass is here."

"Wonder what the hell they want?" Jimmy asked warily.

"Ole Bev must be on one of his goodwill missions. Yep, three thirty. Evenin' 'trol troops gettin' ready for roll call right now," Bloodsworth said when he saw BCPD Commissioner Beverly Ober exit his cruiser.

Ober was Baltimore born and lived in Canton where he had grown up. He was forty-nine years of age, five feet eleven inches tall and in excellent physical condition. He had been a uniformed officer his entire career and looked sharp in his. He rode an *Indian* in the motorized unit until he was forced to leave when the bike went down after skidding on wet pavement and caused permanent damage to his right knee. The department tried to retire him, but he refused; he loved being a cop too much to leave. He asserted himself and was promoted to police commissioner.

When he got out of his cruiser, Ober rubbed the toes of his spit-shined cordovans on the back of his trouser legs. Although he had never served in the military, he maintained a US Marine look. He felt that a sharp appearance showed self-confidence and commanded respect.

Ober was of the 'old school' and loved his 'pachyderms,' as he affectionately referred to members of the bureau of patrol. "Like a herd of wild elephants passin' through. No tellin' where they're goin, but ya *sure* as hell can tell where they been," he would say and grin.

As a result of his fondness, most were content to remain in the BOP and seldom applied for transfer to specialty units. Ober wasn't crazy about detectives, but tolerated them knowing they served as a necessary component of the department.

At least once a year, Ober visited every police squad during roll call.

He quietly sat in the back of the room then would take the lectern when the sergeant was finished. The officers loved him and felt comfortable in his presence; his enthusiasm was contagious and they were energized after he spoke. In conclusion he would say, "Stick 'em, mace 'em and cover 'em with leaves!" Inevitably they responded by clapping and howling, to Ober's great delight.

"Blood, what ya up to, boy?" Lieutenant Eugene Fallin, Ober's aide and police-academy classmate of Bloodsworth said.

"Butchie, or do I have to call you lieutenant now?"

"Your majesty will do."

Bloodsworth acknowledged Ober with an informal salute and said, "Afternoon, sir. Good to see ya."

"Commissioner, Detective Saukas here."

"Jimmy Saukas?"

"Yes, sir, that's me."

"Does your father own the Garden Bar?"

"Yes, sir, bakery, too. Just came from there in fact. Donut?" he asked as he pointed the open bag in Ober's direction.

"Don't mind if I do. Ya know what they say 'bout cops and donuts," he answered, as he pulled out a honey dip.

"Thank you, sir," Fallin said as he bit a cinnamon twist.

"Keep on the good side of him, Jimmy. Boy's goin' places," Bloodsworth said.

"Saw your father just this morning in the mayor's office. They were makin' plans to kick off the campaign," Ober said.

"Yeah, Dad and Mr. D'Alessandro are good friends: had dinner with them and Governor McKeldin in the Annapolis Statehouse last week."

"Sure hope Tommy wins again. Hate to lose my job. That damn Republican's gonna give 'em a run for his money this time."

"Almost four, sir. Roll call's about to start," Fallin said.

"Gentleman, it's been a real pleasure. Thanks for the donut, Jimmy," Ober said as he rubbed his hands together to shed off the sugar. He then popped a quick salute and went inside.

* * *

"Guy's hungry?" Jimmy asked the boys in the holding cell.

"Thanks a lot, Detective. I really needed somethin' to eat," Alec said.

"Where're the other two?"

"Victor's inside with the homicide guys. When Nick started moanin' and pukin' they called an ambulance and took 'em to the 'mergency room. What's gonna happen to us, Detective? We goin' to jail?" Reds asked pitifully.

"Maybe, just hafta wait'n see."

When Jimmy entered his office, Conroy was critiquing the investigation. "Okay, we've talked to all of 'em and they say the same thing. Essentially, that the dead guy attacked the Nicholson kid and was stranglin' 'em with this belt. Gotta believe it belonged to 'em because the initials CAO on it match the name we found on his military ID. After seein' the Nicholson kid and listening to the others, I feel confident they're tellin' the truth and acted in self-defense. I've decided to cut 'em loose and see what the state's attorney says. Anybody got anything to add?"

When they heard a loud roar and clapping come from the squad room, Bloodsworth said, "Roll call's over."

"If nobody has nothin' else, that'll do it. Thanks for all the help, guys," Conroy said in closing.

Dom let out a sigh of relief and immediately ran to the lobby and told the Bazeys and several other parents of Conroy's decision. While waiting for the paperwork to be completed, Dom polished off two butter rums and a lady finger. He then escorted Victor and Alec to the front.

"Dad, it wasn't our fault," sobbed Victor. "Guy was tryin' to kill us."

"We'll talk about it when we get home, Vic," Luke calmly said as he put his arm around Victor's shoulders.

Bloodsworth called Conroy into one of the interrogation rooms and said, "Gunner, what's with that guy, Rogers? I get a funny feelin' just ain't somethin' right about 'em."

"Me, too, can't put my finger on it though. Haven't known 'em that long. Just transferred into the unit last week."

"What was that shit ya said to 'em 'bout havin' flat feet?"

"Told me they kept him outta the army, but I don't believe it. Seems physically fit enough to me."

"Hmmp, he's weird."

While Bloodsworth and Conroy conversed, Detective Jordan approached Rogers as he was completing paperwork. "You're Detective Rogers, right?" Jordan asked.

"Uh-huh," Rogers replied as he took note of Jordan's attitude change.

"I'm Eddie Jordan, glad to meet ya," he answered with a Dudley Do Right smile.

"Friends call me Kenny. Glad to meet you," Rogers replied as he took Jordan's hand.

* * *

After Rogers' signals appeared on Jordan's 'gaydar' screen at the trestle, he watched him closely and noticed how he subtly perused the other men, especially in the groin area, then casually looked away. He also detected a hint of a swish and softness about him, particularly in the eyes. "It's over a hundred degrees out here and he looks like he just stepped outta the shower," Jordan said to himself.

Jordan's assessment of Rogers was accurate. In 1942 when Rogers was drafted, his flat-footedness was detected but didn't disqualify him from military service, but the check mark in the 'yes' box of his induction questionnaire regarding homosexual tendencies *did*. Although his foot malady was noted on the file, no mention of his sexual penchant appeared.

In 1945 at age twenty-one when Rogers made application to the Baltimore City Police Department, the recruiting officer was interested in filling vacancies created during WW II and ignored it when Rogers informed him of his foot deficiency.

"Anything else wrong with ya?" the recruiter asked.

"Not that I know of."

"Your feet won't keep ya out. After a couple years walkin' a beat they'd go flat anyway. Report to city hall Monday and take the written exam."

Rogers passed with flying colors. During his physical examination, the doctor said, "You do have fallen arches, but that shouldn't be a problem."

Rogers graduated second in his academy class and was assigned to the central district walking a foot beat on the 'Block'—a section of East Baltimore Street lined with bars and strip joints similar to those in the French Quarter of New Orleans. Prostitution ran rampant in the *Villa Nova* and *Two O'clock Club*; the *Gayety Theater* where Blaze Starr regularly performed, featured live burlesque shows nightly. The area the Block encompassed was a bevy of activity where foreign dignitaries, movie stars and US Congressman often roamed the crowded streets.

The Block was an excellent source of revenue for the city and corrupt politicians, and patrol officers were discouraged from making arrests or using physical force. Rogers fit in well and liked it. He became friendly with the bartenders and never paid for a meal or drink. He partied there with other officers until a whore said to him, "What're ya some kinda fairy?" after he refused oral sex from her.

After three years of 'poundin' the ground,' Rogers was accepted to the detective bureau and transferred to the northern district where he gained a reputation as a good investigator and was looked upon as a 'lone wolf.' Four years later he went to homicide where he was forced to team up with Conroy.

* * *

Following a few minutes of small talk, Jordan and Rogers were sure of one another's sexual preference. Before leaving, Jordan said, "Get together for a drink sometime?"

Rogers found him attractive and thought for a moment. After deciding Jordan wouldn't endanger his secret, he said, "Sure, when?"

"Gimme your number."

"Call anytime, I don't go out much," Rogers said as he handed him a business card.

"Neither do I," Jordan answered and winked.

When they got home, Luke sat the boys down and said, "Now tell me everything that happened. And I mean *everything*."

"The guy tried to kill us, Dad. We had to stop 'em," Victor said.

"He really did, was chokin' Nick with his belt," Alec added.

"I said, from the *beginning*, dammit."

As Victor related the epic saga, Luke and Lucy sat slack jawed.

"That's it, Dad. The whole entire story," Alec said.

"Can you believe this shit? And where's all the stuff ya bought at Sunny's?"

"Left it all on the train. All I have is this watch and duffle pants."

"Would've killed for one of those on Iwo," Luke said to himself when he recognized the watch's vintage. He then took notice of the jumper-cable handle holding the slack in the pants' waist and asked, "Where's the Bible you were gonna buy?"

"Lied about that, Dad. Bought the equipment at Sunny's with the money."

"Sweet Jesus, Vic, what in hell were you thinkin' of?"

Victor offered no explanation and shrugged.

"Ya think this is funny?" Luke said with raised eyebrows to Lucy as she held back a smile. "Lord have mercy on this bunch, for we know not what we do," he said when they all began laughing.

"Think I'm gonna jail, Dad?" Victor asked.

"Only if we're lucky!"

When they recovered from their laughter, Luke said, "Y'all are gonna be held responsible for your actions from either the court or God."

Hope it's from God, Victor thought.

"Okay, you're both grounded indefinitely. No TV, no radio, no movies, no friends, no nothin'. Is that clear, fellas?"

"Yeah, we understand," Victor said.

"And I was looking forward to watching Winky-Dink and Howdy-Doody on Saturday," Alec said to himself.

* * *

At the time, The Coroner's Office for the State of Maryland was responsible for conducting autopsies in Baltimore City and all of Maryland's twenty-three counties. Coroners were not required to be medical doctors and served on a part-time basis until Dr. Russell Fisher professionalized the system and converted it to the Office of the Chief

Medical Examiner. Dr. Fisher served as the Chief Medical Examiner until his death, and was considered the foremost authority on postmortem examinations. He headed the autopsy of President John F. Kennedy in 1963.

When Conroy showed the ID card to Helen Rasmussen, she was able to identify the person in the photo as her brother, Caspar Olszewski, and confirmed he had been a POW and an incorrigible alcoholic since his return from the war. Further, that she had not been in contact with him for several years, and to her knowledge he was living on the streets in Highlandtown. After viewing the body at the coroner's office, she confirmed it as that of her brother.

After Dr. Fisher was apprised of the identification, he officially declared the deceased as: Caspar Alfred Olszewski. When given the circumstances surrounding his demise, Dr. Fisher determined the cause of death to be a result of sharp-force injury to the neck and back from a pointed object, possibly a bayonet as used by Japanese forces during WW II. The manner of death was ruled undetermined homicide, pending further investigation.

The next morning, Conroy responded to the Felony Screening Section of the Maryland State's Attorney's Office where after explaining the details of the death to an assistant state's attorney, 'RECOMMEND NOT TO PROSECUTE,' was rubber stamped on the application and forwarded to State's Attorney Hall Hammond, who concurred with the recommendation: Dr. Fisher then finalized the death as justifiable homicide.

When Conroy called Bloodsworth and informed him of Hammond's decision, he asked him to notify the Bazeys. "Sure thing, Gunner, I'll call Dom, he'll let 'em know."

"Thanks again for all the help. Be sure and tell Jimmy he's a shoo-in for homicide if I have anything to say about it."

"No, he's a keeper. I'll just tell 'em ya said thanks and that he did a good job. I won't mention none of that other shit to 'em."

"Trade ya even up—him for Rogers."

"Not on your B-seventeen ass, buddy."

"What about you? Ever think of transferrin' over?"

"Thought about it. Not right now though, happy here with my burglaries and stuff."

"Lemme know if ya wanna change course."

"Sure thing, Gunner. Talk to ya soon."

* * *

"Did they ever find out who the guy was?" Luke asked Dom after learning of the state's attorney's decision.

"Yeah, had a Pollock name, Ozinski or somethin'. A POW they said."

"Could his name have been Olszewski?" Lucy asked.

"Yeah, that's it. Olszewski—Caspar I think. Hadda brother killed down Sparris Point some years ago they said. Fell down a smokestack or somethin'. You all right, girl?" Dom said as he grabbed Lucy's arm when she staggered and turned pale.

"Come over here and sit down, honey. Want a glass of water or somethin'?" Luke asked.

"Yeah, water."

"Here, drink this. I'll call Dr. Houska and he'll come right over," Luke said when he returned.

"No, don't bother him. Just give me a minute and I'll be all right."

A few minutes later, Lucy's color began to return and Dom said, "Ya looked like ya saw a ghost or somethin'. Ya all right now? Did I say somethin' that upset ya?"

"The man who fell down the smokestack and died was my first-husband Paul's best friend, Alec Olszewski. We named our Alec after him. Paul said he had a younger brother named Cas. Never met either one of them, but Paul talked about them all the time. My God, the dead man would've kinda been Alec's uncle. I can't believe it."

"What next, cuz?" asked Luke.

"Hard to say, Lukie, hard to say."

* * *

It had become customary for the firefighters of Forty-one Engine's 'B' shift to converge for breakfast after their last night of evening shift at the *White Coffee Pot*, a chain restaurant in the Baltimore area famous for its pancakes and sausage. Luke passed on breakfast on the first day of school, and hurried home to see the boys off. Just as they were leaving, Luke pulled up. "Have any fires last night, Dad?" Alec asked.

"Didn't get one run."

"Too bad."

"Where's your lunch, Vic?"

"Don't need lunch. City's gotta cafeteria, gym, swimmin' pool, showers and everything."

"Wow. Can't wait 'til *I* get to go to high school," Alec said.

Luke felt good that Victor seemed interested in his new school. "Got enough for lunch?" he asked.

"Mom took care of me."

Luke grinned and said, "Now if the teacher asks you boys what ya did this summer, don't tell her," he then changed to a falsetto voice and finished, "I killed a man, teacher, got arrested and stayed locked down at home."

"Luke, stop," said Lucy who had joined them. "They've been through enough."

"Go on now. Don't wanna be late on your first day."

"Think they'll be all right?" Luke asked.

"Certainly hope so," Lucy answered.

"What ya doin' home?"

"Mr. Haussner gave me the day off."

"How come?"

"Because it was Labor Day yesterday and I worked. He told me I didn't have to come back until Wednesday."

"Does that mean we have the whole house to ourselves?" Luke asked with a devilish glint.

"Sure does."

"Get naked, baby, we got lost time to make up for."

When they got in the vestibule, Luke goosed her. "Be patient," Lucy said as she wriggled from her housecoat.

After completing a two-hour 'zesty session,' Luke rolled over and said, "When was the last time we did it, baby?"

"I can't remember. Been such a long time."

"Good to be back in the saddle. Missed my pancakes at the Coffee Pot this mornin', what say we get dressed and go get some?"

"It's ten o'clock, haven't they stopped serving breakfast?" Lucy asked as she looked at the Westclox wind up on the night stand.

"Breakfast there twenty-four hours."

"Sounds great, let's go. I'm starved."

* * *

There is an old riddle: what are people who use the Rhythm Method called? 'PARENTS,' is the correct answer. Murphy's Law states: what *can* go wrong, *will* go wrong, and at the worst possible time.

In their lust, they had forgotten Lucy's ovulation time had not been calculated recently. Although Luke considered it while making love, he thought, one time won't matter; Murphy's Law held fast and the riddle's answer was reinforced.

When she was two weeks late, Lucy went to Dr. Houska. "Let me be the first to congratulate you—you're pregnant," he said after running a series of tests.

Lucy reacted calmly as she was quite sure she was. "Tell him what you just told me," she said after calling Luke in.

"Luke, you're gonna be a father."

"I'm gonna be a father?" he answered with a stunned look.

"Are you upset, honey?"

"Hell no, I'm on cloud nine. I was hopin' you were pregnant. When's the baby due, Doc?"

"From what Lucy told me, I figure sometime around the first of June."

Lucy thought about when Alec was born and Paul was killed. Hope it's earlier, she said to herself.

"That's great news, Doc," Luke said as he beamed with pride.

"Lucy wants Dr. Rysanek to deliver the child, the same doctor that delivered Alec. He's still at St. Joseph's. Make an appointment as soon as possible. It's important she begin her prenatal care right away."

"I'll call the minute we get home. Anything else?"

"No, that's it for now. Again, congratulations."

"Thanks, Doc. We love ya."

When they got home, Luke gave Lucy a glass of orange juice and made her sit. "I'm not an invalid," she said.

"Just tryin' to look out for you and the baby, sweetheart."

"I loved Paul, Luke, but you are the *true* love of my life. I don't know what we would've done without you, darling. I'm so happy to be giving you a child of your own."

"I love ya, too, baby. You and the boys are the best thing that's ever happened to me." He then led her to the bedroom, and they made love.

When the boys got home from school, Luke said, "Got somethin' to tell ya guys."

Victor looked at him warily and was suspicious of his good spirits. "What we done now, Dad?" he asked.

"Your mother's gonna have a baby."

When they didn't answer, Luke said, "Doesn't that make ya happy?"

"Yeah, Dad, it does," Victor answered.

"When's the baby comin'?" asked Alec.

"In June," answered Lucy.

"Hope it's on my birthday."

Hope it's not, she thought.

Alec knew his natural father had been killed in action, but wasn't aware it occurred on the day he was born. As Lucy didn't want his birthday to be stigmatized, she draped the ribbon over the date on the plaque holding the Medal of Honor. Alec became accustomed to the decoration and ignored it. Victor never connected the two events.

That night, while celebrating Lucy's pregnancy at Josie and Maria's, Luke poured a small amount of wine for the boys and Lucy. "Ah saluta, to the finest woman in the world and our forthcoming addition to the family," he said while offering a toast.

When the glasses touched, some wine spilled from Luke's. He had been told by his grandfather of the Italian superstition whereas if any falls during a toast, bad luck will come upon the holder of the glass from which the wine came. Luke blew it off and continued with the celebration.

THE DEVIL AND ME AND THE BABY MAKES THREE

On April 2, 1953, the Minor League Orioles and Major League Yankees met for an exhibition game at *Memorial Stadium*. Luke had only seen the Yanks play on one occasion when he and Dom visited relatives in the Bronx. The 'Yankee Clipper,' 'Joltin' Joe DiMaggio, was out injured then, but in good shape and ready to go for this match up.

At the time, *Memorial Stadium* was known as *Babe Ruth Stadium* in honor of the Baltimore native. The voice of the Orioles and Colts, Chuck Thompson, dubbed it 'The Old Gray Lady on 33rd Street.'

Heavy thunderstorms and reports of tornadoes forced the game to be cancelled after six innings with the visitors leading 16-1. DiMaggio hit two home runs that day: the first one off the starting pitcher, Duane Pilette; the second from reliever Hoyt Wilhelm, who was vindicated in 1957 when he threw a no-hitter against the Yankees—one of three pitched at Memorial Stadium.

Despite the disparity in the score, Luke and the boys had a great time. Not only did they see DiMaggio perform at his best, they stuffed themselves and bought a Yankee cap. "Wonder what the score'd a been if the game went nine?" Luke asked.

"Probably a hunnert to nothin'," Alec answered.

"The Orioles did score *one* run," Victor reminded him.

"Yeah, how'd that happen?" Luke asked.

"When ol' number eleven, Gus Triandos, the 'Golden Greek,' knocked one a Whitey Ford's fastballs over the right-center fence," Victor said.

"Forgot about that."

When they got home, Lucy asked if they were hungry. "Couldn't eat a thing," Luke answered as he rubbed his protruding stomach. "Had three hot dogs, at least a pound a peanuts, a large bag a popcorn, drank two 'Nattys' and one Coke. Boys did pretty good, too. Doubt if they're hungry. How ya feelin', babe?"

"Good. Got some ironing done, then took a nap. Just woke up a half hour ago."

"Think I'll go lay down awhile myself. If I'm not up by seven, wake me. Don't wanna miss the Milton Berle Show. Donald O'Connor and Frances the Talkin' Mule are guests tonight."

"I'm *sure* you'd be devastated if you missed Frances."

* * *

On June 11, 1953, Lucy went into labor. "Ready to go, huh?" Snake asked Luke when he arrived.

"Yeah, my wife's on the sofa in the livin' room."

"Gotta back door? Don't wanna take a chance on droppin' 'er down those damn marble steps."

"Yeah, good idea. Meet ya out back."

Luke and Snake, accomplished short-order chefs, became acquainted by exchanging recipes. "Call me if I can be of service when the time comes. Pulled eighteen from the chute and ain't missed one yet. Hell, one of 'em's even named after me and my partner—Jake Andy Johnson," Snake proudly said.

"Sure will, buddy."

After securing Lucy onto a gurney, Snake said, "Where to, City Hospital?"

"Hell no, wouldn't take ma dog to that bone factory. St. Joe's."

"Ten-four. Ya ridin' with us?"

"Drivin'. Gotta make a quick call first."

"See ya there."

Luke knew Snake was well experienced in giving aid and saving lives. He was all business on the job and maintained an excellent bedside manner. "Be right there, baby. You're in good hands with these guys." Lucy smiled and felt secure by Luke's assurance.

"Hello."

"Dom, Lucy's on her way to St. Joe's. I'm headed there now. Meet ya?"

"Yeah, I'll call the others. Anything ya need?"

"Just for ya to be there."

"See ya soon."

* * *

Teresa Sophia Bazey—'Terri,' weighed in at seven pounds even.

"Ain't she a beaut'?" Luke said as he gawked at Terri's shriveled-up face.

"Look at 'er hair," shouted Dom. "Ya done good, Lukie, she's gorgeous."

Dom then began opening and closing his palms while making blowfish faces.

"Stop, man, before they put ya in the frickin' psycho ward," Luke told him.

Dom ignored the comment and continued. "Look, Luke, she thinks

I'm funny."

"You're funny all right, funny in the head. Now stop, you're embarrassin' me."

"What in the world is he doing?" Luke's sister asked him when she arrived.

"Just bein' his usual asshole self. Don't ya know the damn fool well enough by now?"

"Yeah, you're right. Lost my head there for a minute, haven't seen 'em lately."

When Luke visited the maternity ward, Lucy was breast feeding. "Hi, baby. Love ya. How ya feelin?" he asked as he kissed her on the forehead.

"Got two of us to call baby now. I feel wonderful," she answered with a glowing smile.

"Ain't she beautiful?" asked Luke.

"Looks just like you, darling."

"No," Luke said in strong disagreement, "looks like 'er mother."

"Think she's finished yet?" a nurse asked.

"Think so," answered Lucy.

As she began walking away with Terri, Luke said, "Can I hold 'er?"

"Sure, sorry I didn't ask."

Terri let out a loud burp and spit up. "Sounds like her father after drinking a Natty," said Lucy. While wiping her face, Luke detected a strong odor.

"Smells like her father after eating half pound of Conte Luna and marinara," Lucy said.

"I think she's ready for *you* now," Luke said to the nurse.

* * *

"I love her, Mom. She's so pretty and has such nice hair," Alec said when he first saw Terri.

"Me, too," said Victor.

As it was impossible to resist her natural charm, Victor didn't feel the animosity toward Terri he held for Alec. Above all, he had come to love and respect Luke, and she was *his* daughter.

INVIDIA

At first, Alec couldn't do enough for Terri. When he realized she had replaced him as the center of attention, however, he displayed his resentment by ignoring her and through bad behavior. Luke and Lucy noticed the change, but overlooked it until the principal sent him home for telling the teacher to 'fuck off' when she asked him to erase the blackboards.

After conversing with Alec, Dr. Houska determined his change in personality was a result of two factors: first, an increase in his testosterone level; second, a delayed reaction to the killing at the railroad trestle. Houska said the problem would correct itself, and advised everyone to be sympathetic and understanding in the meantime.

In actuality, the problem was created by the *Sixth Deadly Sin—Invidia.*

* * *

A few days later while shopping for comic books, Alec noticed a booklet entitled, 'Protecting Your Child from Crib Death.' The first page informed parents that a small percentage of children die in their sleep for no apparent reason, and warned them to tuck all bedding under the crib's mattress so as not to enable the child to become choked by it if placed in their mouth. Also, to encourage the child to sleep face up, as most victims appeared to have died while asleep face down. Alec tucked the booklet in his shirt pocket then bought a copy of Superman, Batman and The Green Lantern.

When he returned home, he stepped lightly and stopped at the top of the steps leading to the basement where he could tell from the sound of steam being released that his mother was ironing. He then crept to his room and sat on the edge of his bed where he began reading the booklet. When he finished, he went to his parent's bedroom.

Before Terri was born, when Alec had a bad dream or became frightened, he would bring his blanket and pillow and curl up on the floor where the crib now was. "Look at the little bitch, sleepin' in my spot," he said with great contempt. He then rolled her onto her stomach and watched. When she continued to breathe, he turned her face up.

Alec had seen a movie starring Dan Duryea where he put a cushion over his wife's face in an attempt to murder her and when he didn't see condensation on the mirror he placed under her nostrils, he knew the job was done.

As Terri began to awaken, Alec covered her face with a pillow. When she coughed lightly and began to wiggle, he applied more pressure until she stopped moving then placed an eyebrow mirror under her nose. When there was no fog, he said, "Got 'er like the heron got that fish. She never knew what hit 'er."

He then turned her over and stuffed one end of the blanket in her mouth, and replaced the pillow and mirror. He gathered his comics and took the booklet outside and threw it in a sewer hole. "Mom, I'm home," Alec said loudly when he re-entered the house.

"Okay, honey, be up in a minute, have to check on the baby."

When Lucy got upstairs, Alec was sitting on the sofa reading. "See you got your new supply," she said while rubbing his head.

"Yeah, gotta new one this time, the Green Lantern, ever heard of 'em?"

Lucy thought Alec seemed in better spirits. "Maybe the trip to the doctor's office helped," she said to herself. "No, never heard of him. Gotta go check on Terri, she's due up anytime now."

"Alec come quick, something's wrong with Terri, she's not breathing," Lucy shouted when she got upstairs.

Alec stopped reading and stuffed his comic books under the middle cushion of the sofa. "Gotta protect the Green Lantern from Victor," he said.

Alec then darted upstairs and saw Lucy holding Terri above her head and shaking her lightly while frantically saying, "What's wrong, baby? What's wrong? Please start breathing. "God, please don't let her die!"

Terri's glazed eyes and mouth were partially opened, and her lifeless head bobbed like a rag doll. Alec faked a look of concern and said, "Mom, what's wrong? Is Terri all right?"

"Go next door and get Mrs. Varipapa!"

"Mrs. Varipapa come quick, Mom needs ya, somethin's wrong with Terri, She's not breathin'," Alec shouted while beating on the door. "Gotta make this look good," he whispered. "Open the door, please open the door," he shouted as he hammered the knocker.

Mr. Varipapa, home alone at the time, had been asleep. "What the hell's wrong, boy? The place on fire or somethin'?"

"Ya gotta come quick. Mom needs help with the baby. Hurry!"

When he got there, Terri was lying face up on the bed. "Please God, don't let her be dead. Please, please, please, Lord," Lucy repeated over and over.

Mr. Varipapa, a WW II veteran, was familiar with dead bodies and said, "Terri's with God now," as he covered Lucy's praying hands with his.

Lucy lowered her head and said, "My baby, my sweet little girl is dead."

Wish Mr. Varipapa'd go home so I could get back to my comics, Alec said to himself.

"Where's Luke?" Mr. Varipapa asked.

"I don't know. Him and Victor went to fix a car. Would you call Dom and see if he knows? His number's next to the phone."

The two had become acquainted when Dom visited, and were on a first-name basis. "Dom, Gus Varipapa. Ya know where Luke is?"

"Got no idea. Is anything wrong, Gus?" Dom asked when he heard Mr. Varipapa's somber tone.

"Ya should come over here right away, Terri's dead."

A feeling of surrealism came over Dom and he asked, "Terri who? Not the baby."

"Yeah, Dom, the baby. Get over here right away."

"What the hell happened?"

"Not sure, just come."

"On my way."

While traveling at a breakneck pace, Dom was stopped by a Maryland State Trooper just before he got to the city limits on Route 40. "I stopped you for operating your vehicle in a reckless manner," Trooper Long politely informed Dom.

Damn troopers, don't they have anything better to do than stop honest citizens? Dom thought. He flashed his badge and said, "Police emergency."

"What happened?"

"Not sure how, but my baby niece died."

"Where is she now?"

"Six-hundred block of Macon Street in Hollandtown."

"Know it well. Grew up on Tolna, a few blocks away. Follow me, get ya there in a couple minutes."

"Good man. Lead the way."

With red lights and siren, five minutes later they turned onto Macon Street. "Thanks for everything, Trooper. If I can ever help *you* with anything call southeastern and ask for Sergeant Sabitini."

"My pleasure, Sergeant," Long said and proceeded back to his patrol area.

Mr. Varipapa met Dom at the front door and led him to Lucy's bedroom.

"What happened, Luce?"

"I don't know. When I came to check on her she wasn't breathing. I just don't know what happened."

"Where's Luke and the boys?"

"Luke and Vic went to Waverly to work on a car. Should be here anytime. Alec's downstairs."

"How's he takin' it?"

"He's really upset. He really loved Terri."

"I'll go check on 'em."

"Alec, ya down 'ere, boy?" Dom said as he walked down the stairs.

"Yeah, I'm here, Uncle Dom," he answered while stashing his comics in a closet.

"How ya doin', kid? Doin' all right?"

It's workin', things gettin' back to normal already, Alec said to himself. "Is Terri really with God like Mr. Varipapa said?"

"Afraid she is, Al. God loved her and wanted her with him."

"If she's with God, she'll be all right."

Alec was delighted when he realized he was crying real tears: Dan Duryea couldn't have done a better job himself, he thought.

After coddling Alec for a few minutes, Dom called the southeastern precinct. "Sounds like a crib death to me, what about you?" Blooodsworth said.

"Yeah, I was thinkin' the same thing."

"General order requires homicide to investigate CDs. I'll call 'em, then head over myself."

"Thanks, Blood. See ya when ya get here."

When Luke and Victor turned onto Macon Street, they saw a conglomeration of fire department and police vehicles blocking the intersection. "What in hell's goin' on here?" Luke asked as he saw Dom walking toward them.

Dom considered death notification the worst part of his job. He tried a variety of ways in which to deliver the 'blow,' but came to the conclusion the direct method was best. He balled his fists, straightened his arms and set them on Luke's shoulders. "Brace yourself, cuz'... Terri's dead."

Denial is the first stage of acceptance; "Don't be fuckin' with me, Sabitini. Everybody knows you're a clown, but this ain't no way to fuck aroun', God dammit," Luke said in shrouded hope that Dom's message was untrue.

"Do I look like I'm jokin', Lukie?"

When Luke stared into his eyes, he knew the truth. His head began to spin, his knees buckled and he staggered. "What happened, Uncle Dom?" Victor asked.

"Don't know, Vic. Homicide's inside now tryin' to put it together."

"How's Lucy?" asked Luke.

"Pretty shook up."

When they went in, Luke said, "How ya doin', baby?"

"I'm your only baby again. Terri's gone."

"What happened, how'd she die?"

"Don't know. I found her dead in the crib. What difference does it make? She's gone, no matter what."

Luke and Dom went to the bedroom where Bloodsworth and Detective Rogers were examining the body. "We meet again, sailor," Bloodsworth said to Luke with an extended hand and sympathetic smile.

" 'Deed we do, Girene."

"Detective Rogers from homicide, sorry to meet ya under these circumstances, Mr. Bazey. Didn't meet ya the last time."

"Good to make your acquaintance, Detective."

Rogers, who interrogated Victor during their first encounter, said, "Been keepin' straight, Vic?"

"Yes, sir. Grown up a lot since the last time I saw ya."

Rogers turned to the others and said, "I've found no evidence of foul play to the body. When I arrived, Mrs. Bazey explained to me the child was fine when she lay her down for a nap, but when she returned, found a corner of the bed blanket in her mouth. I seriously doubt if she choked on it as no petechial hemorrhaging has been noticed. It's my opinion she died as a result of the Crib Death Syndrome. Dr. Fisher at the coroner's office requires autopsies to be performed where this phenomenon is suspected."

"Is an autopsy really necessary, Detective?" Luke asked.

"Yes, sir, I'm afraid it is. It's required by law," Rogers explained gently.

"Okay, I understand, but don't tell my wife, she'd freak out knowin' her little girl was gettin' sliced up like a roll of baloney."

"We'll keep it to ourselves, sir," promised Rogers.

"What now?" Luke asked.

"The ambulance crew is standing by ready to go."

"Hold on, gimme a few minutes with my family before ya take her away, okay?"

"Take all the time ya need, sir."

"Dom, stay here. Be back inna minute," Luke said as he slapped him on the shoulder.

"Okay, Lukie, be waitin' for ya."

When they returned, Luke tied a white embroidered ribbon around Terri's head and put a pair of booties on her Lucy's mother had crocheted. They knelt and delivered several prayers and asked God to accept her into heaven, kissed her, cried and left. When they got back downstairs, Luke looked pitifully at Rogers and said, "Okay, Detective, you can have 'er now."

Alec cried like a baby when the ambulance driver carried Terri down the steps. Good riddance, bitch, he said to himself as they went through the door.

* * *

Terri's body was laid to rest at the Most Holy Redeemer Cemetery next to Luke's grandparents. A small head stone with her name and inscription, 'Terri we will meet again in heaven,' marked her grave. Alec put on his best performance in front of relatives and friends when he sobbed about how much he would miss his beautiful little sister. Luke's father reminded him that God sometimes acts in strange ways. Alec loved it; *he was number one again.*

THE CICADA

After Terri's death, Lucy lost all interest in life and became depressed. Fearing she might suffer a relapse of her mental illness, Luke took her to Dr. Houska for an evaluation. After writing prescriptions, Houska said to Luke, "If she displays *any* sudden mood swing, especially in the form of euphoria, bring her in immediately."

"Sure thing, Doc. I'll let ya know if anything changes."

* * *

In mid-September, Lucy 'suddenly' became her old self and began rising early and completing chores. Her interest in sex renewed, and she wasn't satisfied after making love.

"Looks like Mom's gettin' back to normal," Alec said to Luke.

"Yeah, she's a lot better," Luke answered with a contented look on his face.

One morning when he got home from night shift, Luke discovered Lucy at the kitchen table completely naked writing Christmas cards.

"How come ya don't have any clothes on, hon'?"

"Had a hot flash, must be those pills the doctor gave me. Think I'll stop taking them; they slow me down too much."

"Ya writin' *Christmas* cards? Hell, Christmas ain't for three months yet," Luke said with a confused look.

"Luke, how many times have I told you there is no such word as ain't?"

"Never," he answered curtly.

"Well, I'm telling you now, it's not a word. And I don't want to hear you using it again. As far as the cards go, I thought I'd get an early start, that's all."

Luke detected an air of arrogance and superiority in Lucy, along with an 'in-charge' attitude he had never seen before. "Don't talk to me in that tone, God dammit. I'll say whatever the hell I feel like sayin'."

"I'm sorry I yelled at you, sweetheart. It's that medication," Lucy said as she put on her housecoat.

When she started crying, Luke rubbed her shoulders and said, "We'll go to the doctor and see if he'll change your meds."

"Want to make love?" Lucy said.

"Let's go."

When they finished, she said, "I called Mr. Haussner last night and told him I was ready to go back to work."

"What'd he say?" Luke answered with surprise.

"He told me I could start tonight."

"Ya really think you're ready? Hell, a month ago ya couldn't stay awake."

Who in the fuck does he think *he* is to question *me*? He's not a damn doctor, she said to herself. "Oh, yes. I feel a lot better now than I did then. I need to get around other people."

Luke pondered closely and thought: maybe it *will* do her good; she hasn't been out of the house since Terri died.

"I'll agree under one condition."

"What's that, honey?"

"We go see Dr. Houska tomorrow and ya let me say ain't."

"That's two conditions. Okay to both."

* * *

"You an hour early," Mr. Haussner said as he looked at his watch.

"Couldn't wait to get started," Lucy answered.

"Good to have you beck."

"Good to be back."

"Sherman, someone here to see you," Mr. Haussner chirped through the kitchen door.

"Mizz Lucy! Lawd have mercy, good ta see ya, honey. Haven't seed ya since ... "

"Since the funeral. I never got a chance to thank you all for coming. What tables are mine tonight?"

"Vun trew five. Same as before."

As her adrenal glands began overproducing, a local businessman who had previously complained about Lucy's service was seated at table two. "Don't I get any water tonight, young lady? I'm thirsty, had a hard day," he impugned.

Reminiscent of the demon-possessed Regan MacNeil vomiting on Father Karras, Lucy spit in the customer's face. "Drink that, you fat fuckin' prick," she roared at him in a deep, throaty voice.

"And what do you do for an encore, shit on the table?" the customer said as he wiped spittle from his glasses.

While hitting him with the edge of a serving tray, she yelled, "How's that for an encore, you cock sucker?"

As she was about to plunge a butter knife in his eye, a plain-clothed police officer sitting at the next table blocked the thrust. "Somebody call the 'rollers,' " he shouted as he wrestled her to the floor.

"God, you're a cruel and selfish mother fucker for taking my baby. You're a no-good God, you son of a bitch. I love the devil, I hate you, I hate you, I hate you. Long live the devil. Fuck God!"

When the uniforms arrived and saw Lucy's wild behavior, they called for Mariah. After Mick and Dick got there, they restrained her with handcuffs and leg irons then took her to Pine Street where she was put in a straight jacket and placed in solitary confinement.

* * *

Luke planned on checking on Lucy, but never got the opportunity as his company was called to a two-alarm blaze at McCormick Spices. When he returned at eleven, a marked police cruiser was waiting out front. "Luke Bazey?" Officer Reynolds asked.

"That's me, what's up?"

"I was by earlier and the watch man told me ya were out on a fire. Thought I'd give it another try before quittin' time."

When Reynolds turned his head to avoid eye contact, Luke knew he was in for bad news and said hastily, "Please, Officer, get to the point."

"Your wife was arrested after trying to kill a man at Haussner's."

"My wife? What the fuck ya talkin' 'bout? My wife wouldn't hurt a fly."

"Lucy Bazey, that's your wife right?"

"Yes, sir. Lucy Bazey."

"She went off on a customer and tried to stab him with a butter knife. Detective havin' dinner there arrested 'er and took 'er to Pine Street."

Luke thought about Lucy's aggressive behavior and asked, "She still there?"

"Yes, sir, far as I know. She was in pretty bad shape. They'll probably bypass a hearing and take 'er right to Spring Grove."

"Thanks, Officer."

After learning Lucy had been transferred, Luke requested the remainder of his shift off. "Sure," Lt. Fox said, "call if we can help."

"Thanks, Lieut. I can stay and hang hoses if ya want."

"Don't worry about it, other guys'll do it."

Luke met Mr. Haussner at his restaurant where he poured them each a shot of Drambuie. When he saw a painting of a beautiful naked woman in the stag bar, he thought of Lucy writing Christmas cards.

After he returned to his car and digested what Mr. Haussner had told him, he said, "Ya dumb son of a bitch, why didn't ya listen to the fuckin' doctor? Ya asshole, ya shoulda never agreed to let 'er go back to work, especially with the way she was actin'. What were ya thinkin' of?"

He slapped himself in the face and began crying. "God, what did she ever do to deserve all this? Only *you* know what happened to 'er real parents, then ya let 'er husband get killed in the war. After that, ya put 'er in the nut house, then ya took 'er baby away. Now ya got 'er back in the loony bin; havin' fun God? What else ya got planned for 'er?"

* * *

Dr. Ingmar Janssen was renown in Europe for his success in dealing with patients suffering from what later would be known as Manic Depression or Bi-Polar Disorder. Janssen fled his native Sweden in 1938 to escape the Nazi scourge sweeping Europe and practiced in New York's Bellevue Hospital until 1946 when he moved to Baltimore after accepting the position of Head Psychiatrist at Spring Grove.

"Has your vife been hospitalized in the past for any such behavior?" Janssen asked Luke when he arrived the next day.

"Yes, sir. Ten years ago she spent thirteen months here for the same thing after 'er first husband was killed in the war," Luke answered.

"Has she suffered any recent trauma?"

"Yes, sir. We lost our daughter a few months ago."

"Any member of her family similarly afflicted?"

"Don't know anything 'bout her parents, she lost 'em at a young age. Her two sisters seem all right."

"I'm certain you vife is suffering from an episode of Manic Depression."

"Can ya explain that a little, Doc?"

"Ya. The patient suffers changes in moods. For avhile they are euphoric, then become depressed. Usually they get better, but it alvays returns. It is like a cicada that lies dormant until suddenly avakened by external forces of nature, then goes avay, then comes back."

"How long before she recovers?"

"Only time vill tell. She's been heavily sedated and vill remain asleep for some time. In a few days ve'll begin her on Lithium."

"I heard 'em say she was really wound up when the police took 'er away. Have ya ever had one this bad?"

"Yes, many. I treated a man at Bellevue a few years ago who broke a police night stick in half vith his bare hands after an officer hit him vith it. The man vas so far out of control the blow had no effect. After six months of isolation and regular doses of Lithium, he recovered and vas released. But remember, the 'cicada' *vill* at some point return."

"When can we see 'er, Doc?"

"In her present condition, I'm not allowing visitors. After a few weeks I'll re-evaluate and decide. Give me a call then and I'll let you know."

"Thanks, Doc, I know you're a good man. Please do your best. I don't know what I'd do if anything else happens to her, she's been through so much already."

"I alvays do my best," Janssen said as he smiled.

"I know she's in good hands with you, sir. I can feel it in your touch."

DOMINO I

When Janssen's evaluation sunk in during the drive home, a sense of frisson engulfed Luke. During the rapture, he realized their little 'dream house' had become a horror chamber to Lucy after Terri's death, and decided that she wouldn't return there after her release. "I'll not only move 'er from Macon Street, I'll take that job in Florida and move her outta the whole state. Too damn cold fightin' fars in Balmur in the winter anyway. Change'd do us all some good. We'll beat that frickin' cicada or die tryin'," he proclaimed with renewed spirits.

As he neared 'Little Italy,' hunger pangs hit. While savoring the 'grinder' from Vellegia's, he gazed at *The Shot Tower*.

* * *

The Phoenix Shot Tower, also known as the *Old Baltimore Shot Tower*, is a red-brick structure, 234 feet tall; it is cylindrically shaped, upwardly tapered, and when completed in 1828, was the tallest structure in the United States.

In order to produce 'drop shot' for pistols and rifles, and 'molded shot' for larger weapons such as cannons, molten lead was dropped from a platform at the top of the tower through a sieve-like device. As the lead fell, centrifugal force and gravity caused it to form shape; after it landed in a vat of water, the hot lead cooled and hardened. The newly formed shot was then dried, polished, sorted and placed into twenty-five-pound bags. The tower normally produced 100,000 bags of shot a year but was capable of double that amount if needed.

The tower ceased its production in 1892 and was designated a national historic landmark in 1972.

* * *

Luke watched pensively as 'Felix the Cat's' bulgy eyes and tail moved from left to right. "Ain't had nuthin' but bad luck since Dom gave the black bastard to Lucy for her birthday," he said as he removed the clock from the kitchen wall.

When they got home, Luke called the boys for a 'pow-wow' and explained Dr. Janssen's prognosis. "In the meantime, fellas, we're on our own. If we work together and do right, we'll get by this. We'll have to do our own warshin', arnin' and cookin'. Any problem with that, guys?" They acknowledged and felt relieved by Luke's pep talk.

The next morning, Luke found the want ad for the job in Florida. The contact person informed him the starting salary in Dade County for firefighters with professional experience was $4,950; $450 a year more than he was earning with the BCFD after eight years of service. Further, as he was serving as a firefighter, he could laterally transfer and not be required to complete twelve weeks of training.

Upon filling out the application, Luke didn't mark the block, 'date available to begin employment.' "Cross that road when we come to it," he said as he licked the envelope and placed a three-cent Liberty Head stamp on it.

* * *

"Mr. Bazey, I vas just about to call you," Dr. Janssen said when Luke called. "Mrs. Bazey is showing definite signs of improvement, but I don't think she's quite vell enough for visitors yet. I'm going to allow her to mingle vith other patients one hour a day during mealtime. Give it another two veeks and call back, okay?"

"Glad she's doin' better. Keep up the good work, talk to ya in a couple. Call me anytime. Thanks, Doc."

Although somewhat improved, Lucy was still arrogant and irritable when she joined other patients for lunch the following afternoon. "You don't expect me to eat this slop, do you?" she said when served a bowl of beef stew.

The server, a patient himself, suffered a multi-personality disorder and often assumed other personas. Before answering Lucy's question, he brushed back his pencil-thin mustache, crooked his brow and replied, "Frankly, ma deuh, I don't give a flamin' fuck what ya do with it. For all I care ya can stick it up a baboon's ass."

Bells, whistles and fire alarms went off in Lucy's head. When the attendant recovered from the scalding substance Lucy had thrown in his face, he began strangling her until she stopped breathing. "Save your Confederate money, for the South shall rise again," he shouted as orderlies subdued him.

When notified of Lucy's murder, Dr. Janssen was mortified. "How could I have let her enter patient population so soon? How could I have done such a stupid thing? How vill I ever be able to explain this to Mr. Bazey?"

"How could you have been so fuckin' stupid?" Luke echoed when given notification of Lucy's death by Dr. Janssen.

"Mr. Bazey, I just don't know vat to say. She seemed to be responding so vell to the Lithium I thought she could handle the interaction. Please forgive me, my most humble apologies go out to you and your sons."

"You bein' sorry won't bring 'er back, ya quack bastard. Damn your soul, Doctor. I'll own you and that fuckin' hospital before this is over. Do ya read me?"

"Quite clearly, Mr. Bazey. Quite clearly, sir."

After throwing the phone, Luke punched a series of holes in the plasterboard. "God what the fuck is *with* you? Why have you forsaken us so badly? What have we ever done to you?" he shouted as he repeatedly pounded his head against the wall. "How in hell am I gonna tell this to the boys?" he said as he wiped blood from his forehead.

"What's wrong, Dad?" Victor asked when he saw Luke on the sofa crying.

Before he could answer, Alec arrived and dropped his book bag. "Your mom's dead, boys. She was killed by another patient in the hospital today," Luke said as tears rolled down his face and reached for his sons.

"Boys, I know it's hard for ya to understand now, but I've found that sometimes if a tragedy don't kill ya, it can make ya stronger. Okay, guys?" Even though they didn't fully comprehend the meaning of Luke's comment, they nodded.

* * *

Although quite taken by his mother's passing, Alec quickly accepted it. He concluded that had God intended for her to live, why would he have allowed her to be murdered?

Victor lost all focus after his mother's death and found it impossible to concentrate on his schoolwork. Against Luke's advice, he dropped out and took a job delivering auto parts.

"Ya must be outta your mind if ya think I'm gonna pick that thing up."

"You're right, Vic. I was outta my mind to hire your worthless ass. Collect your pay and hit the bricks," his boss said.

"Finky, this is Victor. I'm inna jam, can ya help me?"

"What ya need?"

"Got fired from Marsheck. Can't go home, my father'll kill me. Pick me up?"

"Yeah. See ya in front of the Pulaski Memorial in about an hour."

"Thanks, Fink."

* * *

"Ya can sleep here for now. When my parents get back from New York we'll ask 'em if ya can stay longer," Finky said when he showed Victor the guest room.

"Thanks, buddy."

When Luke got home that evening, he read a letter from The Dade County Fire Department accepting him as a lateral transferee, then filed it with monthly bills.

"Have ya seen Vic, Al?"

"Nope."

"He was supposed to get off at one. Wonder what's keepin' 'em?" Luke asked as he looked at the fat-chef clock and opened an American.

Luke changed brands as it reminded him of Lucy when he saw 'Mr. Boh,' on National's label. "You'd think they could come up with something better than that for a picture," she would jokingly say when she saw the round-face caricature with one eye and a black handlebar mustache.

"Balmur's best, baby. Can't beat the stuff," Luke would answer.

With three Americans under his belt, Luke called Victor's boss. "Frank, Luke Bazey here. Seen Victor?"

After a few seconds, Luke said in an irritated voice, "Frank, ya still there?"

"I'm here, Luke. I fired Victor this mornin' after he came in late again and refused to lift a rebuilt on the truck."

"What the fuck's wrong with that boy? Did he say where he was goin'?"

"No, he just collected his pay and left."

"Thanks, Frank. Gotta big repair job comin' up next week. I'll come by and get the parts."

"Anytime. Glad to be of service."

Luke seethed and opened another beer. "After all I've done for that little bastard, he goes and pulls a stunt like this. Wait'll I get my hands on him."

"I know what his problem is," Luke said after he pondered on Victor's dismissal. "Old Vic's been through as much as any of us 'round here. He's embarrassed he got fired and don't wanna face me. He'll be home when he runs outta money."

"Ya doin' all right, bub?" Luke asked as he 'woolied' Alec's head and smiled.

"Fine, Dad. How 'bout you?"

"I'll get by, Son. Thanks for askin'."

Luke finished the six pack as he watched The Ted Mack Amateur Hour.

* * *

Victor and Finky saw a John Garfield movie on television where he and an accomplice robbed a bank. "Ever think about stickin' up a bank?" Finky asked Victor.

"No. I know one that's prime pickins' though."

"One what?"

"A bank, asshole."

"Oh, yeah. Where?"

"On Ponca and Eastern. No guard, no alarm, no nothin'. It'd be easy."

"Let's go by tomorrow and check it out."

"Ain't no harm in lookin."

The next morning, they entered the bank. "Can ya cash this for me?" Finky asked a teller.

"Do you have an account with Atlantic Federal, sir?"

"No, sure don't."

"Company policy doesn't allow me to cash a check unless the holder has an account with us. There's a First National a few blocks up next to Goldenberg's, I'm sure they'll accommodate you."

"No problem. Wasn't thinkin', I'm headin' in that direction. Thanks anyway."

"Glad to be of service, sir."

"Ya right, place's a piece a cake, a pushover," Finky said when they returned to the car.

"Told ya."

"Whatta ya think? Wanna try it?"

"Fuck it, let's do it. But first we gotta prepare."

After agreeing on a plan, Victor said, "All right, all we need is a couple a guns, a pair a nylons, a big bag and some rope. Anything else ya can think of?"

"That sounds like it. My mother's got a pair hangin' in the bathroom, and 'ere's an old canvas mail bag in the basement with a drawstring. Some clothesline down 'ere, too."

"Perfect, what about the guns?"

"Can't help in that department. What about you?"

"I know what we'll use. Get the car keys."

Finky drove to the shopping center on Pimlico Road and parked in front of the G. C. Murphy store where Victor purchased two water pistols. After they got back to the house, he carefully carved out the spouts and smoothed the ragged edges.

"We're all set, brutha. All we gotta do now is find out what time the bank opens," Victor said.

The next morning, they parked on Eastern Avenue directly across from the bank, when at nine thirty the bank manager approached and began fumbling for his keys. After unlocking the door, he retrieved the articles he placed on the ground and entered.

When they returned the following morning, Victor said, "Unlocked the place at the same time two mornings in a row. Let's get 'em tamar, okay?"

"The sooner the better," Finky replied.

* * *

As they put their 'tools' in the mail bag, Victor said, "Nylons, pistols and rope. Anything else?"

"Can't think of nothin 'ceptin' some balls."

"We got plenty of those. Ya ready?"

"Ready, let's go. Just like Garfield and Cagney."

They parked the 'getaway car,' a sky blue, torpedo-backed '49 Nash, on Oldham Street next to the bus storage lot of the Baltimore Transit Company—BTC: 'better take a cab' as deciphered by locals, then walked across Eastern Avenue and positioned themselves between the New Nemo Movie Theater and Garden Bakery.

Jimmy Saukas, inside the bakery at the time chatting with Fritz, said, "Gonna take the sergeant's exam next month. Hope I pass."

"I'm sure a sharp fella like you will do fine. By the way, thinkin' 'bout throwin' my hat into the political arena and running for city council."

"Get with my father, he'll get ya started in the right direction."

"I'll be sure and do that."

When Jimmy turned to leave, he saw Victor and Finky dash across the street. "Good Christ, they're stickin' the place up," Jimmy said when he saw them point guns at the bank manager.

Jimmy ran behind the counter and grabbed the telephone, never taking his eyes from the bank. When the call taker answered, he said in a calm, clear voice, "This is Detective Saukas from southeastern. I'm inside the Garden Bakery at the corner of Eastern and Ponca, directly across from the Atlantic Federal Bank. As we speak, I'm watchin' two armed suspects rob it. I'm gonna take a position behind a black Chevy parked in front and wait for 'em to come out. I'm a white male, five ten, one seventy-five, black hair, wearing a tan jacket with brown pants. I'm armed with a three fifty-seven. Send help quick. Got all that?"

"Yes, sir. Help's on the way."

"I'm headed over now. Advise the incomin' cars, no red lights or sirens. Don't wanna tip 'em off. I'm gonna put the manager of the bakery on the line. He'll keep ya apprised of what's happenin'."

"Good luck, Detective. God be with you, sir."

Fritz's 'blood lust' was whetted, and he experienced a feeling of rapture while listening to Jimmy. He took the telephone from him and covered the mouthpiece. "Anything I can do to help? Got a Luger under the counter here."

"No, uniforms'll be here shortly. Just stay on the line and keep communications aware of what's happenin'."

Fritz disappointingly agreed and uncovered the voice piece. "Fritz here," he said to the call taker. "Detective Saukas is on his way to the bank."

"Okay, sir. Let me know what's goin' on."

"Will do."

The dispatcher cleared the channel by activating the loud, ominous-sounding electronic warning alert. "BEEEEEP, BEEEEEP, BEEEEEP". "All cars standby-Signal Thirteen at the Atlantic Federal Bank at Ponca and Eastern. Plain-clothed off-duty Detective Saukas out front behind a black Chevy. Units respond Code Two. *Do not transmit,* keep the channel clear. Only call out when you arrive on the scene."

A *Signal 13* is an advisory to police officers that one of their 'blue brethren' is in trouble and requires immediate assistance. The term is used cautiously and sparingly as officers stop whatever they are engaged in and respond at a breakneck pace.

When the dispatcher put out the hue and cry, *every* available police unit in the southeastern district went *'en route.'* Food, coffee and soft drinks were thrown from the windows as the 'cavalry' charged to the rescue.

While in the midst of their *'flagrante delictio,'* Victor and Finky discovered they hit the mother lode. As the Highlandtown branch of the Atlantic Federal had never been robbed or burglarized, it was chosen as the place in which to store worn US currency shipped into the United States from London. An armored carrier was scheduled that afternoon to pick up the cash totaling over $1,000,000, and transport it to US Treasury Department Headquarters in Washington, DC. When they were only able to put a third of the cash in the mail bag, the duo stuffed their pockets and shirts until they bulged. Using a James Cagney line, Victor said, "Time to blow, others'll be showin' up for work soon." After taking the manager's door keys and tying him up, they headed out with the swag.

In their haste, they failed to notice Jimmy when they got outside. "Unit four-fifty on the scene. They're comin' outta the bank now with guns drawn. Have the other units step it up, radio," the first on-duty unit to arrive said.

"Units responding to the thirteen, step it up to Code Three, red lights and sirens authorized," the dispatcher urgently advised.

When the rollers heard the radio transmissions, their adrenaline levels soared to a higher plane. After activating the emergency equipment, they depressed their accelerators to the floor causing the fuel supply to increase and rush into the throttle bores of their 239-cubic-inch Ford Police Interceptor engine. As gasoline spewed into the combustion chamber of the oversized-Holley-four-barrel carburetor and sucked in more air, the distinctive 'throaty roar' bellowed from beneath the hood. At hearing the reverberation and feeling the RPM of their engines increase as their cruisers leapt forward in response, exhilaration swept through the officer's bodies and the hair on the back of their necks hackled.

The uniformed officer jumped the sidewalk with his cruiser and stopped it directly in front of the bank, putting the suspects in a crossfire position. "Police officer, drop your guns or I'll blow your fuckin' balls off!" Jimmy ordered with Finky in his sights.

Finky dropped the money bag instead of the weapon and started to raise his hands in surrender. When the gun pointed in his direction, Jimmy fired one shot that struck Finky in the right cheek bone causing his head to explode and brain matter to be splattered onto the bank wall.

After hearing the shot, the uniform responded by firing two rounds from his Remington twelve gauge. Of the eighteen lead pellets expelled from the shotgun, twelve of them struck Victor in the 'kill' zone between his waist and head.

"Ya all right, Sarge?"

"Yeah, how 'bout you, Jimmy?"

"Fine, everything's fine here."

When they saw no movement, they cautiously approached the bodies. After kicking the guns away, Jimmy removed the nylon stocking from Finky's mangled head, oozing brain matter and chunks of congealed blood.

"Oh my God what have I done? Lord have mercy on my soul," Dom shouted when he recognized Victor's face under the covering.

"The Bazey kid. I remember him," Jimmy said as he holstered his weapon and disarmed Dom, leaning against his cruiser in a semi-delirious state.

As cruisers rained in, Jimmy dragged his right forefinger across his throat.

"Ten twenty-two, ten twenty-two, ten twenty-two all units to the Atlantic Federal," an officer cried out over the police radio. "Both officers are okay, two suspects down. Start at least two ambulances this way."

"Ten-four. All units responding to the Signal thirteen at Ponca and Eastern, ten twenty-two. That's ten twenty-two all units responding to the Signal Thirteen. Channel's back in full service."

"Ya okay, Jimmy?" a uniform asked.

"Yeah, got a cigarette?"

"Get Dom to City Hospital psych ward right away; he's fucked up in the head right now. Suspect he smoked was his nephew," Jimmy said after he took a long drag from the Viceroy.

"Jesus Christ, man, what happened?"

"Didn't recognize 'em with the mask on. Call homicide, both suspects DOA. Call for the shootin' team, too."

"Ten-four, brother."

Despite the order canceling additional units, the cruisers continued to roll in. "Ten twenty-two all units to the thirteen at Ponca and Eastern," an officer said.

"Ten-four."

The police dispatcher re-sounded the electronic tone and repeated, "All units ten twenty-two, that's ten twenty-two the Atlantic Federal."

When Bloodsworth arrived and saw the stressed look on Jimmy's face, he immediately recognized it as *The Two Thousand Yard Stare*. The term is used to describe the unfocused gaze of a battle-weary soldier and was coined by *Life Magazine* war correspondent and artist Tom Lea in 1944 after the Battle of Peleliu. Victims of the 'stare' show no emotion in their eyes and appear as though life has been sucked from their bodies.

Bloodsworth had seen the look on many Marines during his military service.

Most police officers go their entire careers without firing their weapons anywhere other than the practice range. However, when forced to shoot and kill a person, many display a modified version of the stare. It is further exacerbated when fellow officers try to console the shooting officer by offering words of encouragement or expressions of congratulations for the action.

"Great job, Jimmy. Blew them sons of bitches to pieces. No-good bastards had it comin, ya did the world a favor," one officer said.

"Dumb bastards didn't even have real guns," said another as Jimmy nervously smiled.

"How ya doin', kid?" Bloodsworth asked.

"I don't know, boss. Maybe I shot too quick."

"Ya did the only thing ya coulda done, lookin' down the barrel of a forty-five," Bloodsworth said as he put his arm around Jimmy's shoulder.

"But the forty-five. I think it's a water gun."

"Did ya know it was a water gun while he was holdin' it, Jimmy?"

"Course not, if I did I wouldn't've shot."

"Well then ya were protectin' your life, Jimmy, and Dom's, too. Ya did the right thing."

"Did ya know the kid Dom shot was his nephew?"

"Jimmy, get one thing straight. The dead guys weren't *kids* out playin' hopscotch in the fuckin' street. They were grown men in the act of commitin' a damn felony. Look at that money stuffed all over 'em. Get that 'kid' shit outta your mind, they were dangerous criminals. No tellin' what they woulda done if they'd a gotten away. Shit, from the looks of things, musta hauled three, maybe four-hundred thou' outta there. Fuck with the bull, ya get the horns, Jimmy. Now get that clear in your mind, okay?"

"Okay, boss. Had no choice in the matter, I guess."

"Guess my ass. Tell ya what, Jimmy, the next time somebody points a gun at ya, examine it *real* close before ya shoot. Then ask 'em if the fuckin' thing is real or not. See where that gets ya. It'll get ya a six-foot hole, that's what it'll get ya."

"Thanks, boss. I love ya, man. You're absolutely right. I acted in good faith when I shot. I truly believed it was a real gun."

"One other thing, don't listen to what those airhead 'trol cops tell ya. The ones doin' the most talkin' were too young for WW two and the others got a deferment for Korea when they joined the department. They don't know shit from Shinola when it comes to killin'. They think it's cool, like when John Wayne does it in the movies. If somebody likes it, they're a sick fuck. Did my share in the Corps and hated it. Was glad as shit when it was over and I got back to the farm."

"Okay, boss. I'll ignore 'em."

"Here comes your dad now. Stay with him 'til homicide and the shootin' team gets here. They'll drag ya over the coals, but be cool; they have a job to do, too. Better they do it to ya now and not some prick attorney in court. They'll treat ya right. I'm gonna go to the hospital and check on Dom. I'll catch up with ya when I'm finished."

"Thanks, boss."

"Ya can start callin' me Blood now, okay?"

"Only if ya call me Jimmy all the time."

"Deal."

* * *

Detective Sergeant Rogers and his partner, Detective Carl Jones, a newcomer to homicide, had the grim task of notifying next of kin.

Jones was twenty-six years old, pear shaped and attempted to hide his baldness with a 'comb over.' He enlisted in the United States Marine Corps a month before the Japanese surrendered, and told 'war stories' even though he never left Parris Island.

Jones constantly tried to impress fellow officers with his superior intelligence. When attempting to make a point, he had an annoying habit of smacking his lips and tugging his groin area.

"We'll notify the Bazey kid's parents first, they only live a few blocks from here; met 'em on another case earlier this year," Rogers said.

"I can do it if you want me to, Sarge. Made lots of notifications when I was inna Corps," Jones replied as he smacked and tugged.

Rogers found Jones irritating, similar to the sense of weirdness Conroy felt toward him. "I figured you did. I'll take care of it."

"Let's get it on," Jones said, ignoring Rogers' snide answer.

As Luke opened his seventh American of the day, he heard a knock at the front door. "Mr. Bazey, Detective Rogers, remember me?" he asked when Luke answered.

"Yeah, I remember ya, how ya been?" he said as he guzzled down half a can.

"I've been good, thanks for askin'. This is my partner, Detective Jones, may we come in?"

"Sure, come on in. Jonesie, glad to meet ya. Want a beer?"

"Naw, too early in the day for me. Were you in the Corps?" he asked when he saw the photo of Luke.

Oh, Christ, hope he doesn't start that, 'when I was in the Corps,' shit *again,* Rogers said to himself.

"Yeah, I was in. How 'bout you?"

"Yeah," he replied, leaving it there as if to read Rogers' mind.

"What brings you fellas to this neck of the woods?"

When Rogers hesitated, Luke remembered he was a homicide detective and said, "Has something happened to Victor?"

"Is Mrs. Bazey here?"

"No, the Mrs. passed on a couple a months ago."

"No wonder he's drunk, poor bastard's been through enough already. First his daughter, then his wife. Wait'll he gets a load of this."

"Got some bad news for ya, Mr. Bazey."

Luke put the beer can to his lips and sucked the last few drops, then said, "Victor's dead, ain't he?"

"I'm afraid you're right, he is."

"What happened?" Luke asked calmly as his heart began to pound.

"He was killed by the police while robbing the Atlantic Federal. His accomplice was also shot and killed by an off-duty officer, Detective Jimmy Saukas. Sergeant Dominic Sabitini shot Victor."

"Dominic Sabitini, he's my fuckin' cousin. He woulda never shot Vic. No man, you're wrong. Not fuckin' Dom. Uh-Uh, no way," Luke shouted as his eyes bulged and the veins in his neck appeared ready to burst.

"I'm afraid I'm not wrong, Mr. Bazey. Both were wearing nylons stockings over their heads at the time of the shooting and couldn't be recognized," Rogers apologetically replied.

"Face it Mr. Bazey, he was in the middle of committing a felony and suffered the consequences," Jones arrogantly said.

Luke sprang up and delivered a smashing right to Jones' left eye and said, "Face that, ya mutha fucker!"

After kneeing him in the balls and landing an upper cut to Jones' chin, Luke vented his pent-up frustrations and began kicking him in the abdomen as he lay on the floor causing Rogers to strike Luke in the back of his head with his blackjack until the spring popped out from the leather binding in its handle.

When Jones regained consciousness, Rogers said, "Why in the fuck did ya talk to the man the way ya did? Didn't ya hear 'em say he'd just lost his wife? What the fuck is wrong with you, Carl, ya nuts or somethin', or don't ya give a shit about people's feelings?"

"Ya lost control, Sergeant."

"That's your biggest problem, ya asshole. All ya wanna do is control shit. You're not near as smart as ya think ya are, ya dumb fuck. The man not only lost his wife, his daughter died of a crib death earlier this year. Didn't know that, did ya? Mr. Smart Ass. He's a tough bastard, fought on Iwo. Thought I was gonna have to shoot 'em to save your worthless ass."

The only part of Rogers' admonishment that got through to Jones was the part about him not being as smart as he thought he was. "We'll see who's smart and who's not when I tell the captain how ya mishandled the situation, ya dumb cock sucker."

'Cock sucker' infuriated Rogers and he replied, "Shut the fuck up before I take a piece of your ass myself. Bazey gave ya just what ya deserved. As far as tellin' the captain, after he hears what really happened, you'll be poundin' a beat on Calhoun Street and the brothers'll take care of your fat fuckin' ass."

"Everything all right here, Detective?" asked Officer Cooper when he arrived for assistance.

"Yeah, everything's under control now. The gentleman got a little upset when I made death notification to him. Had to subdue him, that's all. He'll be fine now. Waitin' for an ambulance to carry him to City Hospital and stitch him up a little."

"A little my ass. By the looks of his head and all that blood, he'll get about a forty-stitch zipper."

"Fuck you, too. Uncuff me and I'll kick your ass just like I did his," Luke said while looking at Jones.

"Like father, like son," replied Cooper.

"Not this time. Mr. Bazey there's a good man, just had a lot on his mind and lost it for a time, that's all," Rogers said.

"Yeah, he must've, from as drunk as he is this early. Did he fuck your partner up that bad?"

"Yeah, didn't give 'em anything he didn't deserve though."

"Like the man told Cooper there, fuck you, Sergeant," Jones yelled.

When the ambulance crew arrived, the driver asked, "Which one first, the suit or the civilian?"

"The civilian, the other one can wait," Rogers answered.

Jones scowled while rubbing blood from his face and turned his head.

"Let's see if we can stop some of that bleedin' for ya before we put ya in the wagon, okay?" the driver politely said to Luke.

" 'Bout time we got somebody with a little respect around here. Do what ya gotta do, doc. What house ya from?"

"Truck eleven. You a farman, too?"

"Yeah, hose man at Forty-one Engine."

"Sorry to meet ya under these conditions. Let's see what we can do for ya now."

"Yeah, cops fucked me up pretty good, I guess."

"Looks like they did their best work," the driver said as he wound bandages around the dressing on Luke's head. "There, 'at oughta hold ya for awhile." He then turned to Jones and said, "Sit down, Detective and let me see what I can do for you."

"Thanks, I was beginning to wonder if anybody around here gave a shit about me. I *am* an officer of the law, ya know."

"We know," Rogers said. "Just sit there and let the man do his work and don't start any of that Marine Corps bullshit, okay?"

"Okay, *Sergeant,* whatever you say, sir," Jones replied arrogantly along with a salute.

"You girls been quarrelin'?" the attendant asked.

"Good line there, Saint Nick," Luke said, in response to the attendant's red-and- white tasseled hat. "How 'bout goin' downstairs and gettin' me a beer. Could really use one right 'bout now."

"Ya know I can't do that, brutha. Besides, looks like you've had your fair share already."

"Yeah, guess I have had enough for one day."

When the second ambulance arrived, Luke and Jones were loaded separately. Before he left, Rogers called his commander. After hearing of Jones' conduct, he said, "We'll deal with that later. In the meantime do ya need anything from this end?"

"Yes, sir, I do. Can ya have someone make death notification for me? I have to go to the hospital and wait for them to stitch up Mr. Bazey, might be as long as three or four hours."

"No problem. Gimme the name and address of the next of kin and I'll send somebody by right away."

"According to the guy's license, he was Theodore Arthur Finkelstein. White male, seventeen; forty-nine seventy-three Winner Avenue in Pimlico. His body's at the morgue. Got all that, sir?"

"Yep, got it. How's Jones doin' by the way?"

"He's at the hospital. He'll be pretty sore in the rib area for awhile. Guy did a pretty-good number on 'em. Thanks, Captain. Catch ya later."

"One more thing. Got a message here from Eric Johns, said he's your cousin from Buffalo. His train was cancelled and won't get in until tomorrow."

"Thanks for the info, Cap'. Really appreciate it."

Edmund Jordan used the pseudo-name Eric Johns, and Kenny Rogers, Kurt Roberson, when they left messages for one another through a third party. "The train has been cancelled," meant the meeting was off, and "the train is running behind schedule," indicated the caller would be an hour late.

"What's up, Eddie?" Rogers asked when he called.

"Dad has some city officials comin' to his house tonight for a little Christmas get together. Wants me to meet 'em, thinks it'll be good for my political future, sorry."

"Okay, I understand. I would've probably had to cancel myself. Caught that bank-job shooting up your way."

"Oh, that's yours, huh? Heard it was really messy, Sabitini killed a relative of his or somethin'."

"Messy's not the word, buddy. Tell ya all about it tomorrow. We're still on, right?"

"Yeah, lookin' forward to it. The only thing I have scheduled is a prisoner transport in the morning. Same time, same place, right?"

"Same time and place."

"Good, got a new pair of bikini underwear just for you. Gotta run; ciao, sweetie."

"Can't wait to see those drawers. What color are they?"

"I'll make that a surprise. Love ya."

"Love ya, too."

* * *

Three hours later, hospital security brought Luke to the waiting area. His blows resulted in thirty-seven stitches and caused his eyes to blacken.

"Sorry 'bout that ruckus back at the house, Detective. Just lost my head when your partner popped off like he did. How's he doin'?"

"He's fine. He was treated and released. Don't worry about him."

"Good, glad he's okay. I'm ready to go and face the music for what I did to 'em."

"If I take those cuffs off, ya promise to behave yourself? Ya already cost me one blackjack today, can't afford to lose another. Damn things are expensive."

"No problem, Detective. Ya can take 'em off, I'm better now. Broke your blackjack on my thick skull, huh?"

"Thing sprung out all over. Never seen the insides of one before."

"Damn, doesn't surprise me ya broke it with the way my head feels right now."

"Mr. Bazey—"

"Call me Luke."

"Luke, you assaulted a police officer, it's not like gettin' a speeding ticket, it's a felony in the State of Maryland. Ya could serve as much as ten years and suffer a heavy fine. And even if you're found not guilty, the fire department's gonna can your ass."

"Looks like I'm really in deep shit, huh?"

"No, Luke, you're not."

"I'm not?"

"No. I've decided that Jones' attitude and shitty comment to ya is what instigated the episode. In light of that and all the other things you've had to deal with, ya don't need this hangin' from your neck like a dead albatross."

Luke was prepared for the worst and shocked by Rogers' revelation. He thought, this is the best thing that's happened to me lately and it had to come as a result of Victor's death. "Does Jones know about this?"

"Don't be concerned over Jones. I'll deal with him."

"Don't know how I'll ever be able to repay ya for this, Detective. Ya don't know how much it means to me. All I have to live for now is my son Alec."

"I think I know how much this means to ya, Luke, and your gratitude is repayment enough. Gotta keep you firefighters on the job, never know when I might need one myself."

"Whenever ya do, just holler and I'll come runnin'. Uh, is Victor's body at the morgue?"

"Yeah, somebody from there'll call ya when it can be released, usually two or three days."

"I'm old hat at this; it'll be three days. Thanks again, Detective. You've done right by me. By the way, ya pack a hell of a wallop with that blackjack. Wow!"

"You're quite welcome, Luke. You don't do bad without one. I guarantee Jones'll attest to that," Rogers said as they chuckled.

"By the way, how are you gonna explain those injuries to the fire department?"

"I'll deal with that one later."

"Come on, I'll give ya a ride home."

"Do you know where Sabitini is now?"

"Unless he's been released, he's here. He got unglued at the bank after the shooting and they brought him in for sedation. Let's go see if he's still here, gotta set up an interview with him anyway."

When they got to Dom's room, they were greeted by his wife. When he saw him asleep, Rogers said, "Have him call me at this number when he feels up to it."

"I will. Thank you, Detective."

"My God, Luke, what happened to you?" Claudia asked when Rogers left.

"It's too long of a story to go into now. How's Dom doin?"

"When they first brought 'em in, he was totally out of it. His face was pale and he kept babbling about how he would burn in hell. After they gave 'em a shot, he passed out. He's been asleep for about an hour. Kids are on the way. Luke, Dom didn't know it was Victor. Officer told me he had a mask on and was armed, said it was a toy gun. If he would've had any idea it was Vic, he wouldn't have shot 'em even if it was a real gun. Please don't hate us, Luke. Dom loves you. He loved Lucy, Terri and the boys, too. Please, please, please forgive him, Luke."

Luke took her in his arms and said, "I know, I know. He did the only thing he could do. Now calm down and relax, ya don't wanna be upset when the kids get here."

When Dom's children arrived, they rushed to his bedside and he awakened. "Oh God, what have I done?" he said.

Luke's disheveled appearance startled Dom. When speech failed him, he tightened his grip on Luke's hand. "Ya don't have to say anything, cuz. I understand, I still love ya." Luke sensed his presence was upsetting Dom and said, "Gotta run. Alec's at home alone. See ya soon."

* * *

Dom never recovered from the trauma he suffered after shooting Victor. When he was unable to perform as a police officer, he was forced to retire on a mental disability after nineteen years of faithful service to the Baltimore City Police Department. He left with little fanfare, having refused a going-away party, and maintained little contact with his former police associates after retirement. His relationship with Luke became strained, and they only met at family gatherings.

Many police officers die within ten years of retirement; Dom was no exception. Six years later, at the age of fifty-one, he passed away after suffering a stroke.

* * *

Alec was aghast when he saw Luke's mummy-like appearance. "Dad, what's wrong, what happened to your head and eyes?"

"Got on the wrong side of a ball of lead, Son."

Alec thought Luke was describing an accident he had at work and said, "I thought ya were off today."

"No, Son. I worked as hard today as I ever have in my life."

"Ya gonna be all right?"

"I'm fine now, just look bad, that's all."

As Alec clung to Luke's leg and he softly stroked his hair, it reminded Alec of how it was before Terri was born. I'm really glad God took Terri, he said to himself.

When he looked up, he saw bad news in Luke's eyes as he said, "Son, got somethin' to tell ya—Victor's dead, police shot 'em."

A hot flash shot up Alec's back and he said, "Does Uncle Dom know about this, Dad?"

"Yeah, he knows, Son. It's just you and me now. Just the two of us left," Luke said as he finished his beer.

Alec broke into tears and went to his room. A few minutes later, Luke joined him and said in an attempt at consolation, "We'll make it all right, old buddy. We'll be okay," as he rubbed Alec's back.

"We'll be okay, Dad," Alec mimicked Luke as he hugged him.

"Yes, we will."

When he returned to the kitchen, Luke dropped an ounce shot glass filled with Seagram's 7 in his pewter Yankees stein and filled it with American. After chugging it, he realized he was out of beer and got his empty starch bottle and walked to 'Millie's' for a refill.

While Luke was gone, Alec decided Victor's death would serve him well in several ways: first, there was no one left he would have to share Luke's affections with; next, Luke could do more for him. "I'll play the sympathy angle and maybe I can weasel a Schwinn three speed outta this," he said. Most importantly, he determined when Luke died, he wouldn't have to share his money with anyone. By the time Luke returned, Alec came to the conclusion he had been blessed by Victor's death.

* * *

The next morning, Captain Whittaker called Rogers into his office and said, "Jones is out sick today, said his ribs ached. Wanted for the three of us to meet so I could get his version. Now tell me about what kind of shit he pulled yesterday."

"I'd a kicked his ass, too, if he talked to me that way," Whittaker said after hearing the story.

"Now be advised, Mr. Bazey *had* been drinking, but still acted in a civilized and cordial manner. In fact he offered us a beer," Rogers said.

"What kind?"

"American, I think."

"Did ya take it?"

"No, I passed."

"I would've passed on that donkey piss myself. Now if he'd a offered a Budweiser, that'd be a different story. Sounds to me like Jones stepped on his dick big time. You've been here for two years now and I have confidence in you and your work. Furthermore, you're a sergeant and part of your job is to maintain good relations with the community. If Jones' version is anything like yours, his fat ass'll be back in cordovans poundin' the ground."

"Captain, three officers down. Two DOA, the other one critical," Detective Monroe said as he burst into Whittaker's office.

"Where? Who are they?"

"Southeastern precinct, two uniforms, Pavlik and O'Brien are the DOAs. One dick, Eddie Jordan transported to City."

"Any arrests?"

"Yeah, one suspect, an M. O., DOA as well. As far as I can determine, Jordan was transportin' the whack job to Spring Grove from southeastern. As I understand it, Jordan's some kinda humanitarian and doesn't believe in cuffin' prisoners. Whack disarmed 'em in the parking lot, shot 'em twice, then two uniforms as they got outta their cruisers. Off duty pullin' into the lot took out the whack."

"Okay, get a team over there. Tell 'em I'm on my way."

"Southeastern district turnin' into a bastion of crime. That's where your double was yesterday, right, Kenny?"

After he heard Jordan's name, Rogers' heart jumped into his throat. When he didn't answer, Whittaker said, "Rogers, ya okay? Ya look kinda green there."

"Sorry, Captain, didn't hear what ya said."

"Southeastern, that's where your double was yesterday, right?"

"Yeah, right. What did he say the names of the officers were?"

"Got it right here—two DOA uniforms, Pavlik and O'Brien. One wounded suit—Jordan."

"Jordan, *Eddie Jordan?*"

"Didn't get his first name. Rogers, you all right? Looks like ya need oxygen or somethin'. Ya know this Jordan guy?"

"Met 'em once on a case over there."

"Kenny, ya look like you're ready to faint. What's the problem, man?"

"Just upsets me when officers go down, I'll be all right."

"Ya well enough to go to southeastern?"

"Yeah, if you drive."

* * *

By the time they arrived, Detective Sergeant Conroy had taken charge of the investigation. "What's up, Gunner?" asked Whittaker.

"Cap'n, Kenny, good to see ya. Got things 'bout wrapped up here. Not much to it. Fuckin' idiot detective, Eddie Jordan, didn't cuff a nut job. He's in surgery now, don't know if he's gonna make it. Kenny, you remember Jordan, he was that smart ass on the trestle case we handled when I was breakin' ya in. Bloodsworth wanted to kick his ass."

"Yeah, I remember 'em."

"Kenny, ya all right? Ya look kinda queasy and pale, boy," Conroy said.

"Same thing I told 'em," replied Whittaker.

"I'm okay, don't like it when cops are killed."

"Hell, nobody does. Could've been one of us."
"I'll be all right," Rogers replied.

* * *

The one-mile-long funeral procession consisting of 256 vehicles with police officers from every jurisdiction in Maryland and six states, began its journey from the Shrine of the Little Flower Catholic Church on Belair Road, and ended at the Most Holy Redeemer Cemetery. It took ten minutes from the time the hearse stopped at the gravesite before the last vehicle started the twelve-block trip. After a twenty-one-gun salute was fired by the BCPD Honor Guard, the ceremony ended.

All elected state officials to include Governor Theodore R. McKeldin, Mayor Thomas D'Alessandro, and the Attorney General, C. Ferdinand Sybert, were in attendance. The city council was also there, except for one notable absence: Edmund Jordan, Sr. It was suggested by the mayor he not attend as his presence might be unpopular with the police officers and bring negative attention and defamation to the City of Baltimore. Mr. Jordan was not only the father of the officer responsible for the deaths of the fallen heroes, he was an outspoken critic regarding the use of deadly force and restraining devices by police officers. He continued to defend his son's actions, maintaining his conduct was of a humanitarian nature.

Despite Jordan's desperate lobbying efforts to preserve his son's reputation and police career, it was recommended by the Baltimore City Police Department Trial Board for him to be dismissed from service with prejudice. The recommendation was approved by the mayor and all but one voting member of the city council.

SPILLED WINE

The first attempt to organize a fire unit in Baltimore came on July 16, 1763 when a lottery scheme was proposed by the city to complete the Market House, construct a second wharf, purchase two fire engines and a parcel of leather buckets. Fire service remained on a volunteer basis until February 15, 1859 after the city activated four companies of around-the-clock professional firefighters and sufficient equipment. Ninety-four years later Pierre Alexander and six others were the first African-Americans to graduate from the Baltimore City Fire Academy.

* * *

"Looks like the niggers're finally takin' over, don't it?" one of the firefighters commented as Alexander entered Forty-one Engine the first time.

When he reported in, Lt. Fox said, "Welcome aboard, son."

"Good to be here, Lieutenant."

"What shall we call ya?"

"Friends call me Pete, sir."

"Pete sir, that's a funny name," Fox replied in jest. "Okay, Pete it is. Ya better change into your chambrays before we get a call."

"Luke, just the man I wanna see," Fox said as he and Pete entered the bathroom and dressing area. "What ya got in your hand?"

"Which hand, Lieutenant?"

"The one you're not pissin' with."

"Just a note remindin' myself to do somethin'."

The sheet of paper Luke was holding was a handwritten sign he had removed from the door of the bathroom that said, 'WHITES ONLY.'

"Remindin' ya to do what, wash your hands when ya finish?" Fox asked.

"Naw, my momma taught me not to piss on my hands, sir," Luke said as he grinned and crumpled the paper and tossed it.

"Up yours, Bazey. This is our new man, Pete Alexander."

"Hey, Luke Bazey. Glad to meet ya, Pete."

"At least there's two around here who aren't rednecks," Pete said to himself.

"Pete's gonna be with ya on forty-one, Luke."

"Great. I'm sure he'll do fine."

"I'll try my best."

"Ya hungry?" Luke asked Pete.

"I could eat."

"Just gettin' ready to whip up a batch a S.O.S."

"Sounds good."

"Come on in the kitchen and I'll introduce ya to the rest of the guys," Luke said as he washed his hands.

When they entered, Luke said, "Everybody listen up, this is our newest man, Pete Alexander."

"Don't look like no *man* to me. Looks more like a boy."

"Ain't no call for that kinda talk, Riley. Now mind your manners," Luke said.

When breakfast was finished, Luke said, "Come git it, boys. Fresh biscuits up inna minute."

"Smells great," Pete said as he dropped a scoopful on his plate.

"Don't serve no niggers in this place," Riley said.

"Man didn't order a nigger. Now shut the fuck up before I come over there and stick this spoon up your white ass," Luke said.

After breakfast, Luke and Pete became better acquainted. "I know it'll be hard, but try not to let that asshole Riley get to ya. When Lieutenant Fox told us a Negro was comin', we all got together and talked about it. Mostly everybody 'cept Riley and a couple others said it didn't matter to 'em as long as ya held up your end."

"I think I met the others when I first walked in."

"Easy for me to say, but just relax and ignore those assholes. Like the man says, this too, shall pass. Show 'em you're better'n 'em. That'll shut 'em up."

"You're a good man, Luke. I like your attitude."

"Now tell me 'bout yourself."

"Not much to tell. Born and bred in the city. Graduated from Dunbar, went to Morgan State for awhile then transferred to Howard in DC. Took a job with Baltimore Gas and Electric when I got outta the army. Applied here when they started hiring us."

"What'd ya do in the army?"

"Airborne, five fifty-fifth; ever hear of 'em?"

"Triple Nickels, you bet I heard of 'em. If my history serves me right, you guys fought fars out West, right?"

"Yeah, guess 'at's what made me join up here."

* * *

In 1943, the 555th Parachute Infantry Battalion, also known as the 'Triple Nickels,' became the United States' first all African-American parachute unit. Although combat trained, the 555th saw no action in WW II. Instead, they became known as 'Smoke Jumpers' as a result of fighting forest fires caused by incendiary balloons launched in Japan and carried by wind currents to the western coast of North America where they were detonated.

* * *

"Ya married, any kids?" Luke asked.

"No to both."

"Divorced, huh?"

"No, wife died in a car crash last year. She was sittin' in 'er pride and joy, little yellow-and-white Nash Rambler, waitin' for a light to change when a loaded dump truck with a drunk operator rammed 'er from behind; flattened the car and her both. She was mangled so bad, had to keep the casket closed."

"Damn, man, sorry to hear that."

"Tough when ya lose your wife."

"I can't imagine such a thing."

"You married?"

"Yeah, three years this past February."

"Kids?"

"Adopted my wife's two boys and had our own little baby girl on the eleventh of this month. Great kids, love 'em to death."

* * *

Luke's test of friendship came on the first night of the following evening shift when a firefighter brought up the issue of which bunk Pete would occupy. "I think we oughta put 'at nigger onna floor. Bad enough he gets to use our bathroom, much less sleep inna same bed as him. Whadda ya think 'ere, Rile?" Arnie Corbin asked.

"Floor's too good for 'at jig. Throw his black ass on the pumper hoses. He's your buddy, Bazey, whadda *you* think?"

"I think ya oughta shut your big Alabama- ass-lookin' pie hole, that's what I think, ya fuck stick."

"Got somethin' to say to me about where I sleep?" Pete said when he heard the bantering.

"Yeah, boy. None of us wanna lay down anywhere after you been 'ere."

"Back off, Pete," Luke said.

"Don't need ya to fight my battles, Luke. I can take care of myself."

"There's no doubt in my mind ya could mop up the floor with this piece a shit, but you're a fuckin' probie, Pete, and a colored one at that.

115

Headquarters just lookin' for a chance to jack your ass and send ya packin'. Be cool, dammit."

Luke then turned to Riley and said, "I'll settle this shit right now. When we're on, the only ones who'll sleep in the last bunk on the right is me or Pete. If it makes ya feel better, put a reserved sign on the fuckin' thing so's 'em Prima Donnas from A and C won't get contaminated either. Is 'at good 'nuff for ya, asshole?"

"Yeah, 'at'll work," said Riley.

"Then it's settled, now get outta my sight."

Pete later removed a handwritten sign taped to the foot pole of the bunk that read: 'RESERVED—GUINEAS AND NINNYS ONLY.'

* * *

Upon arriving home from Victor's funeral, Alec tuned in the *Adventures of Captain Midnight.* The show was sponsored by *Ovaltine,* and offered applications in the jars for membership to the 'Secret Squadron.'

"Gotta get me a jar of that stuff so I can join up," Alec said as he watched the captain manipulate his way out of another desperate situation. Luke smiled at Alec's entertainment as he handed Pete a bottle of Seagram's. Following six depth charges, Luke said, "What the fuck's God got against me, Pete? What have I ever done to him?"

"Ain't no God, Luke. Quit believin' in 'em after my wife was killed. No way a merciful god would allow his creatures to get fucked up the way some people do; more like the devil's work if ya ask me."

"Thought the same thing myself on Iwo. Kept the faith though, that's the only way I was able to get through the ugly fuckin' mess. Inclined to agree with ya now," Luke said.

"How 'bout the millions of Jews he let get slaughtered?"

"Yeah, you're right. Fuck it, Pete, I've had 'nuff, gonna turn in. You can sleep in Victor's bed tonight. I think ya know where it is."

"Thanks, buddy. Was hopin' ya asked, couldn't drive in this condition."

After he went to his desk, Luke handed Pete a note: RESERVED FOR NINNYS ONLY TONIGHT—NO GUINEAS ALLOWED. "Thought I'd make ya feel right at home."

"I didn't think ya knew 'bout that sign."

"I saw ya chuck it and picked it outta the trash after ya went to sleep that night."

"Thanks, pal, I'll sleep better with this. By the way, thanks for stickin' by me. Made things a lot easier knowin' I had at least one friend."

"Least I could do for another hairy-assed farman. Besides, ya got a lotta friends at the house. Boys have come to respect ya."

"All the boys?"

"*Almost* all the boys. Night, Pete."

"Night, Luke."

* * *

February 14, 1955, would have been Luke's fifth wedding anniversary. Instead of taking the day off and spending it with Lucy as he had done on the previous four, he reported to work.

"BONG, BONG, BONG, BONG!" "BONG, BONG, BONG, BONG!" the two- hundred-decibel alarm sounded shortly after Luke's arrival.

"Git in your gear, boys, we got another one at Adamco. Fire's spread to buildings on both sides, boat boys can't handle it. Two alarms already," the firefighter on watch bellowed over the loud speaker. "BONG, BONG, BONG, BONG!"

* * *

Basically, the number of alarms is determined by the amount of apparatus sent to a fire. An engine, ladder truck or civilian vehicle, referred to as a 'buggy,' is considered apparatus if it carries fire-department personnel.

* * *

Lieutenant Fox, engaged in a heated game of Pinochle when the alarm sounded, said, "Fuckin' Adamco *again*? This is the third time since July. Didn't know they opened after the fire marshal shut 'em down. Son of a bitch, just when I had a handful of spades."

After taking a 'maintenance' shot of Smirnoff from the rubbing-alcohol bottle kept stashed in his locker, Luke jumped into his boots, asbestos coat and leather helmet, then leapt onto the platform on the back of forty-one.

As the truck sped down Eastern Avenue, the rushing glacial air and production of the siren and bells made Luke feel like he was in the North Pole at an outdoor insane asylum at the stroke of midnight on New Year's Eve.

"Got us a good'n here," Fox said when he saw the inferno. "Get all the hoses off, we're gonna need every inch of line we have with that wind blowin' the flames in our face," he shouted above the growl of the fire.

"Good thing it's not the middle of summer, we'd be like a bunch a steamed Jimmys," Luke said.

When they heard the containers of highly explosive chemicals go off, the firefighters turned their attention to the warehouse and observed a display not witnessed in Baltimore since 1814 when British war ships bombarded Fort McHenry a mile further south on the river.

Shortly after the explosion, a 300-gallon vat of chemicals shook the ground for a six-block area as it blew the roof of the 20,000-square-foot warehouse into millions of pieces. As fiery missiles returned to earth, Fox said, "Fuck this hose, let's get the hell outta here!"

As they dove beneath forty-one, a flaming section of reinforcement beam landed where they had been standing. While under shelter, they heard heavy thuds and felt vibrations as burning debris landed on the hose bed above them.

"Come on, boys. 'Em hoses won't last long under all 'at heat," Fox desperately shouted.

"Fuck it, ain't no worse'n Iwo," Luke said.

"Reminds me of Jap fire-balloons," Pete replied.

The 'no-worse-than' attitude is the reason men of their era are known as *The Greatest Generation.*

When they reached topside, all tucked the collars of their coats beneath the tails of their helmets. Pete grabbed the hard-bristled broom from the tool cabinet and climbed onto the truck bed where he began sweeping the glowing rubble. The molten hailstorm mercifully stopped and the firefighters began removing the hose and dragging it to a position of usefulness.

"Quick thinkin', Pete, good job," Fox said as he flashed him the 'okay' sign.

"Black bastard'll probably gitta merit badge," Corbin said to Riley when he overheard Fox.

After his hose was attached to a water supply, Luke signaled the firefighter at the hydrant with a thumb up. "Let 'er rip, Billy," Luke shouted as he opened the shut-off valve of the brass nozzle.

"Adam's ale on the way, Lukie!" Billy replied as he slowly turned the long wrench.

* * *

The 'Monster' continued gorging itself on the delectable buffet of flammables like a starving animal when the wind increased to gale force.

Battalion Chief Hugo Zappa, second cousin to Baltimore-born, Rock 'n Roll-star Frank Zappa, made the decision to let it burn and try to save as many of the structures as possible. "Foxie, take 'yer guys next door and keep 'em hosin'. Maybe we can salvage somethin' outta this mess," Zappa ordered Fox. "Been on the department twenty-four years and ain't *never* seen anything like this."

"Roger, Chief."

Fox made an assessment and directed his men inside the building adjacent to Adamco. "When we get in, keep the hoses on the fire side of the wall. Luke, you and Pete go upstairs and spray down the walls up 'ere," Fox said as he pulled his gas mask over his face.

"Ten-four, Lieut," Luke answered as he shut off the nozzle. "Ready to go, paratrooper?"

"Lead the way, sailor."

When they reached the second floor, Luke removed his right glove and felt the wall. "Not bad here," he said. After moving to the far end of the room, he felt the wall again and immediately pulled his hand back. "Things hotter'n a firecracker," he said.

When Luke reopened the nozzle and the high-pressure stream hit the brick wall, the 100-year-old mortar melted like ice cubes in boiling water. Suddenly, the wall collapsed and caused the floor section under Pete to give way while flames licked the ceiling. As the crew downstairs was working in the front of the building, they were unaware of the catastrophe and didn't rush to aid the distressed duo.

When Pete fell through the floor, the hose was jerked from Luke's grip and draped over a wooden support beam. As it whipped like a crazed boa constrictor, Pete held on for dear life and was able to snatch a support rod protruding from the opposite wall. As the Monster nipped at Pete's boots, Luke pulled off his mask and grabbed Pete's free arm. "Hold on, buddy. I got ya," he said.

As the flames got higher, Luke said, "Let go a 'at rod, then grab my arms and I'll drag ya up, okay?"

Pete nodded at Luke, and said to himself, I hope I'm wrong about God, as his high-school graduation, his wife's death, and his first day at Forty-one Engine passed before his mind's eye.

* * *

When it became a ten alarmer, Zappa said, "Okay, sound the Mayday."

"Everybody not on a hose grab a horn, bell, whistle or anything that makes noise," the second in command said over his loud speaker.

All at once it was like VJ day in Times Square, as the bizarre-sounding instruments created a 'circus-from-hell' atmosphere.

When Pete heard the Mayday, he ripped off his mask. "Luke, get your ass outta here, save yourself, brutha," he said.

"Bullshit," Luke answered as he struggled even more.

"Please, Luke, lemme go."

"Fuck you, ain't leavin' without ya."

"Love ya, man," Pete said as he gazed in Luke's eyes and released his hand.

Luke watched in horror as his friend and confidant was gobbled alive; Iwo Jima, Lucy, Terri, and the wine spilled from his glass, passed before his eyes when the floor let go.

* * *

"Where's Bazey and Alexander?" Fox called out after he took a head count.

"Hadn't seen 'em since they went to the second floor," answered Billy Norris.

"They *had* to hear all 'em sirens and bells go off. God damn, we gotta find 'ose boys," Fox shouted in near panic.

"Bazey, Alexander, get your asses out here. Fire's outta control," Fox yelled through a megaphone as his eyebrows singed.

When he got no response after a second call, Fox double-timed to Zappa. "Chief, Chief, sound another Mayday. Two a my boys not accounted for!"

"Crank 'em up again, Danny. Two men still inside!"

When Luke and Pete didn't appear, Zappa said in a crackling voice, "Okay, Danny, shut 'em down. They must be goners. Keep your eyes peeled for 'em, Foxie, if they show up, let me know right away."

"Looks like they're done for, men. Chief says we'll look for 'em when things cool some," Fox said to his company as he blessed himself.

* * *

When the wind died down, the blaze lost intensity and was slowly brought under control; as the heat lowered, icicles formed on the firefighter's helmets.

After fourteen hours, the Monster was crippled and reduced to a heap of smoldering rubble. Debris strangled the river around the warehouse and bobbed like flotsam and jetsam, while active hoses continued to drench the embers.

"Need volunteers to go inside and look for Bazey and Alexander. All those willing, take one step forward," Fox said dramatically.

"Didn't expect anything less from you fine gentlemen. You're *all* blue to the bone," he said when they all took the step.

"Lieutenant, Lieutenant, c'mere quick," Jaworski shouted after entering the building.

When Fox arrived, he saw two humanoid figures lying face up. Both had assumed a 'boxer's stance' when their arm and leg muscles constricted from the intense heat; the rubber boots melted around their legs, created a surreal appearance, like inner tubes burned around spindly tree trunks, while the absence of hair, and tiny slits that replaced their eye wells and lips, gave them a look of macabre mannequins.

"Alexander here," Fox said as he blessed himself.

"How can ya tell?" asked Thompson.

" 'At's Pete all right," Thompson said as Fox held the corpse's scorched upper lip open and he saw Pete's trademark gold tooth.

"Hell of a way to go," Fox said as he hung his head and wept.

"With the fire as bad it was, probably didn't take 'em long to die," Thompson said as he gazed at the remains.

"Long 'nuff, long 'nuff," Fox answered.

After opening Luke's turnout coat and unbuttoning his shirt, Fox was startled at how well the asbestos outerwear had protected his body. He then reached in and found a medal of the Virgin Mary holding the Christ Child. "May you be protected always. Your loving wife, Lucy—2/14/54," was inscribed on the back.

"It's Bazey all right," Fox said as he clutched the medal. "Gonna have to leave 'em here 'til the investigators look things over." After leading the others in the Lord's Prayer, he said, "Okay, men, still got work to do."

As the company was exiting the building, Zappa arrived. When he saw their long looks, he knew the men were no longer missing. "Got 'em, Foxie?" he asked.

"Yeah, we got 'em, Chief. Both of 'em in the back of the building. Looks like the floor caved in, poor bastards never had a chance. "Shouldn't a sent 'em upstairs alone, Huey," Fox howled. "It's all my fault, Chief. My fault."

"Nonsense. Ya did the right thing, Lieutenant. How'd you know the damn floor was gonna cave? Don't blame yourself, ya didn't do anything wrong. Danny, c'mere, take the lieutenant to the aid station and get 'em some coffee or a drink if anybody's got a bottle, okay?"

"Sure thing, Chief. Come on, Paul, a little snort'll fix ya right up."

"Thanks, Danny. I could use one right 'bout now."

"Dino, ya next in command?" Zappa said.

"Yes, sir, sure am."

"City set up an aid station 'cross the street. Send yer guys over four at a time. I'm sure all their bellies are empty by now."

"Affirmative, Chief. Thank ya kindly, sir," Dino replied as he tendered a half-hearted salute.

"Carry on."

"Located the missin' men: both DOA. Have the investigators speed it up. Not sure how long that building's gonna last," Zappa advised the dispatcher.

"Ten-four, Chief."

A few minutes later, the dispatcher called back, "Investigators tied up now. Said to transport the DOAs to the morgue."

"Yeah, they're tied up all right, probably by a couple a bimbos on the Block. Danny, go tell Dino to get the bodies on the move 'fore that whole fuckin' building goes."

"Roger that."

When the morgue wagon arrived, the local television crews swarmed it like piranha fish. As the bodies were being carried, Channel two Newscaster Keith McBee, asked one of the attendants, "Do you know the identity of the dead men yet?"

"Better get that fuckin' mike outta my face, Mac, 'fore I shove it where the sun don't shine—comprendo?" he answered.

Acting Lieutenant Mark Dino, in a more diplomatic fashion explained their identity was being withheld pending notification to the next of kin.

* * *

The incident became known as 'Baltimore's St. Valentine's Day Massacre,' as five firefighters lost their lives that day. The names, Pierre Lamont Alexander, Lucca Mayo Bazey, Donald Francis Edwards, John Paul Robertson and Michael Alan Vickers were added to the *Roll of Honor* at Baltimore City Fire Department Headquarters.

Edwards and Vickers were killed when a wall collapsed and crushed them; Robertson perished from a fatal heart attack while frantically removing bricks in an effort to save the two. The artist assigned to inscribe the plaque made the observation that when the first letter of their last names were rearranged, it spelled, BRAVE: appropriately, all were referred to as the 'BRAVE WAVE.'

SENTIMENTAL JOURNEY

After having dinner with the Varipapas, Alec returned home and turned on the television where he saw a news bulletin reporting the blaze and watched intently while the announcers dramatically reported it.

"The wind is whipping with the vengeance of a cat of nine tails as the fire burns hopelessly out of control. At this point, efforts to contain it have proven futile and firefighters continue to dodge falling debris as Satan's brew is cast upon them."

After hearing the commentary, Alec returned to the Varipapas where they were glued to the television. "Your dad'll be all right. Don't worry, honey," Mrs. V said when she saw Alec whimpering. He snuggled close to her as he became engrossed in the nightmare.

"It's way past your bedtime," Mrs. V said to Alec at ten. "Spend the night with us why don't ya?"

"Okay."

"Michael won't mind if ya sleep in his bed, he has another one in Germany now."

* * *

Reds had enlisted in the US Air Force and was assigned to the Strategic Air Command, headed by General Curtis E. Lemay. When he took over SAC in 1948, it consisted of little more than a few understaffed and untrained B-29 groups left from WW II. Within a few years, it became the most powerful and effective military force the world had ever known.

Lemay served as a USAF General Officer for seventeen years, longer than any other man in the history of the United States military. Other than the Medal of Honor, he received every award his country could bestow upon him. In 1961, he attained the highest position in the USAF as Chief of Staff.

The 'Old Warrior' died on October 1, 1990, and was buried at the United States Air Force Academy Cemetery in Colorado Springs, Colorado.

* * *

"Alec all squared away?" Mr. V asked as he was leaving for work.

"Got 'em tucked in snug as a bug."

"Kinda nice havin' a kid around again," Mr. V said.

"Sure is. See ya when ya get in, honey," Mrs. V said as she kissed him good-bye.

When he arrived home the next morning, Mr. V said, "Luke here yet?"

"Haven't seen 'em."

"I'm sure they're holdin' 'em over 'cause of that fire. Where's Alec?"

"He left for school a few minutes ago, surprised ya didn't pass 'em on your way in."

"No, musta just missed 'em. Brrr, it's cold as a witch's tit out there," Mr. V answered as he unbuttoned the chin straps of the USAF pile cap Reds had given him for Christmas.

"Stu Kerr callin' for snow," Mrs. V said.

"How much?"

"Maybe six inches."

"Damn, that's all we need, frickin' snow."

"Oatmeal and raisins okay for breakfast?"

"Hell, woman, when ya gonna learn? This is dinner time for me," he answered as he opened a bottle of Natty. "How's 'bout puttin' on a steak and some a your famous home fries, darlin'?"

"Anything for you, lover boy," she answered as she went to the freezer. "By the way, Luke left money for Alec's board in that envelope on toppa the fridge."

As Mr. V opened it, he heard a knock at the door. When he answered, Captain Mannion from the fire department said, "Excuse me, sir, are you familiar with the Bazey family next door?"

"Not but two of 'em livin' there anymore: Mr. Bazey and his son Alec. Anything we can help ya with?" Mr. V answered as his wife joined him.

"Yes, sir, ya can. I'm Captain Mannion and this is Father Paige, one of the department's chaplains."

"Please to meet ya. I'm Gus Varipapa and this is the Mrs., Ellen," he replied as he shook hands with Mannion and nodded at the chaplain. "What can we do for ya, Captain?"

"We just came from Firefighter Bazey's parent's home and no one answered. Neighbors said they were vacationing in Florida with their son and daughter. Do you by any chance know how we can contact 'em?"

"Yeah, we gotta number. Ellen, what'd ya do with it? Y'all come in outta that damn cold."

"The number's in the book by the phone, I'll get it."

"Is there a problem, Captain?" Mr. V asked.

"Mind if I smoke?"

"No, go right ahead," Mr. V answered as he handed him an ashtray.

"I'm not supposed to say anything until after the next of kin is notified, but I guess it's all right to tell you in the absence of his family,"

Mannion said as he French inhaled. "Are you familiar with the ten-alarm blaze at the fertilizer factory on the Pratt Street Wharf?"

"Yes, sir, I am. Saw it on the television."

"Firefighter Bazey and four other firemen were killed there last night. His body's awaiting an autopsy at the coroner's office," Mannion said as the bill of the Pall Mall glowed from another long drag.

"Lord have mercy," Mr. V said as he removed the pile cap and flopped into an armchair, "do you know what that family's been through in the last year, Captain?" Mr. V asked as the chaplain assisted his wife.

"I'm well aware. I represented the fire department at his daughter and wife's funerals. Woulda been at his son's, too, but Mr. Bazey refused. Said it was confined to family members only."

"I thought ya looked familiar. Remember seein' ya at the cemetery. Sounds like ya got a great job there, Captain," Mr. V said facetiously.

"It does get a bit trying at times," Mannion answered as he flicked ashes into the tray. "Fortunately for me, I just have this one notification, they spread it out a little this time."

"Thank Christ for small favors, huh?"

"Every little bit helps," Mannion answered as he crushed out the Pall Mall.

"How'd it happen?" a teary-eyed Mrs. V asked.

"All we've been able to confirm so far is that a floor caved in on Mr. Bazey and another firefighter, Pete Alexander, and they fell one story into the fire."

"Pete, he's a Negro, right?"

"Yes, he was Mr. Bazey's assistant hose man."

"Yeah, we met 'em several times. Him and Luke got real close after Lucy was killed. He was really a nice man," Mr. V said with a crackle.

"Good firefighter, too."

"Is this the number?" Mannion said to Mrs. V.

"Yes, Luke gave it to me last week when his family left for Miami. They just bought a canal-front cottage there. Said they were thinkin' about relocating. Luke wanted me to have it in case of an emergency. We take care of his son when he works, uh, worked evenings. I guess he had some kinda premonition."

"Where's his son now?"

"At school."

"Okay if he stays with you all until we can get in contact with Mr. Bazey's next of kin?"

" 'At'll be fine, we like havin' 'em here. Just talkin' 'bout that last night," Mrs. V said.

"When we get back to the office, I'll contact the Miami Fire Department and get them to make the notification there."

"Got by with one this time, huh?" Mr. V jokingly asked.

"Just like Baltimore Colts number forty-four, Bert Rechichar sendin' one through the goal posts," Mannion said as he feigned drop kicking a football. "Here's my number, if ya need anything, please call. I'll be in touch after I speak with the parents. Now what's your phone number?"

"Broadway six-two-one-five-eight," Mr. V answered.

"Okay, B-R-six-two-one-five-eight," Mannion answered as he wrote in his *Spiral* pad. "Gus and Ellen Varipapa, V-a-r-i-p-a-p-a, right?"

"Very good, Captain," Mr. V said.

"My mother was a Panadoulis before she was a Mannion, quite familiar with Greek names. Can't ya tell by the hair?" Mannion asked as he ran his fingers through his thick, black, wavy locks.

"I knew there was somethin' 'bout you I liked," Mr. V answered.

"Okay, we'll be on our way. Call anytime. If I'm off duty, answerin' service'll pick up and get me at home."

"Thanks for everything, Captain, Father," Mr. V said as they shook hands and embraced.

"Poor Luke, I just can't believe he's dead," said a teary-eyed Mrs. V after the fire officials left.

"I seen lottsa burned-up bodies in Europe, ugly damn sight, terrible. Don't even look human. Look more like big chunks a charred meat," Mr. V said.

"No doubt they'll keep the casket closed. Lord have mercy, I just can't believe it. Wonder what'll become of Alec?"

"Don't know, but if push comes to shove I think we should try and adopt 'em. After raisin' a hellion like Reds and all the shit him and his hooligan friends put us through, raisin' a nice kid like Alec'd be a pleasure. Do ya know who his godparents are, hon'?"

"Met 'em once. If memory serves me right their names are Henry and Lena, live in that new Welsh development out by Belair Road. Henry's the brother of Alec's real dad."

"Don't remember meetin' 'em myself."

"Still want that steak?"

"Naw, not in the mood for a big meal now. Oatmeal and raisins sound good after all."

As Mr. V finished the last of his brew, he said, "What time's Alec get home from school?"

"Usually around three. If it snows, they might let 'em go early."

"Okay, whatever time he gets here, wake me up. Ain't gonna be easy, but we gotta tell 'em about his father before he hears it on that damn television set."

"How do ya tell a ten year old he's just become an orphan?"

"He may be an orphan technically, but he'll always have a real home and family here if I have anything to say 'bout it. Don't worry, honey, he'll be all right," Mr. V said as he consoled his weeping wife.

"Okay, sweetie, go to bed now. I'll come get ya when he gets here."

Mr. V tossed and turned as he contemplated how he would break the news to Alec.

* * *

The schools were closed after four inches of snow had fallen. On the way home, when he saw a fire truck in front of Baltimore Market, Alec walked to it in hope of finding Luke.

"Too bad about Bazey and Alexander and 'em other guys," Alec heard a firefighter say.

"Yeah, they were good men. Heard they were burned beyond recognition."

"They'll really be missed. Wonder when the funeral'll be?"

"Excuse me, sirs. My name is Alec Bazey. My father is Luke Bazey, he's a fireman at forty-one. Were you all just talkin' 'bout him and Mr. Pete?"

"Oh, shit," Carey said to himself. "Did ya say Luke is your father, little boy?"

"Yes, sir, he is. Is he all right?" Alec asked in a semi-panicked voice as he pulled back the hood of his parka.

"Lieutenant, Lieutenant Fritsch, c'mere right away," Carey called out.

"What's the problem?" Fritsch, an Artie Donovan look alike said as he stuffed in a hot dog he had scrounged from the Garden Bar.

Carey then put his arm around Fritsch's massive shoulders and quietly said, "Luke Bazey's kid," as he thumbed toward Alec. "Overheard me and Smitty talkin' 'bout Bazey and Alexander. Guess he doesn't know yet."

"Ya dumb shit. Your mouth's always gettin' ya in trouble. God damn, man," Fritsch barked.

"How could I have known it was Bazey's kid, Lieutenant?" Carey answered with palms up.

"We told ya at roll call next of kin hadn't been notified yet and to keep your yap shut, ya shit-for-brains fuckin' idiot."

"Didn't know, Lieutenant."

"Okay, get back on the truck and shut the fuck up. I'll handle this."

* * *

Although Fritsch came across like a mountain lion, he was actually a kitten. As a result of his size, he volunteered at various charitable organizations as Santa Claus and contributed his own funds for gifts.

When he saw Alec, Fritsch remembered the first time they met during a shift change. Being enamored by his charm, he said to Luke, "Take Alec over to the Grand and tell my deadbeat brother-in-law to let 'em in. If he tries to charge ya, remind him he still owes me for when he dipped in the till to bet that *sure thing* at Pimlico. Saved his ass from the hoosegow when that plug ran DFL. Tell 'em to throw in a large pop corn and soda; some Jujubeads, too"

"Mighty nice of ya, Lieutenant. Thank the man, Alec."

"Thanks, Mr. Fritsch."

"My pleasure, son."

* * *

"Do ya remember me, sir?" Alec asked as Fritsch approached.

"Sure do, Alec," he tenderly replied as he smiled and gently wiped snow from Alec's hair and pulled up his hood for him.

Alec, trembling from fear, pitifully asked, "Did my daddy really get burned up like that fireman said?"

"Big-mouth bastards," Fritsch said to himself.

"Collins, call dispatch and have 'em hold us ten-ten. Got some business to tend to."

"Got ya, Lieut, take your time."

After entering the Garden Bar, Fritsch said to Alec, "Can I get ya anything, pardner?"

"Could go for a hot chocolate."

"Me, too. Beertender, a hot chocolate for me and my little buddy here."

"Comin' right up," the elder Saukas answered.

Fritsch then took in a deep breath and swallowed the basketball in his throat. "Alec, uh, uh, Alec your dad, your father, he's uh, uh,"

"My dad's what?!"

"Your dad was killed in the fire last night."

The Lord made a mistake this time, Alec thought. My dad wasn't supposed to go like the others.

"Is there anything else I can do for you gentleman?" Saukas asked as he placed down two cups of hot chocolate with floating whipped cream and half of a maraschino cherry on top.

"Thanks, at'll do for now," Fritsch replied.

"Is everything okay, Lieutenant?" Saukas asked when he looked at Alec.

"We'll be fine. Thanks, Jimmy."

The two walked hand in hand, and Fritsch put Alec on his lap when they got in the truck. Alec's lifelong dream came alive as the driver put Forty-one Engine in gear and headed down Ponca Street with him in the front seat.

When they pulled up to their house, the Varipapas met them. "I take it ya know 'bout the boy's father," Fritsch said to a bleary-eyed Mr. V.

As he let go a yawn, Mr. V answered, "Yeah, a Captain Mannion and Father Paige came by this morning and told us. How'd Alec find out, Lieutenant?"

"He overheard a couple a my guys talkin' 'bout it outside Balmur Market a little while ago while we were 'ere on a false box. They didn't know he was Bazey's son."

"Good Christ," Mr. V answered, "helluva way to find out."

"My sentiments exactly. The firefighters have been admonished. Hopefully they'll be more tactful in the future 'bout who they run their mouths in front of."

"Hope so," Mr. V answered. "God damn, poor kid's been through enough."

"I know all about it. Can the boy stay with you all, sir?"

"Stay as long as he needs to. I already worked that out with the captain."

"Bless you, uh, what did ya say your name is?"

"Gus, Gus Varipapa."

"Wally Fritsch, been a pleasure, sir."

"Pleasure's been all mine," Mr. V answered sarcastically.

"Lieutenant, got a hot one at Western Electric on Broening Highway," the driver yelled.

"Gotta run. Thanks for everything, folks."

"God be with all of ya," Mr. V answered sincerely.

* * *

"Hello, Ellen Varipapa here," Mrs. V said when she answered her phone the next morning.

"Yes, ma'am. This is Henry Pinski, Alec's godfather, how're you today?" a soft-spoken voice said.

"Fine, and yourself, Mr. Pinski?"

"As well as can be, considerin' everything that's happened."

"Know what ya mean. What can I do for ya?"

"Captain Mannion from the fire department said Alec was stayin' with you all, is that right?"

"Yeah, he's here. Kept 'em home from school today. Poor thing's really takin' it bad."

"They tell me it's not easy when ya become an orphan."

Mrs. V saw an opening and said, "As long as me and Gus are alive, he'll always have a home. Come to grow fond of 'em."

"Yeah, us, too. In fact, that's why I called."

Mrs. V's heart sank when Henry indicated his feelings. "I'd like to visit with you and your husband at your earliest convenience and discuss Alec's future. What's a good time for ya?"

"Well, my husband works the midnight shift at GM and is home most evenings."

"How 'bout tonight?"

"What time?"

"Around seven?"

"See ya then."

* * *

Henry had seen action with the US Army's 17th Airborne, 194th Glider Infantry Regiment during WW II. Resulting from his diminutive stature, he was assigned to carry a Browning Automatic Rifle so he could be easily concealed during combat operations.

The war ended for him at the *Battle of the Bulge* during *Operation Varsity* when he was sprayed with flaming napalm. Although cosmetic surgery improved his appearance some, the right side of his face remained like melted candle wax.

As a young child, Alec was intimidated by Henry's looks, but grew fond of him due to his friendly nature.

* * *

"Alec'll stay here 'til after the funeral then come with us, right?" Henry asked Mr. V.

"Yeah, that'll be good. That way we can spend a few days with him and get to say our good-byes properly. How's that sound to ya, Alec?" Mr. V asked.

"That'll be okay, I guess."

"Don't sound too enthused there, Alec," Lena said.

Alec recognized her tone of voice and diplomatically answered, "Oh, I'm lookin' forward to comin' with you all, but I hate leavin' my friends here, that's all."

"You'll love our new neighborhood," Henry said. "Parks and ball fields just down the street; lots of other kids there, too."

"Sounds like a lotta fun, sure I'll like it. Where will I sleep?"

"We're fixin' up the basement for your room. Got some friends comin' over this weekend to put up some knotty pine. It'll be real nice by the time we're done with it."

"Knotty pine, that's the stuff with the brown spots on it, right?"

"Right."

"Yeah, I think I'll like that."

"I'll go by and see the lawyer who handled the trust and let 'em know what's goin' on," Henry said to Mr. V.

"Guess we'll be puttin' the house up for sale, know anybody in the market?" Henry asked.

"I was thinkin' 'bout that, might wanna buy it myself and use it for a rental. If Ellen agrees, we'll make ya an offer. Nothin' like livin' next door to your tenant."

"Good and bad. Every time a light bulb goes out or a commode gets clogged, guess whose door they'll be knockin' on."

"I'll keep my equipment handy," Mr. V said while gesturing as if thrusting a plunger.

"Okay, see ya after the funeral."

"Make it the day after, I'm sure none of us'll feel like doin' much afterwards."

"Okay, the day after then."

* * *

Luke's burial instructions stated that his remains be placed next to the others at Holy Redeemer; Pete's called for cremation, and the ashes deposited on top of his wife's grave in the Druid Park Cemetery.

The service began at Sacred Heart on Conkling Street where thousands of firefighters and police officers from all over the United States were in attendance, as well as contingents from Great Britain and France. The streets were clogged for blocks by fire equipment and official vehicles adorned with American and Maryland flags draped with black shrouds. An outdoor P-A system was installed to accommodate the overflow crowd.

After Father Biancamelio's sermon, in an unprecedented move, Reverend Tobias Johnson, Pete's former Baptist Minister, took the pulpit.

"Ah knew Mr. Alexander as a chil', held his beauty full lil' body in ma arms when ah dip him in the water. Ah prayed for Jesus Christ Almighty to guide and protec' 'em throughout his life. Ah know 'dat war took a lot outta Peteie, as it did lots a other good men. He loss faith in da Lawd, but ah know God has accepted and welcome him anyways, cause Peteie was a righteous brutha 'n a special human bein'. Let's have a big amen!"

"Amen, brother, amen!" the exhilarated crowd responded.

The organist then depressed the generator board of the Hammond C5 and began to play. In the deepest and most velvet-sounding baritone voice imaginable, the reverend began to sing. "On a hill, far away, stood an old, rugged cross, the emblem, of sufferin' and shame ... Everybody join me now!"

All voices sang back, "And I love, that old rugged cross. Where the dearest, and best, for a world of lost sinners slain."

The crowd sang on and finished with a rousing last verse. "To that old, rugged cross, I will ever, be true, its shame and reproach gladly bear; Then he'll call me someday, to my home far away, where his glory, forever, I'll share!"

"Thank y'all, and may God be wiff ya!" the reverend sounded as he exited the pulpit.

Not a dry eye could be found: bravado firefighters, police officers, city officials and clerks, wept shamelessly and embraced one another in death grips. When they returned to earth, Colonel Robert W. Blanchard of the United States Marine Corps, took the pulpit.

"Ladies, gentleman and well wishers from all over the world, I welcome you here today in order to pay respect for the two heroes who lie before us. I didn't have the honor of meeting Firefighter Alexander in life; however, I'm told he was a dedicated public servant as well as a brave and honorable man, having gallantly served his country as a member of the US Army's Five-Hundred and Fifty-Fifth Airborne Division. My heartfelt condolences and sympathy go out to Firefighter Alexander's family and friends seated before me," Blanchard said as he waved an opened hand.

After a long period of applause, Blanchard continued. "It *was* my privilege and deepest honor to have met Firefighter Bazey ten years ago on this very date on a small volcano-formed island in the Pacific some six hundred and fifty miles south of Tokyo: that island is better known as, *Iwo Jima*. Signalman Third Class Bazey, aboard the USS Guam, was temporarily assigned to the USMC Fifth Division as a corpsman and went ashore during the invasion. On that day, I witnessed Mr. Bazey with total disregard for his own safety, cross a field of enemy fire and rush to aid a wounded Marine. Miraculously, Mr. Bazey was able to drag him back to safety where he later recovered from his wounds. That Marine was my younger brother, Lance Corporal Martin P. Blanchard, who was later killed on Okinawa. Signalman Bazey's extreme bravery and unselfish action on that day inspired me to recommend him for the Medal of Honor. My hat's off to you, sailor!"

When Detective Bloodsworth heard Blanchard, he jumped to his feet with tear-filled eyes and a baseball-size lump in his throat and shouted, "Give 'em hell up 'ere, sailor!" as he looked upward and shook his fist.

The congregation then broke out in euphoric uproar, everlasting applause and wild cheering.

When order was restored, the USMC Honor Guard from the Marine Barracks at 8th and I in Washington, DC, followed by the United States Army Honor Guard Team from Fort Holabird in Baltimore, marched down the center aisle. After positioning themselves around the flag-covered caskets, USMC Gunnery Sergeant Oden Strapper, shouted, "Front, two!" at which the bodies were carried to the hearses.

The procession then began to form two rows behind Engine Forty-one. With ten BCPD motorcycles in the lead, it stayed together until reaching Eastern Avenue. Citizens lined the streets along the route to both cemeteries in order to pay their respect to the fallen heroes. The masses sobbed, waved American flags and saluted as the endless stream of vehicles passed.

The path to Luke's gravesite was lined with sailors, Marines, firefighters and police officers, in succession. The trail to Pete's burial site was equally adorned, with former members of the 555th replacing the navy personnel. After the Alexander family was seated, Reverend Johnson led the gathering in prayer, while Pete's mother spread his ashes over Esther Laverne.

During the prayer session for Luke, Lieutenant Fox removed an animal shelter from his vehicle. Fortunately for the cat inside, she had wandered from her mother who was accidentally crushed under forty-one as it exited the firehouse on a run. Luke appropriately named her 'Boots' when he discovered her hiding place. Luke nurtured her, and she became a permanent member of forty-one's household. She was familiar with Alec, as he fed her when he visited.

"Alec, me and the other men want ya to have Bootsie here for your very own," Fox said as he handed her over.

Alec gently stroked her as she curled up on his lap to escape the cold air. "Thanks, Mr. Fox. Is it okay if I keep her, Aunt Lena?" Alec asked with teary eyes.

"Sure, hon', it'll be fine."

* * *

Six navy blue Grumman F9F-8 Panther jets circled an area thirty seconds from the cemetery after taking off from the Naval Academy ten minutes earlier. The pilots, USMC Captain Pete Olson and US Navy Lieutenants Ed McKelar, "Wild Bill" Gureck, Ken Wallace, Zeke Cormier and Nello Pierozzi, were the US Navy's Blue Angel Team.

"Ground control to BA-one," the sailor said over his radio transmitter.

"BA-one bye. Go ahead, GC," Captain Olson answered.

"Party's awaiting your arrival, sir."

" 'At's a Roger, C. BA leader to team. Ya ready, boys? Sound off individually."

"BA-two, ready."

"BA-three, 'ats a go."

"BA-four, set."

"BA-five, let 'er rip."

"BA-six, let's do it."

" 'At's a Roger, team. All units ten-eight, C. Form 'em up for a fleur-de-leis, boys. Here we come, ground."

The Panthers took on a cross formation and lined up five abreast with Olsen in front of the pack. At precisely the moment they flew over, all six fighters turned at a ninety-degree angle and headed skyward in separate directions, forming a perfect fleur-de-leis.

As they soared toward the heavens, red-white-and-blue smoke expelled from their port openings. The crowd was awestruck by the precision surgical movements and stood in astonishment as the air became electrically charged.

"Damn, make ya proud to be an American," Bloodsworth shouted above the oohs and aahs of the crowd.

"What a site, 'ol Lukie certainly got his propers," Dom shouted over the roar of the jet engines.

As a final tribute, the lead aircraft slightly tipped its right wing then quickly leveled off, as did the others. After tipping their left wings, they flew to Druid Park and performed the same magnificent act for Pete's gathering.

When the Panthers vanished into the western sky, Gunny Strapper shouted to his riflemen. "Ready!"

Seven chrome plated M-1 Garrands were then placed at port arms.

"Aim!"

All weapons were snapped up and slammed against their shoulders, then elevated to a forty-five-degree upward angle and sighted by the shooters.

"Fi-yah!"

All seven discharged simultaneously.

The squad leader from the army then issued the same orders to his team: "Ready … aim … fi-yah!"

Seven more shots rang out.

After the honor guard from the fire department completed the twenty-one-gun salute, all three groups marched away twirling their rifles in unison.

A bugler then led in for a female Marine who began singing *Butterfield's Lullaby*, better known as *Taps* in a crystal-clear soprano voice:

Fading light dims the sight
And a star gems the sky, gleaming bright
From afar drawing nigh,
Falls the night.
Day is done, gone the sun
From the hills, from the lake, from the sky
All is well, safely rest;
God is nigh
Then goodnight, peaceful night;
Till the light of the dawn shineth bright,
God is near, do not fear,
Friend, goodnight.

Alec and his family began weeping hysterically. Why have you done this to me, God? Why did you take *him* away? I'm only ten years old, God, I didn't deserve this. Now I don't have anyone. Why, Lord, why? Alec thought as he looked at the graves of his mother, sister, brother and Luke's casket.

Alec remembered catechism class when the nun spoke of the Antichrist. "This man of sin will possess a number of characteristics, one of them as performing all sorts of evil," Paul wrote in Thessalonians Chapter Two. Could I be the Antichrist and God's getting even with me for killing Terri? My first two initials *are* A. C., Alec thought as he gazed, pondered and wept.

* * *

"Okay, folks, could I have your attention please?" Firefighter Sam Lukehardt said over the public-address system. "In his burial instructions, Firefighter Bazey requested that his favorite song be played in closing."

As Lukehardt took the forty-five RPM on the black-yellow-and-white Specialty label and placed it on the turntable, he said to his assistant, "Here goes nothin'," as he rolled his eyes and curled his lips. The 120-decibel speakers then blasted out, "Ah womp bomp a lou bomp a lomp bam boom! Tutti frutti, all rootie, tutti frutti, all rootie, tutti frutti all rootie, oooh, tutti frutti, all rootie, tutti frutti, all rootie, ah womp bomp a lou bomp a lomp bam boom!"

When the crowd heard Little Richard wailing out Tutti Frutti, they were dumbfounded. "What the hell?" said Luke's father.

"Sir, is this some kind of perverted joke?" Mrs. Bazey asked.

"No, ma'am. The chief said it was in Luke's will that we play this song at the end to lighten things up. Just followin' orders, ma'am."

As the music progressed, the initial shock wore off and the crowd began to groove. "Fuckin' Lukie. He always did have style," Dom said with a broad grin.

"Way to go, sailor," Bloodsworth yelled out.

"Semper Fi, brother. Semper Fi," a former Marine and current BCFD Firefighter shouted.

When it finished, Lieutenant Fritsch hollered, "Play it again, Sam!"

"You're the boss, Lieutenant."

"Ah womp bomp a lou bomp a lomp bam boom!"

RITES OF PASSAGE

According to Dr. Arnold Van Gennep, the Rite of Passage has three phases: in the first phase—Separation—people withdraw from the group and begin moving from one place or status to another; in the third phase—Incorporation—they re-enter society, having completed the rite.

* * *

When Henry bought his new home, he was unaware of another development in the area due to begin construction. After the announcement became public, many of the homeowners got up in arms.

"That's just wonderful," Henry said to his next-door neighbor Frank Cusnarski, a city traffic cop. "Had to work my ass off to get outta the slums and here the federal government comes and puts it in our backyards. It just ain't right."

"Yeah, bound to be some of my clients movin' in 'ere, too. Now they'll know exactly where I live," Frank added.

Complaints and petitions were filed, but had no effect on the plan. When the editor of the Baltimore Sun got wind of the dissidents, he referred to them as middle-class 'snobs' who had no compassion for the less fortunate. As *Claremont* was completed years before Equal Housing Legislation was passed, the federal government restricted the residents to that of Caucasian families so as not to disrupt the racial balance of the surrounding neighborhoods.

* * *

Alec was warmly greeted by his cousin Carol, who escorted him to his living area. "Boy oh boy, this is great," Alec said as he touched the knotty-pine walls.

"I set you up with a little desk and lamp in the back for your school studies," Carol brightly said.

Carol was five months younger than Alec, and although she carried the Pinski surname, her Italian heritage dominated her appearance.

"It'll be so nice having you live here. Mom and Dad said God wouldn't let us have any more children, but now he's sent you to me for a brother," Carol said gleefully.

"Where's Bootsie gonna sleep?" Alec asked while he stroked her arched back as she purred.

"Dad's gonna take us to the pet store on Belair Road later and buy a bed for her, then we can put it right next to yours."

"Where's the candy store?"

"About eight blocks away on Chesterfield Avenue."

"Eight blocks away, I'll starve to death by the time I get there."

"Don't be silly, it's only a ten-minute walk. You and I'll go after lunch."

"Okay, I guess that'll be all right. Where will I go to school?"

"Brehms Lane Elementary, about a mile away."

"A mile away?"

"Yeah, Mom drives me most of the time. You'll like it, there's a big playground and a cafeteria and all."

"Cafeteria sounds good."

* * *

Alec quickly adapted to his change of environment and felt loved and secure, but was stand offish to the other kids in the neighborhood. When he would venture off, he and Boots usually walked to nearby Herring Run. On one of his outings, Alec was followed. "Hey, whacha doin' throwin' rocks in my stream, punk?" a male voice said shortly after he entered a wooded area.

Startled by the intruder, Alec quickly turned and said, "Sorry, didn't know it was yours. I'm finished anyway."

"That violation'll cost ya one blow job, kid," the older boy said as he stroked his erect penis.

"Come on ,Bootsie. Time to go home, girl!"

"Get on your knees, ya little bastard."

Alec delivered a blow with his right elbow that caught the other boy completely off guard. "Who ya think you're fuckin' with? I'm Russell, the baddest mutha fucker around," he said as he wiped blood from his chin. "Now you're gonna suck my dick, or I'll cut your little balls off," he said as he pulled a black scrimshaw-handled Buck Knife and held the four-inch blade to Alec's throat.

"Help, help, somebody please help me!"

"Ain't nobody can hear down here, asshole. Now get to suckin'," he said as he nicked Alec's left ear.

When Boots heard Alec's cry for help, she charged to the rescue. "God damn," Russell yelled when he felt her claws dig into his penis.

As she made another pass, Russell plunged the knife through her tiny body and twirled her like a shish kebab then flung her away. "The same thing's gonna happen to you, if'n ya don't suck my dick. Now get to work, ya little fucker."

Alec looked at the bleeding penis as he wiped blood from his ear, then capitulated and dropped to his knees. While moving his hips to and fro, Russell touched the knife to Alec's cheek and said, "All you're doin' is lettin' me mouth fuck ya. Now suck it, God damn it."

Russell placed his free hand on the back of Alec's head and forced himself further in. During ejaculation, Alec felt the penis convulse as semen trickled down his throat.

"Ya liked it, I can tell ya did by the way you sucked," Russell said with fiendish eyes as he pulled up his zipper.

Alec went to the stream and spit out a remaining bit of semen, then rinsed his mouth. "If ya tell anybody, I'll come back and cut your balls off. Understand?"

"I understand," Alec answered as Russell trotted back to the street.

Alec buried Boots' bloody remains and said, "God, why are you doing this to me?"

He then sat by the stream and contemplated: he considered telling Henry, but decided against it as it would be too embarrassing, and thought perhaps he would consider him a homosexual. He came to the conclusion that had he been with other people, he wouldn't have been forced to commit the evil act. More importantly, Boots would still be alive. There is strength in numbers he determined. "I'll get acquainted with the other guys in the neighborhood," he said. He also came to the realization that if he were bigger and stronger, he would've been able to put up a better fight.

Above all, he remembered what Luke told him and Victor after Lucy was killed. "Boys, I know it's hard for ya to understand, but I'm gonna tell ya what my grandfather told me always to remember—if it don't kill ya, it'll make ya stronger."

"I know what Dad was talkin' about now," Alec said. "This *will* make me stronger and I'll get even with that dirty bastard. He made one big mistake today; *he shoulda killed me and let Bootsie live.* I'll make 'em sorry for that," Alec vowed to himself.

On that day, Alec entered the second phase of the Rite of Passage—the Liminal Period—where people leave one place or state, but have not entered or joined the next.

* * *

When he got home, Alec explained that Boots had been swept away in Herring Run and he cut his ear while trying to rescue her.

"We'll get you another kitty," Lena said.

"Thanks, Aunt Lena, but I don't want another one. Nothin' could ever replace Bootsie."

"Poor, baby," Carol said as she hugged him.

"Uncle Henry, would you buy me a set of weights?"

"Sure, fella. The trust provides for ya to have pretty much whatever ya want within reason. How come ya want weights, sport?"

"I was lookin' at *Your Physique Magazine*, and thought I'd like to look like one of 'em guys in the book: 'at British guy, George Efferman, especially. Also like to take some judo lessons, never know when it might come in handy."

"Sounds good. We'll start lookin' into it tomorrow. We can set up a gym downstairs for ya. Might even do some liftin' myself."

"Ha, fat chance," said Lena. "The only thing you'll lift is your fork to your mouth."

"Now, now, sweetheart."

EIGHTY-EIGHT RED RIGHT

A few days after his encounter with Russell, Alec, now anxious to make friends, approached a boy who lived a few doors away. "What's with that red fedora?" Alec asked him.

"Just started a club in the neighborhood. Call ourselves the 'Rebels' and the hat's our trademark. Got somethin' to say about it?" the boy with a Southern drawl answered in lead-dog fashion.

"No, I'd like to join. What do I have to do to get in?"

"Are ya a Yankee or Confederate?"

Easy question, thought Alec. "I'm a Rebel. What else would I be?"

"You're in. My name's Jerry Greenwell, what's yours?"

"Alec Bazey, glad to meet ya."

After being introduced to the other members and obtaining appropriate head wear, Alec asked if any were familiar with an older kid named Russell. None said they were, and Alec stayed on the lookout for him hoping they would cross paths while in the company of his troops.

The next day, Alec overheard his neighbor tell Henry that a young man named Russell Palmieri from Claremont had been arrested for molesting a policeman's son under the bridge over Herring Run on Sinclair Lane.

That has to be the same guy that killed Boots, Alec said to himself. I'll have to wait for 'em to get outta jail before I can get even with 'em.

* * *

As Henry parked his '53 Ford in front of the Louis J. Smith Sporting Goods Store on Conkling Street, Alec spotted Lieutenant Fox sitting in front of the firehouse.

"Oh, there's Mr. Fox. Can we go over and say hi?"

"Yeah, sure. He's the one who gave you Boots at the cemetery, right?"

"He's the one."

When Fox saw Alec, his face glowed. "Alec, how ya doin'? So good to see ya. What's it been? Let's see, February, March, April, May, June, July, August. Six months," he counted off on his fingers.

"Nice to see you, too, Mr. Fox."

"How's ol' Bootsie doin'?"

Alec didn't answer and looked to the ground and began circling his right foot on the pavement.

"We lost 'er a few days ago," Henry said. "She fell into Herring Run and got swept away."

"That's terrible. We have a lot more cats around here. Want me to get ya another one, Al?"

"No, that's okay, sir," Alec said with watery eyes.

"If ya change your mind, come see me. I'll take care of ya in the house-cat department. Now what brings you boys to this neck of the woods?"

"Goin' next door to get Alec some weight-liftin' equipment. He wants to build himself up," Henry said as he rolled his good eye.

"I'll go over with ya, maybe we can chisel ol' Butts down on the price a little. Smitty, goin' next door for a few," Fox yelled to the watch-desk officer.

* * *

After a year of spirited training, Alec gained thirty pounds of pure muscle, and had grown four inches.

"Damn," said Henry as he felt Alec's flexed bicep. "Nobody's gonna mess with you, boy. Feel 'at arm, Lena."

" 'At's really somethin' all right. Good goin', Alec."

* * *

In conjunction with weight training, Alec began taking Jiu-Jitsu instructions. Jujutsu or Jiujitsu, meaning the 'art of softness,' is a Japanese martial art that consists of grappling and striking techniques. It evolved from the Samurai of feudal Japan as a method for dispatching an armed opponent in situations where the use of weapons was impractical or forbidden. The techniques were developed around the principle of using an attacker's energy against them, rather than directly opposing it.

* * *

In September of 1959, Alec entered Baltimore City College High School; the same one Victor had attended. Now just a whisker short of six feet tall, and weighing in at a strapping 210 pounds of rippled muscle, he easily made BCC's varsity football squad. Despite his maximum effort, Alec couldn't outperform upperclassman Tommy Simpson for the position of starting quarterback.

Simpson's father was a former Olympian, and served as the Chief Executive Officer of Maryland National Bank, headquartered in Towson. His mother was a socialite, and had inherited her parent's home in prestigious Dulaney Valley, where her only child began his education.

His parents transferred him to football-powerhouse BCC in the public school system where many players won athletic college scholarships.

Simpson drove to school in a '57 black Thunderbird, and was provided a private parking place in the faculty lot. The school administration and teachers coddled him, especially the principal and football coaches. When he strutted down the halls, the other students would split ranks and let him through.

As Simpson was always conveniently involved with athletic activities when exams were given, his were administered one on one and he carried straight A's. He held himself above the other pupils and considered it an honor for them to be in his company. He constantly questioned the coaches when they gave him direction, and often refused to comply with plays sent in during games.

After Simpson's sixty-five-yard touchdown pass on the final play defeated rival Calvert Hall, he was interviewed on WCAO—'60' on the radio dial, by Gene Creasy.

"It was a tough game, but we snatched victory from the jaws of defeat," Simpson cockily testified over the airwaves. "Took my best effort, but I knew I had it in me."

"That's great, Tommy. All us down here at CAO were pullin' for ya. We knew ya could do it. What about the big City-Poly game comin' up on Thanksgivin' Day, who's gonna win that one?"

"Is there any doubt in your mind with me at the helm? C'mon, Crease, you tell me who's gonna win."

"Sorry, Tommy, lost my head there for a moment."

After the interview was blasted throughout the school over the P. A., Simpson began referring to himself as the 'Unitas' of BCC and insisted his jersey number be changed to '19.'

* * *

The BCC-Poly Thanksgiving Day tradition began in 1889 at Clifton Park where BCC emerged victoriously. The public-school football rivalry was the first in Maryland and is the second oldest in the United States, predated only by that of Boston Latin and English High.

In 1959, BCC was a slight favorite over Poly; on a clear cool day, fifteen thousand were in attendance at Memorial Stadium for the event.

"Let 'em receive," the team captain said, "this buncha chumps need an advantage."

" 'At boy's got all the talent any player could possibly ask for," BCC Head Coach George Young said when he saw the referee signaling that Poly would receive after his team won the toss. "His biggest fuckin' problem is between 'is ears. He keeps 'at attitude and he'll never make it in this game, God damn," he said in frustration.

When Simpson came to the sideline, Young said, "Tommy, what the hell are ya thinkin' 'bout, boy, lettin' 'em take the kickoff?"

Simpson quickly turned his head from side to side and shouted back, "Ya callin' *me* a fuckin' boy, Coach? The only boy I see 'round here is 'at little flunkie of yours carryin' your clipboard."

"I have half a mind to bench you and put in Bazey!"

"Then what, lose? Bazey can't hold a candle to me. I know it, you know it and *he* knows it."

Alec ripped off his helmet and locked a death grip around Simpson's throat. No one intervened until they saw Simpson begin to turn blue. "Watch 'at shit, Bazey," Young said as he winked and smiled while Simpson gasped for air. "Defenders take the field. Let's kick some Poly asses, oohrah!"

"Oohrah!" the 'D' responded.

* * *

The first half ended in a scoreless tie. After returning the opening kickoff of the second half to Poly's forty-five, BCC was forced to punt when the 220-pound left defensive end sent Simpson flying for a seventeen-yard loss on third and six.

"Do I have to do the fuckin' blockin' too?" Simpson barked as he removed sod from his face guard.

"Shut the fuck up or we'll call Bazey in and let 'em finish the job on your lame ass," the center yelled back.

"Bazey got lucky. He caught me off guard."

"Yeah, ya looked off guard when your face turned purple."

* * *

At the start of the fourth quarter, Poly's quarterback connected with a forty-two- yard scoring touchdown pass to the right split end. They failed to convert the extra point and led 6-0.

The Poly defenders had Simpson's number that day. By the end of the third quarter, he completed only six passes for short gains in eighteen attempts. With one minute and eleven seconds remaining, Simpson hit on a long pass to *his* split end who was knocked out of bounds at Poly's six. On first and goal with the clock running, Simpson called a quick opener over the left tackle and was stopped cold. He then tried the same play over the right side, where the runner was tripped up at the two. With thirty-one seconds remaining, Coach Young called time.

144

"Okay, Tommy, show everybody you're as good as ya say ya are. We haven't used our power sweep all day, now's the time. Forty-three right on two, okay?" Young said when Simpson returned to the side.

"Forty-three right on two. Okay, got it, Coach. Bazey, don't fuck up and blow the extra point after we score. Hear me, dammit?" Simpson yelled at Alec who ignored him and continued to stretch his leg muscles.

"Okay, eighty-eight red right on three," Simpson called in the huddle.

"Eight-eight red right: that's a crossover in the middle of the field. Ya sure that's what the coach called?" Artie Gibson, the fullback asked.

"Fuck the coach, he doesn't know anything. I watch Unitas do it all the time. Catches the defense off guard. Never fails."

"You're *not* Unitas."

"I'm better'n him. Now shut the fuck up and do it. Everybody got it? Eighty-eight red right on three. Let's go!"

As Simpson faded back to pass, Young shouted at the top of his lungs. "Is he fuckin' deaf or just plain stupid? I called a runnin' play!"

"Tryin' to play hero again," the assistant answered.

When Simpson released the ball, everyone on BCC's side crossed their fingers and held their breath. A few seconds later, the scoreboard showed: time remaining-0:00, Poly-12—BCC-0, after the safety snatched the ball and returned it 102 yards for a touchdown.

"Nice goin', Johnny U," Gibson hollered.

"What kinda shit was 'at?" Young ventilated when Simpson came back.

"Don't worry 'bout it, Coach. We'll get em next year," Simpson said cavalierly.

"You won't be *my* fuckin' quarterback next year."

He won't be *anybody's* quarterback next year, Alec said to himself.

COVE ROAD

On Alec's sixteenth birthday, he said to Henry, "Unc', does my trust fund have enough in it for me to buy a car?"

"Alec, I guess you're old enough to know. After everything was settled, the fund ended up with nearly three hundred and twenty-five thousand dollars. Lena and I've been real careful and you haven't cost that much to raise, and now there's about three-fifty in it. I'd say ya could have a car, what about you, Lena?"

"Sure, I think it'd be a good idea. Alec's been a good reliable person. After all, it is his money."

"Wow, I had no idea it was that much. I spotted a hot yellow-and-white fifty-six Chevy convertible with four on the floor when me and Edjew drove past Schaffer and Strominger a couple days ago on our way to the Circle for hamburgers. I really liked it." "How much?" asked Henry.

"Fifteen hundred."

"That doesn't sound bad. Let's ride up now and see if we can cut us a deal."

"But I don't have my license yet."

"No problem. If we buy it, I'll drive it home and Lena can drive the old Ford back."

"You're the greatest, Unc'. One other thing, I wanna buy you all a new car. Carol, too, when she turns sixteen."

"We couldn't take your money, Al. We'll keep the old Ford, it's still in good shape."

"Please, Unc', do it for me."

"Whadda ya think, Lena?"

"We'll see. If one's on sale or somethin', we might consider it."

"What kind are ya gonna buy me?" asked Carol.

"Whatever kind ya want, Sis."

"Can't wait, come on November," Carol shouted with glee.

* * *

"Got that thing for a steal," the salesman said as he turned over the keys to Henry. "Your uncle drives a hard bargain. Now enjoy your car, son, and be careful."

As they entered the gorgeous piece of machinery, Alec said, "Aren't we gonna look for a car for you?"

"We'll wait awhile. No sense in rushin."

"Let me know when you're ready."

On the last day of school, Henry picked up Alec and drove to the Maryland Department of Motor Vehicles on St. Paul Street to apply for a learner's permit. After two weeks of daily training, he passed his driver's test.

While driving down North Point Boulevard in the direction of the Bethlehem Steel Plant, the area began to look familiar to Alec. When he got to the river and saw a ship in the channel passing close to shore, he recognized Goo-Goo Minnie.

On the way back, he turned onto a one-lane road. "Have to remember this place. Gotta car now, might wanna bring a chick down here and park."

* * *

On a Sunday afternoon while cruising with Christine Racioppi, an elementary schoolmate Alec had become reacquainted with on his part-time job at Eddie's Supermarket in the Freedom Village Shopping Center on Erdman Avenue, he spotted Simpson driving his Thunderbird. When he turned and followed, Christine said, "I thought we were going to Loch Raven, Al," as he parked on the shoulder a safe distance from the driveway of a home Simpson had pulled into.

"Gotta check the oil, light just came on."

While fumbling with the dip stick, Simpson came out of the house escorted by a female. Must be his girlfriend's place, Alec said to himself. "'Bout a quart low, I'll take care of it later. Now onto the reservoir," he said to Christine who smiled and snuggled close.

When Alec returned the next night, he followed Simpson and the female when they left the house. After staying at a motel for two hours, Simpson dropped off his girl, then drove to a local bar. "Must have a phony ID," Alec said.

The next day, Alec drove back to the desolate road off North Point Boulevard where he noticed a path leading into woods. Once in, a vehicle couldn't be seen due to the heavy vegetation and thick trees. It was obvious no one had been on the path recently as the underbrush was high and unmolested.

That evening, Alec went back to the bar. When he saw Simpson's car in the lot, he parked and ducked below the steering wheel. While waiting for him to leave, Alec thought about Terri and said, "If I *am* the Antichrist, so be it. As long as I don't get caught, it's okay."

The moment he saw Simpson exit, Alec quietly got out and hid between cars until he heard gravel crunching. Before he hit the ground,

Alec wrapped duct tape around Simpson's neck in order to secure the plastic bag he mushroomed over his head to contain the blood flow. "Stealth—just like the heron," Alec said as he stuffed the body in his vehicle and tossed the two-pound maul in behind it.

After the burial, Alec tamped the ground, covered it with shrubs and gathered the pickax and shovels he left there when he dug the grave. He then switched off the Coleman Lantern and drove to North Point Boulevard from Cove Road.

"Thanks for lettin' me use the old Dodge," Alec said to the manager as he handed him the keys of the store's delivery truck when he arrived for work the next afternoon. "Cleaned it up for ya, filled it up, too."

"You're welcome, Al. Anytime ya need it, just ask," the manager said as he took the keys.

* * *

When the news media discovered Baltimore's homegrown football prodigy had gone missing without a trace, they went into a speculative frenzy. The local newspapers and sports broadcasters couldn't imagine what became of the 'warm, friendly and talented superstar.' One sportswriter published a theory that he had been kidnapped by the KGB and brainwashed into becoming a hockey player in the USSR.

"Until Simpson returns, Bazey'll be our starting quarterback," Coach Young said on the first day of practice at Kirk Field.

"Wouldn't surprise me none if the coach didn't off Tommy for callin' that dumb-ass eighty-eight red right last year," Artie Gibson whispered with a grin to Alec.

"Never can tell, Artie."

* * *

Under Alec's leadership, BCC beat Poly 30-26 in the 1960 Thanksgiving Day match up. In the fourth quarter of the 1961 game against Poly with BCC leading by 30-0, Alec took a blindside hit and was replaced. Poly scored a touchdown on the last possession of the game and converted a pass for two more points; the final score stood at: BCC 30—Poly 8.

MOLLY

Alec was unsure as to what path he should follow to his future after a permanent injury to his right knee on the *last* play of his *last* high-school football game disqualified him from any of the athletic scholarships he had been offered by several major universities. As he had maintained a 3.75 grade-point average, he knew any school in the nation would accept him, especially with Uncle Sam footing the bill. He decided against college for the time being, however, and considered joining the military.

* * *

"Hello, Lena, this is Mary Antonelli. Do ya remember me?"

"Oh sure, Mary, how ya been?"

"Fine. A little arthritis here and there, but okay otherwise. How you been?"

"Couldn't be better, especially hearin' from you."

"Is Alec there?"

"Sure, I'll get 'em for ya."

Alec took the phone and said, "Zia, Maria. Come stal?"

"Buono, buono."

"What ya been up to, Aunt Mare?"

"Same old stuff. Uncle Joe's still drivin' a truck, bought a nice little waterfront home in Bowley's Quarters. Ya should come and see us."

"Finally moved from Lakewood, huh?"

"Yeah, got a deal on this place and decided to make the move."

"I loved that house on Lakewood. All ya hadda do was walk out the back door and boom, you were at the Belnord Theater."

"Yeah, we miss that and walkin' to the grocery store. Gotta drive five miles to the nearest civilization down here. It's nice though, got our own crab pots and everything."

"Before we hang up, I'll get your number and address. Maybe we'll drive down Sunday."

"Sunday sounds great. I'll get Joe to bait up plenty a chicken guts and eels Saturday so's we'll have a nice batch a hard shells for ya."

"Good, haven't had any yet this year."

"Listen, the reason I'm callin' is because your grandmother called me a little while ago."

"*My* grandmother? Grandma Pinski died before I was born, and I see Grandma Bazey all the time. What grandma are ya talkin' about?"

"The one on your mother's side. Her name's Molly Gardner now and she lives in a small town in upstate New York—Cortland."

"I thought she was dead."

"No, honey, we were never sure what happened to her and your grandfather. For all we knew, they *were* dead."

"Damn, how'd they find ya?"

"Well, she said she's been tryin' for years, but the authorities wouldn't give her the information until all the foster parents were gone. She and her husband Clarence hired a private detective and they found us. Isn't that exciting?"

"I'm not sure if it's exciting, but it comes as a hell of a surprise. Is she comin' to see us?"

"I told her to let me contact the family before they came. Get a pencil and paper and I'll give ya my address and phone number and we'll talk about it on Sunday. I'll call your Aunt Elizabeth and invite her and Uncle Mike, too, okay?"

"Sounds good to me. All right, I got a pen and paper, shoot."

After Alec hung up, Lena asked with a quizzical look on her face, "What was that all about?"

"Seems like my natural grandmother found her family here in Baltimore. Mary invited us to her house for crabs and beer Sunday. Y'all up to it?"

"No, leavin' for Buffalo Friday for Henry's airborne convention. Maybe next time."

"Okay, I'll tell ya how it went when we ya get back."

* * *

Two weeks later, when they saw a new Cadillac pull into Mary's driveway, everyone took a deep breath, then walked out to greet the guests. The group presented a dignified appearance, and were clearly Alec's mother's relatives. When Molly spotted them, she clutched her heart and began crying.

"My beautiful little girls," she cried out as she showered them with hugs and kisses. "God has finally brought you back to me. Thank you, Lord. If Lucy could be here my prayers and dreams would have been completely answered!"

When Molly spotted Alec, she immediately knew he was her grandson. With shortness of breath, she said, "Except for the lighter eyes and hair, you're the spitting image of your grandfather. Lord have mercy, you've brought him back to me, too."

While chatting under the sun porch on the Middle River Basin side of Mary's home, it was learned that Molly's brother Frank, had inherited the La Blanc Leather Company in Brooklyn; the only place he worked after having relocated there from Barton, Maryland. "I knew Mr. Lippenstein liked me, but had no idea he was gonna leave me the place. Coulda knocked me over with a feather when they read the will," Frank told everyone with a sly grin.

"Frank gave us the money to hire the private eye so we could find you," Molly said.

"Yeah, I was in New York when my mother sent you girls to the orphanage," Frank said as he looked apologetically at his nieces and nervously fidgeted with his two-carat diamond ring. "Didn't find out about it for nearly two years when I came home for Christmas. I swear to ya, if there was anything I coulda done, I woulda. I wasn't much more than a kid at the time and could barely support myself. I'm sorry girls," he said as he held them close and sobbed.

After the men loaded in Joe's twenty-six-foot Chris Craft for a tour of Miller Island and Bay Shore, Molly and her daughters conversed privately. "I didn't know you all were gone until I got outta the hospital. As soon as we could, Frank and I took a Greyhound to the orphanage in Baltimore where they told us all of you had been adopted out, and they weren't allowed to tell us who the foster parents were. We gave up lookin' for ya after a week, and I went back to New York and worked on the assembly line at La Blanc until 1940, when I met Clarence who was in town for an apple-grower's convention. We got married a month later, and I've lived in Cortland ever since."

After hearing of Lucy's perils and the circumstances of her death, Molly said hysterically, "Oh my God, it sounds just like me when I was in the hospital. If it wasn't for me, none of this would have happened!"

"Now, now, mother, it wasn't your fault," Mary said.

"At least we still have Alec to remember her by," Molly replied.

"Yes, we do, and he's a wonderful young man."

Molly and the others departed the next morning following a Sunday breakfast feast. After giving their fond farewells, the group vowed to meet again soon, and stay in contact.

* * *

A month later, while at Clarence's funeral, Molly asked Mary if it would be in order for her to relocate to Baltimore as she had no family in Cortland.

"Nothing would make me happier," Mary said with great enthusiasm. "There's an empty apartment overtop my beauty shop you can take rent free."

"I wouldn't think of imposing."

"Mother, please. We have lost time to make up for, take the

apartment."

"Okay, if your husband doesn't mind."

"Joe won't mind."

"All right, I'll be in contact after I make the arrangements at this end."

"Can't wait."

* * *

Alec's neighbor, Frank, frequented various 'oval' sites throughout Maryland. His favorite was off Northern Parkway, and known as the *Pimlico Race Course.*

Pimlico officially opened in the Fall of 1870, with the colt *Preakness*, winning the first running of the *Dinner Party Stakes.* Three years later, the horse would have the 1873 *Preakness Stakes* named in his honor. The race is the second leg of the *Triple Crown* and run at a distance of 1 3/16 miles. The track is also noted as the home for the match race in which *Seabiscuit* beat *War Admiral* in the Second Pimlico Special on November 1, 1938, before a crowd of forty-three thousand.

Frank taught Alec how to decipher a racing form and the basics of handicapping; as picking a winner involved a certain amount of skill, planning, patience and tact, Alec was a natural for the game.

* * *

After Molly relocated, she and Alec became quite close as she resembled his mother and possessed many of her attributes. On one of their outings, Alec suggested to Molly they try their luck. "Oh, I've never been to the horse races. I wouldn't know what to do," she answered naively.

"I'll teach ya, Grandma, nothin' to it."

"Okay, how much money will I need?"

"Nothin'. I'll show ya how to read the Morning Telegraph so ya can pick your own horses the next time. This time, I'll make the bets for ya, and if we win, we'll split it. How's that sound?"

"Can't lose, let's go."

On a bright afternoon in October, the two headed for Pimlico. They parked in the valet area on the Winner Avenue side and entered through the clubhouse gate.

Alec had been given 'inside information' from Frank, that *Noble Dream* was a 'mortal lock' to win the first race. As most of his 'tips' ran last, Alec was wary, but felt this tout was good as Frank had given him twenty dollars and told him to play it all on the nose. When Alec placed his bets, Noble Dream was at 8-1: by post time, 11-1.

154

When the pack got to the sixteenth pole and Molly saw the white three on the blue background on the blanket of the lead horse, her primal instincts took over. "Come on, baby. Hold 'em 'ere. You can do it, you can do it, you can do it," she hollered.

"It was close, but I think the three won on the nod," Alec said when the 'photo-finish' light came on.

A few minutes later, a wet glossy traveled on a clothespin and wheel down a cable. After what seemed like an eternity for the stewards to examine the photo, a beautiful, '**3**,' lit next to the first-place finisher on the tote board, followed by: '**OFFICIAL.**'

Alec looked at his fifty-six-year-old grandmother in amazement as she slapped him a high five and kissed him on the mouth when he handed her half of $258 after cashing a twenty-dollar ticket. The seven horse, *King's Corsair,* shipped in from Belmont, completed the daily double for them and they split another $522. "My God," Molly said as she fanned the bills in front of her face. "Where have you been all my life? You darling boy."

Molly insisted on buying dinner after the races, and Alec drove to the Backfin Restaurant on Reisterstown Road, directly across from Maryland State Police Headquarters. "You not only look like your grandfather, you act like him, too. He was so kind, considerate and generous. You would've loved him, Alec," Molly said after placing her order.

"Too bad I didn't get to meet 'em. What was his name?"

"Antonio Iadavia. He was from Sicily; we met on the boat over."

"How'd he die?"

Molly looked away. A few seconds later she covered Alec's hands with hers and said, "I loved your grandfather, Alec, and he loved us; but he was not good in *all* ways. He died of syphilis, from having sex with other women."

Alec was dumbfounded by his grandmother's confessional and sat silently. "He was also a murderer; he killed people for the Mafia."

Alec's heart stopped as he gazed aimlessly. After the waitress brought their meals, he said, "How many people did he kill, Grandma?"

"A lot, is all I know. They paid him lots of money to do it."

"Wow."

"I guess I shouldn't have told you. You look upset."

"No, Grandma. I'm glad ya did, I'm *really* glad ya did."

That answers a lotta questions, Alec said to himself. Now I know where it comes from.

PAST PATRONAGE RECOGNIZED

On the way home from their day at the races, Alec said, "Grandma, open the glove box and get the envelope in there with your name on it."

"Oh, Alec, they're lovely, thank you so much, honey. I'll put these in my album," Molly said after she looked at the photos. "I don't see one of your sister. How come?"

The question stung Alec and he answered, "I guess we never took any."

In actuality, there were scads of photos of Terri, but Alec had destroyed them. "I would've loved to have seen a picture of her. Who'd she look like?"

"She looked a little like Mom and Dad, but more like you."

"Did she *really*?"

"Yeah, same eyes and nose. She was a beautiful little girl."

"Oh, that's so sweet. What did she die of?"

"They never were able to determine. Some sort of disease where kids die in their sleep." Anxious to change the subject, Alec said, "Do you have any pictures of Grandad?"

"We had a bunch of all of us, but my mother threw them away like she did my babies. Damn her wretched soul."

"How about your father, what became of him?"

"After having thirteen of us, he up and disappeared. God only knows where he went."

"So your mother was left alone with a bunch of her own kids to raise after he cut out, huh? Maybe that's the reason she sent Mom and her sisters to the orphanage."

"Yes, that's true. But if she wanted, she could've found room for three more."

"How'd you and Clarence get together?"

"I met him through a friend of Uncle Frank who was staying at the same hotel as Clarence during an apple-grower's convention in New York. He was such a kind and lovable man; it really hurt when he passed. We were married for twenty-two years."

"Yeah, he seemed like a nice guy. Would've liked to have gotten to know 'em better."

When Alec got home, he returned the original photos to the chest at the foot of his bed. While removing the plaque holding the Medal of Honor, the blue ribbon fell free.

"Son of a bitch, my father was killed on the day I was born," Alec said when he looked at the newly exposed area.

After reading the account of his father's heroic conduct, he said, "I'm gonna go airborne, too."

* * *

Alec had gone to Hamilton JHS on Bayonne and Sefton Avenues in the Hamilton section of the city. Located nearby, at the intersection of Harford Road and Hamilton Avenue, was the 'Arcade,' an early shopping mall of sorts. At the very end, was one of many movie theaters owned by Durkee Enterprises. Adjacent to the theater and across from the barber shop, was the US Army Recruiting Office.

"Afternoon, son. Sergeant Pervalion, what can I do for ya?"

"Decided I wanna be a paratrooper."

"You've come to the right place. Have a seat and I'll get ya some brochures and have ya fill out an information card."

"That'll be fine."

"Anything to drink? Got some cold Cokes in the back."

"Coke'll be good."

When he returned, Pervalion said, "Ya got the look of a paratrooper. What're ya, 'bout six one, two-twenty?" he asked as he eyed Alec's cut.

"Six even, two-twelve this mornin' when I weighed myself."

"How long ya been liftin'?"

"Seven years now. Started the Weider Method and stuck with it."

"Good goin', it sure popped the trick for ya. Airborne's a tough outfit, what makes ya wanna go there?"

Alec noticed wings on Pervalion's highly starched shirt, and an 11th Airborne patch on his shoulder. "My father was with the hundred and first, and my uncle with the seventeenth. Figure it's my turn to keep up the family tradition."

"Your dad was with the one-o-one?"

"Yes, sir. Jumped on D-Day. Killed at Foucarville, won the Medal of Honor there. My uncle fought the Battle of the Bulge; was nearly killed when a flamethrower melted his face."

"What's your name, son?"

"Bazey, Alec Bazey. B-a-z-e-y."

Pervalion reached in his desk and retrieved a booklet with a light blue cover. As he thumbed through it, Alec noticed the title: *Distinguished Honorees of American Conflicts* "Not anybody listed in *this* book named Bazey," Pervalion said.

The sergeant's tone irritated Alec, and he snapped back, "Try Pinski—P-i-n-s-k-i, Paul Pinski—five-nine-five-seven-seven-seven-one. I was given the name Bazey by my stepfather, Lucca Bazey, who, by the way, won the Silver Star on Iwo Jima. Check that in your little book, and if those names aren't in there, throw the thing away."

A moment later, Pervalion said, "I extend my deepest apologies to you, son. Both names *are* in here. I looked Bazey up in the Medal of Honor section. Again, I truly apologize. Here, keep the book, I can get another."

Alec beamed with pride when he saw the names and replied, "That's okay, Sergeant, everybody makes a mistake."

* * *

On January 2, 1963, Alec arrived at the US Army Induction Center at Fort Holabird, driven there by Carol in her '59 Ford Sunliner he had bought on her sixteenth birthday.

"Was with your father when *he* went in," Henry said.

"Little different this time, Unc'. World War II not goin' on like it was for you guys."

"Be careful, Alec. Stay clear of flamethrowers," Henry said while rubbing his drooped side.

"We love you, Alec," said Lena.

"Write soon," said Carol.

"Soon as I can. Don't worry, guys, I'm a big boy. Can take care of myself."

He then took Christine's hand and led her a few feet away. "Alec, I've loved you ever since I first saw you in the second grade. It's not too late, please reconsider joining up. I don't want anything to happen to you."

"I love you, too, Chris, but I feel compelled to do this. It's only for three years, then we can get on with life and not have the draft in the way."

After a long kiss and embrace, Christine said, "I'll be waiting for you, Alec. Go do what you have to do, and come back in one piece."

"Okay, sweetheart."

When they completed another kiss, Alec entered the induction center.

* * *

Alec was delivered by rail to what was known as *Fort* Jackson, South Carolina. He was more fortunate than his father, as his company was located at the top of Tank Hill. Instead of running up the hill, however, the troops ran down, *then* back up. In any case, 'humpin' the hill' couldn't be avoided.

Alec graduated from basic training with honors. After a week of leave, he returned to Fort Jackson where he completed four weeks of advanced infantry training.

Upon arriving at Fort Benning for jump school, the trainees

assembled on the parade field. During the welcoming indoctrination an eerie feeling came over the commanding officer when he scanned the front row.

After the ceremony, the commander summoned his aide. "There's somethin' 'bout that 'cruit that gives me the willies," he said while thumbing Alec. "Check 'em out when we get back."

Shortly after returning to headquarters, Lt. Downs entered the commander's office and said, "Colonel, that 'cruit's name is Alec Christian Bazey, R-A-one-three-eight-zero-zero-four-six-seven."

"Name doesn't ring a bell. Where's he from?"

"Don't know, sir. Want me to get his file?"

"Yes, please do. Can't shake this feelin'. Seems like I know 'em from somewhere."

A few minutes later Downs returned to the colonel's office and said, "Sir, the file says Bazey's from Baltimore."

"I was there once after the war," the colonel said as he scratched his head. "The name Bazey doesn't do anything for me though. Thanks, Tom. Might just be one of 'em déjà vu things or somethin' weird like that."

Alec sensed a kinship with the colonel as well, but like him, was not able to make a connection.

* * *

"Private Bazey reporting, sir," Alec said to the C.O. at pay call while displaying his ID card.

"Bazey, where in hell do I know you from, boy?"

"Don't know, sir. Feel like I know you, too," Alec said as he scooped the cash and departed.

After having gotten a close look at the colonel, it came to Alec the next morning during physical training. "The big guy in uniform standing next to Mom in the photo is Colonel Boetler, I'm sure it's him."

That night, Alec wrote to Lena for her to mail him the photo. "Can you imagine that?" Alec said when he got the picture.

The next day, he sent the photo and note that read: Colonel, sir. This photo was taken in front of my grandparent's house in Baltimore in 1946. My name at the time was Alec Pinski. I think this is what we were speaking of in the pay line. Respectfully, Pvt. Alec C. Bazey, RA13800467.

"Tom, Tom, Bring Private Bazey to my office right away," Boetler shouted after he saw the photo and read the note.

"He's in a C-forty-seven about to make his first jump. Have to wait'll he gets down, sir."

"Look at this photo. His father was the trooper who saved my ass in

Normandy. The feelin' was just too strong. And some people say that God's dead and Jesus was some sort of magician. This proves they're wrong. They sent that boy so I can thank him for what his father did for me. Hallelujah, brother. Hallelujah!"

* * *

The colonel's staff car was waiting for Alec when he hit the drop zone. "Private Bazey, front 'n center," Downs shouted over the battery-powered megaphone.

After rolling his parachute, Alec ran to Downs, saluted and said, "Private Bazey reporting as ordered, sir."

"Get your ass in the car, Private. Colonel wants to see ya right away."

Downs opened the trunk of the staffer where Alec stashed his equipment. "Colonel damn near shit himself when he saw that picture," Downs said as he chuckled. "Swore you were sent to 'em from heaven."

More likely from the other direction, Alec said to himself.

When Alec entered Boetler's office, he snapped to attention, served up a sharp salute and said, "Private Bazey reporting as ordered, SIR."

"Just like your old man, a true pro. Have a seat, son, and take that damn steel pot off," Boetler said with a foxy grin.

"How'd your first jump go?"

"What a rush, never experienced anything like it. Can't wait to do it again."

"Yeah, I remember my first one, too. Went out right in front of your father, just like in Normandy. Care for a cup of coffee?"

"Yes, sir, black. Thank you, sir."

Boetler picked up the photo and said, "I remember when your brother Victor took this with his Brownie. You were just a little snipe then, look at ya now. What's your brother up to these days? He was quite a little cuss, always tryin' to get cigarettes from me."

"Vic was killed in a car accident a few years ago."

"Sorry to hear that, Bazey. Only met 'em that one time. Kinda liked the little scutter."

"Yeah, he was somethin'."

"What about your mom?"

"Her and Vic were killed together."

"Damn, son. I guess your stepfather raised ya then."

"No, sir. He was a Baltimore Firefighter and killed on duty. I was raised by my godparents."

"Private, you've really been through a lot in your young life. I'm glad to hear your relatives were there for ya."

"Yes, sir. They've done a lot for me. My uncle was with the

seventeenth, one ninety-fourth Glider Infantry."

"Remember 'em well. They were held in reserve when we jumped in Normandy. Dropped 'em when the Germans went on the offensive during the Bulge. Seventeenth was some fightin' sons of bitches they were."

"That's what Unc' tells me."

"What made ya join the airborne?"

"Family tradition I guess, Colonel. Besides, if I hadn't, I never would've gotten to meet you."

"My sentiments exactly, son, my sentiments exactly. Sure glad ya did," Boetler replied as he puffed on a White Owl. "Bazey, words can never describe the admiration I hold for your father. Not only because he saved my life, but also because he was a hell of a man. He was disciplined, dedicated, ballsy and loyal. That's why I met with your mother personally instead of writin' her a letter. I'll never forget when your dad jumped on that grenade—it was exactly twelve noon on June 6, 1944. Been carryin' it around for nigh under twenty years now. Finally, I can say thanks to your dad's blood, next best thing to doin' it personally. If the good Lord's willin', I'll get to meet 'em again someday."

"Gotta be getting' back to my unit now, Colonel. Rappellin' exercises this afternoon."

"Ya certainly don't wanna miss that. I know I'll see ya again 'fore ya ship out. Good luck to ya, son. Tom, come give Bazey a ride back to his unit."

"Thanks, Colonel. It's been a real pleasure meetin' ya, sir."

"Likewise, Bazey. Ya take care now, son."

"That's an affirmative, sir."

Alec replaced his helmet, snapped to attention and delivered a departing salute to the colonel.

* * *

"Control tower, Sergeant McElroy."

"Yeah, Sarge, this is Private Bazey from A Company. Need some information."

"Yeah?"

"What's the time difference between here and Normandy, France—do ya know?"

"Fuckafonno. I'm from the Bronx, not Greenwich—hold on."

A short while later, McElroy said, "Six hours. Ya plannin' to go 'ere or somethin'?"

"No. Just wanted to know. Thanks, Sarge."

"Later."

When Alec got back to the barracks, he located his birth certificate. "That's some spooky shit. I was born at the same time my father was killed," he said as his spine felt like it had been hit by lightning. "Six-six-six: the number of the 'Beast,' " he said after it sunk in.

CRACKER FUZZ

The 173rd Airborne Brigade was originally activated in 1917 as the US Army 173rd Infantry Brigade. It went through a series of reorganizations, culminating in February 1942 as the US Army 87th Reconnaissance Troop, 87th Division.

The unit experienced extensive combat in Europe as part of General George S. Patton's 3rd Army. In 1945, it was deactivated, then activated from 1947-51 as the US Army 87th Mechanized Cavalry Reconnaissance.

Its greatest chapter began on March 26, 1963 when it was reactivated on the island of Okinawa. The 'Sky Soldiers,' as the Chinese Nationalist paratroopers called the members of the 173rd, made thousands of jumps in Pacific area countries and was the first US Army unit sent to the Republic of South Viet Nam in May, 1965.

During more than six years of continuous combat operations, the Brigade earned four unit citations, had thirteen Medal of Honor winners and was awarded 130 Distinguished Service Crosses: 1,731 of its members were killed in action, and another 8,345 wounded. The Brigade took part in fourteen designated campaigns and conducted the only US combat parachute assault of the Vietnam War.

After the Gulf of Tonkin incident promoted the first large-scale involvement of US armed forces in Vietnam, in preparation for combat service, ten members of the 173rd were sent to the US Army Intelligence Headquarters and Language School at Fort Holabird.

* * *

Alec was bewildered as to why he hadn't received correspondence from Christine. When he got to Baltimore for interrogation school, he made several attempts to locate her.

"*Fuck her*," Alec said when he came to the realization she was gone. "Bitch never did anything for me that mattered. Only reason I told 'er I loved 'er was to get 'er off my back about enlistin'. You can kiss my ass, Christine. Stay gone, bitch!" he said in frustration.

In actuality, Christine had done much for Alec. She filled the female gap in his life and encouraged him to perform at his best, despite the adversities that had been thrust upon him. When he knew his future on the gridiron was over, he was disappointed; Christine, acting in her typical optimistic fashion, pointed out that football player's careers often end in permanent physical disabilities. Despite all the good things she stood for, Alec wrote her off as a memory.

* * *

Upon completion of training, Alec returned to Fort Benning where the 173rd continued to prepare for their imminent participation in the Vietnam War. In late April of 1965, the Brigade got their marching orders.

The unit shipped out from Atlanta, Georgia, onboard a commercial American Airlines 747. Via Oakland, California and Anchorage, Alaska, they reached their final destination, Tonsunet Air Force Base in Saigon on May 12, 1965.

Alec's platoon NCO was thirty-eight-year-old Sergeant First Class Geaton Solari, originally from Syracuse, New York. He was a crafty veteran known for his prowess and instincts for survival. When Corporal George Carter learned Solari was their leader, he said to the others, "I served under ol' Sonny in the Dominican Republic. If anybody can get us through this thing, he will."

With those words of encouragement, Alec and the other's trepidations were somewhat abated.

* * *

"Men, this is Lieutenant Lester Hatfield," Solari said as he stood before the assembled troops and introduced their platoon leader. "He has a lot to offer us here in the field."

Hatfield was from Louisville, Kentucky, and took great pride in the fact he was akin to the infamous Hatfield clan of the area.

"It may enlighten *you* people to know I graduated at the top of my class at the Point. With *my* trainin' in advanced leadership, *I'm* sure to produce at least *one* Medal of Honor recipient from y'all."

Oh, Christ, another second looey who thinks he's General fuckin' Patton, Solari said to himself.

"As soon as we receive orders for a mission, be ready, 'cause we're gonna go kick some gook ass!" When Hatfield didn't get adulation from the troops, he shouted in a high, shrill voice, "What's wrong with y'all? Are ya a buncha pussies or somethin'?"

"They been travelin' a long time, Lieutenant. They're pretty tired, sir," Solari said.

"Ya better shape this bunch up, Sergeant, or *your* ass'll be inna sling if they don't perform under fire. Is that clear?"

"Crystal clear, sir," Solari replied somberly with his head lowered.

"Okay, then. Group dismissed. Get your dead asses over to the armory and draw weapons."

Solari turned to the platoon, and while clandestinely holding his right hand by his upper thigh, motioned for the troops to respond.

"Sir, yes, sir!"

"That's more like it. Sounds like ya might have a setta balls after all."

"Now that's the way ya gotta treat the misfits in this war, Sergeant. Most of 'em ain't nothin' but hicks, spicks or nigra draftees," Hatfield said as the platoon dispersed.

"Sonny'll teach 'at Lieutenant Fuzz lookin' cracker bastard a thing or two," Corporal Carter said to Alec.

CHOOCH AND TOOTS

One of the paratroopers who had not traveled with Alec's group arrived and took quarters with the first platoon. "Excuse me, are ya savin' this bunk for anybody?" he asked.

"Savin' it for you, help yourself," Alec answered.

"Thanks, I'm John Baranco—friends call me Chooch."

"Pleased to meet ya, Alec Bazey. Chooch, that means jackass, right?"

"Yeah, you a wop, too?" Chooch replied as he threw his duffle bag on the top bunk.

"Half. My mother was Italian, my father Polish."

"That makes ya a polewop," Chooch said as he shook Alec's hand.

When he chuckled, Chooch was relieved, as Alec was a head taller and fifty pounds heavier than him.

"How'd ya ever get stuck with Chooch?"

"From the Top Cat cartoon show on television. Friends said I looked like the dude. Where ya from?"

"Baldemur. How 'bout you?"

"Marlow Heights," Chooch answered in delight, realizing they were from the same state. "Ever heard of it?"

"Can't say I have."

"It's a bedroom community just outside DC in Prince George's County off Branch Avenue, Maryland Route Five—close to Southern Avenue."

"Not real familiar with DC. Good to meet somebody from home though."

* * *

'Tootsoon,' is a derogatory term used primarily by Italians in metropolitan areas to describe African-Americans. One theory holds that the expression was coined in Italy where people of the *Tutsi* tribe from central Africa were enslaved after being brought there by Roman Legions.

Pvt. Elmore Banks, a short, plump, mild-mannered draftee, had been dubbed 'Toots,' by his friends in Chicago. He had been duped into going airborne by a recruiting officer who told him that becoming a paratrooper would enhance his masculinity, and that they received an extra fifty-five dollars a month in hazardous-duty pay. Toots attended jump school at Fort Campbell, Kentucky, and made it through by sheer determination.

* * *

"What do people who drive a Cadillac always say?" PFC Carling asked his redneck counterpart.

" 'Em white folks sho' make some fine cars."

"Why don't you fuckin' honkies just keep your mouths shut. I'm tired of listenin' to your shit," Toots countered.

"What's your little black ass gonna do if we don't shut up, boy?" Carson asked as Carling looked on and smirked. "It's just you against the seven of us. Ain't none of your *bruthas* 'round to protect ya, is 'ere?"

"Two against six," Alec declared.

"Three against five," Chooch added, standing shoulder to shoulder with Alec and Toots, now smirking.

"Time ain't right, we'll settle this later," Carson said.

"Come on, Toots, these guys are pussies. Let's go get a beer," Alec said.

Feeling as though he gained a victory when Alec discontinued the challenge, Carson said, "You're 'Talian, right, Bazey?"

"What if I am?"

" 'Talian ain't nothin' but a nigger turned inside out."

As Alec approached Carson, he sprang to his feet and assumed an Ali position; before he could react, he found himself staring at the ceiling.

"Get up only if ya want more of where that came from," Alec said.

" 'At's enough for me, Bazey. Fight's over, man," he said, realizing he was no match for Alec.

"I'll take ya up on 'at beer now. In fact I'll buy. You, too, Chooch."

"Let's go," answered Alec.

* * *

"Bazey, ya really did a quick number on Carson," Toots said as he offered his beer in toast to Alec at the enlisted man's PX.

"A little trick I learned in judo school. If ya hold up your right fist, that's what they stay fixed on. Then ya slam 'em with your left elbow. Never know what hit 'em. Like a heron snatchin' a fish."

"Will ya show me some of that judo stuff?" Toots asked.

"Sure, what 'bout you, Choochie? Might come in handy against Charlie."

"Yeah, can't hurt."

"Okay, we'll start tomorrow."

* * *

The 173rd became known as the 'Herd,' with Company A, first platoon, heading the pack. Although Hatfield loved the adulations, he was well aware all of the credit went to Solari.

After being delivered to a 'Hot Landing Zone' by the 17th Cavalry, Solari quickly assessed the situation. "We'll regroup in that grove of banyans," he said when they hit the ground.

"Belay the last. Spread out and form up in the open meadow. Banks, Johnson, Ford, James take the point," Hatfield said.

Toots recognized all of the troops Hatfield ordered to the point were African-Americans. "Yes, sir," he answered.

"Lieutenant, the run between here and that open meadow is suicide. They'll be mowed down before they get halfway."

"Let me remind you who's in charge here, Sergeant—I am. When did *you* graduate from West Point? It's a classic textbook move I learned there. Get those troopers movin' now!"

"Yes, sir," Solari angrily responded. "Ya heard the man. Rest of us are right behind ya," Solari ordered as the Huey took on AK-47 fire.

Before they got twenty yards, all four became part of the 58,379 combat deaths in Viet Nam. In later years, their names would be placed on the *Viet Nam Veteran's Memorial* on Henry Bacon Drive in Washington, DC.

When Hatfield saw the result of his ignorance, he panicked and shouted, "Abort, abort, abort, everybody back onna chopper. Overwhelming enemy concentration. Take 'er up and call for an air strike!"

"Lieutenant, let's form up in the banyans. We can kick their asses from 'ere," Solari insisted.

"I'm not gonna remind you again, Sergeant of who's in charge. I said abort, we're drastically outnumbered. Now back onna *fuckin'* chopper."

"Yes, sir. Pack it up boys," Solari said in sheer disgust as the AK chatter increased.

"What about Toots and the others?" Alec shouted.

"Nothin' we can do for 'em now. We'll send a med-evac unit back for 'em later. Now get this thing up," Hatfield screamed in high-pitched panic tenor to the pilot.

On the flight back, all sat in silence while Solari glared with hatred at Hatfield who wouldn't return a look. Alec pondered the death of his friend and said to himself, I'm gonna have to give Hatfield a ride to *Cove Road.*

* * *

When they returned to base, Hatfield hastily prepared a report of the incident indicating that heavier than expected enemy concentration at the LZ had forced him to abort the mission after four of his platoon members were killed. "Read this over, Sergeant, and tell me you concur with it," Hatfield said as he turned the report over to Solari.

"That's not *quite* how it was, Lieutenant," Solari said, handing it back.

"Oh, so you disagree, huh? Ya know, an extra rocker under your top stripes would look great; I think I could probably arrange that—under the right conditions that is."

"Looks fine to me, sir," Solari said after a review of the paperwork.

"I thought you might change your mind with a second look."

* * *

When Alec and Chooch returned to the LZ with a med-evac unit after a mammoth air strike, Alec bellowed, "If that fuckin' Fuzz hadda listened to Solari, Toot's still be alive!" as he and Chooch shoveled Toots' charred remains into a body bag.

When Alec and Chooch returned to camp, they reported to the NCO quarters where they found Solari. "Sergeant, we just got back from the LZ and there wasn't any NVA or VC bodies there. Doesn't that make Lieutenant Hatfield guilty of some sort of dereliction of duty?" Alec asked.

"What are you, soldier, some kinda fuckin' guardhouse lawyer? Did it ever occur to either one of you weasel dicks the enemy took a powder after we left?"

"The evac team said the strike came fifteen minutes after we cut out. No way they coulda gotten a large concentration of troops out that quick," Chooch barked back.

"Evac team don't know their ass from first base; the strike came two hours later. Shit, they coulda moved a whole army out in that amount of time."

"That doesn't make sense, Sarge. Why woulda they even bothered two hours later?" Alec asked.

"Bazey, Baranco, if you fuckwads know what's good for ya, you'll keep your mouths shut. Hatfield didn't do nothin' wrong, the place was crawlin' with yella."

"That's not what you said out there. Somethin's gotta be done 'bout that son-of-a-bitch Lieutenant 'fore he gets all of us, includin' you, killed," Chooch shouted back.

"If ya go past me with this, I'll send your dead asses so far north a LERP team won't be able to find ya. Now get outta my sight—both of ya!"

The next day, when they learned Solari was being promoted, Chooch said to Alec, "I guess Sonny's gonna get his thirty pieces of silver—that *Judas Iscariot* bastard."

* * *

Two weeks later, Solari addressed the platoon. "Men, Lieutenant Hatfield has some good news for ya. Go 'head, sir," Solari, now sporting master-sergeant stripes, said to the group.

"Wonder what kinda kamikaze mission Fuzz has in store for us today?" Chooch whispered.

"Got somethin' you'd like to share with the rest of us 'ere, Baranco?" Hatfield said.

"Uh, yes, sir, Lieutenant. I was commenting to Cornell here how nice ya look with your new silver bar and how pretty the sarge's new stripes are. Isn't that what I said, Johnny?" Chooch said to Pvt. Cornell, holding back laughter.

The upper command had been so smitten by Hatfield's report, they decided not only to approve *Solari's* promotion, but also promote Hatfield for the excellent leadership he displayed during a perilous encounter with the enemy.

"If no one has any other asinine comments, I have several items of good news for y'all. The first one's right here," Hatfield said enthusiastically as he produced an M-16 from a satchel.

" 'At lifer tryin' to motivate me's like Hitler givin' a pep rally at a synagogue," Chooch whispered to Cornell.

"All right, maybe Sergeant Phillips here, the armory NCO can rouse your interest. They're all yours, Sergeant."

When the military cut back after the Korean War, Phillips, a former Marine, was rifted back to lance corporal after receiving a battlefield commission to the rank of lieutenant during the *Battle of Incheon*. He became frustrated by the lack of upward mobility in the Corps, and transferred to the army where career advancement was more attainable. "Thank ya, Lieutenant," Phillips said in a Midwestern dialect as he took the weapon.

As he held the black beauty, Phillips' command presence shined through and he instantly won over the group. "This here's a M-sixteen automatic rifle. It's originally derived from the ArmaLite AR-fifteen and was developed by the Colt Gun Manufacturers in West Hartford, Connecticut. The weapon's a five-point-fifty-six millimeter, air-cooled, gas-operated, magazine-fed killin' machine with a rotatin' bolt actuated by direct impingement. It's capable of delivering eight hundred and fifty rounds a minute and has a muzzle velocity of thirty-two-hundred feet a second with an effective range of six-hundred yards. Any questions so far?"

When no one asked, Phillips went on. "Plastic stock and smaller rounds makes it a lot more mobile inna bush 'an 'at fourteen ya been totin'. It was originally manufactured with a steel barrel, and bad rumor had it that it didn't need to be cleaned. Buncha Marines up north disproved 'at theory when they didn't oil 'em down, and the barrels rusted up. NVA wiped out a whole platoon who never got a shot off. After 'at, they took 'em back, reissued fourteens and redesigned the barrel with chromium and issued cleanin' kits. She's a real widow maker now, she is," Phillips said as he fondled the weapon with white cloth gloves on his hands. "After ya get some trainin', you'll trade in your fourteens and get one of 'ese babies. Make 'em gook bastards sorry we're here."

"Boo-rah, boo-rah, boo-rah, one seventy-third's comin'. Prepare to meet you maker, ya Luke-the-gook, mutha fuckers. Gonna get you asses!"

"That enlisted swine'll never make it here," Hatfield muttered to himself with contempt. "A good leader is always unpopular."

"Okay, Lieutenant, they're all yours again, sir. Pleasure meetin' ya boys. Good luck, God be with y'all."

After resounding applause and whooping and hollering, Hatfield took over. "The second item of good news is that you'll be issued new name tags and chevrons. At the rate you're goin', Baranco, you'll be lucky to keep 'ose l'il PFC butterfly wings."

"I'll give 'em back now if ya promise to send me home," Chooch answered as he motioned his arms in butterfly fashion.

"The new uniform accoutrements have an OD background with black markings, and you'll all be issued OD T-shirts as well; be better for camouflage purposes. Understand what camouflage is, Baranco?"

"Yeah. Everybody knows camouflage is when a camel farts."

"Baranco, I'ver had enough. When we break, report to the latrine for a shit-burnin' detail."

"Can't live with 'em and can't kill 'em," Chooch answered as Alec grinned sardonically at Hatfield.

"All right, now for the best part," a bright-eyed Hatfield said. "Headquarters has approved my recommendation that every trooper in the first platoon below the rank of E-five be promoted one rank as a result of their exemplary actions in the field since their arrival in country."

"Hush money. That son of a bitch is tryin' to bribe us," Alec whispered to Pvt. Adams.

"What about me, Lieutenant. Am I getting' promoted, too?" Chooch asked.

"Yeah, I'm promotin' ya to Colonel of the urinal."

When the others laughed, Hatfield felt vindicated and said, "That's it for now, men. Does anyone *other* than Baranco have a question?"

At a negative response, Hatfield said, "Group dismissed. Baranco—to the latrine."

* * *

"I say we refuse the promotion and turn Fuzz in," Alec said. "The cock sucker's tryin' to pay us off in blood money."

"Listen, man, Fuzz fucked up, and bad. But I'm a lifer, ain't gonna do my career no good if'n I turn in an officer. I didn't see 'nuffin, undastand? I seed 'nuffin'," PFC Adams said.

"Me neither, blood. I didn't see 'nuffin either. I'm takin' my 'motion and run," Pvt. Clark said in agreement.

"What 'bout you, Brownie?" Alec said.

"Lieutenant did all right far as I'm 'cerned. Got my black ass outta 'ere alive. 'At's all matter to me."

"I'm surprised at you guys," Chooch, reeking of burned excrement and kerosene, said. "Toots was you guy's brother. Thought y'all stuck together."

"What's done's, done, bro'. Don't do no good to stir the shit anymo' than ya has to. Just let it be, white boy. Don't mean 'nuffin'," Brown answered.

"I guess we're outnumbered, Choochie. Speakin' of stirred shit, get outta those clothes and take a shower, man. It's Friday night, no patrol tomorrow Sonny said. Let's go slam down a few at the Memphis."

"Sounds good. Be with ya in ten."

"Better make it twenty from the looks of ya. Here, take some of this stuff; my sister Carol sent it to me for my birthday."

"Didn't know ya had a sister. Man, this shit smells stronger than cat food," Chooch said as he took a long sniff.

"She's really my cousin, but she's like a sister. Now get in the fuckin' shower."

* * *

During the bus ride, Chooch said, "I'm surprised you rolled over so quick with the brothers."

For a split second, Alec considered sharing his intentions with Chooch of how he planned to deal with Hatfield. "Fuck it, headquarters wouldn't believe us anyway, especially without Sonny and the brothers backin' us. Just ain't worth it. Besides, E-five pay's better'n E-four."

175

"Yeah, guess you're right. Sure do miss 'at little Tootsie though."

"Me, too. Shit'll catch up with Hatfield 'fore this war's over," Alec said with confidence.

"Sure hope so."

HONKY-TONK WOMAN

There was one difference between the Memphis Bar and others in Saigon, at least for Alec. That difference's name was Danielle Dao Hiep, a twenty-year-old beauty of Vietnamese, French and African stock. Dani stood at 5' 9", weighed in at a light-running 106, and flaunted the most beautiful set of long, svelte legs imaginable. Her hair was jet black, and her copper-toned skin offered the perfect contrast to her piercing emerald eyes. Dani was best described as, *drop dead gorgeous.*

Dani's grandfather fought with the US Army 369th Infantry Division during WW I, a unit that was embraced by the French after being rejected by General Pershing who doubted African-American's ability and willingness to fight. When he returned to the United States after the war and was denied basic human rights, Dani's grandfather returned to Europe and joined the French Foreign Legion that led him to Viet Nam where he married, and fathered four children.

* * *

When the bar owner, Mr. Rick, saw Alec and Chooch enter, he gave a nickel to a hooker named 'Sophie Fucker' and said to her, "Here comey Alric and da Chooch. Push R-nine on Rock-Ola: dey favrit song."

After Dani heard Charlie Watts clink the cowbell, she looked for her man. As Bill Wyman led in for Brian Jones and Keith Richards and Mick Jagger began singing *Honky-Tonk Woman,* Dani grabbed a shot glass full of water from the bar and belted it down to hold true with Mick's reference to a gin-soaked barroom queen in Memphis as she gyrated her hips while covering her crotch with both hands. Next, Alec followed Mick's instructions and loaded her across his right shoulder. When he put her down, Dani began motioning as if tossing rose petals on Alec, then produced a red silk handkerchief from her black laced panties and held it to Alec's nose while she softly blew in his ear. The crowd, fully lit up by now, joined in with dance and helped Mick finish the song.

"Alric, where you been? No see you in rong, rong time. No makey boom boom," Dani said when Alec sat down and she jumped on his lap, unzipped his pants and began massaging his package.

"Been busy killin' VC, brown sugar."

"You gotty 'nutta girlfriend. No takey me to Balmur. Gottie zootcase and pockeybook all pack in back by zinc. Wantie Polrock Johnnie hotty dog and livey in Hollrandtown. Where Tootsie tonight?"

"Back at the base," Chooch said, in order to avoid an emotional explanation.

"Here, baby, go play some music and get us another Bud," Alec said as he handed Dani a five.

"Me keepie change, too—Okay, Alric?"

"Yeah, you can keep it."

"We makie baby later, go get Bud now."

As the jukebox played *We Gotta Get Outta This Place* by Eric Burden and the Animals, a male voice from a group of Americans yelled, "Only fags from Hollandtown."

When a man familiar looking to Alec began walking toward him from the other end of the club, Alec hollered back, "Ray-Ray Walters. Is that you, ol' buddy?"

"Sure 'nuff is, bro'. I thought it was you when I saw y'all walk in. Then I was sure when I heard that bitch say somethin' 'bout Hollandtown."

"I don't remember the last time I saw ya," Alec said. "What the fuck ya doin' here?"

"Same as you I 'magine. Sam called my number and I ended up in the Big Red One."

"One seventy-third for me; we done a couple ops' with you guys."

"Damn, it's really good to see ya. When *was* the last time?" Walters asked.

"I think it was when we scrimmaged you guys at Montebello Park. Three, four years ago."

"I think you're right, kicked the shit outta us, too. Ol' Mervo never had much of a football team."

"Ray, this is my goomba John Baranco from Marlow Heights, Maryland, just outside DC."

"Good to meet ya, John."

"Friends call me Chooch. Good to meet ya, too, brother."

As the night wore on, conversations between Alec and Walters about their exploits at the Red Shield Boys Club and Camp Puh'Tok in Monkton, led to more serious remembrances. "You really went through some shit there in fifty-four 'n fifty-five."

"Yeah, things were pretty raggy for awhile. Thank God for my Uncle Henry and Aunt Lena."

"Yeah, they seem to be good people. Their daughter Carol was really hot if I recall."

"Never thought of 'er in that regard. I guess she is good lookin'."

"Is that the same one who sent you the Jade East?" Chooch asked.

"Same one," answered Alec as he reached for his wallet. "Here's a picture of 'er."

"Damn, she has the map of Italy on *her* face," Chooch said, while nearly drooling on the photo.

"She's a real sweetheart, unattached, too."

"Wow, can't wait to meet *her*."

At midnight, Walters looked at his watch and said, "Gotta be gettin' on, bus for camp leaves in fifteen minutes. Is this place your regular hangout?"

" 'Bout the only place we come to."

"Good, bound to run into y'all again here if I don't see ya in the field or get aced."

"You still on Macon Street back home?" Alec asked.

"Yeah, still with Mom and Dad. Shoulda got married and dodged the draft."

"Okay, I'll look ya up when I get home. Good luck, brother. Love ya, man."

"Love ya, too, Al. Good meetin' ya, Chooch."

"Same here, bro'."

"What was Walters talkin' 'bout in fifty-four and fifty-five?" Chooch asked Alec when Walters left the Memphis.

Alec's eyes widened as he shook his head and stared into space when the memory of all four deaths played in his mind. "Lost my whole family in less than a year. First, my little sister," he said as he grimaced at the thought of how her little body wiggled under the pillow. "Then my mother and brother were killed in an automobile accident; then my stepdad was killed in a fire."

"I didn't know ya had a stepfather."

"Yeah, never met my natural father; he was killed with the one-o-one on D-Day. Drink up, buddy, gettin' late. Don't wanna miss the bus back to camp," Alec said in an attempt to drop the subject.

As they headed out, Chooch put his arm around Alec's shoulder and said, "I know we're not kin, but I'll always be there for ya, brother."

"I know, Choochie. You're the best friend I ever had, you can depend on me, too."

THE RECKONING

Following a briefing at headquarters, Hatfield called for Solari. "I've been advised the NVA's buildin' troops at this coordinate," Hatfield said while pointing at an area on a map northwest of Plei Me in the Central Highlands. "Got orders for our company to spearhead a search-and-destroy mission there. Hueys'll be ready and waitin' at o-six-thirty."

"My boys'll be ready, too, Lieutenant."

The buildup was a predecessor to the two-part *Battle of Ia Drang*, which took place between November 14th and 18th, 1965.

At 6 a.m., Alec and his platoon climbed aboard the lead chopper—a spanking- new UH-1 with growling teeth painted on the front. After they landed, Solari ordered them to assume assault formation.

"Fall back, fall back," Solari shouted as he twirled his right forefinger above his head when they came under fire. A few minutes later, a cavalcade of pith-helmeted NVA regulars appeared in the wake of a mortar barrage.

When the melee began, Alec saw his chance to even the score for Toots as Hatfield rolled to his left in order to retrieve a loaded magazine from his ammo belt. Without hesitation, he aimed and fired three shots that found their mark directly up Hatfield's anal cavity. As blood gushed from Hatfield's mouth, and he dug his skinny fingers in the ground and cried for his mother, euphoria overcame Alec.

After staving off the assault, Solari, while cutting a malevolent look at Alec, said, "Carruthers, take Evart and Franco back and see if any of our guys are still alive; I saw Hatfield go down."

"Six down, six dead, Lieutenant Hatfield one of 'em," Carruthers said when he reported back.

"What about enemy body count?"

" 'Bout twenty-five, maybe thirty."

"We'll send an air ambulance back for our dead. Meanwhile, get the wounded on the Hueys. Rest of us, back in the bush."

Three hours later, the assault group was ordered to return to base. As they exited the chopper, Solari said, "Bazey, come with me."

Instead of returning to the NCO quarters, Solari led Alec to Hatfield's office. "Sit down, Bazey. You and me gotta talk, boy."

"Yeah, Sarge, what's up?" Alec said as he removed his field equipment.

"The rounds that hit Hatfield came from the area *you* were in."

"Oh, yeah. And how could you tell that?" Alec replied as he maintained steely eye contact with Solari. "Lotta shootin' goin' on out 'ere, coulda come from anywhere."

"I know, 'cause his guts were hangin' out his ass. Wasn't no enemy but *you* standin' behind 'em. I know how pissed you and Baranco were after Banks and the others were killed."

"Sarge, I'm not the enemy, remember?" Alec said as he pointed to the cloth strip above his left shirt pocket where US Army was written.

"You fragged 'em, Bazey, I know ya did, God dammit!"

"Wasn't me, Sarge. No, no, not me," Alec said with equanimity as he shook his head.

"Would ya be willin' to take a lie-detector test?"

"Sure, bring it on. Let's do it right now if that'll clear this shit up. Yeah, I'll take it."

I know they won't give 'em a lie detector in the field, but does he know that? Maybe he *didn't* ace Hatfield, Solari said to himself. "I know ya did it, Bazey. I saw ya aim your fuckin' sixteen at 'em and fire," he said.

"With all due respect, Sarge, ya didn't see anything of the fuckin' kind," Alec replied as he glared directly into Solari's sparking eyes, calling his bluff.

Solari then got up and sat next to Alec. "Listen, Bazey," he said as he pulled in close and touched Alec's knee, "I'm glad that worthless piece a shit's dead. Thought about doin' it myself a couple times. If ya admit it, we'll keep it here 'tween the two of us, okay?" he said as he stroked the nape of Alec's neck.

Alec slowly turned his head, looked Solari directly in his eyes, and remembered Herman and the money bag; Jimmy Saukas and Nick. This time I'm the fish, but I see the heron comin', he said to himself. "I don't know what you're talkin' 'bout, Sarge. Can I go now, or am I under arrest?" he answered.

"No, you're not under arrest, but I'll tell ya this—I'm gonna keep a close eye on ya when we get in the shit again. If ya even *look* at me funny, my sixteen's goin' up *your* ass, understand?"

"Ya don't have anything to worry 'bout, Sarge. I'm a soldier, not a murderer," Alec answered, and an Antichrist who'll slit your fuckin' throat if ya get in my way, he said to himself.

"You're relieved. Go back to your quarters."

On the way to the barracks, Alec saw Chooch being escorted by an MP. "What's happenin', Choochie?" he asked.

"Don't know, bro'. MP here came rushin' in and said Sonny wanted to see me right away. You all right, man?"

"Yeah, everything's cool. See ya when ya get back."

"Later."

When Chooch returned, he quietly said to Alec, "Let's go outside for a minute." After finding a private spot, he said, "Al, Sonny tried to get me to say I saw ya smoke Hatfield, but I wouldn't give ya up."

"Give me up?" Alec answered indignantly with arched eyebrows. "Ain't nothin' *to* give up, man. I didn't ace the L. T."

"I saw ya do it when he rolled over. Don't worry, buddy, your secret's safe with me; I'll take it to my grave."

Ya might just do that, Alec thought. "I don't know what in hell you're talkin' 'bout, really, I don't," Alec answered as he looked deeply into Chooch's chocolate eyes. Wish the fuck he would've kept that to himself, he said inwardly.

VIEW FROM THE PENTHOUSE

The next morning, Solari said to his command, "HQ ordered us to take some prisoners. Who here's been to language school?"

"I have."

Although Solari had serious misgivings about him, he was glad to see Alec had been trained in the Vietnamese language as he knew he possessed the 'killer instinct' and would get the job done. "Okay, Bazey, you work with Sergeant Van Duan here from the South Vietnamese Army. He'll be your interpreter, understand?"

"Got ya, Sarge."

"Now we *really* need information on enemy activity, no funny business. Is that clear, Bazey?"

"As a bell, Sarge. No funny business."

Alec, quite taken with Van Duan, extended his hand. "Sergeant, Specialist Bazey, pleased to make your acquaintance, sir."

"My pleasure, Specialist."

"If I may ask, how'd ya become so fluent in English?"

"I was born in Saigon in 1942, then moved to Paris when my father, who was employed by the French Government, was transferred. Fortunately, we were there during the Battle of Dien Bien Phu and stayed afterward, instead of returning home. When the United States got involved here, father became a consultant for the American Government and was relocated to Washington, DC. I learned French and English along the way. Returned to Saigon in sixty-one and joined the ARVN who sent me to Fort Monmouth, New Jersey for training in microwave radar operations."

* * *

The *Battle of Dien Bien Phu* was fought during the First Indochina War between the French Far East Expeditionary Corps and Viet Mihn Communist Revolutionary Forces. It took place between March and May, 1954, and culminated in a massive French defeat that effectively ended the war. The battle is considered to be the first time a non-European colonial independence movement had evolved from guerilla bands to a conventionally organized and equipped army able to defeat a modern western occupier.

* * *

"Sergeant, I'd appreciate it if you'd help me out today, okay?"

"No problem, Specialist."

"Please call me Alec."

"No problem, Alec, that's what I'm here for. I've been on many missions. I'll show you good solid techniques for obtaining reliable information."

"Good, I'm a quick learner, eager, too."

"We'll get along fine and do well together, I'm sure."

* * *

As they approached their LZ, Van Duan spotted six Viet Cong, and directed the pilot to put the Huey down not far from where he made the observation, about two miles north of the Ho Chi Mihn Trail. After exiting the chopper, Van Duan said to Solari, "The VC we saw, took refuge in a tunnel. They'll come this way and pick up supplies along the 'Trail' when they think the coast is clear. Have your men hunker down and remain still."

"Sure thing, Sergeant," Solari replied. "My guys'll be cool."

"All right, you heard the man. Remember, we want as many of 'em alive as we can handle; dead men tell no tales. Now spread out," Solari ordered the troops.

After sitting passively for thirty minutes, Chooch yelped, "God-damn bugs and shit," as a pack of fire ants crawled down his collar and hosted on him.

"Shut the fuck up, Choochie," Alec responded in a whisper as he placed his right forefinger over his lips.

"Get these fuckin' things offa me," he replied while frantically removing uniform parts and equipment.

While Chooch struggled, Van Duan spotted the group moving toward them. He slowly lifted his right arm and pointed. "VC right on time," he said softly to Alec.

When they got within twenty yards, Van Duan yelled out in Vietnamese, "VC, Stop!"

Hell was turned loose as they began shooting aimlessly. Upon return fire, two of the VC went down, while the other four dropped to their knees and surrendered. After their hands were tied in the back, Van Duan ordered the group to sit, while a ring of security formed around them.

"Call the chopper back, we'll go to the penthouse for a better view. They'll talk then," Van Duan said when Alec got no response from the prisoners.

At five-hundred feet, Van Duan told the pilot to level off, and said to

Alec, "Let me speak with them, okay?"

"Your show."

Bedlam broke out in the Huey when Van Duan tossed the prisoner Alec had started with through the starboard door. "What the fuck is 'at?" PFC Anderson yelled as the liberated captive tumbled toward earth.

"Looks to me like an effective 'terrogation method," said Spec 4 Edwards, a New Orleans Police Officer draftee.

The other prisoners began begging for their lives. "Tell me why the NVA are here building up troops," Van Duan shouted above the roar of the engine.

"Big battle planned, big offense," one of them offered in broken English to Alec. "Please no lettie him throw me out choppa," he shouted.

"Answer all my questions, mutha fucker, and we'll take you and the others back to base in one piece, understand?" Alec replied.

"Undastand mutha fucker. What you want know?"

Van Duan was satisfied with the dialogue until the prisoner became elusive. "Mind if I step in again, Alec?" he politely asked.

"Go right ahead, Sergeant."

"Son of a bitch," yelled Anderson, "here comes another'n,"

"Looks like they're makin' progress up 'ere," Edwards coolly added.

When the chopper landed, Edwards said to Alec, "Looks to me like y'all boys were havin' fun up 'ere."

Alec smiled and nodded.

"Bazey, did ya get the intelligence we need?" Solari asked.

"Got good skinny, Sarge. Best get 'em back to HQ for debriefin'."

"Pack it up, boys. Time to go home," Solari ordered.

On the flight back to camp, Alec said to Chooch, "Did ya get rid of those ants?"

"Fuckin' things nearly sucked me dry. Look at this shit," he answered as he pulled his collar from his red, swollen neck.

"Wonder how many ants'll die of clogged arteries from that oily blood?"

"Yuk, Yuk, Yuk, mutha fucker. Anybody ever tell ya you're a regular fuckin' Red Skelton? What the hell was goin' on with those muthas doin' the Superman act?" Chooch said as he continued to scratch.

"Just gathering data, that's all. Worked good, too," Alec answered as he smiled sinisterly.

"I'm really beginnin' to wonder 'bout you."

"You know very little 'bout me, Choochie."

"I know you're a killin' fuckin' machine. That I do know."

"Be cool, Chooch. Don't let your ass pay for somethin' your mouth charged on a credit card," Alec said to himself.

* * *

After learning the NVA were preparing for a huge offensive move in the Central Highlands, Solari and his platoon were ordered to return for more prisoners in order to confirm the information they received.

When they reached their LZ, the pilot said to Van Duan, "We'll be glad to offer elevator service again if ya need us to, Sergeant—just dial the front desk."

Van Duan responded with a thumb up and salute.

While traipsing through the jungle, Solari smelled cigarette smoke in the dense air. As they proceeded, he signaled the platoon to take cover when he saw a group of NVA smoking. "Oh shit, they got us," Solari said when the group turned in response to a myna bird.

When he saw a large contingent advancing in their direction, Solari ordered Carter to call for an emergency rescue; just as he gave the map coordinates, he was struck by enemy gunfire. As he snatched the radio, Solari noticed two holes protruding outwardly from the back of Carter's fatigue shirt, still emitting smoke.

Before Solari could issue the order to retreat, the area became a blazing field of fire. A few minutes after the first platoon beat the enemy back, they regrouped and advanced in full force. "Bravo-Echo to Air-Six: find us quick, boys. Got at least a half-company, maybe more, bearin' down on our asses!" Solari urgently advised the chopper crew.

" 'At's a Roger, Bravo-Echo. Ten minutes away."

Shortly after Solari's transmission, another wave broke through the foliage. Although Alec had been struck in the left shoulder, upper chest and right thigh, he was able to participate in the fracas. After taking another hit, he went down as the sound of the Huey made its presence known.

"Air-Six to Bravo-Echo," the co-pilot called over the two-way. "Air-Six to Bravo-Echo. Come in Bravo-Echo."

When PFC Carmichael heard the urgent cries over the radio, he saw it lying next to Solari's body. "Bravo-Echo to Air-Six," Carmichael answered.

"We're right above y'all, Bravo-Echo. Get your boys in 'at clearing on your right flank. More Hueys onna way," the co-pilot replied as the Huey's fifty caliber razed the area around the platoon's location.

" 'At's a Roger, Air-Six. We'll wait'll the other birds get here, then make a run for it."

"They'll be here any second. Hang tough, Bravo-Echo, hang tough, brutha. Help's onna way," the co-pilot shouted.

As the bantering continued, Chooch saw Alec pinned down by gunfire and incapacitated by his wounds; in a desperate move from a position of cover, Chooch stepped out to draw fire.

Immediately, his left forearm was severed at the elbow when a burst from an AK struck him. Bleeding profusely while carrying the remains of his limb under his left armpit, Chooch hobbled to Alec's location and dragged him to a spot where others were able to safely deliver him to one of the choppers. While passed out from exhaustion and loss of blood, two paratroopers snatched Chooch and his mutilated arm, and placed them next to Alec. Combat medics then tended their wounds and hooked them to I.Vs.

Alec looked at an unconscious Chooch and clutched his bloody stump. "I'll never be able to repay ya, pal," he said, as the chopper whisked them to the US Army 3rd Field Hospital in Saigon.

WELCOME HOME

The United States Army Medical Center for the east coast is located at 6900 Georgia Avenue NW, in Washington DC. It is named after Major Walter Reed, a US Army surgeon who led the team that confirmed yellow fever is transmitted by mosquitoes rather than direct contact.

* * *

Upon arrival, Alec met with the Commanding Officer of WRAMC.

"Although Specialist Baranco's valor and gallantry indeed sounds worthy of being honored, unfortunately his efforts won't be officially recognized as no one other than yourself can confirm his actions," the C. O. informed Alec.

* * *

It was a heartfelt and warm reception when the Pinskis arrived for their first visit; all broke into tears of joy while they carefully hugged and caressed Alec.

"Looks like ya did your share for the good old US of A," Henry said.

"Oh, Alec, what have they done to you?" Lena asked, while Carol sympathetically stroked the stitches on his partially-shaved head.

"I know I look like I been run through a meat grinder, but I'm really doin' great. Doctors say I'll be outta here before Christmas. Folks, I want y'all to meet my best friend, John Baranco—everybody calls 'em Chooch. Chooch means jackass in Italian, ya know."

"I *know* what it means," answered Lena indignantly. "Have you forgotten I'm a full-blood Italian? My maiden name is Lemme. Know what that means, Chooch?"

"Horn, right?"

"Bena, bena. Very good, young man."

"It's so nice to meet you," Carol said as she shook Chooch's right hand.

"I've heard a lot about you. Alec showed me your picture. Boy, you look just like Sophia Loren."

"Oh, stop, do not," Carol said as she giggled.

"I'd hug ya, but as you can see I have limited equipment," Chooch answered as he displayed the remains of his left arm.

"I bet that wouldn't stop a big strong guy like you," Carol said as she wrapped her arms around him and pecked his cheek.

"Watch what you're doin' now. I'm under heavy sedation, not

responsible for my actions."

"Chooch, you're so silly," Carol answered as she batted her basil eyes at him.

"Heard a lotta good things 'bout you folks," Chooch said to Henry and Lena. "Thanks for savin' our boy. Heard you guys had the fight of your life over there," Henry said.

"Yeah, got kinda wild," Chooch humbly answered.

When Carol sensed the conversation was upsetting him, she said, "Chooch, show me where the cafeteria is. I'm kinda hungry."

"Sure, Sophie. Could go for a Coke myself."

"I'll buy," Carol said.

"She's buyin', guys. What about you, Al, Mr., Mrs. Pinski?"

"Yeah, if Carol's buyin', I'll have one," Alec answered.

"I'm good."

"Me, too," Lena echoed.

"So great to see ya. How's everybody been?" Alec asked as Lena held his hand.

"Everything's 'bout the same with us. Still at Harper Tugboats at the Camden Pier. Boy, this place looks just like it did twenty years ago," Henry said. "Took 'em six months to make me look like I wasn't fresh off a barbeque grill."

"Anything new with you, Aunt Lena?"

"Got a part timer servin' up hamburgers at the Little Tavern up on Conklin' Street."

"The one across from the firehouse, next to the Grand?"

"Yeah, 'at's the one."

"Man, I'd kill for one of those burgers right now."

"Next time we come I'll bring you and Chooch a bagful."

"Make it soon."

"We're plannin' on comin' back tomorrow, bring 'em then."

"Some fries, too."

"Fries, too."

After Alec got his afternoon medications and a shot of Demerol, he dozed off. When awakened by Lena's light rub, she said, "Okay, babe, we're gonna go now. Let ya get some rest. See y'all tomorrow."

"Don't forget the burgers."

"No problem."

"I'll come tomorrow, too," Carol added as she glanced at Chooch and smiled.

"Thanks for the Coke, Sophie. See ya tomorrow."

Carol wiggled her fingers and smiled.

After they left, Chooch said, "Super family ya got there, Al, especially that Carol. Man, she's a real doll baby. Think she'd go out with a semicrip'?"

"If you don't act like your usual asshole self she might."

"Seriously, man, do ya think she'd go out with me?"

"Only if she doesn't mind bein' seen with somebody named after a mule."

"A mule is sexless, a jackass ain't, and neither am I. Come on, man, tell me what ya think."

"I think you're just like Solari said, a real weasel dick. Fuck if I know, ask 'er and see what she says."

"I don't wanna embarrass myself and put 'er onna spot. Please tell me if ya think I gotta chance. Come on."

"Listen, dick breath, here's all I can tell ya: she's unattached, a great kid, and it seems as though she was amused by your stupid shit, okay?"

"Pretty, too, ya forgot that."

"Yup, pretty, too."

"Should I take that to mean ya think she'll go out with me?"

"If that's what ya wanna hear, then yeah, I think she'll go out with ya. Now shut the fuck up and lemme get some sleep. You've given me a headache."

"Good, I agree. I think she'll go out with me, too. Thanks, Al."

"If somebody didn't know better they'd think ya suffered brain damage back in the jungle. Now shut up and watch television and let me sleep."

"Oh, am I keepin' ya awake? Sorry."

* * *

Alec was delighted to see his gleaming '56 Chevy parked on Elmora Avenue when he got there. "She looks great, Unc'. Ya really kept 'er in good shape for me. Thanks for everything."

"Just tuned 'er up yesterday, least I could do for a wounded veteran."

Lena had prepared Alec's favorite meal as a homecoming dinner: San Giorgio #10, covered with a slow-cooked sauce, rich with jumbo shrimp and soft-shelled crabs. As Alec began his second helping, Henry said, "Al, we got a welcome-home party all set up for ya on Saturday. Invited all your old buddies and some relatives. How's 'at sound to ya?"

"Just what the doctor ordered. What time?"

" 'Round seven. Is 'at all right?"

"Seven's fine, can't go dancin'," Alec answered as he pointed at his cane.

No one had mentioned Christine, and although he wondered if she had made contact, he didn't ask. Maybe she'll be there, Alec said to himself.

"We don't have Chooch's number, do you have it?" Carol asked.

"Yeah, right here in my wallet. Ya want me to call 'em?"

"No, I'll do it," Carol answered as she snatched the slip of paper, "I'm more familiar with the arrangements than you."

As Alec returned his wallet, he grinned slightly and said to himself, Choochie boy, I think you're in like Flynn.

* * *

"Good to see ya, *kinda* in one piece," Jerry Greenwell said when he saw Alec in front of Wilke's on Belair Road and Pelham Avenue.

"Good to see you, too, buddy."

"This is my wife, Sharon."

"Heard lots of good things about you, Alec, especially what a great quarterback you are," Sharon said.

"*Was* a great quarterback," Alec replied, as the thought of Simpson's murder flashed through his mind.

"You still at GM, Jerry?"

"Yeah, still puttin' 'em pickups through the line down Broening Highway."

"Edjew, Georgie, is that you guys?" Alec said as he looked over Greenwell's shoulder.

"Sure 'nuff is," Edjew responded.

"You're a sight for sore eyes," Georgie said.

"What ya guys been up to?"

Edjew answered, "Went inna army right after high school. Spent my whole enlistment at White Sands Missile Range in New Mexico. Met Tuki here in El Paso and got married there. Workin' at Hamm's Brewery on O'Donnell Street."

"Good for you, man. Pleasure to meet ya, Tuki," Alec said as she looked shyly at him and nodded.

"How 'bout you, Georgie?"

"Got married and beat the draft. Then went on the city police department, stationed at southern. This is my wife, Carmen. You remember her from the neighborhood, don't ya?"

"Carmen, is that you? Damn, girl, you sure developed," Alec said as they both remembered losing their virginity.

Carmen then kissed Alec and lightly rubbed her tongue quickly over his lips. "Alec, great to see ya."

"Come on, let's go in and get a drink," Alec said as he tingled in response to Carmen's wet greeting.

A few minutes after Alec and his 'old crew' entered, Chooch and his cousin Dennis arrived. "Choocie, over here, buddy," Alec shouted when he saw him perusing the party room.

"Glad ya could make it," Alec said when Chooch got to his table.

"Wouldn't've missed it for the world," he answered as he glanced at Carol batting her eyes at him.

No accountin' for taste, Alec said to himself when he noticed the contact.

"Listen, my parents are havin' a get together for *me* next Saturday night at the Knights of Columbus Hall on Southern Avenue on the D.C. line. If y'all aren't doin' somethin', how 'bout stoppin' by."

Carol jumped up and said, "Oh, we'd love to come. I'll get directions from you later."

"Told ya, Choochie," Alec said with a sly look on his face.

"Told him what?" Carol asked.

"Never mind, just a little thing between me and him."

* * *

Later in the evening, Alec's Aunt Elizabeth's husband, Mike McAndrews, rudely broke into a conversation regarding the Vietnam War and said, "Back in the brown-shoe army I was in, the soldiers were real men, not like the bunch of pussies 'ere now. In *my* army, the men knew how to fight, kill, and die with honor."

"I guess *your* soldiers were 'deader' than ours, huh Uncle Mike?" Alec replied with fire in his eyes and six Budweisers under his belt.

"See, that's what I'm talkin' 'bout. Spoiled brats of this generation ain't got no respect for their elders, or nobody else for that matter. Bastards like you and 'em niggers're gonna get our asses beat over there."

"Respect runs in two directions, Uncle Mike. Ya give none, ya get none. What'd you do in the war anyway?" Alec asked.

"I was inna Eighth Air Force, bombed the shit outta Germany, that's what I did. If you weren't all trussed up with that cane and shit, I'd show ya what a real man can do."

"Mike, shut your mouth. This is Alec's comin'-home party, now sit down. Better yet, let's go," Elizabeth said angrily as she pulled on his shirt collar.

"*You* shut the fuck up, bitch. I'll deal with your stinkin' ass when we get home. Like I said, Alec, if you weren't all bound up like some kinda fuckin' mummy, I'd teach your young ass a thing or two, 'deed I would," Mike said as he snorted.

"I heard you were a grease monkey and never got off the ground, much less made a bombin' run," Henry said. "Ain't no bandages on me. Let's see what ya got."

"Aren't you gonna do something, Mother?" Carol said.

"Best to leave him alone when he gets like this," Lena answered.

"Fuck you, pizza face, let's dance," Mike said.

When Henry delivered his left elbow to Mike's jaw, Chooch said, "Damn, just like ya showed me and Toots," as he and Alec clapped.

"Just like ya showed me, Alec," Henry echoed with a shitty little grin.

"Just like I showed ya, Unc'."

When Mike came to, Elizabeth said, "Are ya happy now? Ya big, dumb, Irish jerk."

"Help me up, I'm ready to go."

I'LL LAY YOUR SOUL TO WASTE

How could a kind and merciful God allow all of the pain and suffering that is present in the world, or let an evil creature such as myself exist? Alec asked himself during his recovery period.

In a quest for a better understanding of a creative force, he became a voracious reader on the subject. Of the multitude of volumes he consumed, the one that held the most logic for him dealt with *Paganism*.

* * *

Alec discovered that in ancient times, Pagans worshipped a number of gods and goddesses. In modern times, *Neo-Pagans* believe everything around them is holy, because all is *part* of a god or goddess, and therefore sacred; they believe Earth itself is a living being.

Alec altered the traditional Neo-Pagan belief, and decided not to attach a human life form to it. He didn't share his view on Paganism with others. As far as the world was concerned, he was a devout Catholic.

* * *

"Yeah, decided to go to college and get my law degree," Alec said to Jerry Greenwell as they sat at the Freedom Inn.

"What makes ya wanna be a lawyer?" he asked.

"I think it'd be interestin' and the money's good. Work anywhere if ya gotta law degree."

"Scum of the earth," Edjew said as he laughed and slugged down three ounces of Carling Black Label while shopping for a heavy crab.

As Alec licked the *Old Bay* spice mixture from his paring knife, he focused in on a customer when he entered the bar. "That guy looks familiar," he said to himself as he sucked the delectable meat from the claw.

"A lawyer, huh?" Georgie asked.

"Yeah, gotta do somethin'," Alec replied, while still eyeing the customer.

"I'd rather suck a dick than be an attorney," Georgie said.

"I heard ya do suck dicks," Edjew quipped.

Suck a dick, Alec said to himself when his light bulb came on.

As the familiar-looking man took a drag from a Marlboro, Alec said to himself, "Palmieri, Russell Palmieri, the son of a bitch that killed Boots."

Alec then pulled a towel from the roll on the table and quickly wiped his hands. "Be right back, gotta whiz," he said.

"Don't hurry," said Edjew. "Down to our last few crabs."

"Order another dozen on me," Alec replied when he got up from the table. As he walked toward the men's room, Alec quickly glanced at Palmieri. "Bastard's gained a lotta weight, but that's him, no doubt about it. I'd recognize 'em in hell, and that's exactly where I'm gonna send 'em. Cove Road, here we come," he said while he stood at the urinal and grinned.

"Order a new batch yet?" Alec asked when he returned.

"Yeah, fresh ones on the way," Jerry replied.

"Only one thing better'n 'steamed Jimmies," Jerry said when the waitress dumped them on the table.

"Oh, yeah, and what's that?" Georgie asked.

"Free Jimmies," he answered as he juggled one of the hot delicacies.

"Thanks, Al, 'preciate it. On my two-week layoff for model changeover. Little low on cash right now. Pay ya back when the line starts up again," Jerry said with sincere gratitude.

"Don't worry 'bout it, buddy."

After finishing his third beer, Palmieri said to the bartender, "See ya tomorrow, Ronnie. Same time after work."

"Okay, Russ. See ya then."

This must be his waterin' hole, Alec said to himself.

* * *

"One roll of sisal rope, hammer and ten-penny nails, filet knife, half gallon of gasoline, funnel, pickax, shovel, hand saw, plywood and strips, saw horses, bit and brace, a two-inch pipe four feet long, campfire matches, Coleman Lantern, duct tape, handcuffs, handgun, phony police badge and ID case, lawn chair, cooler packed with six Buds and ice, bug spray, box of Kotex and a large bottle of styptic powder. That oughta do it, but first I got a little detective work to do," Alec muttered after he checked his list of 'supplies' the next day.

At 5:25 p.m., Alec positioned his car within eyeshot of the entrance to the Freedom Inn. Fifteen minutes later, a small bus with Maryland State Roads and Highway Commission painted on its front doors pulled in the lot. "See ya in the mornin', Russ," the driver said.

"Creature of habit, just like I figured," Alec whispered. "Fucker must be thirty and doesn't even own a car. Guess that's what happens to a bastard that spends time in jail for killin' cats and rapin' kids."

As the Seeburg played the *Viscounts'* latest version of *Night Train*, Alec entered the bar. "Bud draught, please," he said to the bartender.

"The city council today approved the passage of a bill into law requiring all bicycles in the city to be registered, and for a license plate that will be issued to be displayed on them at all times. Baltimore City Council Chairman Meindorf said this action should combat the rash of thefts that have been plaguing the city involving ten-speed English racers," George Baumann said, "now onto the *World News Report.*"

After a commercial and lead in, Walter Cronkite appeared on the television mounted behind the bar. "President Johnson said today, that US policy concerning the escalation of the war in Vietnam is beginning to shows signs of success, as the enemy body count reported by the Associated Press so far this month has nearly doubled from last month's total. Further, enemy movement has been curtailed by increased air strikes directed at strategic enemy locations."

"Things were startin' to heat up when I was over there," Palmieri said to the bartender as he chugged a Marlboro.

What the fuck did he say? Alec asked himself.

"Didn't know you were there, Russ," the bartender answered.

"Yeah, put nine years in the 'crotch.' Forced me into retirin' when I got wounded," Palmieri said as he raised his T-shirt. "Got shot up pretty good," he said as he looked down and rubbed his 'combat injuries.'

In actuality, Palmieri had been stabbed by an inmate he attempted to force into giving him oral sex while serving his ten-year sentence for child molestation at the *Breadthsville Reformatory for Young Men Between Seventeen and Twenty-One* in Hagerstown, Maryland.

"Loved the Corps. Didn't wanna leave, but they forced me to. Took out three of the slimy little bastards 'til they finally put me down."

I oughta go do that lyin' fuck right now, Alec said to himself. Marine my ass. Fuckin'-convict-cat-killin' pervert's more like it.

"After I got out, I started with Maryland State Roads. Been there ever since."

"My kid brother's in the Corps, got back from Nam a few weeks ago. He's in the third division, what outfit ya say you were in?" the bartender asked as he served him another Rheingold.

"Too painful to talk about. Start havin' flashbacks and go outta my mind."

"I'm sorry, Russ, didn't mean to touch a nerve. Won't mention it again."

"That's all right, you didn't know," Palmieri answered as a group of construction workers entered and took him off the hook.

Alec shook his head and whispered, "That counterfeit bastard. This is gonna be more fun than I thought."

"Thanks, Ronnie, see ya later," Alec said as he left.

The bartender acknowledged with a nod and smiled as he scooped the two dollars Alec dropped for him on the bar.

Alec waited in his car for Palmieri to exit, and watched him as he began walking on Erdman Avenue. "Cuttin' through," Alec said when he saw him turn right onto a small dirt path.

Alec then drove to Sinclair Lane and parked. A short time later, Palmieri appeared and walked a quarter mile. "Got the bastard," Alec said when Palmieri entered unit 3863 in Claremont.

* * *

"How ya been, Tommy boy? Beat Poly two years inna row after I took over. Gonna have some company in the next day or two, buddy," Alec said when he located the tree with an X carved on it as he began unloading equipment.

That evening, he said to Henry, "Unc', could we trade cars tomorrow? Engine in mine started missin' and I haven't had time to check it out. Goin' to Havre de Grace tomorrow to do some work on my buddy's barn. Hate to break down on I ninety-five and get stranded."

"If ya want, we can go look 'er over after dinner."

"I'd rather do it when we got plenty of time."

"Sure, we'll take care of it Saturday. Just leave your keys on the television and I'll leave mine there, too."

Before Alec joined the army, Henry took him up on his offer and purchased a black '62 Ford that closely resembled unmarked city police cruisers. "Thanks, Unc'. Aunt Lena, won't be home for dinner tomorrow night, my buddy's wife gonna fix us stuffed pork chops."

"If they're good, see if she'll gimme the recipe."

"I'm sure she will."

* * *

The next morning at nine, Alec left his house to hold consistent with his explanation for the use of Henry's car. Having time to kill, he decided to visit Seidel Bowling Lanes on Belair Road and roll a few games.

After three games, Alec drove to Eastern Avenue for lunch. As he walked past Epstein's Department Store and Gammerman's Camera Shop, he saw a sausage imprinted with G & A, painted on a marquee. He thought of Pavlov when his mouth began to water as he looked through the front window at 'dogs' slowly turning on the rotisserie. After, he walked to Kramer's and got a bag of caramel popcorn and a cherry sticky apple. Before returning to the car, he bought two Banlon shirts at Buddy's Men's Wear and a pair of Cuban Heels at Levi's Shoe Store. He then drove to the Vilma Theater and caught *The Sand Pebbles*: the motion picture for which *Mako* won an Academy Award for best supporting actor.

After the movie, Alec went to Freedom Village and took a position. At five forty-five, the familiar Maryland State Roads bus pulled up and exited Palmieri. When he went inside, Alec retrieved the .38 and shoulder holster he had carried in Vietnam from the trunk of the Ford, then sat in the front seat and waited. Just as the August sun was beginning its descent, Palmieri made his appearance from inside the bar just as *Gimme Shelter* started playing on the Ford's radio.

The sight of him titillated Alec, and he removed his sunglasses. When Palmieri began walking, Alec put his glasses back on, and said with a look of truculence, "It's show time."

Alec drove ahead, and backed the Ford up the small path out of sight from traffic. When he saw Palmieri trekking toward him, he exited and produced his old Captain Midnight badge he had pinned to the inside of his wallet. "City poleece. Russell Palmieri you're under arrest," Alec said.

"Under arrest for what? I ain't done nuttin'!"

Alec handcuffed Palmieri and threw him in the back seat where he placed duct tape over his mouth and secured rope around his ankles. Euphoria consumed Alec as he looked in the rear-view mirror and saw Palmieri completely at his mercy.

On the way, Palmieri looked around and became confused. Alec picked up his thought waves and said, "In case you're wonderin', Russ, I'm takin' ya to a *special* police station."

Palmieri was panic stricken. As he squirmed in desperate efforts to escape, Alec said, "I didn't know you were in the Corps, Russ. I didn't think they took guys who fucked little boys."

Palmieri's head began to swim and he started crying. When they reached their destination, Alec backed the car in and said, "Relax, Russ, It'll be over soon."

Who is this crazy mutha fucker? Palmieri shouted in his mind as he observed what appeared to be a freshly-dug grave. Why's he doin' this to me? He said to himself as he thought of all the young boys he had raped.

"Bet you're wonderin' who I am, aren't ya, Mr. Palmieri?" Alec said as he frantically shook Palmieri's head by the hair. "You killed my fuckin' cat—now do ya remember me?"

The sordid encounter reeled through their minds as they recalled Boots being twirled and flung. "I asked ya a question. Do ya remember me?"

Palmieri nodded.

"If ya utter one sound when I pull that tape off, I'll drop ya dead where ya sit, understand?" Alec said as he pointed the gun at Palmieri's head.

After acknowledging, Alec removed the tape and Palmieri said, "I'm sorry— "

"Nothin' ya say can change things. Now keep ypur fuckin' mouth shut 'til I tell ya to open it, all right?" Alec said after jamming the gun in Palmieri's left ear.

Another nod.

"Okay, now open."

When he did, Alec immediately placed his penis in and said, "Now suck it. All you're doin' is lettin' me mouth fuck ya."

It wasn't Palmieri's first encounter in *giving* head, as he had become 'Bubba's bitch' in prison. When he began to spit, Alec replaced the duct tape over his mouth, forcing semen to ooze from his nostrils.

Alec put the looped end of a length of rope around Palmieri's neck, cut the binding from his ankles, and motioned for him to stand. He then led him to a tree stump where he pulled down Palmieri's trousers and underwear.

"That's perfect, the knife ya killed Bootsie with. Now I won't have to mess up my cutlery," Alec said as a Buck Knife with a scrimshaw handle dropped from a pocket.

When Palmieri's eyes rolled back, Alec slapped him and said, "Stay awake God dammit, it's not gonna be that easy for ya. Ya haven't heard the fat lady sing yet. Now kneel and put your thighs against that stump; gonna show ya a little trick I learned in the Nam. Oh that's right, you were there, weren't ya? Ya probably know this one," Alec said when Palmieri complied.

Alec got the hammer and nails from the supply bag and laid them on the stump, then opened the knife. In order to disable Palmieri from moving, Alec tied another piece of rope to his thighs and wrapped it around the stump several times. When he offered resistance by leaning his upper body back, Alec said, "Ready for that, too," as he taped one end of a 2" x 4" to the back of his neck and placed the other end in a hole he had dug. Alec then returned to the front, and while stretching Palmieri's penis, plunged the nail through, then drove it into the stump with the hammer.

"I figure that's how poor little Bootsie felt, ya lousy hunka fuckin' blubber," Alec shouted as a mask of evil enveloped his face while the lyric, *Rape, murder, it's just a shot away, shot away*, echoed in his mind.

"You're choice. Cut it off or ya can stay there and bleed to death like the stuck fuckin' pig ya are," Alec said as he uncuffed his prisoner and handed him the knife. Palmieri instantly grabbed it and severed his member.

"Good choice, Russ," Alec said as he replaced the cuffs. "Ya like gettin' your dick sucked so much, I figure you'll love this," Alec said as he stuffed the removed penis in Palmieri's mouth and covered it with a new strip of tape.

"Gonna have some more fun before I kill ya, Russ," Alec said as he pushed Palmieri to the ground and dumped the styptic powder on his wound, and topped it with two Kotex pads. "Wanna introduce ya to Tommy Simpson. You'll be roomin' with 'em.., forever," Alec said after he dragged Palmieri to his grave next to Simpson's. "Just in case you're interested, Russ, my name's Bazey, Alec Bazey. Sweet dreams, mutha fucker," he said as he dropped the lid on the coffin.

Palmieri, who had played football under Coach Young several years before Simpson and Alec, thought, Alec Bazey, the kid that replaced Simpson after he disappeared.

"Can ya hear me down there, Russ?" Alec said tauntingly into a length of pipe he had placed through one of the holes in the coffin's lid. "I'm gonna have me a Bud now. Would ya like one?" he asked while pouring its contents into the pipe.

"Okay, Russ, show's over," Alec said as he emptied a half gallon of gasoline into the coffin through a funnel. "You guys sleep tight," he said as he dropped a lit match behind it.

Alec's face glowed as bright as the emitting flames when he heard Palmieri's muffled cries. "Just like Grandad would've done. Got 'em for ya, Bootsie."

* * *

"How'd it go today, hon'?" Lena asked when Alec got home.

"Real good. Got squared up on an old matter," Alec answered.

"Do ya get me the recipe for the stuffed chops?"

"No, everything was burned so bad I didn't bother to ask for it."

COLLEGE BOY

The *University of Maryland* is a public research foundation located in the City of College Park, three miles north of Washington, D.C. It is the flagship institution of the University System for the State of Maryland and is considered a 'Public Ivy'—an institution that provides an Ivy League collegiate education at public-school tuition. It is the largest university in the state as well as the Washington metropolitan area, and is a member of the Association of American Universities.

On March 6, 1856, UM was chartered as the Maryland Agricultural College. Two years later, Charles Benedict Calvert, a descendant of the Barons of Baltimore and a future US Congressman, purchased 420 acres of the Riverdale Plantation in College Park for $21,000. He founded the school later that year with income earned from the sale of stock certificates, and on October 6, 1859, the first 134 students began their education there.

*   *   *

"Is that you, stranger?" Alec heard a deep, sexy female voice from behind him say.

"Yeah, it's me. How's it goin', girl?"

"What's a matter, ya turn shy or somethin'? I remember when ya couldn't *wait* to swap spit with me," she seductively said when Alec didn't open his mouth as she kissed him.

"That was a long time ago. You're married now."

"A little French between old friends wouldn't hurt anything. Improved quite a bit since the last time we did it," she said as she flitted her tongue.

"Carmie, people are watchin'. You're embarrassin' me," Alec said as he retreated from her advances.

"What're ya doin' shoppin' here? Figured a big, rich, good-lookin' guy like you'd go to Eastpoint."

"Two Guys stuff's as good as the expensive places there. Gettin' ready for college; start classes at the University of Maryland on Monday. Goin' for a law degree."

"Oh, a big-time lawyer, huh? How 'bout we go back to my house and do one for old-time sake before ya go away? Georgie's rock fishin' on the Eastern Shore, won't be home for hours. What he doesn't know won't hurt 'em. Guarantee it'll be worth your time. Advanced from that schoolgirl stuff," she said without inhibition as she slowly moved her knee back and forth across his groin.

"She really looks good," Alec said to himself as the fragrance of *Tabu* began to act as an aphrodisiac.

"Listen, it's not that I don't wanna, and Christ knows you're sexier lookin' than Raquel Welch, but Georgie's my old pisan. What he doesn't know may not hurt *him*, but it will hurt me. Sorry, Carmie. I just can't do it to 'em—or you rather."

"Alec, you're a real boy scout. I'm proud of you," Carmen answered as she backed off. "If ya ever get lonely down there in College Park gimme a call and I'll come meet ya," she said as she handed him a business card.

"Carmen's Beauty Salon. That's right, you took cosmetology at Mervo, didn't ya?"

"Sure did. Bought Grande's Barber Shop on Belair Road a few years ago and converted it to a hair salon. Doin' real well."

"Yeah, I was by there a few days ago, remember seein' it. Didn't connect the name to you. Way to go, girl."

"I cut men's hair, too. Come by for a little trim, hair trim that is. Doesn't sound like you'll take me up on the other kind."

"I'll come—for a haircut that is. Good seein' ya, Carmie."

"You, too, Alec."

What a waste, she thought, as Alec proceeded to the checkout counter while she closely eyed his tight buttocks, wide back and narrow waist. "Guess I'll have to hang in there with Jerry Greenwell," she said.

* * *

The day before the fall semester began, Alec arrived at Annapolis Hall where room 2C in the Harford Hall dormitory was assigned as his new residence.

As there had been antiwar protests on campus, Alec decided to keep his military experience private. When asked by his roommate, Jeffrey Rabinowitz, why he hadn't entered college until the age of twenty-two, Alec told him it was unaffordable until he had received a moderate inheritance.

"Ya coulda applied for a government loan like I did. Nobody ever pays 'em back; it's free money for poor people like you and me. We *deserve* it. Government wised up and realized it's *not fair* for the rich to keep it all. Finally makin' the capitalists share the wealth," Jeffrey explained passionately.

Alec didn't become aware of Jeffrey's opposition to the Vietnam War until they watched the evening news and he went into a rage about how the tyrannical United States Government was imposing its will on a nation that didn't choose to conform to the evils of capitalism. He maintained that the billions of dollars being spent on the war should be given to the needy. He made it known that although he was against President Johnson's Vietnam War policy, he zealously supported his 'War on Poverty.' Further, he was an advocate of the social relief programs being created to form 'The Great Society.'

* * *

While recovering from his wounds, Alec not only converted his religious beliefs, he also became an advocate of *Jeffersonian Politics*: a policy that supports a federal government with greatly constrained powers and follows a strict interpretation of the US Constitution. Alec's favorite quote from Jefferson was, *"A government large enough to give its citizens everything they want, is also a government large enough to take away all they possess."*

Jefferson believed that if the individual is allowed to act free from unreasonable intrusion and unnecessary interference from the governing body, the group will also reap benefits. *Jeffersonian Politics* firmly supports and rewards individual efforts instead of punishing and inhibiting them with high taxes and stringent government regulations.

Contrary to Jefferson, Alexander Hamilton, the first United States Secretary of the Treasury, founding father, economist and political philosopher, emphasized a strong central body with implied powers, more in line with a socialistic form of government.

* * *

Shortly after returning from spring break, a group of protestors took over the Adele H. Stamp Student Union Building and set fire to it. Further demonstrations wreaked havoc on campus until a contingent of police officers from several jurisdictions was hastily formed and combined forces.

Alec experienced what he would later consider to be a defining moment in his life when a large group of demonstrators approached six Prince George's County Police Officers standing guard at the Campus Book Store on US 1 and College Avenue.

As the crowd approached them, a young sergeant ordered the team members carrying shotguns with tear-gas launching devices mounted on the barrels, to open fire. After the canisters landed, half of the protestors turned and ran, while the others regrouped.

"Port, arms," the sergeant shouted, "forward, march."

Wearing French blue trousers with black stripes, and gray shirts bearing an embroidered patch of the Prince George's County Coat of Arms, the officers slowly proceeded a half step at a time, thrusting their batons. Gas grenades attached to their flak vests swung freely, and condensation appeared and vanished on the face shields of their riot helmets with each rhythmic grunt. "Umph, Umph, Umph." By the time they reached the disorderly group, all but ten had dispersed.

While the officers subdued the troublemakers, Alec looked on and said, "Those guys are really somethin'. Well trained and disciplined. Took care of that bunch of assholes in short order."

When he saw two of P.G.'s finest split off in his direction, he made a beeline for the dormitory. "Stay in there where ya belong, dickhead," an officer shouted.

"No problem, buddy. Ain't goin' anywhere tonight," Alec said as he ducked in.

COUNTY MOUNTIE

Prince George's County, Maryland, is bordered by the Potomac River, Washington, DC, Anne Arundel, Charles, Howard and Montgomery Counties. The first recorded visit to the area by a European came in the summer of 1608, when Captain John Smith sailed up the Potomac River on an expedition. In 1634, Governor Leonard Calvert traveled on the Potomac from St. Mary's City, Maryland's first colonial settlement, to visit the Piscataway Indian village located on Piscataway Creek.

On April 23, 1696, the Maryland General Assembly named a new county after the dashing Prince George of Denmark, husband of the heir to the throne of England, Princess Anne. During the 1700's, the county grew and the frontier area transformed into civilization, when people from Europe began migrating to it. Agriculture provided the livelihood for every resident with tobacco at the heart of the economy.

Prince George's County grew with Washington, DC and the federal government. Among other institutions, Andrews Air Force Base, the Census Bureau, the Beltsville Agriculture Center and NASA Goddard Space Flight Center became located there.

When the campus protests became unbearable for Alec, he decided to leave school and become a Prince George's County Police Officer.

* * *

Prior to the beginning of class on his first day at the police academy, Alec met Chooch at the El Rancho on Marlboro Pike. "I always wanted to be a county policeman," Chooch said after they were seated. "Guess that's outta the question now," he added as he held up his left arm.

"Yeah, I guess it is. How's it goin' down at the VA?" Alec asked.

"Makes me feel lucky in losin' just an arm when I see some of those poor fuckers roll in on their wheel chairs. One of my clients lost both arms and legs when he tripped over a *Claymore*; lucky he survived."

"If ya call livin' without any limbs lucky, I guess he was. Rather be dead myself."

"Me, too," Chooch replied as their 'bellybuster' breakfast arrived.

"So you and Carol finally set a wedding date, huh?" Alec said as he added a healthy dose of Tabasco to his eggs and home fries.

"Yeah, Saturday October twenty-first's the big day. Don't ya know they use that stuff to kill bugs with?" Chooch asked as Alec screwed the top on.

"Guess ya shoulda had a bottle with ya when we were out fetchin' prisoners that day, huh?"

"Damn, I can still feel those little bastards diggin' in," Chooch answered as he stuck a fork down the back of his collar and scratched.

"Miss, would you please bring another fork for my friend; he's contaminated this one," Alec said to the waitress as he held up the scaly utensil.

"Oh, did I set out dirty silverware? I'm sorry."

Alec snickered as he poured maple syrup onto his pancakes when the waitress scurried to the kitchen.

* * *

When he was a rookie officer, due to his father's political connections, the Prince George's County Police Department's Training Division Commander, after having served the minimal amount of time required as a patrol officer before being eligible for transfer, was assigned as an aide/driver to the PG County Commissioner. While acting in that capacity, he was able to rub elbows with high-ranking police and county officials, and made a meteoric rise through the ranks. After being promoted to lieutenant, he went to the training division to help mold the department into a more professional organization.

"My name is Captain Wilbur J. Street, and I welcome each and every one of you to the Prince George's County Police Department," he said to the bright-eyed recruits after they were seated.

Although Street had little experience in policing, he was expert at 'walkin the walk,' and 'talkin' the talk.' "I know some of ya won't make it through the academy," he said dramatically as his eyelids flitted. "Give it at least two weeks—then if you decide to leave, there'll be no hard feelings. For those of you who *do* make it through, however, a rewarding career awaits you; nothin' like slappin' the cuffs on a bad guy out on the bricks. Best feelin' in the world knowin' you've done your bit to make for a safer society," Street said as he continued to pour it on.

Is this Bozo shittin' me or what? Alec asked himself. Shoulda been in jump school. Or better yet, the Nam, if he thinks this place is tough.

"All right, men, that's all I have for now. Remember—two weeks. Good luck, comrades," Street said enthusiastically as he exited the stage and waved.

Corporal Gorman, another sycophant who considered himself a 'bad ass,' stepped behind the podium. "All right, ya 'cruit scum bags, report to the clothing room at the end of the hall for uniform issue. Now move it."

What the hell have I gotten myself into? Alec asked himself as the other thirty-nine scrambled for the door.

* * *

Police training was scheduled for twenty weeks, four of which would be a tour of duty with the bureau of patrol. "Officer Bazey, I'm Lee Foote. Understand we'll be ridin' together," Alec's training officer said upon introduction.

"Pleased to meet ya, Lee." After a period of small talk, Foote said, "Okay, see ya Saturday afternoon. Shift starts at three. Know where Seat Pleasant Station is?"

"Yeah, Corporal Brooke took us by there a few times during stop and approach."

"See ya there."

Seems to be a decent sort, Alec said to himself.

He's big, but I'm taller, Foote said to *himself.*

* * *

At roll call, Sergeant C. W. Hicks, introduced Alec to his squad members. "All right now listen up. We have a new member here—Alec Bazey, ID number six-one-six."

When the dandruff-collared, roly-poly Corporal Fred Hollandberger heard the ID number, he giggled and said, "Six-one-six: didn't know they could count that high over to the academy."

"Don't pay no attention to ol' Dumbo. With sixty-eight for an ID number, he thinks anybody that has one with three digits is still a fuckin' rookie," said PFC Hartley.

After Hollandberger cackled like a hen, roll call broke and the officers hit the road. Upon entering the black '66 Plymouth, Foote said, "Now forget all that shit they taught ya in the academy; I'm gonna show ya the right way to do it. Understand what I'm sayin', rookie?"

When Alec passively nodded, Foote said to himself, This guy's a real pussy. I'll drum his ass out before he goes back to the academy.

As they pulled up to the 7-11 in Kentland, Foote said, "First thing a good cop does to start off a shift is get a cup of coffee."

"I don't usually drink coffee this time a day."

I might run this cunt off before the end of the shift, Foote said to himself. "Okay, be back in a minute. Our car number's six forty-three; that's six-four-three. Got it? Or shall I write it down for ya?"

"I think I can remember that," Alec replied.

"Be right back."

"Another fuckin' Hatfield," Alec said.

"Where ya livin'?" Foote asked when he returned with his coffee.

"Took an apartment at Kenilworth Towers on Greenbelt Road.

Familiar with it?"

"Yeah, I know it. That's where all 'em fags from DuPont Circle moved to, heh, heh, heh."

"I don't think so. It's really a nice place. Only a hundred and seventy-five a month plus utilities. Plan on buyin' a house when I get off probation."

"*If*, ya get off probation," Foote snippily replied.

"What's that suppose to mean?"

"Just what I said. *If*, ya get off probation."

"Yeah, okay."

"Any niggers in your class?"

"No, no blacks."

"I didn't ask if any blacks were in the class, I asked if there were any niggers."

"No, no niggers either," Alec answered in appeasement. Ya haven't been with this guy a half hour yet; put Cove Road outta your mind, Alec said to himself.

At the time, thirty percent of Prince George's County's population consisted of African-Americans. Of the eleven hundred plus members of the police department, only seven were black.

* * *

The PGPD employed a shift plan for the bureau of patrol known as the 'Kansas City Swing.' Although it minimized manpower, the plan was exhausting for those forced to endure it. Of the four squads assigned to each precinct, three were scheduled to work seven continuous eight-hour days of alternating shifts, with only one off in between. The schedule provided a four-day break after three tours.

The most grueling time period came during midnights, when Foote became a tyrant. "Gimme that mike, ya dumb ass. Car four forty-three, correct our location to Landover and Manson. My partner went into some kinda coma and forgot where he was," Foote arrogantly growled when Alec misinformed the dispatcher of their location.

His admonishment inspired the other officers to make cat calls over the air and beat their open mikes against metal objects. "See what happens when ya fuck up? Listen to 'em, the other guys think you're an idiot. Your mother and father must be some kinda morons to have produced a re-tard like you," Foote barked.

While covering Foote's holstered service revolver with his left hand, Alec leaned over and grasped his throat with his right. "Don't ever talk about my parents, ya piece a shit," he shouted as he applied pressure.

Fearing for his life, Foote put up his hands in surrender while he slammed on the brakes. After the cruiser came to a screeching halt, Alec withdrew Foote's revolver and threw it on the passenger-side floorboard. "I'm gonna give ya a break and let ya go, okay?" he calmly said.

Foote nodded as his eyes bulged and saliva spewed from his lips. When he regained his composure, he said, "Can I have my gun back?"

Alec retrieved the revolver and handed it to Foote, while unsnapping his holster. "Guess you're kinda sensitive about your folks, huh?" Foote said meekly.

"My family's none of your business."

"Sorry, Alec, didn't mean to offend ya. Won't happen again."

"Ya been fuckin' with me since day one, just because ya could. Does that make ya feel like a big man or somethin'?"

"Car four forty-three, citizen advises of a suspicious person in the area of eightieth Avenue and Sheriff Road. Four forty-three?" the dispatcher interrupted.

"Ten-four, radio," Foote answered.

Saved by the bell, Alec said to himself.

* * *

"Car five forty-three, ten-eight," Alec advised the dispatcher as they exited the parking lot on Sunday morning of day shift.

"Ten-four, five forty-three. Five forty-three, respond code three to a holdup in progress at the seven-eleven, seventy-fifth and two-o-two. Five four-three?"

"Ten-four," Alec answered as Foote turned the cruiser right onto George Palmer Highway from Addison Road and activated the emergency equipment.

"Bad guys at it early today," Foote said when he looked at his Timex.

A short time later, Alec said, "Bet that's the holdup men," when he saw a car traveling at a high rate of speed.

"Bet you're right," Foote said as the Plymouth's left wheels nearly lifted off the ground as it turned onto the exit ramp.

When they fell in behind and signaled for the vehicle to stop, Alec said to the dispatcher, "Five forty-three behind holdup suspects on Landover Road just east of Barlowe. Red, sixty-three Impala. Maryland registration, B-T-H-one-nine-seven."

"Ten-nine; siren cut ya out."

"They're runnin' radio," Alec shouted when a cloud of blue smoke blasted from the tailpipes of the fleeing vehicle as the suspect's heads jerked back.

"What's your ten-twenty?"

"On Landover toward the Beltway. Sixty-three red chevy. Maryland, boy-time-Henry-one-nine-seven."

"Ten-four, five forty-three. All cars respond to the area of Landover Road."

By the time the next cruiser cleared Seat Pleasant, the chase had reached I-495 and Maryland Route 4, three miles from the closest unit. "Advise Maryland State and Oxon Hill," Alec shouted into the mike above the howl of the siren.

Shortly, the dispatcher advised, "Closest MSP car's in Accokeek. Oxon Hill hasn't come ten-eight yet."

"Looks like just you and me, partner. Oxon Hill slugs are down Indian Head Highway at Sunnybrook's breakfast buffet," Foote said to Alec.

"Headed toward the W-W. Call and get 'em to lift the span," Alec said to the dispatcher.

Thirty seconds later, the dispatcher came back. "DC says the controls on the Wilson Bridge are ten-seven: take fifteen, maybe twenty minutes to fix."

"Too late anyway. Halfway across in triple figures," Alec answered as the speedometer needle tickled 106. "Call Virginia State."

Shortly thereafter the dispatcher responded, "VSP says they can't find ya, five forty-three. What's your twenty now?"

"Rollin' up on ninety-five!"

"Five forty-three, be advised—holdup at the seven-eleven's been confirmed; female suspect armed with a handgun, possibly a forty-five shot the manager and assistant; manager DOA. Copy, five forty-three?"

"Five forty-three, a-ffirmitive."

As he pressed the release on the shotgun rack, Alec unkeyed the mike and said, "Grab my gun belt, Lee,"

"What?"

"Grab my fuckin' gun belt."

When the Plymouth veered close to an eighteen wheeler, Alec ducked back in and said, "Hold 'er steady this time," as he leaned out the window for a second time.

When the cruiser got to the rear window on the driver's side of the Chevy, Alec unloaded the Wingmaster as the female passenger began firing in his direction.

"Ya okay, man?" Foote asked excitedly.

"I don't know. Am I bleedin' anywhere?" Alec asked as Foote pulled the Plymouth onto the shoulder while the engine steamed and the tires smoked.

"I don't think so, buddy. Get out and lemme check."

As Foote looked Alec over for wounds, a blue-and-grey Ford pulled up behind their cruiser. "V-four redio. Found 'em boys from Murlin, just south a the Dulles cutoff. Send the far department and 'vestigators 'is away."

"Ambo, too?"

"You PG County boys just cain't stay outta trouble, kin ya?" A voice under a grey Stetson said. "Either y'all hurt 'iny?"

"I think we're okay," Alec answered.

"Don't see no need for one, redio," Trooper Wright told the dispatcher as he winked at Alec and Foote and watched as the gas tank of the guardrail-speared Chevy exploded.

When they got back to Seat Pleasant, Foote said to Alec, "I had you figured all wrong, boy. I apologize, you're a hell of a man; glad I drew you from the recruit pool."

"Thanks," replied Alec as he stuffed equipment in his car.

"I promise I won't be such an asshole when ya come back after graduation."

Maybe, but you'll always be a jerk-off as far as I'm concerned, Alec said to himself. "Yeah, we'll start over then," he verbally replied as they shook hands and locked eyes.

* * *

The investigation revealed that the suspects had stolen the Chevrolet in Whiteville, NC, after having escaped from a nearby penal farm. While headed to Philadelphia, they replaced the NC tag with one they removed from a vehicle parked at the welcome center in Newburg, Maryland, just over the Governor Harry W. Nice Bridge on US Route 301. When running low on fuel, they left I-495 at the Landover Road exit.

Armed with a Charter Arms .45 they discovered under the seat, the female suspect held up the 7-11, shooting the assistant manager and fatally wounding the manager, while her male accomplice remained in the car. They made good their escape until they crossed paths with the Prince George's County Police.

Alec and Foote were exonerated by VSP from any wrongdoing in the incident. The Prince George's County Police Commander of the Internal Affairs Section concurred with the decision after reviewing the investigative report.

THE PHANTOM

The night before the wedding, Alec met Chooch and several of his friends for a bachelor party at the Quonset Hut in Marlow Heights. As the group began to trickle in, Chooch said nervously to Alec, "Ya all set for tomorrow, man? Got everything?"

"Relax. Lena and Carol have it under control."

"Yeah, no sense in worryin', I'll just drink tonight," Chooch said as he finished his Bud and waved the empty bottle at the bartender.

"Now don't forget, meet me in front of my building at nine, and I'll lead ya to the church."

"I can probably find it myself. Was there the other night for rehearsal, remember?"

"*Meet me at nine Choochie;* Carol'd kill me if you got lost or were late or somethin'."

"You're right, better not take any chances. I'll meet ya."

Two hours later, Alec said to the group, "Hey, it's nine thirty. Big Al's about to go on at Rands. What say we go down and listen to 'em rap out a couple a sets?"

"Sounds great to me, I love Big Al," Chooch's cousin Dennis said as he finished a gin and tonic.

"Yeah, me, too, Big Al's the cat's ass," Chooch said.

"Where's Rands?" Bobby Donato asked.

"On Fourteenth Street in Northwest, half block from I, just up from the Speak Easy," Alec answered as he finished his drink.

"Oh, yeah, the joint where they give ya salted peanuts in the shell and the broad swings on the trapeze overtop the bar, right?"

"That's it," answered Alec. "Come go with me, I'll drive."

"Cool," answered Bobby as they all got up and headed for the men's room.

* * *

Al Downing was an African-American singer, songwriter and pianist, born on January 9, 1940, in Oklahoma. Although he was a 'soul' sensation in the DC area, he didn't achieve international stardom until 1979 when he returned to his 'roots' and began recording country music.

* * *

The crew was thrown back through the front door when they entered

Rand's as Big Al belted out his rendition of the *Midnight Hour* in an overpowering and booming baritone voice.

"Man, that mutha can wail," Alec said as he began grooving.

"Tootsie loved the Pickett," Chooch said.

"Ain't nothin' more disgutin' than watchin' white people dance," Alec said as he watched Chooch non-rhythmically bob and jerk as Al finished his set.

When the group returned to the Quonset, Alec said, "You gonna be all right, right?"

"I'll be fine, no problem," Chooch assured in slurred and incoherent speech.

"Come on, buddy, I'll take ya home."

"No, I'll be fine," Chooch insisted as he fumbled for his car keys and staggered.

"I better follow the fool," Alec said as he put his car in gear. "Good thing he only lives six blocks away."

After Chooch arrived safely, Alec drove to his apartment.

* * *

The following morning, with his head pounding, Chooch followed Alec onto the Baltimore-Washington Parkway at the Greenbelt Road entrance. Lucky we're traveling on this side of the BW, Alec said to himself. The traffic on the other side's barely movin'.

At the same time, the announcer on WTOP advised of the antiwar protest taking place on the Mall in Washington.

* * *

After the wedding ceremony, the procession gathered at Overlea Hall. As he popped open a Bud, Chooch said, "With the way my head was drummin' when I got up this mornin', I thought I'd never make it."

"Good thing you staged a miraculous recovery. Carol woulda kicked your skinny ass if you'd a been a no show," said Alec.

"Feel great now; hair o' the dog works every time."

After Mr. and Mrs. John Baranco finished their last dance, the limousine pulled up to the front entrance. "Off to Niagara Falls. Thanks, everybody," Carol said as they entered the black Cadi.

"See ya in ten days, bro'," Chooch called to Alec.

"Y'all enjoy yourselves," said Alec, as he clung to Lena soaking her tears with a fringed handkerchief.

"Niagara Falls, that's where Mom and Luke went on their honeymoon."

* * *

At the time, every police district in Prince George's County was divided into two sectors. The geographical size and population of the sector determined the amount of beats, or patrol areas within each.

Seat Pleasant Precinct contained sectors four and five, and was divided by Maryland 214—Central Avenue. The population of sector four consisted primarily of African-Americans, while sector five was inhabited by a racial mixture, predominately white.

On Friday, October 2, 1971, Alec was assigned to sector five, and 'line-beat' four.

"Car, six fifty-four."

"Six fifty-four bye."

"Six fifty-four, take the report of a dead body on eastbound Maryland Route Four approximately a half mile from the DC line. Victim's feet are allegedly protruding onto the shoulder of the road from a grassy area. Six fifty-four?"

"Ten-four, six fifty-four. Complainant?"

"Citizen."

"Ten-four."

"Damn, just drove through there," Alec said after he unkeyed the mike.

Upon arriving at the intersection of Pennsylvania and Southern Avenues, he slowly proceeded into the uninhabited area of Maryland. Four tenths of a mile later, he spotted a pair of pink sneakers. With Kel-Light in hand, he exited and walked forward a few steps.

"*Six-five-four*," Alec said dramatically over his hand held radio.

"Six fifty-four," the dispatcher answered.

"Send homicide and evidence. Signal eighty-one's been located: black female, approximately ten years old."

"Ten-four, six fifty-four."

A few minutes later, the dispatcher came back, "Homicide's enroute. ETA—five minutes."

"I'll leave my three-sixties on."

Upon examining the body, Detective Rose said, "Looks like the Freeway Phantom got 'em another one."

* * *

Beginning on April 21, 1971, and suddenly ending on September 5, 1972, six young African-American girls were abducted from their neighborhoods in Washington, DC: four of the bodies were discovered in the District, and two in Prince George's County. No substantial leads or suspects were ever developed in the cases, and still remain open.

Although four of the victims' middle name was Denise, it's believed the similarity was strictly random. Since the last murder, a similar M.O. has not occurred.

Speculation holds that the murderer suffered death rather than imprisonment for another offense; the fact that the killer still lives, cannot be ruled out.

SPECIAL OPS

After clearing the murder scene, Alec drove to the small strip shopping center in the 5200 block of Marlboro Pike next to the Hillside Drive-In. As he composed his officer's report, he heard a beleaguered voice cry out, "Six fifty-two, radio."

"All cars standby. Station's ten-three. Go ahead, six fifty-two."

"Six-I in a white-over-turquoise fifty-seven Chevy just ran off the road in the fourteen-hundred block of Nova Avenue. I'm with 'em now, 'bout a hundred feet inna woods. When I attempted to assist him from the vehicle he punched me in—"

"Ya split my fuckin' head open ... "

"Standby a second, radio," Officer Daniels said as the drunk yelled in the background.

When the other officers heard the chaos, they began the 'charge.'

"What ya got there besides a fat lip, Brucie boy?" Alec asked as Daniels wiped blood on his shirt sleeve.

"Things under control. Ten-twenty-two the other units," Daniels replied as he thumbed toward the driver he 'jacked.'

Just as Alec was about to issue the cancel order, two officers brought their cruisers to a screeching halt and stormed out. While they performed a pilot for the Rodney King Show, Lieutenant Hicks arrived and shouted, "Enough. Put cuffs on 'em and call fire board."

Alec watched in disgust as the duo dragged the driver to the ambulance when it arrived. "Teach you to fuck with the county poleece, nigger," one of the officers said in farewell to the arrestee.

"I just don't know what gets into some of these guys," Hicks said to Alec.

"Do it because they can, L.T. Easy for a fat loser like Watkins to be a bad ass when he has a badge, gun, tear-gas canister, blackjack, night stick and five or six guys on his side. Bet he wouldn't've been so tough if he was up against that dude by himself."

"Amen to that, brother. Probably woulda shot 'em."

Despite Alec's shortcomings, as with most police officers he was 'tit for tat.' When it became clear that a suspect no longer posed a threat, he would discontinue the use of force and take appropriate measures.

"Gotta favor to ask of ya," Hicks said as he touched Alec's shoulder.

"Anything, L.T., just name it."

"Along with my promotion, I'm gettin' transferred to the special-operations division, and I'd like you to come over with me. After your promotion to corporal comes through, I'll make ya one of my squad leaders. Without workin' midnights it'll be easier for ya to finish school. Still in, right?"

"Yeah, been takin' University of Maryland courses off campus. Gettin' close to that law degree."

"We can get ya an unmarked take home and you'll make a lotta overtime. Whadda ya say?" Hicks said attempting to close the deal.

"Let's do it."

The Prince George's County Police Department is quite progressive, as is the county itself. Among other innovations, it was the second urban police organization in the United States to implement a 'take-home-cruiser program,' where every officer was issued their own car, and allowed to operate it on *and* off duty. The policy was put into practice after the City of Indianapolis proved it successful when the crime rate there dropped dramatically as a result of increased police presence on the streets.

* * *

One of the communities developed by Levitt & Sons is *Belair at Bowie* in Bowie, Maryland. The historic *Bowie Mansion and Estate*, located in the heart of the city, was the home of Maryland's Colonial Governor Samuel Ogle and his *Belair Stables*; the area they encompass is known as the birthplace of thoroughbred racing in the United States.

Although Alec had intended on purchasing a home, he hadn't pursued the matter until he was swept by the charm of Bowie after his first visit there. The house he bought, a rancher with a brick front and white trim, was located on Birdseye Lane in the Buckingham Subdivision.

When Chooch first visited, he said, "Maryland flag's weird lookin'. Wonder what all that stuff on it means?" as he watched it wave under the American on the flagpole in the front yard.

"Everybody knows that: it bears the Calvert and Crossland Coat of Arms. Calvert was the surname of the Lords Baltimore who founded Maryland, and their colors of gold and black appear in the first and fourth quarters of the flag. Crossland was the family of the mother of George Calvert, the first Lord Baltimore. The red-and-white Crossland colors, with a botany cross, appear there in the second and third quarters," Alec rattled off unhesitatingly as he pointed at the flag.

"Where'd ya learn that?"

"In elementary school, knucklehead," Alec answered as he smiled and produced a pamphlet from his back pocket that was enclosed with the Maryland flag he purchased.

* * *

On the evening of Thursday, May 11, 1972, Alec and his T-10 squad were detailed to the US Secret Service as a support team. Their assignment was at the Belair Community Center located on Stoneybrook Drive at the intersection of Annapolis Road in Bowie, to provide security for Hubert H. Humphrey, the former United States Vice President and hopeful Democrat candidate for the upcoming presidential election. When Humphrey's visit ended without incident, Alec and his squad members went backstage to meet the senator from Minnesota.

On the following Monday, Alec and his squad were again assigned to the US Secret Service to assist with security for another presidential candidate from the Democrat Party.

At 10 A.M., the squad arrived at the Laurel Shopping Center where they met the U.S. Secret Service detail in front of the Equitable Trust Bank. After being briefed, the squad of seven visited a nearby McDonald's for an early lunch. After, they returned to the bank and waited for the 'Fightin' Little Judge' to arrive.

* * *

George Corley Wallace, Jr., was born in Barbour County, in southeastern Alabama to George Corley Wallace and Mozell Smith. He became a regionally successful boxer in his high-school days then went directly to law school at the University of Alabama in 1937. After receiving a law degree in 1942, he enlisted in the US Army Air Corps, and flew combat missions over Japan in WW II. He served under Curtis LeMay, who would be his running mate in the 1968 presidential race.

After entering politics, Wallace was elected Governor of Alabama for four terms. He ran for the presidential nomination three times as a Democrat, and as the American Independent Party candidate once.

* * *

While waiting for Wallace and his entourage, Alec milled around the entrance of the bank where the landing had been converted to a stage. When Corporal Michael M. Landrum observed an odd-appearing individual in the slowly rising crowd, he said to Alec, "That guy's a pecker shaker if I ever saw one."

As Alec sweat in the ninety-degree heat, he turned toward the crowd after Landrum made the comment and observed a white male in his mid-twenties with very blond hair wearing 'Super Fly' sunglasses. What made his appearance outstanding, however, was his apparel: a heavy, wool sport coat, a Wallace button on his left lapel, red-white-and-blue socks, a white shirt, and a necktie with 'Wallace' written downward.

"I think you're right, Mike. Better keep an eye on that weirdo."

The man melted into the crowd when he saw the officers eyeing him.

When Wallace arrived at three thirty, he took a position behind the lectern and began addressing the crowd of approximately one thousand. The gathering listened quietly as a few hecklers shared their opinions above Wallace's amplified voice. In closing, he said to his supporters, "I appreciate all you citizens of Princess George County comin' here today to visit me. Now I'm gonna come down 'ere and meet some a y'all fine folks."

"Princess George? What the fuck was he, some kinda cross-dressing' perv'?" Alec said to PFC John Smalley.

Wallace then proceeded toward the crowd and began shaking hands with the seemingly friendly group. As he mingled, the man spotted earlier by Landrum began pushing his way toward Wallace. When he got within an arm length, the man shouted, "George, George, George. Over here, George. Shake my hand."

When Wallace reached out, the man fired all five shots from a two-inch, chrome-plated, .38 Rohm revolver: three of the four bullets that passed through Wallace's body struck Alabama State Police Captain E. C. Dothard, campaign-worker Dora Thompson, and US Secret Service Agent Nick Zarvos.

When he heard two shots fired in quick succession, then three more, Alec thought balloons were being popped, as the gunfire was muffled by the density of the closely-gathered crowd. After he saw Wallace and the others on the asphalt, and Zarvos clutching his throat, he knew the sounds he heard was that of gunfire.

Before acting, Alec carefully perused the crowd for an accomplice. As the 6' 2", 240-pound Landrum wrapped his huge left arm around the man's neck, Alec and other officers closed in and removed the suspect from the shocked crowd, now acting in mob fashion. "Kill the son of a bitch where he stands," shouted an elderly man while shaking his cane and attempting to remove Alec's service revolver from his holster.

After pushing the man back, Alec yelled, "Get 'em outta here quick. Don't want another JFK."

As the five officers surrounding the suspect moved toward their unmarked cars, an olive-drab-and-black Maryland State Police cruiser zoomed up from the rear of the bank where the suspect was whisked into the back seat by Landrum and two other officers.

After getting in the cruiser, Landrum looked to the floor and noticed that although there were three sets of handcuffs on the suspect's left wrist, and two sets on his right, none had been attached to the opposite wrist.

"Oh my God," said Senator Humphrey, Wallace's chief opponent in the primary race in Maryland when he was informed of Wallace's shooting while he spoke at a daycare center in Baltimore. "All I can say is that it is a sad business. It's getting so you can't know what's going to happen in our country anymore in politics," Humphrey said as he suspended his campaign and went to Holy Cross Hospital in Silver Spring where Wallace was hospitalized.

* * *

Arthur Herman Bremer, was born on August 21, 1950, and grew up in Milwaukee, Wisconsin in a working class and somewhat dysfunctional household. He didn't fit in well with other people, and was an adolescent in emotional trouble.

On March 23, 1972, Bremer attended a Wallace fundraising dinner and rally at Milwaukee's Red Carpet Airport Inn; although he stalked Wallace, his goal was to assassinate President Nixon in hopes of attaining infamy, and finally be recognized.

Despite his lack of enthusiasm for assassinating Wallace, on May 8, 1972, one week before the shooting, Bremer left his Milwaukee apartment and traveled east in a 1967 blue Rambler. On May 9, he visited the Wallace headquarters in Silver Spring, Maryland and offered to work in the campaign.

On May 15, Bremer was present for a Wallace rally in Wheaton, Maryland at noon. As Wallace was not warmly received by the crowd there, he refused to shake hands, denying Bremer the opportunity to carry out his plan of assassination. His plan came to fruition at the Laurel Shopping Center later that day.

* * *

On August 4, 1972, Bremer was convicted of four counts of assault with intent to murder by a jury of six men and six women after just ninety minutes of deliberation at the Upper Marlboro Courthouse. When the prosecutor, Arthur A. 'Bud' Marshall, mentioned to the jury in closing that society needed to be protected from someone like Bremer, he responded, "Well, Mr. Marshall. Looking back on my life, I would have liked it if society had protected me from myself."

Bremer was sentenced to sixty-three-years imprisonment which was later reduced to fifty-five. He served his sentence at the Maryland Correctional Institution in Hagerstown, Maryland, where he was released from custody on November 9, 2007.

Bremer would serve as the inspiration for the character Travis Bickle, played by Robert DeNiro in the 1976 film, *Taxi Driver.* The movie would subsequently be called a motivating factor in John Hinckley, Jr.'s decision to shoot President Ronald Reagan.

* * *

As Bremer was being treated for wounds sustained during his arrest, he said to Landrum, "Stick with me, Corporal. I'll make ya a star."

After the Wallace shooting, Alec responded to the PGPD Bureau of Criminal Investigations located at 8005 Cryden Way in Forestville, where he completed a written statement concerning his participation in the event.

"Corporal Bazey. You're the one who smoked that salt-and-pepper team on the Capital Beltway a few years back," Homicide Commander Lieutenant Strump said when Alec handed him the statement.

"Yeah, that was me. Hell of a way to start my career, huh?"

"Kinda made ya a legend on the department, hangin' out the window with a shotgun like ya did at a hundred plus."

"Didn't have much choice when I saw the bitch pointin' a forty-five at me."

"No choice at all."

"Hell of a statement ya wrote," Strump said when he finished reviewing it.

"Put everything in I could remember."

"Did Landrum really say that about Bremer lookin' like a pecker shaker?" Strump asked with raised eyebrows.

"Sure did," Alec replied as he looked at Landrum seated at an investigator's desk completing his account of the event.

"FBI'll be interested in that; they're startin' up a profile unit on assassins. I'll be sure and let 'em know. Listen, there's openings in the detective bureau, gonna be lookin' for some new investigators. Why don't ya apply? A man of your many talents would do good as a dick. If an officer doesn't put at least one tour in as a detective during his police career he's slightin' himself. Reads good on a resume after ya retire."

"I'll give it some thought."

Although Alec didn't intend on retiring from the police department, he decided a stint in an investigative section would enhance his career as a defense attorney. After being accepted, he was assigned to the juvenile section.

* * *

Alec soon distinguished himself as an excellent investigator after cultivating several 'snitches.' His favorite was Steve Maloney who resided in the Booker Estates Apartments in Seat Pleasant.

Alec first met him prior to Steve's twelfth birthday, when a Seat Pleasant Town Officer arrested him for breaking and entering. Under state laws at the time, a person under the age of twelve couldn't be charged with a crime: rather, a *delinquent* would be taken into custody as a 'CHIN'—Child in Need of Supervision—and appear before a juvenile master who would decide the child's fate. Unless the offense was of a serious nature or the youth was a habitual wrongdoer, they were placed under some sort of probation and released to their parents or legal guardian.

As his latest arrest was the fourth in less than a year, Steve was sent to *Boy's Village*, a reform school in Cheltenham. After spending ninety days there, he was released to his mother's custody.

* * *

"Detective Bazey, may I help you?" Alec said when he answered the phone at his desk.

" 'Tective Basil, 'is be Steve Maloney. 'Member me, bro'?"

"Yeah, Steve. Thought ya were still in the Village."

"Got sprung yesterday. Muva say I need a summer job. Wanna go to work for you."

"Doin' what?"

"I knows a whole lotta shit goin' on 'round here. Wanna be yo' 'formant."

"What about school?"

"School start back up in September. Muva think a job do me good. Knowm' what I'm sayin'?"

"I think so, Steve. Where are ya now?"

"Pay phone at People Drug Sto' in Seat Pleasant Shoppin' Center. Pick me up?"

"Depends on what ya got for me."

"I knows where ya can get a load of stolen telebisions and a bunch a herb. Dude name Marcus keep the shit in his 'partment on Capitol View."

"Gimme fifteen minutes. I'm driving a light blue seventy Plymouth."

"I waits fo' ya in front of People."

As Alec snatched his keys, he said, "Sergeant Meade, got some business to take care of. Won't be gone long."

"Okay, keep your portable on in case we need ya."

"Ten-four."

* * *

Steve was street savvy and reminded Alec of Victor. On the way, he thought about when the Seat Pleasant Town Officer brought him in. Even though he had been caught carrying a new portable radio and a loaded piggy bank a block from where the burglary occurred ten minutes earlier, he refused to admit involvement in it.

"Ain't done nuffin'," Steve insisted when he met Alec.

"Where'd ya get the radio and bank?" Alec asked as Steve scowled and pouted with crossed arms while handcuffed inside one of the interrogation rooms.

"Got the shit fo' my birfday."

"The record I have here says your birthday was February twentieth; today's June sixteenth, how do ya figure?"

"Must be some 'stake on that record. My birfday June sixteenf. I mean June fifteenf."

"Willin' to take a lie-detector test?"

"Sho', I take a 'tector tess."

"Be back in a minute. Gotta get it ready."

While preparing the 'lie detector,' Alec said to himself, Kid's got his shit together. Knows better'n to cop.

Alec went to the kitchen and attached three stretched springs from ballpoint pens to each leg of a colander then carried it to the copier. After writing, 'The suspect is telling the truth' on two sheets of paper, he wrote, 'The suspect is lying' on a third, then placed the paper in the machine.

Alec then escorted Steve to the men's room and told him, "Now take a piss or do whatever ya gotta do. When you're finished, be sure and wash your hands thoroughly as the lie detector is highly sensitive and requires the suspect to have clean hands or it won't work properly. Understand?"

Steve nodded and Alec left him in the room alone, or at least Steve thought. When he finished, Alec took him back to the interrogation room and said, "Gotta give the machine a few minutes to warm up. Be right back."

Alec went to Detective Booth and said, "Well?"

"All the little bastard did was piss, then turn on the water and stick one of his fingers under it," said Booth, who had been spying on Steve while hiding in a stall with his feet on a commode. The two chuckled, and Alec returned.

"Okay, machine's all ready to go. Come on."

While placing Steve's right hand on the copier lid and the colander on his head, Alec said, "Do you solemnly swear and affirm the answers you're about to give are the full truth and nothing but the truth?"

"Yo', it'll be the troof."

Steve looked like something out of the Twilight Zone as the green fluorescent light from the copier shined on his face; when he saw the truthful response fall in the carriage, he smiled.

"Are you as stupid as you look?" Alec asked next.

"No."

The positive response appeared again.

"Doin' good, Steve. Now for the last question. Did you break into a house today on A Street and steal the owner's personal property?"

"Hell no!"

After the 'The suspect is lying' showed up, Steve ripped the colander off and stomped it flat. "I guess ya got me, 'Tective Basil," Steve said before giving a full confession.

* * *

Steve's first information grossed over $50,000 worth of stolen property and marijuana. As he was not registered with the PGPD as an informant prior to giving the initial data, Alec settled the account with ten dollars from his pocket, and a three-piece combo from Colonel Sanders. Subsequently, Alec enrolled him as a C. I. which qualified him to be paid from departmental funds.

* * *

After a year in juvenile, Alec was transferred to homicide. When he first arrived, he felt like a 'Maytag Repairman,' as murders had considerably lessened in the county. During the lull period, he continued his education; one block of his instruction dealt with the history of organized law enforcement.

The *Bow Street Runners* have been called London's first professional police force. They were founded by the author Henry Fielding, and originally numbered just eight members.

Similar to the original 'Thief Takers,' men who would solve petty crimes for a fee, the *Bow Street Runners* represented a formalization and regularization of existing policing methods. What made the *Runners* different from others was their formal attachment to The Bow Street Magistrates' Office, and being paid with government funds.

The Runners worked from Fielding's office at number four Bow Street and did not patrol. Instead, they served writs and arrested offenders on authority passed to them by the magistrates, and traveled nationwide to apprehend criminals.

Bow Street Magistrates' Court closed in 2006, breaking its long association with law enforcement. *The Bow Street Runners* were the predecessors of the detectives at Scotland Yard.

After becoming familiar with them, Alec called himself a *Runner*, rather than a detective.

* * *

Homicide is defined as the killing of a human being by another human being, and is broken down into four categories: illegal, legal, justifiable and accidental. Within the realm of illegal homicide is murder—the *intentional* killing of a human by another person with malice aforethought. The two degrees of murder are determined by premeditation, or a lack thereof; therefore, a homicide is *not* necessarily a criminal act, whereas murder always is. Manslaughter is considered the unlawful killing of a human being without express or implied malice.

After he learned the legal definition of homicide, Alec came to the conclusion he wasn't a murderer as his actions fulfilled a cause. He then began referring to them as necessary 'events.'

* * *

On the morning of October 24, 1974, two armed suspects entered the *Sheriff's Liquor Store* located at the Kentland Shopping Center, in the 7500 block of Landover Road. The establishment was a 'mom-and-pop shop' owned and operated by eighty-year-old Roger Sheriff, the former Sheriff of Prince George's County, Sheriff Sheriff, and his seventy-six-year-old wife, Claire. As they offered a check-cashing service for patrons, a large amount of currency was always on hand.

While two gunmen demanded money, a truck from Kronheim Liquor Distributors parked in the rear. When the deliverymen unwittingly interrupted the holdup, one was handcuffed to a water pipe, and the other along with the Sheriffs, were ordered to lie face down on the floor. As the gunmen poured gasoline on them, the unhandcuffed deliveryman made a break and was shot in the back as he ran toward the front door. After the shot was fired, the gasoline was ignited.

While the victims burned, the suspects relieved the register of a small amount of cash and a .38-caliber revolver hidden under the counter; having missed over $10,000 in cash in the office, they made good their escape.

Upon the arrival of the Kentland Volunteer Fire Department Engine 33, all had expired except for Mr. Sheriff who was transported by the Maryland State Police helicopter to the Baltimore City Hospital Burn Care Center. Before his death, Mr. Sheriff was able to give a composite artist a detailed description of both suspects.

As the murders were the most infamous to ever have occurred in Prince George's County, the case was given top priority. After months of top-notched investigative efforts on the part of every police investigative agency in the DC area, Detective Arthur Hale, the lead investigator came to his wit's end when a good lead wasn't developed. When the Sheriff's son offered a $15,000 reward, the police switchboard and private line in BCI rang constantly.

Three months after the murders, Hale, at his choice, transferred to the sex squad and the case was reassigned to Alec. In less than two years, Alec had been the lead investigator on ten murders, all of which closed with arrest.

After the .38 was recovered by uniforms from a botched drug rip off in DC, detectives got a hit on it through the *National Crime Information Center*. Upon receiving the news, Alec and Hale responded to DC Police Headquarters on Indiana Avenue NW.

When advised he was a suspect in the murder of four people in Maryland, the person who 'rented' the gun named his girlfriend's cousin as the person who had furnished it.

The perpetrators were brothers from Northeast Washington. During one of the surreptitious taped conversations recorded before arrests were made, the elder brother, a career criminal who had served time at the *Lorton Correctional Facility* for various crimes of violence, admitted to having shot an off-duty DC Police Officer in the face a few years earlier at the *Aquatic Gardens* apartment complex in N.E. Washington when he attempted to rob him—a crime for which he was never connected to. Another taped conversation revealed that the younger brother had worked as a driver at one of the trucking companies in the Ardwick-Ardmore Industrial Center on Pennsy Drive, close to the liquor store.

After being given an order by Strump to obtain arrest warrants, Alec said, "L. T., I don't think we have enough yet. Morgan runs a tight ship. He's gonna want more."

"After they cop, we'll have what we need. Lock 'em up. Boss is gettin' on my ass 'bout overtime."

"But Lieutenant—"

"No buts about it. Do it."

* * *

The brothers were interrogated for sixteen straight hours and held firm to their claim of non-involvement. Finally, the career criminal admitted to having been in the area during the incident, but denied participation in it. The two were subsequently charged with the murders and incarcerated in the Prince George's County Jail on Main Street in Upper Marlboro.

After the suspect's arraignment, Alec, Strump and Hale met with State's Attorney Alan A. Morgan to 'screen' the case. After hearing the evidence, Morgan looked up from behind his bifocals and said, "I take it you *have* arrested the right people here; *haven't* you?"

"They're the right ones," Alec answered defensively.

"Look at these witnesses. Nothin' but a bunch of cutthroats and thieves," Morgan said as he shuffled mug shots.

"We didn't believe the Buddhist Monk, nun and priest they usually hang out with. Had to settle for these guys instead," Alec snapped as he began gathering his paperwork.

"Settle down, Alec," Strump said as Morgan looked on irritatingly and Alec stormed out.

* * *

Normally, the prosecutor will send a felony or serious misdemeanor case to the grand jury for indictment—this time, however, was the exception. Rather than dismissing the charges for what he considered to be a lack of evidence, and possibly undergo public scrutiny for not prosecuting a high-profile offense, Morgan, the elected official, chose to send the matter to the district court.

The judge there chose not to be the goat, and held the suspects over for trial. When he heard the decision, Morgan capitulated and dropped the charges.

* * *

"Chief Street, haven't seen ya in awhile, sir. How ya been?" Alec said as he casually saluted.

"All right. How 'bout, you?" Street answered curtly.

"Was doin' okay 'til Morgan's DTP."

"That's why we're here, sit down," Street said coldly. "Is there anything else you can do on the liquor-store murders?"

"Maybe more surveillance. But I can't imagine anything short of a confession'll change Morgan's mind," Strump answered.

"Then just drop it. It's already cost the county a fortune, and considerable embarrassment. Enough's enough."

"So be it," Alec said disgustedly.

On the way home, Alec said, "Cove Road? Fuck it, not worth the bother. Not anything in it for me except a boatload a shit. It *would* be nice to see those two fuckers go out the same way they sent out those old people though."

* * *

Two months later, the elder brother was rendered paralyzed from the neck down after being shot in the throat by his girlfriend. "Couldn't've done better myself," Alec said after learning the news. "Now if somethin' good like that'd happen to the other bastard, that'd make things a little more square."

ALEC BAZEY. Esq.

When Alec and several white officers got passed over for sergeant, he called the President of the Fraternal Order of Police Lodge 89. "Donny, Alec Bazey."

"If you're calling to bitch about the promotions, I'll tell ya like I told the other guys. The union won't take a stand 'cause black members'll be adversely affected if the department promotes according to the order of the list," the president flatly said.

"Then why did I spend all that time studyin', and why do they even have a list?"

"Search me. All I know is that the county can promote however they see fit."

"That's bullshit, man."

"Bullshit, cowshit, flyshit. Call it whatever ya want. It's their department," he answered flippantly.

"You're a hell of a union man."

"I'll get elected again."

"Thanks."

Click.

* * *

His last day on the department, Alec reviewed the homicide log book for the period he had spent in the unit. After compiling his numbers, he proudly said, "Fifty-nine homicides investigated, fifty-six homicides closed. Not bad for a little polewhop from Hollandtown."

* * *

Alec was warmly greeted by Winfield Bradley, of Bradley, Bradley and Claggett, on Main Street in Upper Marlboro. "You'll be workin' with Gary Nielsen. He's a former prosecutor from the PG State's Attorney's Office."

"Welcome aboard," Nielsen said.

"Good to be aboard."

For the first few months, Alec was assigned civil cases and traffic offenses; his mettle would be tested when a fifteen year old shot and killed a PG Police Officer.

The incident began when the youth was arrested for breaking into coin-operated machines in the Palmer Park Shopping Center. Tyrone

Jackson, a spirited high-school wrestling star, albeit small in stature, was quick and wiry.

"Back off, your breath stinks," Officer Schwartz said when Jackson got nose to nose with him while answering questions for the arrest record.

"Fuck you," Jackson replied, spraying Schwartz's face.

Schwartz grabbed Jackson by his collar, and dragged him in the fingerprinting room and shut the door. "I'll show ya fuck you, ya little son of a bitch," Schwartz shouted as he reached for his blackjack in the slit pocket.

After Jackson evaded a swipe, he grabbed the handle of Schwartz's service revolver holstered in an open-top Bucheimer that had been gifted to him by his father after his retirement. As the stitching was weak, Jackson was able to rip the weapon clear from the retaining clip.

As they wrestled for the Smith & Wesson, Jackson was able to get off two shots. While Schwartz lay dying, Jackson emptied the gun, narrowly missing other officers. Before they could return fire, Jackson ran through the entrance door as an officer walked toward him. 'Clicka, clicka, clicka, clicka, clicka, clicka.'

When Jackson realized the weapon was empty, he slid it in the officer's direction like a shuffleboard quoit, and the officer reholstered his Colt. Jackson was arrested and sequestered while Schwartz gurgled blood and edema.

* * *

Jackson quickly became a *Cause Célèbre* after local activist groups supported his claim of self-defense. Community fundraisers and donations soon provided sufficient funds for the Jackson family to employ the Law Firm of Bradley, Bradley and Claggett for their son's defense.

"Think Alec can handle it, or should I assign someone else to ya?" Bradley asked Nielsen.

"Alec's sharper than cheddar, he'll do fine. Besides he knows his way 'round the police department."

"Don't know if that'll be good or bad. Might not give it his best effort defendin' a cop killer," Bradley, a millionaire attorney and owner of a 300-acre tobacco farm in Croom replied.

"Don't worry 'bout Alec, boss."

"What about that incident when he shot those robbery suspects. Do ya think the news'll try and make somethin' outta that?" Bradley asked as small bursts of flames emitted from tobacco being lit as he puffed on a jumbo ivory-bowled pipe carved in the shape of a Viking's head.

"Just proves how ballsy he is. He was also hangin' out the window of the cruiser goin' over a hunnert miles an hour, if ya remember. Viet combat vet, too."

"Any problems in Nam?"

"Only if ya call gettin' a Purple Heart and Bronze Star a problem. Believe me, he'll do fine, boss."

"Okay, keep 'em. I agree with ya."

* * *

The Barnum & Bailey Three-Ring Circus couldn't hold a candle to the display put on by the media in front of the Upper Marlboro Courthouse on Main Street the first day of trial. Interview and camera teams were lined up from Water Street to the entrance of the Marlboro Volunteer Fire House interviewing anyone willing to speak. Nearly all maintained the same theme—'Free Tyrone Jackson.'

"The Prince George's County Poleece havin' been murderin' innocent black people for years. It's high time we fought back. I think they oughta give Mr. Jackson a medal," said an angry demonstrator profiling before a camera.

"It's an injustice even puttin' the innocent victim on trial. Should release the poor chil' and let 'em go on," said another.

When a crew from WRC set up a transmitting tower twenty feet tall in front of the firehouse, the chief said, "If you don't get that shit outta here, I'm gonna have y'all arrested."

As Jackson and his family walked down Main Street, the crowd began to chant like they were at a Redskin playoff game in RFK. "Free Ty-rone, free Ty-rone, send him home, he's innocent to the bone, free Ty-rone!"

The consummate politician chose to stand as the prosecutor, although several members of his staff advised against it. Nevertheless, Morgan maintained it was his civic duty and moral obligation to handle the matter himself; it was also an election year.

* * *

"Mornin', Mr. Morgan," Nielsen said as they entered the courtroom.

"G'morning, Gary. Long time no see," he said, ignoring Alec's presence.

"Same church, different pew. You familiar with my partner, Alec Bazey?"

As he cut his bulgy blue eyes at Alec, Morgan said, "Yes, we've had occasion to meet on another matter a few years back."

"All rise," shouted the bailiff as the judge entered the room. "The honorable Edgar Sasscer sitting for the State of Maryland and Prince George's County. Be seated and come to order please."

After two days and 157 strikes from the panel of jurors, a jury was selected. "Good group," Nielsen said as six African-American males, two white males and four females filed into the box.

"Ya sure you're okay with this?" Nielsen asked Alec.

"Yeah, I'm good. Cops and fireman are killed every day. That's life in the big city. Besides, it's what I do now, defend criminals," Alec said as thoughts of Luke's death and his mother's murder flashed through his mind.

* * *

After two weeks, it appeared the trial could go either way, until a noted psychiatrist from Los Angeles took the stand. Phyllis Drone was a respected expert in the field of persons abused by authoritative and/or superior forces; she charged $1,000 an hour, with a five-hour minimum.

Drone's testimony included dialogue between her and Jackson whereas he admitted to having been physically and verbally abused by his father. Further testimony on her behalf included Jackson acting out against Schwartz in an extreme fit of anger, causing him to lose his sanity during the nine seconds the incident lasted. She further testified that Jackson regained his senses when he observed the armed police officer in the hallway. Despite Morgan's objections, all of her testimony was admitted into evidence and savored by the jury.

"She fried us," Morgan whispered to Deputy State's Attorney Michael Weller when Drone left the stand.

"Didn't help us any at all," Weller replied when he saw two female jury members in tears.

"She slayed 'em. Was worth every penny," Nielsen said lowly to Jackson with his right hand against the left side of his face.

When Alec saw looks of anguish on the officer's faces, his zeal cloyed.

* * *

"Hello," Alec said at 4 a.m.

"Alec, this is Addison Bradley. Did I wake ya?"

"No, I had to get up and answer the phone. What's up?"

"Gary had a heart attack 'bout an hour ago. He's in intensive care at Prince George's Hospital. You're gonna have to go it alone tomorrow."

"Is he gonna make it?"

"Too early to tell. He's in surgery as we speak."

"Yeah, I'll be okay. Gary was gonna let me give closin' anyway."

"Great. I'll keep ya posted on his condition."

"Please do."

Alec got up, made coffee and began rehearsing. When *Sympathy for the Devil* came on the radio and he heard the comparison between cops and criminals in the song, he thought of the daunting task that lay before him. "If this little bastard walks like I think he's gonna, I'll be goin' back to *Cove Road*," he said.

"Therefore, my client, a mere youth of but fifteen years, fearing for his life at the hands of Corporal Schwartz, disarmed him and defended himself against serious bodily injury or death—I rest my case."

"Order in the court, order in the court, order in the court," Judge Sasscer shouted as he pounded his gavel when the crowd went berserk.

Although eloquent and emotional, Morgan's closing was pale in comparison. With defeat seemingly imminent, Morgan said to Weller as the jury left the courtroom to begin deliberations, "Tyrone Jackson hasn't been on trial here, the Prince George's County Police Department and their sordid reputation has."

When the jury returned, Edward Claggett, Bradley, Bradley and Claggett's junior partner, nudged Alec and whispered, "They were out less than three hours; no doubt about it—they found our boy *not guilty*."

Alec glanced at his Seiko, nodded and replied, "Two hours and forty-six minutes to be exact. I agree with ya, Eddie."

After the judge opened the envelope and read the verdict, he returned it to the bailiff and said, "Mr. Foreman, how do you find the defendant?"

"We the jury, find the defendant, Tyrone Aloysius Jackson, not guilty of all charges."

Nearly everyone in the courtroom reacted as did those in Times Square when the end of WW II was announced. "Hallelujah, hallelujah, hallelujah. Justice has been served!"

"Order in the court, order in the court," Judge Sasscer insisted as Alec sighed and began gathering his belongings.

"Great job, Alec," Claggett said as he patted him on the back.

"Congratulations, Alec," Morgan said in frustration as he extended his hand.

Alec didn't react to the accolades and watched as the stunned widow and her three fatherless children left the courtroom in tears and disbelief.

"Thanks, Mr. Bazey. Ya done your best work, sir," Jackson said.

Ya ain't seen nothin' yet, Alec said to himself.

* * *

In order to avoid contact, Alec slipped out the back door of the courthouse. "How's Gary doin'?" he asked the secretary as he entered his office.

"Last report we got said he was in ICU. When he's able, they're gonna transfer 'em to the Washington Hospital Center."

"Can he have any visitors yet?"

"Immediate family only."

"Do ya know the address at WHC?"

"Yeah, one-ten Irving Street in Northwest D.C., right off Michigan Avenue."

"Thanks, Marcie."

"Heard ya won the trial."

"Yeah, we won," Alec said.

"Don't sound very happy 'bout it."

Alec raised his eyebrows and bit his lip as he tucked away the address. When he got to his office, the intercom buzzed. "Line one's for you, Alec."

"Alec Bazey, may I help ya?"

"Yeah, you can go fuck yourself, ya miserable piece of turncoat shit," the unidentified voice said.

"I guess that's all I deserve," Alec said after the caller hung up.

"Line two, Alec," the secretary said while all the lights on the phone panel blinked.

"Alec Bazey."

"Do ya feel proud of yourself? Ya Judas bastard."

Click.

"Marcie, I'm gonna take the rest of the day off. No doubt I'll be gettin' a *lotta* calls today. Take a message if they'll leave one, okay?" Alec said as he headed toward the door.

"I understand," she said as she picked up the phone. "Bradley, Bradley and Claggett—just a moment, I'll see if he's in. Alec, it's the FOP President," she said with her hand over the voice piece.

"I'll take it in my office."

"Donny, Alec Bazey. What can I do for ya?"

"Alec, I'm gonna be up front with ya."

"How's that?"

"The board and I along with the membership are quite disappointed with the zealousness ya displayed in your defense of that little piece a shit. We expected more from a former brother in blue. Whadda ya got to say for yourself, boy?"

Alec's first inclination was to explain his position as defense counsel. He realized, however, that was exactly what the president wanted him to do. He remembered what Ronald Reagan said to one of his opponents during a debate: "If you're explainin', you're losin'."

"Alec, ya still there?"

"I'm still here, Donny."

"Then whadda ya got to say for yourself?"

"Nothin' *to* say. Anything else ya wanna talk about? How's your golf game? Heard ya won the FOP Tournament last month."

"Okay, I'll just tell the guys ya don't give a fuck."

"Do what ya think's best, Donny."

"Don't look to the FOP for any support in your practice."

"The lack of support from the FOP's the reason I left the department when I did."

"If that's the way ya wanna play it—that's the way we'll play it."

"Bye, Donny."

When Alec got home that afternoon, he took a muscle relaxer. Before dozing off, he remembered the look of bewilderment on the Schwartz family. "The first thing he'll do is buy some weed," Alec said as his wheels turned.

* * *

"Mr. Bradley, Alec Bazey here."

"Alec, I tried several times to call you last evening and your line kept ringin' busy. Was it outta service?"

"No, sir. Kept gettin' crank calls, so I disconnected it. C&P's gonna gimme a new number this afternoon; I'll call and give it to Marcie when I get it."

"Cops harrasin' ya, huh?"

"Yeah. I guess they're frustrated over the verdict."

"Alec, ya did an outstandin' job. A seasoned veteran couldn't've done better. Congratulations, son. Now what can I do for ya?"

"I'd like to take the rest of the week off. Got some personal business to take care of."

"Been neglectin' your girlfriend, huh?"

"Nothin' like that. It's a family matter I have to deal with."

"Take as much time as ya need, son, you deserve a little time off after that ball buster of a trial."

"Thank ya, sir. Any word on Gary?"

"His wife called a bit ago and said he's still in ICU."

"Takin' any visitors?"

"Not yet."

"Thanks, Mr. Bradley. See ya Monday."

"See ya Monday, son."

That afternoon, after Alec located the carved X, he said, "Glad to see you guys're still workin' *undercover*," as he unloaded 'gardening' equipment from his rented van.

* * *

The following day, Alec drove to Palmer Park and waited until

Jackson left his residence and began walking. After he entered the last duplex on Greenleaf Road, Alec said, "Should I take 'em when he comes out, or wait'll later? Fuck it, no time like the present."

Alec then parked the van bearing 'dead' tags he had replaced the good ones with, adjacent to an open area. After repositioning the driver's outside mirror and sliding open the side door, he jumped in the back and watched as Jackson approached. With the speed of a Himalayan Snow Leopard, he placed a noose around Jackson's neck and jerked him in as he slid the door shut. While sitting on Jackson's chest, Alec said, "If ya think I did good work in court, whadda ya think of this?" as he clinched the ligature.

When Jackson's eyes stopped bulging and he went limp, Alec stuffed him in a body bag. "Nobody in sight," he said as he snatched a small plastic bag from the rear floorboard. "Acapulco Gold. Celebratin' with the good stuff," Alec said when he threw the bag from the window as he passed Landover Mall.

* * *

While he was *looking for the passage back to the place he was before,* Alec saw *a shimmering light in the distance,* and turned in. *"Relax, said the night man, we are programmed to receive. You can checkout anytime you like — but you can never leave,"* Alec sang after he killed the beast and registered him in — *The Hotel.*

LOUIE XIII

Disgruntled police officers continued to badger the Law Firm of Bradley, Bradley and Claggett, especially its junior member. Following a scathing article in the FOP Newsletter, 'traitor scum,' was sprayed painted on Alec's new Monte Carlo while parked at the Prince George's County Service Building in Hyattsville. Subsequent to a paint job from Tommy's Auto Body in Upper Marlboro, Alec kept it locked in his garage and purchased an old Toyota from Foreign Car Parts on Brown Station Road.

* * *

The 1978 Maryland Gubernatorial Election produced Democrat Fritz Aldo Meindorf, the former Chairman of the Baltimore City Council as the new governor. Retired Baltimore City Police Captain Kenneth A. Rogers, also a council member, was elected lieutenant governor.

"Says here in the Washington Post the governor and his wife are originally from Illinois, and settled in Hollandtown in the late forties," Alec said as he read the Maryland Metro Section. "Also says Rogers was the BCPD Homicide Section Commander until he retired in 1975. Seems like I oughta know 'em both."

* * *

Shortly after the election, the attorney recruiter from Bennett & Lock, LLP, left a message for Alec.

"Linda Smythe, how may I help you?"

"Alec Bazey returning your call."

"Mr. Bazey, thanks for calling me back so promptly."

"No problem. What can I do for ya?"

"I don't know if you're familiar with our organization or not, but we're the largest law firm in D.C."

"Yeah, I heard a you guys, but didn't realize you were the biggest in town. What can l'il ol' *me*, do for you?"

"Messrs. Bennett and Lock would like to make an appointment to interview you for employment with the firm. Might you be interested?"

Alec, taken completely by surprise, replied, "Sure? When?"

"Can you come in this afternoon around three?"

"Yeah, I can do that. What's the address?"

"Fourteen o-one Fifteenth Street in Northwest at the corner of G."

"Room number?"

"We occupy the entire building. Come to the fourteenth floor and we'll meet in the conference room. Park in the underground lot."

"All right, see ya at three."

At two thirty, Alec pulled his Toyota between a Cadillac and a Bentley then proceeded to the fourteenth floor. "You must be Mr. Bazey. So nice to meet you," Linda said with a glow.

As he walked to the conference room, Alec gaped at the fixtures and expensive art work like someone out of the hills would gawk at skyscrapers the first time they saw them.

"Mr. Bazey, have a seat. I'm Harold Bennett and this is my partner, Martin Lock."

"Pleased to meet you, Mr. Bazey," Lock said.

"Call me Alec."

"Care for a drink, Alec?" Lock asked.

"Yes, a drink sounds good."

While removing the cork from the semicircular hand-blown glass container by *Baccarat*, Lock asked, "Have you ever tasted Louie the Thirteenth de Remy Martin?"

"No, sir. Only heard of it."

As he poured, Lock said, "Louie is manufactured from the grapes of Grande Champagne Terroir of Cognac. It's blended from eaux de vie, some more than a century in age, then aged again in tiercons—barrels that are several hundred years old. A quart sells for around fourteen hundred; the hand-blown crystal decanter alone sells for a hundred. The limited-edition, Spectaculaire, comes in a vessel embedded with a four-carat diamond. The company recommends dealers sell the limited edition for forty-three thousand. Louie the Thirteenth Black Pearl, is also limited, and packaged in individually-numbered Baccarat crystal carafes."

When Alec tasted the superb mixture, he said to himself, "If Mom and Dad could only see me now."

"How do you like it?" Bennett asked.

"Outstanding, sir."

"Care for more?" Lock said as he held the decanter by the neck.

"Sure," Alec replied as he extended his glass.

"Alec, would you consider coming to work for us?" Lock asked.

The decadence of the office and cognac aroused Alec's hedonistic nature, and he replied, "What would be the starting salary?"

"Our entry-level attorneys begin at fifty. In your case, we're prepared to offer sixty. Is that acceptable?"

Alec nearly choked when he heard the figure. Maintaining his cool, he answered, "What about expenses?" as his heart rate shot to ninety beats a minute.

"Expenses are paid in addition to the salary."

Alec nodded. While savoring the astonishing aftertaste on the back of his tongue, he said, "I have two questions."

"And they are?" Bennett said as he snipped the end of a cigar.

"First, what sort of work would I be doing?"

"Mostly civil-rights issues connected with a contract we have with the federal government. And the second question?"

You already answered it, Alec said to himself.

"Why me? Seems like your firm could hire any lawyer, especially one more experienced and not from 'Mayberry,' " he asked anyway.

"We do usually recruit more seasoned attorneys. When we go after young ones, they're graduates of Harvard, Yale, Dartmouth, Georgetown, and occasionally American. You graduated from Maryland, correct?"

"Yes, sir, I did. Quit after my freshman year, and finished through the University of Maryland University College; took all my classes off campus."

Bennett showed a slight scowl as he swished the cool end of his cigar in his glass. "Despite that, we want you because of your reputation in the minority community. By the way, did they ever find your defendant?"

"Not as far as I know," Alec answered as he sipped and looked at Lock.

"Haven't heard," Lock said as he shrugged and held up his palms.

"What's the verdict?" Bennett asked as he took a long drag and short taste.

Wracked with anticipation, Alec calmly finished the last of his Louie and replied, "The Bradleys have been awfully good to me; don't know if I can leave 'em."

"It's now or never, Alec," Bennett said as he tugged the pinpoints of his Eagle shirt.

Now or never. Dad always said that means they got more to give, Alec said to himself as Luke's image appeared before his mind's eye. Playing 'cat and mouse' appealed to Alec, and he said, "Is it okay if I have, say a day to consider it?"

"No, sir. If you turn us down, we're prepared to hire a female from Howard."

"I'm not prepared to answer now, pleased to have met you," Alec said as he walked toward the door. When he saw Lock cut a look at Bennett, he said to himself, Hold on—I think the fat lady's about to sing.

"How's seventy sound?" Bennett asked.

"Eighty."

"Seventy-five."

"Deal."

"Welcome to the firm. Are you by any chance a chess player?" Bennett said, as he cut Alec a sly look and handed him a cigar.

"No, sir, I'm not. I *have* been told I'm a great poker player though."

"No doubt in my mind."

SMALL BLOOD-SUCKING ANIMALS

HEROES, Inc., an acronym for Honor Every Responsible Officer's Eternal Serving, is an organization that supports the families of fallen firefighters and police officers in the Washington, D.C. metropolitan area.

Although he was an exceptional athlete, golf didn't come easy to Alec. When the pro at the Bowie Golf and Country Club pointed out that golf spelled backwards is flog, Alec laughed and agreed, but stuck with the game anyway, and participated in the HEROES Golf Tournament held every July at the Indian Springs Country Club in Silver Spring: a two-day affair, and the organization's largest fundraising event.

On Alec's last visit, noted political-humorist, Mark Russell, emceed the dinner banquet and offered his interpretation of the word politician. "The dictionary defines poli, as many, and tics, as small blood-sucking animals. Therefore, politician is defined as many small blood-sucking animals," Russell quipped.

* * *

Despite the considerable number of Prince George's County Police Officers who resided in Bowie, Alec's first bid for a seat on the city council there won him election.

As with most politicians, he became intoxicated with the power and prestige of elected office. When the Maryland Secretary of State suddenly died, Alec's name appeared on the list of possible replacements. "Kenny, are you familiar with Alec Bazey on the Bowie City Council?" Governor Meindorf asked his lieutenant.

"Yeah, I know 'em. He's from Hollandtown. In fact, his brother was killed by the police when him and another kid held up the bank across from the bakery."

"I remember that. Detective Saukas was in when we saw it go down. Offered my Luger and services. Have state police do a background on 'em. All I know about 'em is that he's a Democrat, and popular with the black community in PG because of that kid he defended for killin' a cop."

"I'll take care of it."

"Thanks, Kenny."

* * *

When the investigation was complete, Rogers met with the governor. "Bazey's clean as a Safeway chicken. Hell of a background."

As he removed a Reemsta Peter Stuyvesant from a silver case and tamped the labeled end on his desk, Meindorf said, "Go on."

"Born on June sixth nineteen forty-four at St. Joe's before it moved to Towson."

June six, forty-four, remember that date well, Meindorf said to himself as he French inhaled the smoke. Was having breakfast with Himmler when we received news of the invasion.

"His natural father, Paul Pinski, was with the hundred and first airborne. Killed at Foucarville and won the Medal of Honor."

Fourcarville: the first French town to fall to the Allies; beginning of the end for the Reich, Meindorf's mental conversation continued.

"He graduated from BCC in sixty-two. His stepfather, Luke Bazey, with whom I was quite familiar, was a city fireman killed at the Adamco Fertilizer Company in fifty-five. He also won the Silver Star on Iwo Jima."

"I remember that fire—called it Baltimore's Valentine's Day Massacre. If I remember correctly, four fireman were killed."

"Five."

"Yes, five," the governor replied as he took another drag and shook his head.

"Joined the army in sixty-three; served with the hundred and seventy-third airborne in Vietnam; awarded a Purple Heart and Bronze Star; went to college for a year, then joined the PGPD; was present when Governor Wallace was shot in Laurel, helped apprehend Bremer; assigned to homicide for five years, handled some fifty-plus cases, most of 'em closed; finished law school at night; started with the Bradley Law Firm in Marlboro, who he was with when he defended the cop killer; went to Bennett and Lock, the big firm in DC; elected to the Bowie City Council in the last election."

"That *is* a hell of a bio," the governor replied as he choked out his Stuyvesant. "Any criminal background?"

"None that'll show up."

"What's that mean?"

"Got in a scrape when he was a little kid when his brother and some of his Yahoo friends killed a derelict. State's attorney called it self-defense."

"Married? Kids?"

"Bachelor, no kids."

"He's thirty-six and never been married?"

"Yes, sir. Never married."

"Any indications of homosexuality?"

The hair on the back of Rogers' neck tingled. "Being a bachelor doesn't necessarily mean you're a sissy. Look at me."

The governor nodded and said, "Call and see if he'll accept the position."

* * *

"Of course I'll take it," Alec answered enthusiastically.

"Good, I'll call ya back before the week's over and let ya know when the appointment's approved. The governor has a lotta pull with the general assembly. I'm sure they'll go for it."

"Thanks, Kenny. Looking forward to meetin' ya."

"Same here," Rogers answered as he gazed at Alec's manly cut in the photograph of him he was preparing for a press release.

After the swearing-in ceremony in Annapolis, Rogers said, "Welcome to the team, Mr. Secretary," as he shook Alec's hand. When Alec looked in his eyes and felt the touch, he knew Rogers was gay.

"Thanks, Kenny. I know which team *you're* on, and you can add me to the list," Alec said as a ploy. Rogers' heart skipped a beat when Alec winked and smiled.

"This isn't the *first* time we've met, Alec. In fact, we've met a couple a times."

"Really? When?"

"The first time was when I was a rookie homicide detective, and you were eight years old. The second time was when your sister died; I handled both investigations."

"I guess ya know about my mother and brother as well, huh?" Alec asked defensively.

"Yes. In fact, I investigated your brother's death when your uncle killed 'em."

"When my *uncle killed 'em?* You talkin' 'bout Dom Sabitini?"

"Yeah, Sergeant Sabitini. I figured ya knew."

"Ya figured wrong. Thanks for sharing that with me," Alec answered as he stressfully frowned.

"I meant no harm, Alec. I really didn't."

"No offense taken, Kenny," Alec said as he patted him on the shoulder. "Listen, why don't you and the governor join me and my family at Middleton's. We reserved the party room."

"Oh, I'd love to. The governor won't be able to attend; he has a speaking engagement in Baltimore," Rogers answered as his heart fluttered.

"Just you then. 'Bout a half hour, okay?"

"Ciao. See ya shortly."

THE ADAPTATION

In college, Alec learned that contrary to popular belief, Darwin never used the term 'survival of the fittest.' Instead, he said those organisms possessing characteristics that enable them to *adapt to changes in their environment* have the best chances of survival.

* * *

Middleton Tavern is a popular hangout in downtown Annapolis for local politicians, and is housed in an eighteenth-century building where slaves were once traded. It's a half block from the city dock, and adjacent to 'Ego Alley,' a canal off the Severn River where extravagant watercraft are often profiled by their owners.

"Over here," Alec shouted when he saw Rogers enter.

"Sorry I'm late, Alec. Stopped off on Duke of Glouchester for a trim."

"Gotta keep up that Caesar Romero image, huh?" Alec said with a grin. "This is the Maryland Lieutenant Governor," Alec said in introduction of Rogers to his party.

While Rogers waved as if campaigning, Chooch said, "Lieutenant— not like Hatfield I hope."

Choochie's been loose lipped with that Hatfield shit lately, especially when he's drinkin', Alec said to himself. "Hey, Chooch, lighten up, okay?" Alec said with derision.

"Oh, sorry, Mr. Big Time."

"Have another shooter," Alec said as he handed him a plastic cup.

After he sucked down a combination of a raw oyster, vodka, worcestshire sauce, Tabasco, lemon juice, and chased it with a gulp of Bud, Chooch said, "Ol' Alec, *my buddy*. Forgot his little friends and what they did for 'em way back when. Or should I say, what they *didn't* do to 'em?"

Alec glared as Chooch sulked. You're beginning to pose a security risk, Choochie, Alec said to himself.

When the party broke up, Alec said, "Thanks for comin', everybody, really appreciate it."

"Alec, ya know where your office is, right?" Rogers said as he headed out.

"Room three-ten: same as my mom's birthday," he answered with a smile.

"All right. See ya."

"We're really proud of ya, Alec," Henry said.

"Thanks, guys. Couldn't've done it without ya," he answered as he hugged them all.

"Come on, getting' late," Chooch yelled angrily from the front door.

"Hold on a minute," Alec said to the others as he walked toward Chooch.

"Man, what's your fuckin' problem?" Alec asked with sparks.

"*You're* my fuckin' problem. If it wasn't for you, I wouldn't be a crip'. Look at me, half a man. Gotta a mind to give your murderin' ass up," Chooch answered acerbically.

"Chooch, be cool," Alec said as he looked at the attentive customers.

After Alec shoved him outside, he said, "I love ya, Choochie. I'm sorry things turned out the way they did."

"I'm sorry, man. Please forgive me, brother. I'm happy for ya."

As they embraced, Carol exited and said, "What's goin' on here?"

"Choochie just had a little too much to drink, that's all. He'll be all right now."

"Yeah, I'm good. We're still buddies. Right, Al?"

"John, you gotta quit drinking. This is the last time. No more, understand?" Carol said angrily as Chooch nodded shamefacedly. "He just hasn't been himself since he got turned down for promotion."

"I understand, Sis. You drive, okay? Traffic's murder on three-o-one this time a day."

"We'll be okay. Love ya. C'mon, Choochie," Carol said as she took him by the hand.

On his way home, Alec stopped at the 7-11 in Hilltop Plaza and bought a cup of coffee. As he sipped, he reflected on the events of the day. "Dad was a hell of a man. He knew if he told me Dom did Victor, it would've broken my heart. God, I miss him," Alec said as he broke into a crying jag.

* * *

"Hello," Alec said when he answered his telephone the next morning

"Alec, boy. How ya doin', man?"

"Damn, I thought you'd still be in bed after the one ya tied on yesterday," Alec replied as he looked at the alarm clock on the vanity.

"No. Carol and me got up early and did some serious talkin'," an upbeat Chooch said.

"Oh?"

"She convinced me to do somethin' 'bout my drinkin'. Gonna call AA today and see if I can enroll with 'em at Parkside Methodist on Mannasota. Group of alkies meet from seven 'til nine every Monday and

Thursday night."

"That's great, pal. If there's any way I can help, please call."

"Thanks, man. After yesterday I wasn't sure if you'd still be talkin' to me."

"Shit did get pretty rank there for awhile. Glad to hear you're gonna take care a business."

"Me, Carol and Y. A. are gonna celebrate with breakfast at the White Coffee Pot on Pulaski Highway. Care to join us? We'll wait for ya."

"No, buddy. Due in court at nine."

"Hook up on the weekend?"

"Sounds good. Y'all come over on Saturday. Just got a new gas barbie. Can't wait to try it out."

"Sounds like a plan. See ya Saturday."

* * *

"My name is John Marco Baranco, *and I am an alcoholic,*" Chooch said at his first meeting. After applause, Chester Karczewski explained how support from AA members helped him manage his disease. Later, Chester agreed to act as Chooch's sponsor.

* * *

Chooch adjusted well to life without spirits and things returned to normal in the Baranco household. Four months after he began the *Twelve Step Program,* Carol enlightened him with news of a forthcoming addition to their family.

A week later, Chooch met with a group of coworkers at *Johnny Unitas' Golden Arm Restaurant* on York Road in Towson. He dined on the house specialty that night: a soufflé consisting of six monster shrimp, covered with a garlic and butter-based crab batter. When he saw a carafe of wine, he said, "Hell, one drink won't hurt."

When the party broke up, Chooch went to the bar and ordered straight Smirnoff and a Bud chaser. When several Baltimore Colts arrived, he reminded them of the team's humbling defeat at the hands of the New York Jets and Joe Namath in Super Bowl III, some eleven years earlier. "Ain't nothin' but a fuckin' bunch of Prima Donnas. You dickheads *belong* in the AFC. Even the Redskins could beat your lame asses," he shouted as he was escorted out by two bouncers.

When he got home, Carol said furiously, "John, you've been drinking."

"That's right, I have. What're you gonna do about it? Ya two-bit whore."

When Carol looked through the storm door and saw steam rising from their car along with front-end damage, she screamed, "What in God's name happened to our car?"

"Shut the fuck up and sit down, bitch," he answered as he pushed her on the sofa.

"I most certainly will not," Carol responded as she sprang up. "I'm gonna call Alec."

"Alec ain't nothing' but a lousy back-shootin' bastard. Doesn't have the balls to meet me face-to-face, even with my one arm," he shouted as he snatched the phone from her.

When Carol scooped her son and headed for the front door, Chooch grabbed the back of her collar and threw her down. "You leave my mommy alone," Y. A. yelled as he pushed Chooch away.

"Get outta my way, boy," Chooch answered as he delivered a backhand.

Carol then punched Chooch in the balls. "Auuuugh," he screamed as he doubled over. Carol snatched Y. A. and headed toward the door again.

Before they could get away, Chooch pushed Carol on the floor and beat her in the face with a fly swatter; when she rolled over, he kicked her in the ribs.

"Stop, stop, stop," Y. A. shouted as he kicked his father in the balls for a second time. He assisted his mother and they made good their escape as Chooch gasped for air.

Carol and Y. A. ran three houses up and began frantically beating on the door. When the owner answered, Chooch had Carol by her hair and yelled, "Take that, ya haughty bitch," as he kicked her in the solar plexus while she lay on the sidewalk. "Take that, shit breath," the neighbor, a city cop said as Chooch 'tasted teak.'

* * *

"Alec, can you get over here right away?" Henry said when he called.

"Sure. What's up?" Alec answered anxiously.

"Chooch got drunk and beat up Carol and Y. A."

"You gotta be shittin' me. Where are they now?"

"They're here with us."

"On my way."

"Has he gone outta his mind?" Alec said as he entered the Harbor Tunnel Throughway. "I'll rip the Adam's apple from that pencil-necked-geek's throat. Better yet, I'll rip off his other arm—and both legs. Son of a bitch!"

* * *

"Who's there?" Henry asked when he heard a knock.

"It's me, Unc'."

When Alec entered, he saw Carol and Y. A. pitifully sobbing. "How'd ya get those marks on you face?" he asked as he rubbed Carol's matted wounds.

"John beat me with a fly swatter. Boo-hoo-hoo."

"Beat ya with what?" Alec asked furiously.

"A fly swatter," Carol answered as she showed him the weapon with a bent wire handle. "He said you were a back-shootin' bastard, too."

"What else did he say?" Alec asked pensively.

"Said you didn't have the nerve to meet 'em face to face."

"Is that all?"

"Isn't that enough?"

"Yeah. I'd say he said plenty. Did he hurt the baby?"

"X-rays didn't show any injury. Dad's gonna take me to the doctor tomorrow."

"How *you* doin', tiger?" Alec asked his namesake as he rubbed his bandaged face. "Daddy hurt me and Mommy, Uncle Al."

"I know, sport. Everything'll be all right, I promise."

Y. A.—Young Alec, idolized his 'Uncle' Al, and was placated by his assurance. "Where's Chooch now?" Alec asked.

"Locked up where he belongs. I have to go to his hearing in the morning."

"What time?"

"Nine thirty."

"I'll meet ya there."

"You can be my attorney, okay?"

"No problem, Sis. I'll see to it he doesn't go anywhere."

* * *

The next morning, Alec and Carol reported to the district court located in the basement of the eastern-district police station on Edison Highway. When the prisoners were brought in mutually bound, it reminded Alec of himself and the Hawks thirty years earlier.

Prior to Chooch's case being called, Alec met with the prosecutor and introduced himself. "Alec Bazey. I'm familiar with you," Jacob Silverstein said. "What brings you to our humble abode?"

"One of the defendants is my brother-in-law. He lost an arm in Vietnam savin' my life; frustration over it lead 'em to hittin' the bottle pretty hard. Came home drunk last night and beat up his wife and son.

He's not a bad person; think ya could recommend a psych evaluation?"

"Is that all right with you, Mrs. Baranco?"

"If Alec thinks that's best, it's fine with me."

"Consider it done."

* * *

"Mr. Baranco, do you understand the charges against you?" Judge Grindstaff asked Chooch standing before him wearing a gauze turban.

"Yes, sir, I do," Chooch replied as he glanced at Carol and his son.

"The prosecutor has requested that you undergo a mental observation. Are you in agreement?"

"A mental observation is fine with me, sir."

"Good answer. Had you said no, I wouldn't have set bond and let your hind parts set in central for sixty days," the judge answered as he looked at Carol's and Y. A'.s injuries. "You look to be a decent sort, Mr. Baranco. The prosecutor advises you're a war hero. Imagine that's where you lost your arm, correct?"

"Yes, sir, it is."

"Then lay off the booze, enroll in AA and stick to it. In your thirty-eight years you've never been arrested 'til now—isn't that telling you something? Why do you think it's called devil rum?"

" 'Cause it brings out the devil in ya," Chooch answered in a humble manner.

"Exactly right. Okay, enough. Mr. Bailiff make arrangements for Mr. Baranco. Next case."

* * *

The following evening, Alec visited Chooch in E wing at City Hospital. "How ya doin', buddy?"

"Okay, I guess. Dugan gave me a twenty-two stitcher."

"Hmmp," Alec said as he gazed at the bandages. Ya deserved more, he thought.

"How's Carol and Y. A.?" Chooch asked.

"They're at Henry's. Gonna stay there for awhile."

"Man, I really fucked up this time, huh?"

"I'd say ya caused some damage. Nothin' ya can't repair though."

Although Chooch was surprised at Alec's attitude, he was encouraged by it. "Man, I was dreadin' seein' you. I thought you were gonna rip my dick off."

"You know me, Choochie. Bein' the back-shootin' bastard I am, I'd have to wait 'til ya turned around before I did anything. Right?"

"What're ya talkin' 'bout?"

The son of a bitch doesn't remember, Alec said to himself.

"Nothin', man—nothin' at all," Alec answered as Chooch stared quizzically.

"Call your job tomorrow and tell 'em you got in an accident and need some time off. That'll explain your injuries and car. By the way, how'd ya wreck it?"

"Hit a group a Jersey barrels on the beltway, hell of a sight. Water and shit exploded all over the place," Chooch answered as he chuckled.

"At least ya didn't kill anybody—did ya?"

"No, just my car."

"All right, don't worry. I'll help ya work your way outta this mess."

"Thanks for everything, Al."

"Least I could do for the man who saved my life. Gettin' late. Gotta be in court in the morning."

As Alec kissed Chooch, he saw Michael Coreleone when he delivered the *'bocca de morte'* to Fredo; he then thought of Darwin, and remembered the heron.

* * *

"How's it goin', man?" Alec asked Chooch when he called a month later.

"Finally had the turban removed. Man that thing was a pain in the ass. People looked at me like I was Boris Karloff or somethin'."

"Been goin' to AA?"

"Yeah. Chester picks me up for the meetings. Keeps right on my ass. Ya know how 'em Pollocks are."

"Talked to Carol lately?"

"Yeah, she called for some money. Henry came by and picked it up."

"How'd that go?"

"He was kinda cool."

"He'll get over it. Just show 'em you're tryin'."

"I'd ask you to come by for a beer, but that ain't gonna happen. What's up with you?"

"That's why I called. Wanna show ya a piece of waterfront property I'm thinkin' about buyin' on Bear Creek. Ya familiar with it?"

"Not far from Eastpoint, right?"

"Few miles away."

"I know it. Been by 'ere a couple times. Nice area."

"Yeah, it is. Usta swim down 'ere."

"How much they askin'?"

"Gettin' it for a song—five thousand. Owner wants to sell it and move to Arizona."

"Sounds good. When ya wanna meet?"

"Let's say, Saturday around four thirty. Should gimme plenty a time to clean up after golf. Meet ya at Eastpoint by Fairlanes."

"Okay, see ya."

* * *

On Saturday, Chooch was waiting in his car when Alec arrived. "Choochie, follow me. Gotta stop by Two Guys, okay?"

"Lead the way."

After parking their vehicles, Alec said, "C'mon get in. I'll go in on the way back."

"Good to see ya. What kinda round ya shoot?" Chooch asked as he entered.

"Forty-four, forty-four."

"Man, this thing is sweet," Chooch said as he caressed the saddle-colored leather seats in Alec's new pickup. "Ya gonna bury somebody?" he asked when he looked in the bed.

"Was doin' some yard work at Kim's. Forgot to put the shovels and stuff back in the shed."

"How's it goin' with you and her?"

"Okay. She's a good kid. Got a great job with the US Department of Justice downtown."

"Engaged yet?"

"Not yet."

"Maybe one day," Chooch said.

"Yeah, maybe."

As *Night Moves* played on the cassette, feelings of nostalgia gripped Alec. He remembered Christine's voluptuous breasts and her warm sensual tongue softly lashing the underside of his penis before she kissed his scrotal area. "I'll check and see if she's in the motor-vehicle database," Alec said to himself when *Old Time Rock 'n Roll* broke his trance.

"Right up that way," Alec said when he stopped in front of a stake with a red ribbon tied on it and pointed.

As the two walked into the woods, Alec said to himself, "Maybe there's another way—it's not too late." As they ventured deeper, he remembered what Solari said on their last mission. "It's only a matter of time before he gives ya up. Gotta do 'em now," Alec whispered as he purposely dropped the satchel he was carrying and Chooch walked ahead. A few seconds later, Chooch said, "Alec, somebody *has* dug a grave."

"Blam!" the .45 in Alec's hand reported.

"Son of a bitch, he's still alive," Alec shouted when he saw Chooch taking short breaths as he lay face up on the ground. "Blam, blam, blam."

"Solari was right: dead men tell no tales," Alec said as he checked in another guest at *The Hotel*.

* * *

Before going home, Alec stopped in to visit his family and begin an alibi. "Anybody seen Choochie today?" Alec said.

"No. Why do you ask?" answered Carol.

"He was supposed to meet me today at the bowlin' alley in Eastpoint to look at some waterfront property, but he never showed up."

"Probably drunk again," Carol answered.

"Don't think so, Sis. I think he really learned his lesson this time."

"We'll see," Carol said skeptically as she rolled her eyes.

Alec picked up the phone and called Chooch's number. "Not home yet. I drove past the house and his car wasn't there either."

Carol shrugged her shoulders as she poured a glass of tea.

After dinner, Alec said, "Lemme try 'em again," as he picked up the phone and dialed Henry's number. "He's home now, line's busy," Alec said as he held the phone out for the others to hear the busy signal. A few minutes later, Alec dialed again and said, "Must've gone back out. I'm gonna go over and see what's goin' on. See y'all in a few minutes. Y. A., wanna take a walk, buddy?"

"Sure."

"Carol, gimme the house key."

When they got to Dudley Avenue and didn't see Chooch's car, Alec and Y. A. unlocked the door and entered.

"No car, no Chooch," Alec said when he returned and handed Carol the key.

"Probably at Leo's Hollywood Park, the Van Dykes are playing there."

"I'm gonna call it a day. Y. A., don't forget, Maryland-Penn State game Saturday."

"Ya gonna pick me up, right?"

"Be here at ten. On second thought, how 'bout I pick ya up on Friday after school and ya spend the night with me?"

"Okay, Mom?"

"Fine with me."

"Tell ya what. Spend Saturday night, too, then me, you and Kim can go over to Arlington and see the Iwo Jima Memorial and the cemetery. All right?"

"Can we come?" Henry asked boyishly.

"Sure. Meet us at my place on Sunday then you can bring Y. A. back. Save me a trip."

"It's a plan," Henry answered.

* * *

"Kid's better off without the drunk bastard," Alec said as he exited the Harbor Tunnel and headed toward the tollbooth. "Bastard woulda ended up killin' both of 'em. Did all of us a big favor."

* * *

"Alec, Chooch's boss just called and said they haven't seen or heard from him all week," Carol said when she called Alec the following Wednesday.

"Have *you* heard from 'em?" Alec asked.

"No, we were hoping you had."

"Not a word, Sis. Have ya talked to his family?"

"Yes, none of them have heard from 'em either."

"How 'bout his AA sponsor? Chester uh, uh, whatever."

"Karczewski. Yeah, I called him, too. I've tried everyone I can think of," Carol answered desperately.

"Called the police yet?"

"No. Think I should?"

"By all means, better yet, let me call."

As usual, Alec had all bases covered so as not to cast suspicion on him. "Okay, step one going into effect," he said as he dialed the number.

"City poleece," the call taker said.

"Good morning, missing persons unit, please."

"Hold on, I'll connect."

"Missing persons, Detective Smoltz."

"Detective Smoltz, Alec Bazey, Maryland Secretary of State. I'm sorry to bother you, but I need your help."

"Yes, sir, glad to be of assistance."

"Seems as though my brother-in-law's come up missing."

"How long?"

"Since last Saturday. He has a drinking problem and was recently arrested. He seemed to be doin' all right, then suddenly disappeared. Anything you can do to help?"

"Have ya checked the local shelters, family, friends and all that?"

"His wife said she's been in contact with everyone. I'd consider it a favor if you'd at least call and talk with 'er."

"Do better'n than that, Mr. Secretary. Gimme 'er name, number,

262

address and I'll go by. How's that?"

"Sounds great, I owe ya one. If ya ever need anything just call."

Smoltz was sitting in Henry and Lena's dining room interviewing Carol within an hour of Alec's call. After compiling a list of contacts and associates, Smoltz said to Carol, "Has he ever been missing before?"

"No, never, but he *does* have a drinking problem."

"I know, Mr. Bazey told me. Who's the last person that you know of that had contact with 'em?"

"My brother, I guess. He was supposed to have met him last Saturday at Eastpoint and he never showed. Later, around nine, Alec called him from here and the line was busy. After that, my son and him walked over to the house and he wasn't there."

"What kinda car does he drive?"

"A navy blue seventy-seven Chevy. Maryland tag GTH-three-two-seven. I have the other information about the car on the insurance papers," Carol replied.

"Okay, as soon as ya get it, call me and I'll put a lookout for him and the car. Anything else?" Smoltz asked.

"Yes, here's the name and number of his AA sponsor."

"Thanks, Mrs. Baranco. I'll get right on it," Smoltz said as he wrote.

* * *

After completing the necessary paperwork and entering Chooch's identity and vehicle information in NCIC as a critical missing person, Smoltz contacted Alec. "Mr. Bazey, line three's for you. Detective Smoltz from the police," the receptionist called over the intercom.

"Step two," Alec said before he picked up the phone. "Alec Bazey, how may I help you?"

"Mr. Bazey, Detective Smoltz. The reason I'm calling is because Mrs. Baranco told me you were the last person known to have contact with her husband. Is that accurate?"

"As far as I know."

After confirming what Carol had informed him, Smoltz said, "And you got a busy signal at his house around nine, right?"

"Yeah, I called and the line was busy, then called back and it just rang. When my nephew and I went to his house, neither Mr. Baranco or his car was there. What's up? Have you had contact with 'em?"

"No, sir. Just trying to verify information."

"Know how that goes. I'm a former police officer myself."

"Oh really, what department?"

"I was one of Prince George's County's finest."

"Good department," Smoltz said.

"For the most part, I would agree. Anything else I can help ya with, Detective?"

"No, sir, that's it for now."

"Feel free to call if I can help in any way."

"Thank ya, sir. I'll keep ya informed."

"That oughta take care of that," Alec said after he hung up the phone.

* * *

On Saturday afternoon, as they were watching the football game at Byrd Stadium, Alec fantasized that he was leading the Maryland Terrapins. "Your Uncle Alec was a football player in high school," he said to Y. A.

"I know, mom said you were a really good quarterback for City. I'm gonna be a quarterback, too," Y. A. answered. "Is my dad ever gonna come back, Uncle Al?" a misty-eyed Y. A. asked.

"When he's ready, buddy," Alec answered stoically.

"Do ya think he's okay?"

"I'm sure he's fine wherever he is. Hey, how 'bout some peanuts?" Alec said as the vendor stopped at their aisle.

"Yeah, peanuts."

"Two please," Alec said.

* * *

Two weeks after Chooch was reported missing, the manager of Two Guys reported to the Baltimore County Police Department that a Chevrolet appeared to have been abandoned on the store parking lot. The responding officer confirmed the vehicle was registered to John and Carol Baranco, and was wanted in connection with a critical missing person. Upon notification of the discovery, Detective Smoltz responded to the point of recovery.

After conducting a canvass of the area in an attempt to locate anyone who had observed activity connected to the vehicle, Smoltz had it seized and placed in storage at the Baltimore City Impound Lot. The vehicle was subsequently searched and processed for fingerprints, then released to Carol.

THE V

"Alec, I have a favor to ask of you," Governor Meindorf said.

"Just name it, sir."

"As you know, the election's coming up next year and Rogers and I are gonna get a head start on the campaign. In that you're a former police officer, I'd appreciate it if you would accompany us from time to time as additional security. Are you agreeable to that?"

"Of course, just let me know where and when."

"Good. Do you own a handgun?"

"Yes, sir, a thirty-eight and forty-five."

"Excellent. Get with state police and have them expedite a permit for ya. Wouldn't want one of my security team illegally carrying a weapon."

* * *

In early December, the governor and his entourage arrived at the Baltimore Civic Center to address the Baltimore Jewish Businessman's Coalition. Shortly after entering the lecture hall, Alec observed a short, fat man of about fifty, wearing glasses with lenses that magnified his eyes. His suit was stained with what appeared to be blood, and his sleeves were well above his wrists, as was the inseam above his ankles. The collar of his dingy white shirt was frayed, and he wore a string necktie. He had on white socks, and a pair of ripple-soled oil shoes. "Somethin' just ain't right about that guy," Alec whispered as he kept the man under surveillance.

Alec watched as the man went to the appetizer table and frantically stabbed three cheese squares at a time and popped several white grapes in his mouth behind them, then stuffed in two meatballs and gulped punch from paper cups in both hands. "Looks like the guy's gettin' ready to go to the gas chamber," Alec said. As Rogers and the other members of the security team were at the opposite end of the hall, Alec was on his own.

When the governor entered the hall and started mingling, the man stopped eating and retreated toward him. As the man strategically positioned himself, Alec moved closer and watched as he completed a cavalcade of gestures as an athlete does in preparation for a sporting event. After the man threw back his head and wiggled his shoulders, he opened his coat and started walking. Alec drew his weapon as the man pulled a revolver from his vest pocket and pointed it at the governor.

Blam, blam, blam, blam, blam, blam, blam, the .45 sounded off as

Alec emptied the clip into the man's chest. After he depressed the release button of the Colt, Alec inserted a loaded clip, then jacked a round in the chamber.

"Governor, ya all right?" Alec shouted.

"Yeah, I think so."

"All of ya stay down," Alec said as he scanned the hall for an accomplice.

"Is everybody all right?" Rogers asked when he and the troopers got to the governor's location.

"I don't think anybody's hit except the suspect," Alec replied as he looked at the gunman's remains, laid strewn and bleeding.

"Anybody else with 'em?" Trooper Hernandez questioned.

"I'm pretty sure he was alone," a stressed Alec answered as he took in deep breaths and kept his gun pointed at the dead man. "You guys check 'round. Y'all stay where ya are," Alec ordered the congregation lying face down on the floor as he kicked the .38 from the body. The governor responded with a hand wave and remained still.

After taking a quick perusal of the area, Trooper Langston said to Alec, "I think the place is secure. City uniforms just pulled up."

"You can get up now," Alec said.

As Alec assisted the knee-buckled governor to his feet, he said, "Alec, I'm glad you saw him before he started shooting, great work."

Rogers glared with envy, and said to himself, I guess Alec'll be a hero now. Alec caught Rogers' thought waves and peered into his eyes as he helped brush off the governor's clothing.

"Does anyone know that man?" Hyman Epstein, the President of the BJBC asked as he turned his head back and forth at the others while they gawked at the body.

"Yeah, I know 'em," Sid Bernstein, a local store owner and membership recruiter of the organization replied as he glared at the corpse. "His name's Schlomoe Edelweiss. Joined our group a week and a half ago, he's a meat cutter at Gruenberg's over in Jewtown, right off Lombard Street."

"How'd a meat cutter become a member? Thought our bylaws required everyone to be a business *owner*," said Jack Roth, a psychiatrist from Liberty Heights.

"He told me he owned ten percent of Gruenberg's and he had the twenty-five- hundred membership fee, so I issued 'em a temporary card pending verification of his credential claim. I turned in his application to Sy for final approval yesterday—I don't see him; guess he's not here tonight."

"No, it's his bowlin' night," another member commented.

"Pfft, bowlin'. He doesn't know what he missed," Epstein said as he threw his hands in the air and shook his head.

* * *

"What made you suspicious of the guy?" Detective Leveille of the BCPD Homicide Unit asked Alec as he examined his gun permit.

"He was actin' really hinky."

"*Hinky?*" Leveille asked as he peered above his bifocals.

"Yeah. Didn't fit in with the others. Ya know?"

"With the other Morta Cristos?" Leveille said.

"I'm not familiar with that term. What's it mean?"

"Christ killer," Leveille answered as he snickered.

Alec ignored the comment and continued, "Through past experiences, I learned that when somebody looks outta place they usually are."

Leveille, an unpromoted and cynical twenty-four-year veteran of the department, had sized Alec up as a 'wuss' who was born with a silver spoon, and had things handed to him. "And just *what* past experiences would those be? *Mr. Secretary,*" Leveille asked witheringly.

The timbre of Leveille's voice provoked Alec, and he responded coolly with, "Well, I guess ya got me there, Detective. I really haven't done much in my life—"

Leveille interrupted and said with indictment, "Watched a lotta television and movies, huh? Heh, heh, heh."

"Yeah, I probably have seen too much on the tube. Guess ya can't count the six months I spent in a combat zone in the Nam as a paratrooper, and the fifty-nine homicides I investigated with the PG Police."

Clearly, Alec's reindictment irritated Leveille, and he bantered with, "How long were you in homicide?"

"Five years."

"That's bullshit. I been here for fifteen and ain't handled half that amount."

"What's your closure rate?"

" 'Bout three-quarters. How 'bout yours?"

My dick's longer than yours, Alec said to himself. "Ninety-four-point-nine-one percent to be exact," he answered.

"Get the fuck outta here."

"Are you the lead investigator on this case?"

"Detective Warren's in charge."

"Lemme talk to him; you and me just ain't gettin' it."

"Suits me."

"Figured it would."

Detective Warren, an upbeat and rising star with the department, then took over the interview. "Damn, Mr. Secretary, that's amazing. And ya say the reason ya kept a close eye on 'em is because he acted like Bremer did before he shot Governor Wallace?"

"Yeah. His demeanor was quite similar. But the way he was dressed was the tip off. He just didn't fit in."

"Wow, I'll be more observant when I'm under similar circumstances."

Alec nodded, and Warren said, "I see no problems at all with the shooting, sir. You're free to go."

"Thanks, Detective, do me a favor, will ya?"

"Yes, sir, whadda ya need?"

"Send me a copy of your report of investigation when it's finished. I'm anxious to see what comes up on the guy."

"Consider it done, that it?"

"Yes, sir, here's my card. Send it to that address."

"Ten-four."

* * *

"Edelweiss, that's the whacko who showed up here Monday and said the governor was a Nazi war criminal," Sy Robkoff, the BJBC Secretary, said incredulously when Epstein called and informed him of the shooting. "Wanted us to open an investigation concerning the governor and his background."

"What'd you tell 'em?" Epstein asked.

"I told 'em that the governor was an American, born in Illinois and had never left the United States. Also that he was a friend of the Jewish community here in Baltimore, that's what I told 'em," Robkoff answered defensively.

"How do you know all these things about the governor? Have you ever checked his background? How could you be sure Edelweiss wasn't telling the truth?"

"The governor showed me his birth certificate when he tried to join our organization after he disclosed that his grandmother was Jewish, that's how I know. I told Edelweiss to go to the FBI if he had proof."

"Did he go?"

"Said they threw 'em out."

"Okay, Sy, calm down. There's probably nothing to his claims."

* * *

Schlomoe Eli Edelweiss, born on April 9, 1932 in Berlin, Germany to Frederic and Deborah Edelweiss, tailors, who owned and operated a thriving business in Berlin, was known to his friends as 'Flower.'

Edelweiss: one of the best known European blooms, belongs to the sunflower family and grows in inaccessible places in many countries of the Alpine Region.

* * *

In May of 1943, the Edelweiss family was moved by train to the infamous concentration camp in Auschwitz, located in Nazi-occupied Poland. When Flower's mother slipped as she exited the boxcar, his father and brother went to her assistance as she lay helpless in the muddy path leading to the gas chamber. "Leave the filthy vermin lay where she is," a German sergeant ordered his father.

"I cannot do that. Look, she is hurt," he pitifully replied as his wife lay helpless.

When he noticed the group not moving, the officer in charge rushed forward and said, "What's the problem? We have a schedule to keep."

"This Jew bitch has broken her leg, Colonel," the sergeant replied.

"A lame animal must be put out of its misery," the colonel said as he unsnapped the cover of his holstered Luger.

As he pointed the weapon at the impuissance woman, her husband and oldest son grabbed his arm while another prisoner snatched Flower and pushed him back with the others. The colonel pulled away, and shot both between their eyes, then turned and responded in kind to the woman. "Put them in the crematorium with the other garbage," he ordered.

When the soldiers looked at him quizzically, he realized his error and called out the order again in German. "You heard Colonel Meindorf," the sergeant said.

Flower, peering around a man's legs, watched in shock and awe as his dead family lay before his eyes. As the crowd began to move, he noticed a large birthmark shaped in the form of a jagged 'V' of the backside of the colonel's right hand as he reholstered the Luger.

Miraculously, Flower survived two years of incarceration. After being liberated, he was shipped to Ellis Island by the Red Cross, and placed in an orphanage in New York. By his sixteenth birthday, he had saved enough to purchase a one-way bus ticket to Miami. During the trip, he sat next to Abraham Gruenberg, who after learning of Flower's trials and tribulations, offered him a job as a meat cutter in his company in Baltimore.

* * *

The name Meindorf stimulated Flower when he saw it written on an election flyer beneath a photo of the gubernatorial candidate. As his mind had formed a block of the colonel's face, he was unable to connect the two until he heard Meindorf speak during the campaign. Flower would never forget the Midwestern dialect and tone of his family's murderer.

The coup de grace came when Flower looked through his binoculars and saw the telltale 'V' on Meindorf's right hand as he massaged a baseball for the ceremonial first pitch at the Orioles' 1980 home opener.

Alec's actions in saving the governor's life made him a national hero and a near godlike figure in the State of Maryland, especially in the Baltimore-Annapolis area.

"Here comes the *man of the hour* now," the head bartender at Middleton said as Alec entered his favorite haunt on his first visit there after the deed.

"Hip hip, hooray, hip hip, hooray, hip hip, hooray," the crowd shouted as they clapped. Alec casually smiled and waved as he passed and sat at Kim's table. "What's happenin', baby?" he asked as he bussed her cheek.

"Nothin' much compared to you, *big boy*. I see your fan club gave you a rousing welcome," Kim replied as she smiled adoringly.

"Had two women proposition me on the way over here," Alec said tongue in cheek.

"Can't blame 'em for wantin' to get next to an essential piece of merchandise like you," Kim answered as she licked her lips and batted her black eyes. "Tell me all about it," she said as she leaned closer.

Alec reeled off the entire account with emphasis on his keen powers of observation and experience in the Wallace shooting.

* * *

During a celebration for Alec at the governor's private home on Gibson Island, Meindorf invited him into the library. As he handed him a glass of Macallan Single Malt Scotch Whisky—1925, the governor said, "Alec, Rogers has been a true asset to my administration, and I intend on keeping him on the ticket in the upcoming election. However, if anything happened to change that, you'd be my first choice for his replacement."

Alec looked deeply into Meindorf's stolid eyes in search of a clue. He's inviting me to arrange an event, penetrated through.

As Meindorf sipped, Alec's silent communiqué was received. He knows exactly what I'm talking about.

"That's very flattering, Mr. Governor. Have one?" Alec said coolly as he offered him a cigar.

"Don't mind if I do. Won't ask where you got this," Meindorf said as he sniffed the rich blend and looked at the label.

As he accepted the cutter, Meindorf said, "Men like you and I are a rare breed, Alec, *a very rare breed indeed.*" After taking a long puff, he added, "We know what must be done and are willing to do it," as he exhaled the aromatic smoke.

This son of a bitch is exactly like me, Alec said silently in self-revelation.

"We're two of a kind, you and I. We can go a long way together," Meindorf said after he entered Alec's mind.

* * *

Meindorf recently learned of Rogers' sexual preference when he picked up his telephone and overheard a conversation between him and his current partner. "Where are you calling from," the effeminate male voice asked.

"My office," Rogers replied.

"Wow, you must really be hot. Thought you wouldn't dare call me from there."

"Just a quick one. Listen, make it eight rather than seven, got some pressing business to finish up."

"Pressing, that sounds exciting. Anyone I know? Tee-hee-hee."

"Gotta go. Eight at the same place, okay?"

"Okay, sweetie. I'll keep it warm for ya."

"Love ya, see ya at eight."

* * *

"Now remember what I told you," the governor said as Alec left.

"Yes, sir, I sure will."

"Remember what?" Kim asked.

"Just a legal matter he wants me to look into on Monday."

"Anything I can help with?"

"No, not a big deal. I'll have an intern take care of it for 'em."

"Becoming the Lieutenant Governor of the State of Maryland is just a whisker away," Alec said to himself, "all that stands in my way is *Rogers*."

* * *

Knowing Rogers' home was a waterfront property in Davidsonville on a dead-end street situated in a gorgeous location on a cliff top, Alec decided it would be the least risky place for him to execute the event.

"Should I go in by boat or car?" Alec asked himself as he located the house through binoculars while parked on the shoulder of eastbound US Route 50 where it crosses the South River. "Better go by car. Gotta do it at night, might run onto that damn water-ski jump," he said as he stuffed the glasses back in its case.

As he came to the fork on Constellation Drive, Alec was reminded of how sparsely populated the area was when he counted seven homes on the three-mile drive between Rogers' house and St. George Barber Road. "Piece a cake," Alec said as he turned in the roundabout where Rogers' driveway began.

* * *

"Hello," Rogers said as he answered his home phone.

"Lieutenant, someone from the past. How are ya?"

Rogers immediately recognized the voice and answered, "Great, Eddie. What about you?"

"Can't complain, practice is thriving."

"Good, glad to hear that," Rogers replied as his heart pounded. "What can I do for ya?"

"It's what I can do for you."

"Oh, and what's that?"

"I called to invite ya away for a long weekend at the oceanfront home I just bought in North Carolina; great place. Not a lotta freaks and long hairs like in Ocean City and Rehoboth. Bunch a golf courses nearby, too."

"Where in North Carolina?"

"Small town, 'bout halfway between Myrtle Beach and Wilmington. Ocean Isle, close to Shallotte. Ever heard of it?"

"Can't say I have. Say it's nice though, huh?" Rogers answered as his mind raced with memories of the fantastic sex the two had enjoyed together.

"Quite nice, even at this time of year. Average daytime temperature's around seventy."

"Wow, beats this brutal cold."

"Think ya can get away for a few days?"

"When do ya wanna go?"

"What about the weekend after next?"

"Let me check," Rogers answered in an attempt not to sound overly anxious. A few seconds later, with his Day Planner still in his car, Rogers answered, "Let me see now— the weekend of January seventh, right?"

"Yeah, good to go?"

"Don't have anything planned, good to go."

"Great, where do ya wanna meet?"

"Meet me here at my house. You can park in my garage. Nobody'll ever see ya come and go."

"Still in the closet, huh?"

"Of course. Think we'd get re-elected if anybody knew?"

"Never can tell, the times they are a changin'. Hadn't hurt my practice."

"I'm not gonna take the chance, at least not yet. Besides, it makes it more exciting this way."

"You're probably right, and yes, it does make it more exciting."

Rogers gave Jordan directions and hung up. "Oh God, I can't believe it, Eddie's back in my life. Thank you, Lord," Rogers said with praying hands as he looked up.

* * *

On the last evening of their reunion during dinner at the Old Pro's Table in North Myrtle Beach after having played a round at Robber's Roost, Rogers looked romantically with soft eyes at Jordan and said, "Eddie, I've had such a wonderful time with you these past few days. Think we can take another shot at it?"

Just what I hoped he'd say, Jordan said slyly to himself as he took a bite of his barely-cooked filet mignon. "I was hoping you'd ask, Kenny," Jordan answered as he caressed Roger's face, "I'd love to."

"Eddie, the governor and I are a shoo-in for re-election; poll's got us ahead by nineteen points. I wanna go out on a high note. If it makes a difference to ya, I promise after this next term I'll come outta the closet if ya want me to."

"It doesn't matter to me, Kenny. I just want ya back under any condition," Jordan answered as he subtly blew a kiss.

After a zesty lovemaking session that night, the two began their journey back to Maryland the next morning. As they entered the ramp for I-95 north, Jordan cut a sideways look at Rogers. When he sensed his feeling of well being, Jordan said to himself, The time is right.

"Kenny, do you remember when you were on the city council and made that under-the-table arrangement for me?"

"It wasn't *exactly* under the table," Rogers, caught off guard answered defensively, "just didn't mention your name because of your history with the city, that's all."

"Call it what ya will; your influence landed me the deal," Jordan responded gently.

"Yeah, I remember. What of it?" Rogers answered in a timorous voice.

"Well, I got another one I want you to 'arrange' for me."

"*Really?*"

"Yeah, are ya willing?" Jordan asked politely.

"Not if it involves anything underhanded, I'm not."

Jordan's demeanor then radically changed, and he said brusquely, "Kenny, I didn't wanna have to get rough with ya but…"

"But *what?*"

"If you're not willing to play ball, I'll see to it that your dirty little secret becomes public. Then see what happens to that nineteen-point lead," Jordan said venomously.

"I should've known, the same old Eddie. Only want what's in it for you, ya selfish bitch."

"Enough with the compliments, will ya or won't ya do it?"

Rogers surrendered and said, "Ya would've been a great politician, Eddie. Let me know what it is ya want when we get home and I'll see what I can do."

"When we get home is soon enough," Jordan answered victoriously.

MATTHEW 7:15

"Have a good trip, Kenny?" Alec asked Rogers when he returned to the statehouse.

"It was okay."

"Ya feelin' all right? Sound a little down."

"Flu or somethin'," he answered as he placed the side of his balled fist against his mouth and coughed slightly.

"Should've stayed out a few days," Alec answered in an attempt to goad Rogers into remaining at home.

"I may do that tomorrow," Rogers said as he began checking his telephone messages. When he got to Jordan's, he put it in his vest pocket and said lowly, "Son of a bitch didn't waste any time."

* * *

When Rogers took the next day off, Alec said, "He who hesitates is lost; tonight's the night."

"Kenny, anything I can do for ya?" Alec asked when he called Rogers at home in order to ensure his presence there.

"No, I'm just gonna lie around and take it easy. I'm sure I'll feel better tomorrow. Thanks for askin'."

"If ya need anything, don't hesitate to call."

"Thanks, buddy, I will."

"Too bad things didn't work out between Alec and me. He's really a nice person," Rogers said after he hung up the phone.

That night, Alec parked his rented car on the shoulder of St. George Barber Road, and covered the license plates with fitted cloth bags. He then drove to Rogers' home and saw the light in the living room on and his car parked in the driveway. "Mighty thoughtful of 'em not to have parked in the garage tonight," Alec said wily as he passed by.

After he got back to St. George Barber Road, Alec uncovered the tags and drove to the 7-11 in Crofton and bought a cup of coffee. An hour later, he returned and recovered the plates. When he drove past Rogers' house and saw all the lights off, he parked in the woods and put on a set of dark coveralls and black watch cap, then proceeded on foot.

Knowing that Rogers' bedroom was at the left end of the home, Alec went to the opposite side and was able to open the first window he tried. "Think an ex-cop would've locked the house up," Alec mused.

After entering, he looked and listened; when he heard no sounds, he quietly proceeded through the living room. "Creeeeeeek." Alec stopped abruptly on the loose floorboard, then changed his position and listened again.

A few seconds later, he began walking toward the kitchen. As he passed through the unlit home, Alec felt something hit him head on. He quickly drew back, pulled his .38 and gasped for air. A moment later, he recognized the figure standing before him to be a human body hanging from a clothesline tied around a ceiling rafter.

Alec removed the Penlight from the top pocket of his coveralls and shined it on the corpse's face. Its tongue was almost touching the bottom of its chin, with the neck stretched to twice its normal length. When he pointed the light down, he noticed the corpse's feet lying flat on the floor.

He then spotted a note pinned to the shirt: For the record, this is a suicide—known by Baltimore Police as a Signal 66. No one in any way, shape or form, assisted, or coerced me into doing it. As I am a good Catholic, I hope God forgives me for my actions and accepts me into heaven. Kenneth P. Rogers—former Lieutenant Governor, State of Md.

"Thanks a lot, Kenny. Ya did me a great favor," Alec quipped and smiled as he returned the flashlight to his pocket. "Statehouse, here I come. Now lemme get the fuck outta here; I'd hate to catch a burglary beef over this shit."

As he drove north on Davidsonville Road, Alec brought the vehicle to a screeching halt when he suddenly remembered the license plates were still covered. "Oh shit," he said as rocks and dust from the shoulder permeated the air as he slammed on the brakes.

* * *

"Good afternoon, Law Firm of Bennett and Lock. How may I help you?" the receptionist said as she answered the phone the following afternoon.

"I'd like to speak with Mr. Bazey."

"Whom may I say is calling?"

"Governor Meindorf from the State of Maryland."

"Just a moment, Governor."

"Alec, Governor Meindorf's on line five."

"Thanks, Sally."

"Bet they found the body already," Alec said as he reached for the phone. "Governor, what can I do for ya today, sir?"

"Alec, I have some very bad news."

This is it, Alec said to himself. "What's that, sir?" Alec asked in a concerned tone.

"When Kenny didn't call in this morning, his assistant called him at home and got no answer. After my security troopers broke into his house, they found 'em hanging from a rafter with a suicide note pinned to his chest, and a stepping stool close by."

Fuckin' troopers couldn't find their asses with both hands, Alec said to himself. "That's terrible, sir. Are they sure it's a suicide?"

"No question, his note was very explicit."

"Did he say why he did it?"

"No, just something about hoping God forgives him. I just can't believe it."

"Can't believe it? It's exactly what you were prayin' for," Alec said to himself. "*Quite* unbelievable," Alec answered, "anything I can do?"

"Not right now. When are you due in your office here?"

"I was plannin' on comin' by tomorrow afternoon."

"Good, we'll talk then."

* * *

The next afternoon, the governor said, "Alec, are you still interested in being my running mate in November?"

"The lieutenant's not even buried yet, sir. I feel embarrassed by the question," Alec answered.

You couldn't wait for me to ask you that question, Meindorf said to himself.

The primordial communication between the two vipers resumed. When Meindorf's thoughts entered Alec's mind, he recalled Matthew 7:15—*Beware of false prophets which come to you in sheep's clothing but inwardly are ravening wolves*. Quit playin' games, this guy's got your number; he can see your dripping fangs just like you can see his, Alec said to himself. "I'd love to be your running mate, sir," he replied.

"That settles it then. I'll get our legal team to organize the paperwork and run it through the general assembly; glad they're still in session. You're quite popular with everyone around here, don't see any problem with gaining their approval."

"Thanks, Governor. Ya won't be sorry ya chose me," Alec said as the two demonic sprites shook hands and sealed their pact.

* * *

"Kim, did ya hear about the lieutenant governor?" Alec asked when he called her immediately after the meeting with Meindorf.

"Yes, heard it on WTOP. That's awful, he was such a nice person. Any idea why he did it?"

"No idea, pulled a Richard Cory, I guess."

"That's really ashame."

"Yeah, it is, but listen to this, the governor just asked me to be his running mate in November. Whadda ya think of that?"

"Oh, Alec, that's wonderful. What'd you tell him?"

"Yes, of course."

"Wow, Lieutenant Governor Bazey. I'm so proud of you."

"Not bad for a little polewhop orphan from Hollandtown, huh?"

"Not bad at all, sweetheart."

"Listen, meet me at my house when ya get off. Gotta run up to Carol's. Then I'll take y'all to Shula's for dinner."

"What time?"

"I'll be there at five."

"Me, too."

* * *

"Hey, Sis, how ya doin?" Alec asked as he hugged Carol.

"Fine, I guess."

"How *you* doin', big man?"

"Good, Uncle Al," Y. A. answered as Alec patted him on the head.

"Nice to see ya, Kim," Carol said as the two embraced.

"Nice to see *you*, been awhile."

"Listen, got some big news for ya. But first, let's me and you go downstairs, all right?" Alec said.

"Sure. What's up?" Carol answered.

"Kim, mind stayin' with Y. A. a few minutes?" Alec said.

"Go right ahead. Hi, Y. A., how're you?"

"Fine, Miss Kim."

When Alec and Carol sat down at Chooch's poker table, Alec reached into his vest pocket and handed her an envelope. "Alec, this is a cashier's check for a hundred-thousand dollars made out to me," Carol said in awe as she gawked at the six figures.

"Sis, you're the best friend I've ever had. You and your parents were there for me when I was a kid and you've always stuck by me, no matter what. I love you and Alec more than anything. I know things've been tough for y'all since Choochie cut out with the insurance not payin' off right away. This oughta hold ya over 'til ya get on your feet. Please accept it as a symbol of my love and appreciation."

"But, Alec, it's so much."

"I've done well through the years thanks to your parents lookin' out for me and not blowin' my inheritance like most people would've. I invested in an upstart stock fund, Fidelity Magellan, when I got outta the army. It's worth well over a million dollars now. Please accept the check, I want you and Y. A. to have it. Go on a vacation or somethin'."

"Alec, we love you, too. Thank you so much. I'll repay you when I get the insurance money."

"It's a gift, I won't accept repayment."

"Thank you, Alec. You're the best brother anyone could ask for."

"If ya only knew the half of it, Sis," Alec said under his breath. "Now for the good news."

"You have more good news?"

"Yeah. Governor Meindorf asked me today if I would be his running mate in November."

Carol then looked quizzically, and said, "What, is Lieutenant Rogers not gonna run this time?"

"Haven't ya heard? Rogers committed suicide."

"Where did they find him?"

"In his house."

"He was such a nice man. I feel so sorry for his family. Kinda know how they feel."

I'm really glad he saved me the trouble, Alec said inwardly. "Yeah, he really was a nice guy. I liked 'em, too."

"When's the funeral?"

"Before the end of the week, I'd guess. Are your parents home?"

"No, they left for Florida yesterday. Won't be back 'til the end of the month."

"Yeah, I forgot. I'll call and give 'em the news tomorrow. You and Y. A. go change, gonna take you to Shula's for a steak."

"I can fix somethin' here."

"Just like your mother, always tryin' to save a buck. Now go get ready."

Carol smiled, waved the check and headed upstairs.

"Oh, one more thing," Alec said.

"More good news?" Carol asked.

"The governor said it'll be all right to hire you as my private secretary after the election. Job starts at nineteen-five a year—interested?"

"Ya got my vote."

* * *

As expected, the Meindorf-Bazey team won the election by a landslide. The charm and style of the pair, coupled with support from the media, created a feeling of security in Marylanders knowing they were in the competent and trustworthy hands of such enlightened leadership.

Alec was ecstatic with his new position, and was out to change the world. His hero image was reinforced when he submitted an outline of a bill to Maryland State Delegate George for a plan that removed

281

restrictions inhibiting free enterprise and promoted tax reform in the State of Maryland. George was enthusiastically backed by other conservative legislators from western Maryland and the Eastern Shore when he submitted the bill to the liberal-controlled, 'tax-and-spend' general assembly.

After it was rejected, Alec personally paid for television air time in order to directly lobby the public for the bill's passage. While standing in front of an easel that held a display board, he illustrated the details of *his* 'trickle-down' plan that *reduced,* rather than *increased*, the tax percentage as income rose.

"And let me ask you this, which wage earners are more likely to avail themselves of state services? Those at the higher level of income, or those at the lower level?" Alec said as he pointed to the figures on the chart. "It's high time the working class in this state are rewarded for their efforts rather than punished for them. Contact your state delegate and insist on the passing of this bill. Thank you for tuning in," he said in closing as he retired the pointer.

The names and telephone numbers of each delegate and their district then appeared on the television screen for thirty seconds. When President Reagan viewed the airing, he asked his press secretary, "Is this guy really a Democrat?"

"Yes, sir, he is."

"Hard to believe. Make a release endorsing that bill. Let's see what we can do to help."

When the phone lines at the Maryland Statehouse were deluged with calls supporting the bill, and the endorsement from 'Ronnie the Popular' made national headlines, the politicians in Annapolis called for an emergency session and unanimously voted to pass it into law.

NO SYMPATHY FOR THE DEVIL

On the morning before his attempt on the governor's life, Flower mailed a letter to Simon Wiesenthal of the *Jewish Documentation Center* in Linz, Austria, that elucidated his captivity in Auschwitz, and identified the current Governor of the State of Maryland as a former Nazi officer who murdered his family there. It explained that all of his efforts to expose the governor's past identity were ignored by authorities, and had caused him considerable ridicule and embarrassment. Edelweiss informed Wiesenthal of his intention to serve justice on Meindorf, and enclosed a current photo of the governor and an appeal for the JDC to pursue the matter in the event of his failure.

After reading the letter, Wiesenthal handed it to his assistant and said, "Jacob, read this."

When he got to the paragraph regarding Meindorf, Jacob stopped and said, "Now where is that thing? Simon, you must clean off this desk," as he rummaged through stacks of clutter and documents.

After he found a recent copy of Newsweek Magazine with a photograph of Meindorf and Alec on its cover he had placed there a week earlier with a handwritten note, Jacob said, "Have you read this?"

"No, I haven't," Wiesenthal answered as he compared the photos of Meindorf.

Upon finishing the article, Wiesenthal said, "Do we have a file on Meindorf?"

"I haven't checked, sir."

"Please do. I believe Mr. Edelweiss was telling the truth."

A few minutes later, Jacob said, "I have located a file, sir," as he waved a thin manila folder.

"What does it say?"

"Fritz Aldo Meindorf: SS member; top aide of Himmler; possibly assisted in plans for the *Final Solution*. Also suspected of killing Americans at Malmedy."

"Photo?"

"No photo."

"Family?"

"Wife and son—possibly named Helena and Karl."

"Have we ever tried to locate him?"

"One of our teams did in the early fifties, but could find no record of him or any trace of his family. It's like he never existed before the war."

"It would fit that he was one of the German-Americans who came to the aid of the Fatherland. Get our best team on the case; I think Governor

Meindorf is hiding a past we should know about."

* * *

When no additional information was uncovered in Europe, BCPD Homicide Detective George Warren was contacted. "Detective Warren, this is Conrad Nagelman of the Jewish Documentation Center. How are you today, sir?"

"Fine. And you, Mr. Nagelman?"

"I'm well, thank you."

"What can I help ya with?"

"We need your assistance with a matter of interest to us," Nagelman eloquently replied.

"What organization did ya say you're with?"

"The Jewish Documentation Center."

"Where ya callin' from?"

"Linz, Austria."

Puzzled and intrigued, Warren said, "Whadda ya need from me?"

"Information regarding the attempt on your governor's life."

"That case is closed," Warren said guardedly.

"I know. If possible, I would like you to send me a copy of your report. Can you accommodate?"

"For what reason?"

"It involves your governor's past."

"What exactly do you do for the JDC?"

"Investigate acts of barbarity to Jews during World War two."

"Gimme your contact information and I'll get back to you."

"That will be fine."

* * *

"What the fuck interest does the Jewish Documentation Center in Linz, Austria have in our governor?" Captain Schrader, Commander of the BCPD Homicide Section, said after being apprised by Warren.

"Don't have a clue, Captain," Warren replied.

"What do they do anyway?"

"Investigate Nazi war criminals, I think."

"Fuckin' governor's American as apple pie. Fuck 'em Heebs, let 'em get a hold of the FBI. Ain't gonna go stirrin' up shit in the governor's office, especially durin' a 'lection year."

When Warren returned the call and explained his boss' reluctance to accommodate the JDC, Nagelman said, "I expected that would be your commander's reaction. Thank you anyway, Detective."

"You're quite welcome, Mr. Nagelman. Ya might wanna get with the

FBI. Good luck, sir."

* * *

Good fortune came Nagelman's way when he called FBI Headquarters. After explaining the situation to Special Agent Byron Meyers of the FBI's Public Corruption Unit, he said, "Baltimore City wouldn't help, huh?"

"No, sir. They told me to contact the FBI," Nagelman replied.

"You've come to the right place. I'm familiar with your organization and the great work Mr. Wiesenthal and his staff has done in nabbin' Nazi fugitives. It would be best if you came here, can that be arranged?"

"Yes, sir. My partner and I will be on the next flight to Washington."

"After you find out what flight you all are on, call and I'll make arrangements to pick you up."

"Good, I will. Thank you for everything, Agent."

After meeting Nagelman and his partner at National Airport, Meyers drove them directly to FBI Headquarters where he was briefed. The following day, after a federal judge issued subpoenas for release of information regarding the assassination attempt, Meyers and two other agents, along with Nagelman and his partner, arrived at the Homicide Section of the BCPD. Subsequent to collecting the documents, Meyers informed the city detectives they were under a gag order, that if violated would cause their arrest. The group then returned to FBI Headquarters and examined the case file.

"Look, here is a copy of the letter Edelweiss wrote to Simon," Nagelman said.

"I hope that helps in your quest," Meyers said.

"Immensely," answered Nagelman.

"I'm sure this is the right man," Nagelman said as he closely studied the photo of the birthmark. "If we only had one person who could identify him, or some other evidence."

"I think we should travel to Berlin and find his wife and son," Jaeger suggested.

"Yes, there's bound to be something or someone there."

* * *

"Meindorf is a very common German name," the clerk at the Berlin Office of Vital Statistics said.

"How many males around the age of forty?" asked Nagelman.

"Impossible to tell, thousands probably."

"Try Helena Meindorf again, please," Nagelman requested politely.

As the clerk peered overtop his glasses, he replied, "I have checked the name Helena for you already, but if you promise to leave, I'll check it again."

"We promise to leave. Thank you, sir."

As he slid his forefinger down a page, the clerk stopped and said, "No, no Helena. However, there is a Helga."

"How old?" Nagelman asked.

"Let me see. Date of birth, December seventeen, nineteen-twenty. That would make her, sixty-two on her last birthday," the clerk replied as he counted the years on his fingers.

"Is there an address?"

"Yes. Here, I'll write it down for you."

After handing it over, the clerk said, "Now will you please go. There are ten people waiting behind you."

"Thank you, kind sir," Nagelman answered as he folded the sheet of paper and tucked it in his shirt pocket.

When they arrived, it was discovered the address had been converted to a McDonald's restaurant. "May as well have lunch," Jaeger said in disgust.

While involved with their 'Big Macs,' Nagelman said, "If what Edelweiss said is true, Meindorf is a criminal of the worst degree," as he sipped Coca-Cola through a straw. "We have to find someone who can identify him."

"Let's return to Linz and pass it around with the others," Jaeger suggested as he stuffed a half-dozen fries in his mouth.

* * *

"I have an idea," Sarah Feinberg, another JDC Investigator said after being apprised of the dilemma.

"Yes?" answered Jaeger.

"Let's do a 'sting.' "

"What is a sting?" Nagelman asked.

"It is when the police offer a reward or prize of some kind to catch criminals or fugitives. We could advertise it as a large estate a Fritz Aldo Meindorf left after his death, and the government is in search of legal heirs. They must of course, be able to prove their relationship to the departed."

"Might work. Let's try it," Nagelman said.

After placing advertisements throughout the Berlin metropolitan area for months, thousands of people responded, mostly criminals and con-artists. A few months after the Gubernatorial Election in Maryland, a sixty-two-year-old female arrived at JDC Headquarters. "I am Frau

Meindorf, and I am here to collect my inheritance," the well-worn decrepit woman in shabby clothes, said to the clerk in a raspy 'cigarette' voice.

"Have a seat, I'll get Mr. Nagelman for you."

As she sat, the clerk dialed Nagelman's extension and said, "Conrad, there's a woman out here who claims to be Frau Meindorf."

"How did she find us?"

"I didn't ask her, shall I?"

"No, I'll be right there."

"Are you the one with my inheritance?" the woman asked when approached by Nagelman as she lit a Reemsta.

"I can help you with that. Follow me," Nagelman replied as she crushed out the barely-smoked cigarette on the floor.

"How is it you came here to claim the inheritance?" Nagelman asked.

"I contacted the police in Berlin when I saw this ad," she answered as she unfolded a clipping she had ripped from a Berlin newspaper she found in the mental ward at the hospital in Linz. "They told me to contact you. Now when do I get my money?" she asked as she lit another Stuyvesant.

"First, you have to prove you are related to the deceased Mr. Meindorf. Can you do that?"

The woman reached in her purse and removed a half-full pint bottle of vodka and placed it on Nagelman's desk. She then produced an expired Austrian driver's license with her photo. "Helga Switzer, is that your name?" Nagelman asked.

"I gave you the wrong card. Switzer was my second husband. Here," she answered as she handed him a frayed identification card with a swastika imprinted in the middle.

"Helga Meindorf, how were you related to Fritz Meindorf?" Nagelman asked as he read from the card dated 1941.

After downing the last of the vodka, she said, "He was my first husband."

"Go on."

"He was an officer in the SS. Worked directly for Himmler, then deserted in nineteen forty-five."

"Where did he go when he deserted?"

"Back to the United States, I guess," she answered as she shivered from the stiff drink.

"Went back to the United States?" Nagelman asked with raised eyebrows.

"Yes, he was an American, born in Carthage, Illinois; came to Germany and joined the Wermacht in nineteen thirty-nine. Now where's my money?"

Chills swept Nagelman's spine when he realized he had hit pay dirt. "That will come later. Now what else can you tell me of him?"

"We had a son named Karl. He was killed by American bombers. I'm in a hurry, when can I get my money?"

"In due time, madam. What else do you know?"

"He has a tattoo on his right arm with his SS number, one-zero-seven-seven-three-nine-four."

"Are you sure that's the number?"

"Yes, I'm positive. Look at the back of my card. I wrote it down after I got it."

Nagelman then turned the card over where he saw the barely-visible number: 1077394.

"Do you have a photograph of him?"

"Yes. Wait a minute, it's here somewhere," she answered as she rummaged through her purse and took short drags from the cigarette dangling from her lips.

"Here it is. That's the three of us in the old days," she said as she handed the relic to Nagelman, then removed the cigarette and crushed it on the floor.

Nagelman's adrenal glands pumped furiously as he viewed the photograph. "Yes, that certainly is you. There is still a strong resemblance even after all of this time," he said as he looked at her image in the photo.

"Of course I was a lot younger there," she said while running her bony fingers through her grey-rooted, dyed-red nappy hair.

"I can still tell it's you," Nagelman said when he put the photo next to her face. She then removed a small mirror and tube of lipstick from her purse. "Of course I was a lot better to do when that was taken," she said as the lipstick crumbled when she applied it.

A once proud *Nazi bitch dog*, Nagelman said contemptuously to himself as he smiled spuriously.

"I have lots of other photos back at the shelter," Helga said as she lit another cigarette.

Nagelman handed her an ashtray and replied, "Which shelter?" as he lit a Marlboro.

"The one I'm staying in until I get back on my feet. The small amount of money my second husband left me is almost gone. That's why I really need the inheritance," she pitifully retorted.

"Where is the shelter?"

"Close by. We can walk there in a few minutes."

"Sharona, call Simon and tell him we have located Colonel Meindorf's wife and for him to come in right away," Nagelman said to the receptionist as he and Helga neared her desk on the way out.

"Can we stop for food? I missed serving time at the shelter," Helga said as she looked at the clock on the wall.

"Sharona, call the deli and have them deliver some food."

"Anything special?" she asked.

"What would you like, my dear?"

"A brat on rye would be nice," Helga said.

"Brat on rye with all the trimmings. Make it two, and order yourself something," Nagelman said as they exited. Sharona flashed him an okay sign and Nagelman responded with a sly and confident wink as he held the door open for Frau Meindorf.

* * *

"This is the photo that will hang the bastard," Wiesenthal cried out indignantly as he examined a shot of Meindorf posing with his right foot on top of a stack of bodies clad in striped clothing. "Look how proud the pig is," he added when he noticed Meindorf's chin high and a smirk on his face. "Show this to the frau and make sure it's him."

"I'll show it, but I know it's him," Nagelman replied excitedly.

He then went into the adjoining room and said, "Is this your first husband?"

"Yes, that's him," Helga answered circumspectly when she focused on the dead bodies as she wiped sauerkraut from her chin.

"Thank you."

"Does that mean I get my money now?" Helga asked as she licked her dirty fingers.

"You'll get paid in due time."

"Look at this," a wide-eyed Wiesenthal said to Nagelman when he returned. "Fingerprint, date of birth, photo in an SS uniform, the whole 'shebang' as the Americans say," Nagelman replied as he examined Meindorf's Nazi identification card discovered by Wiesenthal in the collection of photos.

"The Americans. I wonder what their reaction will be when we prove to them one of their governors is a murderer," Wiesenthal said.

"I assure you, Simon, we will get full cooperation in the matter from Agent Meyers. As I told you, his parents were in Buchenwald."

"Yes, that will make a difference, I'm sure."

"What about the frau?" Nagelman asked.

"She will remain in custody until after the trial. Be sure and inform her that if she cooperates and testifies, she will receive a reward of at least fifty-thousand American dollars, maybe more, after her swine husband is convicted," Wiesenthal answered.

"And if she is not willing to testify?"

"She will spend the rest of her worthless life in an Israeli prison. I'll see to it personally that the Mossad kidnaps her as they did Eichmann and takes her to Jerusalem."

"I'm sure she will accept the fifty-thousand dollar alternative," Nagelman replied.

* * *

Three months later, after a select and highly secretive team from various federal agencies completed an extensive investigation, Special Agent Byron Meyers addressed the members in a soundproof room on the third floor of FBI Headquarters. "All right, people, let me give ya a run down of the case before we head to Annapolis."

With displays and photographs in the backdrop, he said, "We have positively identified the Governor of the State of Maryland, Fritz Aldo Meindorf, as a former member of the Nazi organization known as the *Schutzaffel*, more commonly referred to as the *SS*. Among other atrocities, it has been proven that he assisted in the design of *The Final Solution*, a sinister plot to exterminate every Jew in the world. Also, we have uncovered evidence that he took an active part, and perhaps gave the order to murder eighty-four *unarmed* American prisoners in the Malmedy Massacre in nineteen forty-four during the Battle of the Bulge in Belgium. Clearly, our evidence is limited; however, it is overwhelming and compelling."

The team became engrossed with Meyers' carefully chosen words and listened attentively. "The only known witness in the case is his wife, Helga Anna Meindorf, now being held as a material witness in Jerusalem. She has been interviewed repeatedly by members of the Jewish Documentation Center, and the information she offered has been documented and confirmed," Meyers said as he directed his attention to Nagelman and Jaeger. "After the governor's arraignment and extradition hearing, the state-department team, seated here to my left, has made arrangements with the Israeli Government to have the governor flown directly to Jerusalem for trial. Are there any questions?" When there was no response, Meyers concluded by saying, "All right, you all know your assignments. This case will get international attention, so let's do our very best as the world will be closely watching. Director Webster sends his best wishes and vote of confidence in your professional abilities."

* * *

When the entourage reached the front entrance of the Annapolis Statehouse, pandemonium broke out. As Meyers approached the security team at the door, he held up his I.D. case and said, "FBI, Special Agent

Byron Meyers. Please lead the way to the governor's office."

When another guard picked up the telephone, an agent quickly grabbed it and returned it to its origin. "No calls, just lead the way," the agent politely informed the guard.

"Governor Meindorf, Agent Meyers of the FBI. You're under arrest," Meyers stated as he placed the arrest warrant on the governor's desk and the team followed him into the office.

"What is the meaning of this outrage?"Meindorf asked contemptuously as federal authorities surrounded him. "Get Alec in here and call security, *and my attorney,*" Meindorf shouted to his stunned secretary.

"Governor, please stand up and remove your shirt, sir," Meyers ordered.

"I most certainly will not!"

"Then I'll have to remove it for ya," Meyers responded as he handed Meindorf a warrant for a body search.

As Alec entered, Meindorf was unbuttoning his shirt and said, "Alec, is my attorney on the way?"

"He'll be here shortly. Verna located him at the courthouse across the street, sir," Alec calmly answered.

"One-zero-seven-seven-three-nine-four," Meyers said as he read off the numbers tattooed on the upper portion of the governor's right forearm. "Photograph this please," he said to a team member as he turned the governor's arm with the tattoo toward a camera. "Also get one of that birthmark on his right hand and tattooed blood type under his armpit."

As the governor put his shirt back on, Saul Morgenstein barged his way through and shouted, "What in the world is going on here?"

"And who might you be, sir?" Meyers asked.

"I'm the governor's attorney, *that's who I am*"

"Good, your client needs an attorney. Saves me the trouble of readin' him his rights," Meyers retorted.

"Crimes against humanity? Nazi war criminal?" Morgenstein said incredulously as he read the warrant.

"Yes, sir," Meyers replied as he produced a reproduction on the young Meindorf standing atop the dead bodies.

"It's all bullshit, Saul. A pack of lies," Meindorf replied, as Morgenstein looked at the photograph horror struck.

After recognizing the man in the photo as Meindorf, Morgenstein, a German-born Jew whose parents had fled Germany in Hitler's wake, replied in a passive tenor, "Where are you taking him, Agent?"

"FBI Headquarters at nine-thirty-five Pennsylvania Avenue in Northwest D.C."

"I'll meet you there. Fritz, don't say anything."

"Nothing *to* say. Mistaken identity."

"Mistaken identity my ass; that's you in that Nazi uniform with your foot up and head held high like a hunter posing with a trophy buck," Morgenstein said inwardly.

"I'll meet you there, Governor. I'm sure we'll be able to resolve this," Alec said confidently as Meyers placed handcuffs on the governor.

"Damn straight we'll resolve it. I'll own the federal government before this is over. That fuckin' Reagan's at the bottom of this, I know he is," Meindorf said as Meyers led him out of the office and winked at Alec in passing.

* * *

Alec intentionally arrived at FBI Headquarters three hours later, and waited for Meyers in the lobby while he interrogated Meindorf in his attorney's presence. When he met Alec, he said, "Good to see ya, Lieutenant. Or should I say governor now?"

"Not yet," Alec answered as he smiled.

"I'm sure we could've done it without ya, but your identification of that tattoo sure helped seal the deal. I was hesitant to ask at first, but after we did a background on ya, figured you'd come through; father bein' killed by the Germans, and you bein' a combat veteran, ex-cop and all."

"Thanks, Byron. Ya did the right thing in askin' me. Glad I could be of service. Sure glad the governor asked me to join him in the sauna bath at the statehouse, don't know how I would've gotten a look at that tattoo otherwise."

"Did he try to hide it?"

"No. Arrogant bastard must've thought that as he had gotten by with it all this time, nobody cared. Never saw him in short sleeves though."

"Neither did any of the surveillance team."

"Has he admitted to anything?"

"No, still claimin' it's mistaken identity. When we told 'em his German wife gave 'em up, he laughed and said he's never been outta the US. Just as well, us and the Israelis got 'em cold. They don't mess around with Nazis over there; he'll be swingin' before the year's over. Listen, I gotta get back. I'd invite ya up, but it's off limits, even to soon to be governors unless they're under arrest, that is."

The full-fledged Governor of the State of Maryland before the year's over, reflected in Alec's mind. "Give 'Fritzie' my best, Byron. I'll take you at your word that you and the others *will* keep my involvement mum, correct?"

"No mention of your name anywhere. *I'm* the only one who knows,"

Meyers assured Alec.

The only one, Alec said to himself. Gotta tuck that little gem away.

"Great work, Byron. Do you live in Maryland by any chance?"

"Matter of fact, I do. Prince Frederick in Calvert County."

"If ya ever decide to get into politics, gimme a call," Alec said as he handed Meyers a card with his private phone numbers.

"Ya live in Bowie, huh?" Meyers asked as he looked at the card.

"Can tell by the four-six-four exchange, huh?"

"You got it. Thanks, Governor."

* * *

The morning after the governor's arrest, before collecting the daily egg crop from the coop on his small chicken farm in Denton, retired BCPD Detective Sergeant Samuel Q. Bloodsworth, walked to his mailbox and retrieved the Morning Sun. After reading the seven-page article regarding the governor's arrest, Bloodsworth dug out his old police telephone directory and opened it to the 'S' section.

"Colonel Saukas, how you doin', kid?" Bloodsworth asked in his slow drawl as he held the phone between his ear and shoulder and smiled while pouring a cup of coffee. "Bloodman. I'd recognize that voice anywhere. How ya doin', buddy? Long time no see."

"Still fuckin' around with these here chickens. How come you ain't retired yet, boy?"

"You know me, man, I still love it. What's up, bro'?"

"I told ya when I first met Meindorf at the bakery somethin' wasn't right 'bout that dude. 'Member?"

"Ya didn't come right out and say it, but yeah, I remember; ya asked a lotta questions about 'em."

"From what it says in the Sun, that tattoo I saw on his right arm was the knockout punch."

"Haven't read the paper yet, but that's what I heard on television. Some shit, huh?"

"Imagine, a fuckin' Nazi gettin' elected governor. Mmp, mmp, mmp," Bloodsworth replied.

"Ya do know who the new governor is, right?"

"Yeah, 'at Bazey kid we locked up for killin' that derelict way back when you was a rookie dick."

"Yeah, Sabitini was his uncle. He aced the governor's brother at the Atlantic Federal and I got his partner."

"Small world ain't it? This governor seems to be okay; love his tax reform. We went to his stepfather's funeral. Remember that?"

"Sure do; I'll never forget when they played Tutti-Frutti at the end and the show the Blue Angels put on."

"Listen, Jimmy, if ya ever get over this way, stop in. Got me a little center-console Boston Whaler. Rockfish been runnin' good in this cold weather."

"It's a date, boss. I still got your number; I'll be in touch. Good talkin' to ya."

"Take care, Jimmy. See ya soon," Bloodsworth said with a tear in his eye as he hung up the phone.

"Great man there," Jimmy said as he wiped wet eyes on the other end of the line.

* * *

After three attempts at not being extradited to Israel failed, Meindorf was put on a private flight that landed in Jerusalem. His trial was held in the Beit Ha'am Building, House of the People, the same place where Adolf Eichmann was tried in 1962. After being convicted of crimes against humanity by a three-judge panel, the former Nazi Colonel was sentenced to be hanged by the neck until dead. Despite overwhelming evidence at his trial, Meindorf maintained his innocence.

"Do you have anything to say before your sentence is imposed?" the henchman asked Meindorf as they stood atop the gallows.

"Yes I do," Meindorf said through his black shroud.

"Go on," replied the henchman.

At the top of his lungs, Meindorf shouted, "Death to all Jew vermin. Long live the Reich! Sieg hiel, sieg hiel, sieg—"

* * *

After the execution, Alec was inaugurated as Governor of the State of Maryland. As he sat in his office overlooking downtown Annapolis and the United States Naval Academy, he sipped Louie XIII and lit a Montecristo. "What next?" he said, when he turned and stared at a photograph of him shaking hands with President Reagan in front of the White House after receiving an award for saving Governor Meindorf's life.

Alec's fantasy was broken when his private secretary called over the intercom, "Governor Bazey."

"Governor Bazey—my that sounds good," Alec whispered. "Yeah, Sis?"

"Line three."

"Who is it, do you know?"

"It's a Mrs. Palmieri; said you'd know what it's in reference to."

About the Author

Edward P. Ciesielski, Jr., aka "Ski," was born and raised in Baltimore City and currently resides in Bowie, MD with his wife Janet and son Paul. Mr. Ciesielski graduated from the Mergenthaler Vocational-Technical High School in Baltimore and later attended the University of Maryland University College. He served as a Prince George's County Maryland Police Officer from 1970-90, having attained the rank of Sergeant. Mr. Ciesielski's tenure with the PGPD includes service in the homicide section from 1976-1981 where he was responsible for the investigation of over 400 deaths. Included in those investigations were fifty-nine homicides of which only three remain unsolved.

While a member of the PGPD's Special Operations Division, Mr. Ciesielski and other squad members were temporarily assigned to the US Secret Service and arrested Arthur H. Bremer immediately after he shot Alabama Governor George C. Wallace and three other people at the Laurel Shopping Center in Laurel, MD on May 15, 1972.

Currently, Mr. Ciesielski serves as a background investigator for the federal government.

The impetus for Mr. Ciesielski's debut novel, IN SHEEP'S CLOTHING, is based in large part on his personal and professional life experiences as well as those of friends and relatives, especially his father, a retired Baltimore City Firefighter. He has begun work on a sequel, THE KIT, expected to be completed sometime in 2012.

ALL THINGS THAT MATTER PRESS ™

FOR MORE INFORMATION ON TITLES AVAILABLE FROM
ALL THINGS THAT MATTER PRESS, GO TO
http://allthingsthatmatterpress.com
or contact us at
allthingsthatmatterpress@gmail.com